Franklin B. Sanborn

Memoirs of Pliny Earle, M.D.

With extracts from his diary and letters (1830-1892) and selections from his

professional writings (1839-1891)

Franklin B. Sanborn

Memoirs of Pliny Earle, M.D.
*With extracts from his diary and letters (1830-1892) and selections from his professional
writings (1839-1891)*

ISBN/EAN: 9783337015503

Printed in Europe, USA, Canada, Australia, Japan

Cover: Foto ©Raphael Reischuk / pixelio.de

More available books at **www.hansebooks.com**

Pliny Earle

MEMOIRS

OF

PLINY EARLE, M.D.,

WITH

EXTRACTS FROM HIS DIARY AND LETTERS (1830-1892)

AND SELECTIONS FROM HIS PROFESSIONAL WRITINGS (1839-1891).

Edited, with a General Introduction, by

F. B. SANBORN, OF CONCORD,

Former Chairman of the Board of State Charities of Massachusetts and Inspector of Charities.

"Genius must learn the language of facts."—*Emerson.*

BOSTON:

DAMRELL & UPHAM,

The Old Corner Bookstore,

283 WASHINGTON STREET.

1898.

TO THE KINDRED AND FRIENDS OF

DOCTOR EARLE

IN MANY LANDS AND ALL CLASSES,

AND TO HIS ABIDING MEMORY,

THIS VOLUME IS INSCRIBED.

CONTENTS.

INTRODUCTION.

In writing the life of an American alienist who began his observations on his insane countrymen nearly sixty-five years ago, and traversed Europe, inspecting asylums, in 1837-8-9, one is reminded of the saying of that aged Roman who was brought to trial before the third generation of his countrymen, "It is hard to plead my cause when all the witnesses of my life are dead." So great have been the changes, so incessant the progress, in the study of insanity, its care and treatment, that no single life, however prolonged, can be justly expected to measure them or keep pace with them. That my friend Dr. Earle did so in a marked degree, and was at his death in 1892 in advance of his survivors in some points, as during his life he had been before his associates in nearly·all, is one of his chief claims to remembrance by those who knew not his firm, gentle, and beneficent personality. But, in order to understand how this was so, the reader needs to know something of the history of insanity and its treatment in America up to the present time.

Sydney Smith used to speak of certain events as occurring "before the invention of common sense"; and the traditional, often the scientific, treatment of madness and melancholy in centuries past fell within that absurd period. A curious edition of Æsop's Fables in Latin, printed at Exeter, N.H., in 1799, contained, for the edification of Dr. Abbott's pupils at the Phillips Academy, this account of "The Doctor who took Care of Insane Men":—

There was a doctor of medicine living at Milan who undertook to cure the insane, if they were brought to him before a certain stage in their malady; and his treatment was after this sort. He had a court-yard near his house, and in it a pool of filthy water, in which he tied them to a post, naked. Some of them were in up to their knees, some up to the middle, others deeper still, according to the degree of their madness; and he gave them water treatment in this way until they appeared to be sane. Now one man was brought to him among others, whom he set in the water up to his thighs. After a fortnight he began to grow sane, and begged the doctor to take him out of the puddle. This he did, and so relieved him of the torment, but with the understanding that he should not go outside the court-yard. When this condition was complied with for a few days, he allowed the patient to go all about the house, only he must not go through the gate. His fellow-sufferers, not a few, remained in the water; but he took pains to obey the doctor, and so recovered, remembering nothing of what he had seen before he was crazy.

Stupid as this treatment was, it was reason itself when compared with the exorcism of demons long practised by the reverend clergy, and with the mystic curative quality of the relics of St. Dymphna at Gheel, in Belgium, first observed in the eighth century. The New England Puritans, in the days of Salem witchcraft, still believed in demoniac possession, and had few remedies but the "dark house" of Malvolio, and prayers by the parson, for the frequent insanity of ministers and their wives.* Then came a change for the better, though accompanied by Dr. Rush's profuse bleeding, and the aid of cold water, chains, and the whip, all which seem to have been in use in the first American asylum for the insane, opened at Philadelphia, under Dr. Franklin's eye, in 1752. It was there that Dr. Benjamin Rush, an acute and observant physician, had his long experience with the insane, which bore fruit in his once popular and still interesting work on

---

* The clerical profession give up very slowly their theories of mental and spiritual things. Dr. Hirsch, in his "Genius and Degeneration" in answer to Max Nordau, cites this curious recent utterance of German parsons: "At a meeting of the German ' Union of Evangelical Curates of the Insane ' Rev. Von Bodelschwingh, while admitting that medico-scientific psychiatry had done good service in the recognition, treatment, and cure of the insane, still censured it as at bottom materialistic and temporal. ' It leaves sin and grace, conscience and guilt, quite out of sight, and does not recognize that forgiveness of sins brings life and spiritual health. Speaking broadly, the less the bodily physician uses his *materia medica* in mental maladies, the better. Such things, for the most part, only damage body and soul. The bodily physician may be helpful in the care of the insane, but the prime thing is the care of the sick soul; and this should not be intrusted to the physician in the main.' There is an element of truth in the statement, but it would lead to practical absurdities."

"Diseases of the Mind," published in 1812. Few have made more valuable observations in America on the manifestations of insanity, yet his notion of treatment was but little in advance of the Milanese doctor's. In mania Dr. Rush recommended the strait-waistcoat or the "tranquillizing chair," privation of food, pouring cold water into the coat-sleeves, and, lastly, the shower-bath for fifteen or twenty minutes. This was *moral* treatment, supplemental to bleeding. He adds, "If all these modes of *punishment* fail of their intended effects, it will be proper to resort to the fear of death. By the proper application of these mild and terrifying modes of punishment, chains will seldom and the whip never be required to govern mad people."

This was the height of the medical profession in 1812, after the "humane revolution" of which Rush spoke had occurred under Pinel in France and the Quakers of York in England. He exulted in the fact that in the Pennsylvania Hospital "the clanging of chains and the noise of the whip are no longer heard in the cells of the insane. They now taste of the blessings of air and light and motion in pleasant and shaded walks in summer, and in spacious entries warmed by stoves in winter." He favored separate hospitals for hard drinkers, and the alternation of hot and cold baths to shock the insane into sanity. But his great specific was blood-letting, which he carried to high figures of weight and frequency of withdrawing what he regarded as a noxious fluid. His example, and the virility and vivacity of his truly benevolent mind, made his doctrine pernicious for half a century. Dr. Tuke called him "the American Fothergill," resembling that English Quaker, he thought, "in the independence of his practice, in acuteness of observation, in enthusiastic love of the art of healing, and in popularity as a physician in a great city."

To Dr. Rush, who died in 1813, succeeded physicians of less mark, but who improved the treatment of insanity in some particulars,— Dr. Wyman of the McLean Asylum near Boston in 1818, Dr. Todd of the Hartford Retreat in 1824, and Dr. S. B. Woodward, a trustee of the Hartford Retreat, but in 1833 superintendent of the State Hospital at Worcester, estab-

lished by Horace Mann and others, a year or two earlier.
It was from Dr. Woodward that Dr. Earle drew his first inspiration as professional alienist, and he continued to regard
him as greatly instrumental in the instruction of physicians
and the guidance of the public respecting insanity and its
treatment. He retired before my time, and I had no opportunity to compare him with later alienists. The same is true of
Dr. Brigham, who succeeded Dr. Todd at Hartford, and was
the first superintendent of the New York State Asylum at
Utica. But I believe the superiority of both was less due to
special attainments than to a native vigor of mind, a power of
will, and an impressive personality. They looked forward, and
not backward. They bettered the practices which they found
in use, and they undertook popular instruction; but they made
few discoveries, and left little written evidence of their great
usefulness. Dr. Brigham, indeed, left more of that than Dr.
Woodward; for he founded the *Journal of Insanity*, and wrote
much for it.

The younger contemporaries and successors of these pioneers
were mostly known to me personally, with the exception of
Dr. Bell, whom I believe to have been gifted with the New
Hampshire traits of courage, energy, and good will to mankind,
along with a little more culture than often fell to his rural
contemporaries. I began my inspection of asylums in 1863
with the peculiar establishment of Dr. Rockwell, soon after
visited Dr. Ray in Providence and Dr. Butler at Hartford,
knew rather intimately Dr. Gray of Utica, often saw Dr. Kirkbride and Dr. Chapin, was intimate with Dr. Jarvis, Dr. Choate,
Dr. Tyler, Dr. Clement Walker, Dr. Chandler, and Dr. Bancroft, to mention no others. Few of these men had what
would now be thought a sufficient medical and philosophical
training for one of the most difficult and perplexing branches
of the medical and psychological art. The German psychi-
atrists, as Dr. Earle discovered in 1849, had far exceeded them
in preliminary studies and systematic thought. But most of
them were sensible, practical men, who had learned much as
assistant physicians or superintendents of asylums and hospitals. Several of them were good administrative heads of what

were, in one aspect, great hotels. A few were good organizers, and still fewer were good writers. Dr. Ray was exceptional in this last point. His mind was clear, and his style enviable.

None of these alienists, however, had comprehended the statistical, economic, or even the sanatory relations of the public care of the insane. It was still a new matter. Experience was wanting. Enumeration, even practical definition of the insane, was lacking; and, while their number was much underrated, the likelihood of their recovery was extremely overestimated. The asylums were few and small, received but a portion of the insane, and had no means of determining the exact physical condition of the patients they treated. The microscope had hardly begun to do its work in revolutionizing medicine. The localization of function in the brain was in its rudiments, and was obscured by the charlatanry of phrenology. The classification of insanity by its external manifestations was very little advanced, and had to be the study of each alienist in his own narrow field of observation. They experimented with medical and moral treatment; and, like Dr. Rush, they formed singular notions of what treatment was applicable to the mass of the insane. Still, knowledge advanced under their isolated experiences. They communicated facts to each other and to the public. Unfortunately, like medical men in all ages, with exception of a few physicians of genius, they took guesses and traditions for fact, in too many matters, and were unreasonably sanguine of good results from specifics or hastily formed systems of treatment. Naturally desirous of commending their beneficent mission to the great public, they propagated the hypothesis that all the insane were easily curable, if only intrusted early to their care. This was a pardonable illusion at first. It passed with time into a delusion which they wished the community to share with experts who began to have their doubts and to color their facts. How long it continued to be honestly held by superintendents who made careful observations would be hard to say; but such men should have the benefit of every doubt, since their purpose was good.

Meantime visible insanity increased amazingly; and the impulse given to the public for its better treatment, by the missionary labors of Dr. Woodward, Miss Dix, and others, led to the building of many new asylums, which must be medically officered. By this time, though the real nature of insanity had been but little studied, young physicians perceived that the specialty gave an opening for them in a profession where it was not easy to get a bread-winning position for general practice at the outset of their career. This led to ambition and intrigue for places in the new hospitals and asylums. Personal favor and political interest came in to promote the claims of the inexperienced and self-seeking, and a class of physicians was gradually introduced in important positions who had neither the mental endowment nor the high moral purpose of the pioneers in the American specialty. The pressure for admission to asylums increased with the growth of population and wealth, and the manifest increase of insanity; and the sound principles of the elder alienists, favoring small asylums and greater personal care, were soon set aside, at first on the ground of economy or expediency, and then because great asylums involved larger powers and wider "patronage" in the hands of politicians, medical or administrative. Still, the fiction of easy curability was kept up, and used as an argument for extracting appropriations from legislative bodies, which were then expended in costly structures, from which the insane derived less advantage than did the officials who inhabited such palace-hospitals.

Along with this phase of the specialty went a kind of trade-unionism in the heads of hospitals and asylums, excluding from their guild persons of high attainments and earnest purpose, who might have raised the tone of their meetings and improved the quality of the *Journal of Insanity*, which was their organ. Such was the state of things, concisely interpreted, when the first Boards of State Charities were created, with a general power of inspecting hospitals and asylums, from 1863 to 1870. In every instance, probably, the heads of those establishments opposed the visitation and resented the criticism of the earlier Boards of this class. Instead of welcoming a new ally (which these boards soon became, in the advancement of the true knowledge of insanity and an improvement of its treatment), this medical trade-union of alienists received them as meddlesome critics, and at first thought to put them down. But from that day to this the question of insanity has gradually acquired a fuller and wiser discussion in America, though the treatment of patients still leaves much to be desired. A superficial and often pompous display of knowledge has given way to an earnest search for truth; and the difficulties of the situation (greatly increased as they are by the trebling of our population, the muddy tides of immigration, and a fuller discovery of the statistical facts) are now faced with a better scientific and practical preparation than was possible a generation ago.

It was the peculiar merit of Dr. Earle — in some respects a good fortune rather than a merit — that he began his special career with a far more thorough outfit of experience than most of his contemporaries, and never neglected the means of keeping himself in line with the thought and experience of countries that preceded ours in the improved care of their insane. He was what Lloyd called Sir Anthony Brown, "the best compound in the world, — a learned, an honest, and a travelled man; a good nature, a large soul, and a settled mind." When few Americans had the opportunity, and perhaps none the inclination, to examine the care of the insane in Europe, he explored it, and that twice, — in his first residence abroad and again in his tour of discovery among the German asylums. This placed him above our American weakness of boasting ourselves the foremost in all things, as we are, no doubt, in some things. It broadened his knowledge, and still more his receptivity, so that he no longer took for granted the confident statements of the narrow-minded, while he left a margin for facts and theories that were new to him. His honesty of mind and the habit of his religious sect, long accustomed to look on the fashion of this world not only as transient, but as wrong, kept him from swimming smoothly with the current, as so many of his professional brethren did. His arithmetical turn made him distrust statistics which would not "prove" the result they were added up to show; and his innate frugality caused him to look at the wasting of public money on palatial poor-

houses as worse than a blunder. All this, which kept him
back from advancement in the art he so well understood, was
his best equipment for the final success that he achieved. His
name will stand higher as time passes, because his work was
done, not for present fame and emolument, but for the future
good of a large and unhappily increasing class of mankind. A
part of it also, his refutation of the fallacy of easy curability,
will be remembered as one of the best contributions thus far
made to the science of insanity by the hundreds of American
alienists who have dealt with the subject.

To the new physiological investigation of insanity as a
corporeal disease, which promises better results than it has yet
furnished, Dr. Earle was perhaps a little unjust. He had seen
so many loud proclamations on this subject with so little real
accomplishment, that his practical good sense, joining with the
conservatism of added years, made him less hopeful than he
would have been before 1860. But it will probably always remain true that his moral methods in dealing with insanity are
for the greatest good of all.

The accumulation of thousands of the chronic insane in huge
asylums (so foreign to all the principles of Dr. Earle and his
colleagues of thirty years ago) led him to modify his opinions
in some respects. In his address at the Chicago Conference
of Charities in 1879, he admitted that chronic asylums are a
necessity, but pleaded for their better organization so as "to
preserve the advantages of the small institution with the
alleged economy of support in the large one." To do this, he
would group around the existing hospitals buildings of cheaper
construction ; and he would exclude from asylums the insane
who need no such restraint. "Many patients," he said, "are
now committed, from whom society has nothing to fear, and
whose best interests are thus promoted because they have no
suitable home." Hence a movement had arisen (in Massachusetts chiefly promoted at that time by Miss Dix's early friend,
Dr. S. G. Howe) for placing the insane in family homes, as was
then done in Belgium and Scotland only. While anticipating
little reduction in the over-population of asylums from this
movement, Dr. Earle with his native candor said : "We per-

ceive no serious objection to a trial of the experiment. Success sometimes awaits the efforts of that enthusiasm which is inspired by faith, even when the doubters least expect it." As time elapsed and the Family Care system in Europe showed increasingly good results, Dr. Earle's doubts gave way; and he joined in recommending that the hospitals, as well as the central State authority, should place the insane in Massachusetts families. He went beyond existing opinion in 1890 (see page 278) in suggesting this family care for convalescing patients,—a measure he had found working well on a small scale in the Duchy of Nassau in 1849.

Thus from 1835, when he may be said to have first seriously considered the American problems of insanity, until 1890,—more than half a century — Dr. Earle was foremost in favoring improvements in its treatment; and, where he doubted, he gave the future the benefit of the doubt. I know of no other New England reformers of whom this can be said except Dr. Howe.* These three persons, Dr. Earle earliest and latest, Dr. Howe with the quickest insight, and Miss Dix with the most rapid success, appear to me to have done most to advance the cause in America.

As Dr. Earle's monumental work on "The Curability of Insanity" is still in print, and may be had of the publishers of this Memoir, there seemed to be no occasion to quote largely from it. For a similar reason the "Earle Genealogy," being readily accessible, little has been said of the members of Dr. Earle's family, except incidentally, in connection with his letters and the events of his long life. From the interesting communication of the Rev. Samuel May, a companion of Garrison, a college classmate of Dr. Holmes, and for many years a townsman of the Leicester Earles, some additional information can be had in the Appendix. It has been thought best to reprint there some of Dr. Earle's publications of a time long past, and a few of his later papers. So copious was the correspondence left by him in the hands of his executors that only a small part of it could be used in this volume. Our effort has

---

* Samuel Gridley Howe, born Nov. 10, 1801, died Jan. 9, 1876, was the famous philanthropist and revolutionist of Boston, friend of the blind, the poor, and all who needed help.

been to reproduce in some degree the earlier circumstances of his life, and the scenes in which he moved fifty or sixty years ago, in order to give that interest to these pages which the publication of a correspondence mainly professional or of family significance could not so well impart.

It may be said, however, that his relations with his family, and the mutual interchange of good offices between its members, were such as might be expected from the cordial and practical character of the Earles of Leicester, the Chases of Worcester, and the Buffums of Rhode Island. The pecuniary independence which the elder Pliny Earle secured, until reverses overtook him, was achieved by the diligence and good sense of his son and namesake; and his possessions were used by Dr. Earle to encourage excellence in others, and to promote public interests. Portions of his last Will, at the end of the Appendix, will prove his liberality to the public; his care for those who needed aid was no less liberal.

The portraits in this volume are from a daguerreotype taken about 1846 and from a photograph of about forty years later. The steel engraving prepared for the "Earle Genealogy" and used in a portion of this edition is perhaps of 1875 or thereabout. Without being so speaking a likeness as the later photograph, it has some merits not seen in the other two. The early daguerreotype has suffered in expression from fading.

It may be added that an error of one month crept into the pages that mention Dr. Earle's first voyage to Europe, which began April 25, 1837, and not *March* 25, as printed. In Dr. Earle's brief reminiscences, page 383, this is correctly stated.

F. B. S.

CONCORD, Sept. 12, 1898.

MEMOIR OF PLINY EARLE, M.D.

CHAPTER I.

BIRTH, ANCESTRY, AND CHILDHOOD.

PLINY EARLE, second of that name, was the son of Pliny
Earle of Leicester, a rural town near Worcester, in Worcester
County, Mass., where the subject of this biography was born,
Dec. 31, 1809, at the residence of his father, then engaged
in manufactures and agriculture. His mother was Patience
Buffum, of Smithfield, R.I.; and both she and her husband
were of the Society of Friends, which had early established
itself in the Plymouth Colony and the neighboring colony of
Roger Williams. The first of Dr. Earle's paternal ancestors in
America was Ralph Earle, who came from near Exeter, in
England, and may have been in Rhode Island as early as 1634.
His name appears among the signers of a political compact
made at Portsmouth, R.I., April 30, 1639. He married a wife,
Joan,* no doubt in England, and remained in Rhode Island until
his death in 1678. No successful effort has yet been made to
connect this Ralph Earle (Erle) with the distinguished English
family of Erles in Somerset and Devon, to which belonged Sir
Walter Erle of Charborough, of the generation immediately
preceding Ralph Earle. He was a member of Parliament in
the first years of Charles I.'s reign, and was arbitrarily imprisoned by that king for refusing, with others, to pay a forced loan
under royal authority without warrant of law. A dozen knights,
of whom Sir Walter was one, and seventy-eight other Englishmen of all ranks, were thus imprisoned. They were all released in February, 1628; and in the next March twenty-seven

* Her name was perhaps Savage.

of them, Sir Walter at their head, were returned to the new
Parliament.   Others so elected were John Hampden, Sir Edward Hampden, Sir Nicholas Barnardiston, and Sir Thomas
Grantham,— all Puritans, and opposed to the arbitrary proceedings of Charles and the bishops.   It is every way probable that
the Earles of Rhode Island were distant cousins of these English Erles,— not only for the reasons given by Dr. Earle in his
genealogical volume, "Ralph Earle and his Descendants"
(Worcester, 1888), but also because these New England Earles,
like the English knight, were stanch defenders of liberty and
free speech, which Rhode Island was colonized to maintain.
Ten years later (1638), and about the time Ralph's name appears in Rhode Island, Hampden, Cromwell, and other Puritan
leaders, were entertaining a purpose of emigrating to New
England; and Ralph Earle and his wife, like some of the
Massachusetts and Connecticut colonists, may have been sent
out in advance.

Be this as it may, their son Ralph, about 1660, removed to
Dartmouth, in the Plymouth Colony, but near Rhode Island,
and acquired a large estate in what is now New Bedford and
the Elizabeth Islands.   William, another son, also lived in
Dartmouth, where his son Ralph was born; but about 1717
this third Ralph removed to Leicester, where he also acquired
much land, and where he declared himself a Quaker.   His son
Robert, born in 1706, lived, vigorous and active, in Leicester
to the age of ninety.   The first Pliny Earle was his great-
grandson.   From farming Pliny turned to trade and manufactures, and established a mill in Leicester, where he made
cards for the early cotton-mills from a model of his own, for
which he got a patent early in this century.   This gave him a
competence which enabled him to educate his nine children
well.   Our Pliny was the youngest but one of these, and was
almost sixteen years younger than his eldest brother, John.

Leicester, when Ralph Earle followed his Indian guide,
Moses, from Grafton to its breezy hill-tops, included the present
towns of Leicester and Paxton, and adjoined Rutland.   Within
its limits was the Indian hill, Asnebumskit, fourteen hundred
feet high ; and a portion of Ralph Earle's five hundred and fifty

acres reached the west side of that hill. His homestead and main farm lay on what is now called Earle Ridge, and on both sides of Mulberry Street, extending towards Strawberry Hill, where the churches and academy are, far enough to include the quiet, wooded slope where the Quaker meeting-house stood for more than one hundred years, and where the Friends' burying-ground is ; the meeting-place of the society having been transferred to Worcester about the middle of the nineteenth century. There were no Quakers in that region until Ralph Earle arrived, nor did he declare himself one until 1732; but he was probably the son of Quaker parents, and no doubt shared their opinions, since he would not otherwise have been sufficiently interested in William Penn to visit him in Philadelphia before 1701. The immediate occasion of professing himself a Quaker in Leicester was to avoid the parish tax, then levied on all who were not obviously exempt. Quakers had become practically exempt by the decision of the English Privy Council in 1724, upon the petition of Joseph Anthony, John Sisson (of Tiverton), and John Akin and Philip Tabor (of Dartmouth), who were Quakers, and had been imprisoned a year for failing to lay and collect the ministerial tax in their two townships. This decision set them free, and in substance said that Quakers need not pay such taxes. Ralph Earle, formerly of Dartmouth, his sons Robert and William, and four other men,— among them Nathaniel Potter,— eight years after (1732) asked by petition to be released from paying "any part of the tax for the seport of the minister or ministers established by the laws of this province of Massachusetts Bay," alleging that they were Quakers, conscientiously scrupulous about such payment, and claiming "the Privileges granted" to the people of that name. Seven years later Benjamin Earle, the youngest of Ralph's eleven children, and to whom he had given that part of the farm where the graves now are, joined with Nathaniel Potter in conveying a lot for the Quaker meeting-house in trust to Samuel Thayer, of Mendon, who before the year ended reconveyed it to Earle, Potter, Thomas Smith, and John Wells, on condition that it should be held in common, and should go by shares to their heirs and assigns forever. A small meeting-house was built there in 1741, a larger one fifty years later ; and near them were buried Ralph Earle and his descendants and kindred.

The Earle estates ran along where the present Earle Street, leading towards Leicester Village, crosses Mulberry Street; and there the great-grandfather (Robert) of Dr. Earle had his house. A few rods further south, on Mulberry Street, Robert, Jr. (Dr. Earle's grandfather), built a small house in 1771, afterwards owned by Dr. Earle himself, and now called "Earle Ridge." In 1792 Pliny Earle, Sr., removed his grandfather's house to the east side of Mulberry Street, and made it a factory for his card manufacture, building the next year the larger house, still standing, on the west side. Here his nine children were born, and here both he and his wife died. The Quaker Meeting between there and the village, which had counted but eight male members in 1742, grew to have more than one hundred, male and female ; and in the school district, including the Earle, Potter, and Southwick Quaker farms, there were in 1812 twenty-one grandchildren of Robert Earle, Jr., out of forty pupils. At present no child named Earle is a pupil there, and the broad acres of the Earles mostly pass under other names.

The country itself retains its picturesque features, except that the forests are gone, and are replaced by fruit-trees and well-tilled fields. Noble views are seen from the high hills, and both Earle Ridge and the village hill are nearly twelve hundred feet above the sea. The roads are steep or winding,— sometimes both,— and in summer pleasant. Of his father Dr. Earle thus wrote in his later years : —

My ancestors were mostly either yeomen or artisans, and, with the exception of one or two, took no part that was prominent in public affairs. My father, from whom I took my Christian name, was a man of good intellectual powers, with a love for the science of mechanics, and much inventive faculty. He received little literary education ; but his ciphering-book (that once fashionable record of mathematical work), still in existence, is written in a fair, distinct hand, and would not be discreditable to a good pupil in a country school at the present day. He had a special turn for mathematics, without the opportunity of pursuing its higher branches; and he acquired, though not in the schools, such a knowledge of chemistry as the general student rarely obtained in his active life.

With his habitual understatement, Dr. Earle hardly rendered justice to the prominence of his father and uncles in the early period of cotton and woollen manufacture by machinery in New England, at the close of the last century. Judge Emory Washburn, the historian of Leicester, his native town, gives this account of the small beginnings of what became a large industry, in the hands of Pliny Earle, his brothers, children, and successors : —

The manufacture of cotton and wool hand-cards was commenced in Leicester about 1785, by Mr. Edmund Snow; and among those most early engaged was Mr. Pliny Earle, who possessed much of the mechanical ingenuity (in addition to a great fund of general knowledge) which has characterized those of that name in the town. About the year 1790 Mr. Samuel Slater, the venerable originator of cotton-factories in the United States, having in vain endeavored to procure suitable cards for his machinery in the principal cities of the Union, applied to Mr. Earle. Machine-cards had till then been made in the manner called *plain*. A part of the cards used on a machine is called "filleting," and this part it was desirable to have what is termed "twilled." For this purpose Mr. Earle was obliged to prick the whole filleting with two needles inserted in a handle, in the manner of an awl. This process was extremely tedious; but Mr. Earle at length completed it, and furnished to Mr. Slater the cards on which the first cotton was wrought that was spun by machinery in America. The difficulty with which he accomplished this engagement led to his invention of a machine with which to prick the leather for cards; and about 1797 he accomplished the desired object.

Pliny Earle had engaged in this card-making before 1786, when he was only twenty-four years old. By 1789 he had become so well known that the firm of Almy and Brown of Providence (kinsmen and successors of Moses Brown, a founder of Brown University) engaged him to cover the cylinders in their mill with card-teeth such as he had made for a mill in Worcester, before Mr. Slater had applied to him for a similar purpose. The patent for his machine was not issued till 1803, but it had been in use long before ; and its principle formed the basis of all such machines for many years.

The mother, Patience Earle, was no less gifted and energetic than her spouse. Of her and the events of his childhood, Dr. Earle wrote in an unfinished autobiography : —

My mother, who was but five years old at the opening of the Revolution (1775) had even fewer facilities for education than my father ; but, having a strong literary taste, she became very much of a reader, and carried the habit to the close of her life. From my earliest memory of her till her last illness (November, 1849, when she was seventy-nine), she habitually took an after-dinner nap in bed, taking with her either a book or a newspaper, and reading until she fell asleep. She did the same on retiring at night. When in bed, she always lay on her left side, and held the book or newspaper in her extended right hand. The protracted and semi-continual pressure of her body upon the left shoulder brought into operation a well-known physiological law. At the time of her decease the shoulder-blade of that side was not more than half as large as that of the right side, which had been free from pressure.

My parents had nine children, and the first death in the family was that of my father, who died (1832) when his youngest child was nineteen years of age. Of the nine, seven had learned the letters of the English alphabet before they were respectively twenty months old. , In the two exceptions, the health of the children was so unstable that it was considered unwise to attempt to teach them. This release of the school-teachers from the drudgery of teaching the alphabet was the work of the mother, to whom the children were indebted for that instruction.

It has been said that no person can do three things at one and the same time ; but, if my mother did not accomplish that feat, it must be acknowledged that she came very near it. I have seen her, many a time, during the first three years of my younger brother's life, tending the baby, knitting, and teaching the letters to the baby. My father was a subscriber to the old New York *Herald*, the leading newspaper of the metropolis at that time. Its heading was in plain Roman capitals, an inch or more in height. These letters were used for the instruction of her babies, in so much of the alphabet as they would serve. The large letters of the title-page of the Bible and other books enabled her to complete the alphabet. With the same arrangements of babies and knitting-work, and generally with most of the family present, she read aloud from the Holy Scripture, particularly in the long winter evenings. A neighbor, a prominent minister of the Society of Friends, said of her, "She was the most capable woman, taking her in every respect, that I ever knew; and I have known a great many."

The district school was but about forty rods from my father's homestead, and I began to attend it when very young. I learned easily, and at the age of five years was reading in the highest class, our text-book being Scott's "Lessons," the English publication which to a greater extent than any other supplied the schools of New England prior to the publication of any American work of the kind.

I might relate an anecdote as illustrative of an early facility in the application of acquired knowledge. I was very young, and this is the earliest of my memories; but the circumstances are still as vividly in my mind's eye as if they had occurred much later. One morning, after breakfast, Daniel Jenkins, the man who then had charge of the farm, took me up, and held me with his arms around my legs and face to face with himself, our heads being at very nearly the same height. I pushed his head from me, making him lean backwards, then leaned backwards to some distance, and said to him, "Y!" I remember that I was greatly pleased to find I had discovered, in the group formed by him and myself, a resemblance to that letter of the alphabet. The literary taste of my mother was inherited to a very considerable extent by her children; and, considering the time at which they lived, they became great readers. My grandmother Earle, one of our nearest neighbors, one day remarked to my mother that with her children she had made it a matter of principle not to call away one of them from reading to set them at work. My mother's reply was, "If I should never call upon one of my children while reading to do work, I should never get any work done by them."

My father was a farmer and a manufacturer of (cotton) cards, the latter being what he chiefly relied upon for the support of his family. He was lenient with his children, and did not require us to work regularly, even when we were not at school. He often

kept two farm hands and always one. Either by requisition or for
my own amusement, I often assisted the farmers at their work. I
began by following the mowers to spread their swath (a work which
greatly delighted me), and was soon promoted to riding the horse
for ploughing, which I utterly detested, and always evaded, if possible. Subsequently I made myself familiar with the use of every
farm tool used at that time. The knowledge thus acquired has been
of no inconsiderable use to me in superintending the large farm at
the Northampton Hospital. My father had for those days a great
variety of fruit-trees, in which he took a great interest; and he had
no little knowledge of horticulture and fruit-raising. I learned
from him the methods of grafting and budding fruit-trees when I
was about eleven years old, and had considerable practice upon
young trees raised in our garden. One or two of his experiments
were curious.

Among his pear-trees was one whose trunk was some five inches
through, which had begun to bear fruit. It then began to decay
about five feet from the ground, and so continued till at one point
it reached the heart of the tree. My father then sawed the trunk
half off at two points, above and below the decayed portion, from
twelve to fifteen inches apart. From another tree he cut a branch
about as large as the decaying trunk, and carefully fitted a piece
of this branch into the space from which he took out the decay,
taking pains to match the bark of the branch to the bark of the tree,
so that the flowing sap would pass through the inserted half-cylinder.
He wrapped it at the mended part; and this inserted piece grew,
and formed one-half of the trunk of the pear-tree, which, however,
continued to decay. In two or three years the decayed part extended nearly through the trunk, but the inserted piece had become
so strong as to support the tree. He then sawed out the remaining
and decayed half of the original trunk for a space corresponding
to a new piece which he inserted. Again he wrapped it, and again
the inserted piece grew. The tree flourished for many years, with
no part of its original trunk where the decay had been; and many
a good pear, both of the St. Michael's and the Flemish Beauty
varieties, have I eaten from it. Again, one spring father received
some young pear-trees from New York. They were all planted but
one, which lay in the garden three or four weeks, not "heeled in,"
but exposed to all sorts of weather. I supposed it to be hopelessly

dead; but father took it, and, having gathered some small roots from living pear-trees, inserted their upper ends under the bark of the new tree's roots. He then planted it, and it grew with as much vigor as if its planting had not been thus delayed.

For the business of manufacturing cards and carding-machines, father had a carpenter's shop, a blacksmith's shop, and a foot-lathe. This last was to me of great interest; and I learned upon it the use of the chisel and gouge, while turning tops and fancy articles. In the carpenter's shop I became familiar with all its tools, and practised with them to some extent of usefulness. In the card factory I worked also, in such departments as were within my ability. In making hand-cards, I punched and nailed the handles to the boards, and nailed the cards upon the boards, thus getting the dexterous and facile use of a small hammer. In both hand and machine cards, the teeth were cut from wire by "cutting-machines," which were somewhat complicated. Even as early as my seventh year I was employed, more or less, in operating such a machine, and soon learned to understand its construction, and how to correct some of the simplest forms of its disordered working. Whatever mechanical faculty nature gave me was here called into activity, and so developed that, whenever since I have seen a new machine of any sort, my first impulse has been to investigate all its movements. Thus, when in 1824 a small steam-engine was placed in the card factory, for running the cutting-machine, I learned its use; and, when fifteen years old, in the whole warm season of 1825, I had charge of both the steam-engine and the machine, and practically learned the principles of steam as a motive power. This was my chief occupation until I entered the Friends' School at Providence in the early autumn of 1826.

My school education had not been neglected meantime, for I had just passed my tenth year (in 1820) when I entered the Leicester Academy. I well remember the cold, blustering, uncomfortable, and discouraging day in March. My mother took me in the chaise then generally used,— a covered, one-horse carriage. The preceptor of the English Department, which I entered, was Thomas Fisk, a genial, good-natured man, without much natural taste for his employment, and not specially fond of severe work, but who still performed his prescribed duties without censure. But the preceptor of the Classical Department was an excellent scholar,—

John Richardson,— a somewhat severe disciplinarian, with a countenance really more stern than his character, and silver-bowed spectacles, which, being near-sighted, he constantly wore, and which had
the magical power of making every pupil in the school-room believe
the master was looking right at him.   I remained in the Academy,
excepting a term now and then, until the close of the autumn term
of 1824, and in that term was under Professor Richardson.   In the
following winter term (1825) I was at the town school, in my native
district, and made some progress in mathematics.   In both schools
I learned easily, and my lessons were always thoroughly committed;
but the knowledge acquired was much less than it should have been,
had the Academy been as thoroughly organized and efficiently managed as some others I have known.

No doubt Dr. Earle was here thinking of that excellent institution, still existing, the New England "Yearly-meeting Boarding-school," at Providence, R.I., in which he completed his
academic education, and afterwards taught for some years with
success, leaving on the minds of his pupils, of both sexes, a
vivid impression of his teaching capacity, and most agreeable
recollections of his personal influence and character.   He became an assistant teacher there in 1829, was promoted in 1831,
and in 1835, at the age of twenty-five, became the principal, for
a short time, of this important seminary.   Late in 1835 he resigned his place, and entered the University of Pennsylvania as
a medical student, at Philadelphia, in October of that year.
He had been studying medicine for some years with Dr. Usher
Parsons of Providence (brother-in-law of Dr. O. W. Holmes), a
distinguished surgeon and author, at the same time teaching
his classes in the Friends' School.   He completed his medical
course in 1837, and soon after went abroad.   But all through
his youth his education was more practical than academic, from
the lessons learned in his father's shops and on the great
Leicester farm.   Of these matters the autobiography goes on
to say : —

The persons who did the work of card-making for my father were
chiefly the women and children of farmers, who were thus enabled
to earn a considerable sum in the support of a family.   People in

Leicester and all the adjoining towns engaged in this work; for the holes in the leather which held the card-teeth were pricked by a hand-machine (" pricking-machine "), that could be used in a farmhouse. I often worked at this, rather as a pastime than a labor. We had several "routes" in which a horse and wagon was sent out from the factory for a circuit of from fifteen to twenty-five miles, among the farmers, to carry the leathers and teeth to the "setters," and collect from them the finished cards. Others, living nearer, came themselves to the factory to get the material and return the cards they had set. For some years I drove one of these circuit teams, and thus gained no little experience in the use and care of horses. My father also kept a kind of country store,— not for general customers, but for payment in kind of those who set the cards. There were not customers enough to justify hiring a clerk; and so different members of the Earle family acted as clerk, in due time. I was first promoted to this post when about twelve, and I well remember my feeling of pride at such exaltation. My first entry in day-book of a charge against a customer I considered astonishing.

It will be seen that this discipline and these experiences were just what was needed to make the boy and youth acquainted with the homely details of New England life in the first quarter of the century, when a state of things existed which has long since passed away. In these drives and colloquies with the industrious Yankee farmer, his wife and children, young Pliny Earle, as Channing says of Thoreau in his endless walks and talks about Concord, "came to see the inside of almost every farmer's house and head," — a sight worth seeing and a class worth knowing and spending your boyhood among. The same Concord poet has described them and their habitations as Dr. Earle saw them in the upland region around Worcester, to which he ever loved to return, until he became the last of his family there : —

> I love these homely mansions, and to me
> A farmer's house seems better than a king's.
> The palace boasts its art; but Liberty
> And honest pride and toil are splendid things.
> They carved this clumsy lintel, and it brings

> The man upon its front.   Greece hath her art;
> But this rude homestead shows the farmer's heart.
>
> The wind may blow a hurricane; but he
>   Goes fairly onward with the thing in hand.
> He sails undaunted on the crashing sea,
>   Beneath the keenest winter frost doth stand,
> And by his will he makes his way command,
>   Till all the seasons smile delight to feel
>   The grasp of his hard hand encased in steel.

Among the many virtues of this vanishing class was their frugality, which Dr. Earle learned and commended. He says in his autobiography : —

The disposition to save entered pretty largely into my natural character; and this tendency was fostered by the circumstances into which the family was thrown by the loss of most of my father's property, upon the declaration of peace between the United States and Great Britain, in 1815. His business firm (Pliny Earle & Brothers), which consisted of the three eldest brothers, Pliny, Jonah, and Silas, was formed in 1791; and their business soon became one of the most extensive of its kind in the country. In 1802 they added to it the building of machines for carding both cotton and wool; and in 1804 they placed wool-carding machines upon some stream in each of the towns to which their work extended, even one town in Rhode Island, for the convenience of the farmers who raised wool, but before had it carded by hand in their houses. Grafton, Rutland, Warren, and Northbridge, in Worcester County, and Cumberland in Rhode Island were these towns; and the firm were in part owners of a cotton-mill in Northbridge. The war with England, beginning when young Pliny was two and a half years old, much increased their profits. But the cost of raw material also increased greatly; and the close of the war in January, 1815, found them with a very large stock on hand, with falling prices and very little demand for cards. Such of the business as remained was retained by my father until his death in 1832, his principal agent and manager after 1819 being my brother William, seven years older than myself. My eldest brother, Thomas, who had been with his father in business, removed to Philadelphia in 1817, at the age of twenty-one; and an incident connected with him stimulated my tendency to economy.

Upon his first return from Philadelphia, when I was seven years old, he brought several books for children, which he gave to his younger brothers and sisters,—among them some of the minor tales of Maria Edgeworth, one of them entitled "Waste not, Want not; or, Two Strings to your Bow." Its hero was a boy who one day came across a piece of small cord, picked it up, and put it in his pocket. Some time afterwards, when shooting for a prize in archery, his bowstring broke. Whereupon he calmly took the preserved cord from his pocket, strung his bow with it, shot his arrow, and won the prize. I was greatly pleased with this story, and its moral made a strong impression. Twenty years after, on my first visit to Europe, the multitude of illustrations (not only in Great Britain and Ireland, but in the countries of the Continent) of a degree of economy wholly unknown even in New England, confirmed the impression made by the hero of "Waste not, Want not." At that time also I derived a useful lesson in another direction. I met with the evidences of order and system in the practical pursuits of life, to a far greater extent than in the United States. We were still in our national infancy, our Constitution not yet fifty years old, our territory large, its population sparse, and its business, both in the arts and commerce, carried on under the necessities of the moment rather than by the rules of long experience.

This love of order, system, and economy, however, was quite as much inherited and inbred by the connection of the Earles of Leicester with the Quakers as by any books or observations of early or later years. The traits of Dr. Earle were those so often noted in the English and American Quakers,— patience, perseverance, submission to the will of God as revealed by the Inner Light, even more than in the Old and New Testaments, and, not less, a sober resolution to acquire and retain the means of independent living. This implied industry, frugality, and orderly management of all secular affairs,— virtues visible in the first of the Quaker Earles of Leicester, Ralph, the great-grandfather of Pliny the elder. He had not been called a Quaker until after his removal from Freetown in Bristol County, in 1717, to Leicester. Indeed, he had borne in his youth the military title of ensign. He was a person of middle age and much substance when he became one of the early settlers of Leices-

ter, where his five hundred and fifty acres of land were transmitted to his numerous descendants, and in part to his faithful
negro slave, Sharp, whom he emancipated before his own
death, and presented with thirty acres on the south slope of
Asnebumskit, the highest hill of his region. Though late in
joining the Society of Friends, he was much attached to them,
and made a visit to Pennsylvania (tradition says) to see William
Penn. If so, it must have been about 1700, when Ralph Earle
was forty years old.*

Like her husband, Patience Earle, though descended
through the Arnold family of Lanthony in Wales from war-
rior-chieftains of that land, was born and bred a Quaker. But
she had certain tastes not always cherished in that sect, and
more in accord with the bards of Wales. She wrote verse
with facility, as did her son, who says of this: —

Her natural poetic taste was far above mediocrity; and she read
the verse of standard English poets with close attention, Pope being
her greatest favorite, and, next to him, Goldsmith. I once heard her
say of the " Essay on Man " that, if any person would repeat any
line of it he pleased, she would repeat the other line of the couplet.
Although familiar with Dr. Young, he was evidently not so satisfactory to her as Pope and Goldsmith. I have heard her say that the
" Night Thoughts " would read about as well by beginning at the
bottom of the page and reading upwards. In the last twenty years
of her life she wrote many poetical pieces, some of which found
their way into the newspapers. An unfinished poem of one hundred
and fifty lines, imitative of Goldsmith's " Deserted Village," was
written on revisiting her native village in Rhode Island. Her
school-house, of the Revolutionary epoch, is thus described : —

> In rustic, plain simplicity it stood
> On a broad lawn, encircled by a wood ;
> Within its walls a motley group was seen,
> Of different sexes and of varied mien ;
> Some, hardy, rough, and rugged sons of earth,
> Who never gave one bright idea birth,

* Penn last visited his American colony in 1699, and returned to England in 1701, where he died
in 1718. Ralph Earle may have been a "birthright Friend," who disconnected himself with the
society and afterwards rejoined it. His title of ensign is as late as 1715. He lived to be ninety-six,
dying in 1757, so that the lives of himself and his son Robert covered one hundred and thirty-six years,
from 1660 to 1796.

And seemed by nature from improvement barred,
With minds as callous as their frames were hard;
Some, gentle forms, and delicately wrought,
That scarcely seemed susceptible of thought,
On trifling objects ever prone to dote,—
Their only knowledge what they learned by rote;
And yet another class did there appear,—
Their minds capacious, their perceptions clear;
Like lightning's flash, they caught the vivid ray
Which Learning shed on their illumined way.

She next went on to mention the authors she read with her intimate cousin, Lavinia Buffum, after leaving school and before marriage : —

There on the margin of the rippling brook
We sat, and pored o'er some instructive book;
Read Milton's page, wise, learned, and sublime,
Or soared with Young beyond the bounds of time;
With Thomson viewed the varied seasons roll,
Or searched with Locke the mazes of the soul;
With Goldsmith traversed realms and states unknown,
Or bowed with Burke before the regal throne;
With Hervey pondered o'er the mighty dead,
With Homer trod where Grecian heroes bled, etc.

The same poem contains a tribute to the scholarship and piety of Elisha Thornton, the leading Quaker minister in New England in the period following the Revolution, and also a learned teacher, from whom Patience Buffum received instruction : —

Next the sage Tutor claims my humble lays,
Mild in his manners, wise in all his ways,
Easy of access, gentle, peaceful, kind,
Endowed by nature with a vigorous mind.

.   .   .   .

And when at times he bowed before the Throne
Of the eternal, omnipresent One,
In holy, awful, reverential prayer,
It seemed as if the heavenly host were there.

Dr. Earle goes on to say : —

She commemorated, each by a poem, the arrival and the departure of Lafayette on his visit to this country in 1824–25. When we

visited Worcester, where the Governor of Massachusetts then lived,
she took me with her to see him; and we shook hands with him (in
company with hundreds of other persons) as he stood in the gateway
in front of the residence of Governor Levi Lincoln, a mansion afterwards enlarged and converted into a hotel,—the Lincoln House.
The portrait of Lafayette in the Capitol at Washington is a very
accurate likeness of him as we that day saw him.

My mother was an elder in the Society of Friends, took an active
part in the women's meeting, and always sat at the head of the
meeting when no minister was present. She was liberal and charitable in all her views. At that time great stress was placed by most
of the society upon an adhesion to the custom of wearing its peculiar dress. It was worn by me until I was thirty years old (1840),
when I adopted the fashionable coat,* not being then at my
Leicester home. When informed of the change, her reply to the
informer was, "It makes but little difference what Pliny wears, so
long as he retains his integrity."

It is plain that Patience Earle was the strong religious influence in the household, although her husband is well described by his son as "a conscientious and consistent Quaker,
free from bigotry, and without unchristian prejudice against
any man because of his connection with some other denomination. He took but little part in the church business of the
society, but his house was ever open to its members; and he
took pleasure in seeing it filled at the monthly and quarterly
meetings." Neither he nor his wife seems to have shared in
the controversy which raged about them for some years concerning Elias Hicks and his liberal Quaker following.

Stimulated and united by persecution in the first century of
their separation from the Anglican and Puritan churches, the
Quakers continued to increase and to hold much the same
opinions until about 1820, when the eloquence and novelty of
the discourses of Elias Hicks, the friend of Walt Whitman's
forefathers on Long Island, began to stir up a schism. He
was a Unitarian, while the orthodox Quakers were Trinitarians,
and held to the doctrine of the atonement by the blood of
Christ. They were naturally shocked when Elias, a powerful

* In Philadelphia.

preacher, cried out in one of their great meetings at Philadelphia, "The blood of Christ,— the blood of Christ,— why, my friends, the actual blood of Christ was no more effectual in itself than the blood of bulls and goats,— not a bit more, not a bit." In 1826, when Pliny Earle was beginning his course of learning and teaching at Providence, in the school maintained by the orthodox Quakers of New England, his brother Thomas, then a practising lawyer in Philadelphia, wrote thus to their brother William at Leicester : —

You have probably heard of Elias Hicks being here lately [Dec. 31, 1826], and of the efforts of the Trinitarian Quakers to put him down. The missionaries whom the London Yearly Meeting of late sends so profusely among us are quite zealous in the work. The doctrine of the orthodox may be judged by two facts. The creed of George Keith,* who many years ago separated from the Friends because they would not believe in that creed, was read awhile since to one of the orthodox ministers, he being under the impression that it was the work of an early Quaker, which it was contemplated to republish. At almost every sentence he would exclaim, "Excellent!" "Just what is needed at the present time!" and he concluded by agreeing to take two dozen copies himself. The other instance was Isaac Hopper's reading to an English friend some extracts from "William Penn's Works," to see what he thought of them. So Isaac read from "The Sandy Foundation Shaken" two detached sentences. The Briton was almost enraptured with them. "There it is!" said he. "See, that is just the doctrine of Friends!" But when Isaac had read a little more, to show that what he had so much applauded was Mr. Penn's quotations from Episcopalians and Presbyterians, made for the purpose of refuting them, the man was so vexed that he departed, and has not been at Isaac's since.

Elias's meetings this time have been attended beyond all former example both in the city and country, and, I think, more numerously than those of any preacher of any sort who has been here of late years. Hundreds went away from almost every meeting because

---

* George Keith was indeed "an early Quaker," but a very fickle and pugnacious one, who, from having been a great friend and travelling companion of W. Penn and Barclay of Uri (he was himself a Scot), turned about and denounced the Quakers, and became a parson of the Church of England, subscribing to its creed and obeying its bishops. He lived for a time in Pennsylvania, and years after travelled from Maine to North Carolina, disputing against Quakers.

they could not obtain admittance, although no public notice was given of where he was to be.   This was doubtless mortifying to those who had printed notices of the meetings of the English preachers, sent them to most of the houses, and stuck them up in taverns, and yet were unable to obtain meetings more than half as numerous as those of Elias.   The stenographer who has taken down his sermons (first employed by his opponents) says that in the country near ninety-nine in a hundred Friends, old and young, approve of him.   Indeed, he met with no opposition in the country except at Darby, where X., from London, attacked him.   In Philadelphia there is one monthly meeting nearly unanimous for Elias.   The others are divided, most of the elders and members of the "meetings of sufferings" being against him, and about seven-eighths of the people under the age of forty being in his favor.

At the Pine Street meeting, after Elias had done preaching, Jonathan Evans, "the pope," got up to make "public opposition."   Yet, to avoid violating the letter of the discipline, he was careful not to say a word about Elias, but to proclaim a number of things as the faith of the society, every one present knowing that he wished it to be understood that Elias held the contrary.   At the close of the meeting Elias offered to shake hands with Jonathan,* who refused, saying: "I don't approve of thy doctrines.   He that denies the Son denies the Father."   Elias replied, "If any one says that I deny the Son, he tells what is untrue."   In the afternoon of the same day, at the Twelfth Street meeting, Elias preached to the general satisfaction of the people.   After he had done, Thomas Wistar, a rich and haughty elder, got up to violate the discipline by "public opposition," as J. Evans had done, and probably in pursuance of previous concert.   Immediately a clapping in the gallery commenced, to drown his voice.   Hissing was soon mingled with clapping, and the greatest uproar arose which I ever saw in meeting. "Order!" "Order!" resounded from several quarters,— "Hear what the man has to say!" etc.   Elias rose, and begged the audience to be still and to hear.   He was attended to, and Thomas finished his testimony.   Elias then rose, and said it was a pity the meeting should be so disturbed.   He supposed there was no one present but believed all the Friend had said.   The refractory elders probably

* The customary signal for breaking up a meeting is for two elders sitting next each other on the "high seat" to shake hands.

adopted their course in despair of doing anything against Elias in the manner required by discipline.

The orthodox appealed to the press, three or four years since, in hopes to overthrow Elias Hicks. They published tracts and Elias's sermons; but the other party published tracts also, and the sermons operated differently from what the orthodox hoped. They have now become anxious to muzzle the press, and complained of one Friend for circulating the *Berean*, a Quaker periodical published at Wilmington. The overseers dismissed the complaint, unable to find anything bad in the work except the proceedings of the Bible Society in England, where the Right Worshipful Mr. Somebody (of the Episcopal Church) spoke, and was followed by the Rev. Mr. Somebody, of the Society of Friends. This was published in the *Berean* to show the disposition of English Quakers to amalgamate with the Churchmen and aristocracy, who take the food from the mouths of the laborers of that country. Gould, the stenographer, has commenced a work called *The Quaker*, to be published semi-monthly, each number to contain a sermon by some minister of the society, together with selections from early Friends' writings or the Scriptures in corroboration of the sermon. The first number has a very good sermon of Elias Hicks, preached at Darby. This work has frightened the "meeting of sufferings," which appointed a committee to put a stop to it. Having an idle notion that the law would aid them, they went to Horace Binney for counsel, who told them they could not suppress it. Nevertheless, they put on a bold front, and went to Gould last week, demanding that he should stop the work. He replied that he could not: his support depended on it. They then said that the meeting would not encourage it. He replied it was unnecessary, as he was satisfied with his patronage, having one thousand subscribers. He also informed Samuel Biddle, one of the committee, that the first Quaker sermons he ever took down were in his (Samuel's) own house, at the request of his son, and by him paid for. They were the sermons of William Forster and Stevenson, and were found unworthy of publication. Among other things, they told Gould that Friends never had approved of having their sermons published. He said they must be mistaken, as he had seen the sermons of at least three Quakers in the Friends' Library of Philadelphia.

In a letter of April 24, 1828, Thomas Earle sums up the

points of difference between the Hicksites, whom he calls
"Friends," and the orthodox Quakers, in some terse sentences,
where allowance must be made for some partisan bias : —

The orthodox think much of doctrines, the Friends much of good
works; the orthodox much of wealth, the Friends of a contented
mind; the orthodox would call the righteous, the Friends would call
sinners, to repentance; the orthodox think much, the Friends but
little, of appearances. The orthodox give the Supreme Being a
character less merciful than belongs even to men : the Friends think
his mercy is infinite. The orthodox think men are punished for the
sins of Adam : the Friends do not. The orthodox believe in the
Trinity : the Friends do not. The orthodox subject their reason
and their perceptions to the doubtful language of ancient books : the
Friends try the merit of ancient books by their own reason and sense
of truth. The orthodox think their erring fellow-creatures are to be
shunned almost as wild beasts : the Friends think they should be
compassionated, kindly treated, and reformed. The orthodox appear
proud, or have a proud look, — they speak of "the rabble": the
Friends are of different appearance and conversation. The orthodox
believe a man punishable for his opinions, the Friends only for
actions, as they believe opinions to be involuntary. The orthodox
seem to think that a shade of virtue above a certain point secures a
man eternal happiness, and a shade below that point dooms him to
eternal misery : the Friends believe that every vicious act receives
its appropriate punishment (by mental affliction or otherwise), and
every virtuous act its appropriate reward. The Friends think that
the society at large has a right to judge what measures are proper
and who are its most pious and discreet members : the orthodox
think a small number of individuals have a right to determine that
themselves are the most pious and discreet, and, having so determined, have a right to dictate what course the society shall pursue.

At this time the Leicester Quakers had a large meeting ; and
those of the society living in Worcester came over on First
Days and at other times to worship in the plain house near the
brook, under Earle Ridge. But none of these dissensions seem
to have troubled their united body. In November, 1837, while
Dr. Earle was in Paris, the Worcester Quakers began to hold

First Day meetings in their own town, and the Leicester
Friends to join them; and now for many years the Worcester
meeting has been the only one, and the Leicester meeting-
house has disappeared. The slavery question introduced some
discord, apparently; for Lucy Earle, writing to Pliny Dec. 3,
1837, tells him that at the Worcester First Day meeting of
November 26 "there was a colored man by the name of Roberts,
one of the most respectable in Worcester, and Brother Anthony
Chase (who, by the way, is a zealous Abolitionist) took a seat
beside him,"— a remarkable fact in those days of darkness.

This long report of the stir among the quiet Quakers indicates that Thomas Earle sympathized with the Hicksite
Friends; and this was true of several of the family. But Pliny
was always rather more conservative in politics and religion
than his older brothers,— John, Thomas, and William,— though
ever inclining to liberal opinions. He kept his place in the
Providence school * undisturbed by the contest over doctrines,
and there prepared himself, by the study of books and the instruction of others, for his future career. He hesitated awhile
between medicine and the legal profession, in which his
brother Thomas had distinguished himself before 1830; and he
allowed the success of his brother, John Milton Earle, as a journalist, to draw him early into journalistic work. But, when he
finally took up medicine, he mastered its preliminaries, and

---

* Young Pliny Earle was for a time open to engagement as a teacher elsewhere than in Providence; for a letter of his uncle, Arnold Buffum, April 22, 1830, makes him two offers from Fall River:
first, the editorship of an "Antimasonick paper published in this village, with six hundred subscribers"; and, next, "the school in our new school-house, which will be finished now in a few days."
He accepted the latter, apparently; for he began a school in Fall River July 17, 1830. But what prevented his editing the newspaper is not recorded. Mr. Buffum's statement of the affair is interesting:
"The establishment belongs to a company who will be satisfied with about $75 a year for the rent of
building, press and all, and would give up the concern to the editor, or they will have it conducted
on their account, and will pay a salary. They have been sadly disappointed in the qualifications of
the publisher, and are fully determined to get another person to take his place immediately. They
were about trying to get David Daniels, but learned that he was gone to Baltimore. If thou hast any
inclination to engage in the newspaper concern, thou had better come down here immediately."
Anti-masonry was then being made the basis of a political party; and young Seward came into
prominence, with Thurlow Weed, in that movement, in which, also, William Wirt, the brilliant Baltimore lawyer, and John Quincy Adams were concerned. The Earles had been contributing to a semi-
literary weekly in Worcester, the Talisman; but probably Pliny felt no call to edit a political organ.
Literature and scholarship were native to the Leicester family; and Sarah Earle, ten years older than
Pliny, was not only an active member of the "Leicester Female Literary Society,"— half a century
before the era of women's clubs began,— but the founder of the Mulberry Grove Boarding-school, at
her father's homestead, as early as 1827. She had previously been a teacher in the Friends' School
at Providence.

eventually became eminent in one of its most difficult specialties.   Both these elder brothers were ardent political reformers;
and Thomas, who died in 1849, said of himself, "My democracy
is that which was advocated by Jefferson, my religion that of
the New Testament."   Their father had been an opponent of
Jefferson; and Dr. Earle preserved a letter from the Worcester
Congressman (Seth Hastings) in March, 1806, during Jefferson's second term, in which he told his Leicester constituent:
"I believe it is rather troublesome times with our Executive
and his friends and supporters in Congress: they are in great
perplexity how to manage and guide our political barque."   It
was evidently the wish of Mr. Hastings towards Jefferson, as of
Daniel Webster towards President Madison in 1813, to increase
his troubles and perplexities in holding the helm of state.   Dr.
Earle, and probably his father, had little of this desire to em-
barrass the government of his country, whatever it might be;
and he never took so active a part as his brothers in political
agitation, though always on the side of freedom and civilization.

In entering the Friends' Boarding-school at Providence, as
a pupil, which he did in September, 1826, Pliny Earle was but
going from the companionship of brothers and sisters to that of
cousins; for Rhode Island abounded with his mother's relatives,
the Buffums, and he had as many uncles and aunts there as in
the vicinity of Leicester.   In 1832, while one of the four teachers of this school, which then numbered one hundred and thirty
pupils, of both sexes, no less than eleven of them were his
cousins.   He early displayed a taste for botany and natural
history, and lectured to his classes with zest on those sciences;
but his usual duties at first were to teach spelling, writing,
grammar, and the mathematics.   He was the first to introduce
in the school the now universal method of writing down the
words to be spelled; and he found the usual difficulties in communicating to his pupils the anomalous spelling of our irregular mother tongue.   He says:—

When my spelling-class consisted of twenty-one, I put the names
of the twenty-four United States to them.   They spelled on their
slates; and I found more than two hundred mistakes,— an average

of ten apiece.   Again, when there were twenty-seven in the class, I
made a list of fifty-two words,—the names of vegetables, berries,
fruit-trees, utensils of the farm and kitchen, articles of clothing, etc.,
—things commonly known to them.   They spelled wrong, in the aggregate, three hundred and ninety-one times.   Two words, "mocca-
sin" and "vinegar-cruet," were missed by all.   In an additional
list of sixty-one words, a class of twenty-eight made six hundred and
sixty-eight mistakes.   These, however, were more difficult words.
One youth of seventeen made forty-three errors.

This extract from one of his letters of 1833 shows how early
the statistical habit was formed, and how practical his turn of
mind was, even when his head was full of snatches of verse,
learned from Scott and Byron, and when he had already begun
to publish both verse and prose, and was looking forward with
some longing to a literary life.   In this hope his lectures on
botany were given, as well as for the purposes of instruction.
Writing to his sister Eliza, in May, 1835, he says:—

In the course of my botanical lecture last evening, who should
make his appearance in the room but brother Charles (Hadwen),
bearing a noble specimen of the *Trillium atropurpureum* which he had
brought for my special benefit from Worcester.   It was the first of
the genus that I have seen ; and it came peculiarly apropos, for it
gave me an excellent subject for a peroration.   The uniformity of its
organs, its remarkable adherence to the number three (exemplified in
most of the monocotyledons), furnished a good opportunity to impress on the minds of the class the wonderful harmony and beauty
of organization in the vegetable kingdom.   I have given six lectures, but have only entered the portals of the science.   All the
teachers and about sixty scholars attend the course.   We make long
botanical excursions every Saturday afternoon.   It is ever a pleasure
to me to impart instruction ; but I must acknowledge that one of the
primary motives in attempting these lectures was self-improvement.

The religious seclusion of the Leicester Quakers in the
childhood of Dr. Earle was more marked than it has since
become.   As Worcester and the other neighboring towns grew
in population, the Quaker families made Leicester, and the
Earle region in it, their religious centre, driving up the long

hills and through the winding valleys on First Day and Fifth
Day to take part in the meetings — often wholly silent —
which assembled in the little chapel near the brook and the
wood. As will be noticed hereafter, in a letter of Sarah
Earle's, the Friends seldom tested their faith by attending
other places of worship; and, though they mingled with their
Calvinistic or Unitarian neighbors in the schools of the town,
in literary and political activity, and in social amenities, they
were in most respects a people apart. Their ordinary life was
plain and simple; and certain habits, now outgrown, were found
among them. Tobacco was used more than now by women, in
the form of snuff, and even of smoking; and an aged friend
of the family remembers calling on Dr. Earle's mother, some
half-century ago, and finding her smoking a pipe beside her
broad kitchen chimney.* In politics and philanthropy the
Friends were commonly in advance of other sects. The early
anti-slavery movement found much support among Quakers,
and Dr. Earle had his opinions on that national question early
formed. I do not find that he was ever very deeply enthusiastic, as some of his coreligionists were, in his religious exer-
cises. He was naturally averse to controversy, even in youth,
and had little of that spirit of propagandism which brought
J. J. Gurney to America, in 1837, to advocate the orthodox
theological views, which commended themselves so earnestly
to him. He preached in the Leicester Quaker meeting, but
while Dr. Earle was absent in Europe; and he published fer-
vent and sometimes polemical treatises, upholding the orthodox side of the dispute then going forward. Questions of
slavery and social reform agitated the minds of the Worcester
and Leicester Quakers far more than doctrines of the then
current theology.

* While James I. was persecuting Puritans, he was scarcely less zealous against the use of the
newly discovered American herb,— tobacco. Perhaps for that reason it spread rapidly among
the New England people; and in my boyhood there were many snuff-takers, and not a few pipe-
users, among elderly women. I remember the wonder which struck me as a boy, returning from
school, where we were taught by the "school-ma'am" that all use of tobacco was sinful, when
I stepped into my mother's kitchen, and there found two stout old women, my mother's aunts (one
of them the mother of Moses Norris, then in Congress from New Hampshire), sitting by the great
fireplace, smoking pipes. The mother of General B. F. Butler, a New Hampshire woman twenty
years younger, also had this habit, as I was told by an acquaintance, who said he had often smoked
with her in her kitchen at Deerfield, N.H.

The Quakers, with their traditional dislike of "hireling ministers" and willingness to hear women preach and pray, took a deeper interest than they otherwise might have done in the appearance, in 1837, of those South Carolina sisters, Angelina and Sarah Grimké,* on the platform, pleading against slavery; for the Calvinistic clergy of Massachusetts opposed them fiercely. J. M. Earle, writing to his brother at Paris, Nov. 30, 1837, says:—

The Grimké sisters were lately here, and made their home at my house while lecturing, for about a week, in this and the adjacent towns. We were much interested in them. They are very intelligent and capable, and very much devoted to the abolition cause. Angelina takes the lead in public estimation. She is the best rhetorician, has the best person and voice, with a very imposing manner, and is considered eloquent. S. J. May, in speaking of one of her lectures, says he "never before heard such eloquence from human lips." Yet we were better pleased with Sarah. Her mind is naturally superior to Angelina's, and has been better disciplined. Her feelings, also, have been more disciplined; and that of itself has an important influence on character. The First Day, on the evening of which Angelina was to give her first lecture, Woodbridge, minister of the Union Society, exhorted his hearers, as they loved religion, as they loved him, and by the most solemn obligations which rest upon Christians, not to violate their duty and

---

* Sarah Grimké, born in 1792, and Angelina, a younger sister, were daughters of an eminent judge in Charleston, S.C.,—the latter became Mrs. Theodore Weld; and both had long before 1837 become convinced of the sin and the dangers of negro slavery. In 1836 they published their "Appeal to the Women of the South" on the subject, and early in 1837 they began to address audiences in New York and New England. Samuel Joseph May, above quoted (brother of Mrs. Bronson Alcott), was then pastor in South Scituate; and the occasion of his remark was the close of Angelina's appeal in favor of emancipation, given at his church in October, 1837. The Worcester County ministers were misguided enough to issue a "Pastoral Letter" against the speaking of these women, which drew forth from young Whittier the poem in which occur these oft-quoted lines:—

> Your fathers dealt not as ye deal
>   With "non-professing" frantic teachers;
> They bored the tongue with red-hot steel,
>   And flayed the back of "female preachers":
> Old Newbury, had her fields a tongue,
>   And Salem streets could tell their story
> Of fainting women dragged along,
>   Gashed by the whip accursed and gory.

His allusion was to the whipping of Quaker women from Dover and Hampton, by order of Richard Waldron of New Hampshire, and similar outrages in Newbury and Salem, when Endicott was Governor of Massachusetts.

their principles so much as to go and hear those who trampled under foot that Scripture which declares that a woman is not allowed to be heard in the church. Yet that very evening it is said that both his deacons and a great portion of his church members went to hear her, and I now hear that only four of his church members approve his views on the slave question. The walls of prejudice are evidently giving way. Abolition is looked upon, among Friends, with very different eyes from what it formerly was. An Indiana yearly meeting has recently advised its members, individually, to aid other Christians engaged in the work of anti-slavery.

When these sisters and daughters of South Carolina slaveholders first began to speak in public, only women were expected to attend. An earlier letter of Lucy Earle (August, 1837) makes this remark : —

When the Grimkés lectured in Salem, it was understood there would be no objection to gentlemen attending. Accordingly, at an early hour, the meeting-house was crowded, not only inside, but about the doors and windows. A gentleman who was there remarked, "Those ladies are doing more in the cause than any two men engaged in it."

In the case of Dr. Earle, his sisters and brothers, the tendency was more and more towards science and literature; and, through the efforts of Sarah Earle and a few others, a woman's literary circle was formed in Leicester, before 1820, and when women's clubs were quite unknown. Her Mulberry Grove Boarding-school continued to be a successful establishment for a dozen years. Its name was due to the fact that her father, in his tree-planting, took up for years the industry of growing mulberry-trees, in order to raise silk from the foliage, and at his death, in 1832, left sixty or seventy of these fine trees on his farm. For the same reason the road which now traverses the farm from north to south is called "Mulberry Street." The young teachers — Sarah, Eliza, and Pliny Earle — cultivated poetry and literary prose, and contributed often to publications now forgotten, but which helped to form their style by frequent practice. In these pursuits and incessant occupations,

practical, educational, and literary, the childhood and youth of
Dr. Earle glided along, with no great crises, and no graver
anxieties than usually attend the passage from boy to man.
His family surroundings were happy, liberal, and hospitable.
He was handsome, ingenious, and eager for achievement, but
was fortunate enough not to be thrust too early into the battle
of active life. He began to teach others at nineteen, was ready
for the practice of a philanthropic profession at twenty-seven,
but wisely decided to see more of the world before settling into
a local situation. Hence, the real commencement of his active
career was his tour in Europe in 1837-39.

School-teaching was so natural to the youth of New England
two generations ago that to "take a school" was hardly more
than it now is to take a journey to Chicago. Dr. Earle's first
school was at Fall River, and began July, 1830,—a season
when all schools are now in vacations. We have little record
of it; but in a letter of the following autumn (September 12)
he says, "I am now giving a course of lectures on Astronomy,
and my time is wholly taken up with those and my other
duties." The same letter gives rhetorical expression to the
double desire that was ever dividing his heart,—the wish to
remain among the scenes of his childhood and the love of new
scenes and new acquirements. He says:—

A separation from the scenes and the friends which are rendered
dear by early intercourse—associated with all the fond recollections
of days when care was unknown and sorrow but the shadow of a
name—will be hard for me. I have never until lately learned the
permanency and depth with which the love of home is graven on the
heart. Possessing a passion of an opposite nature,—a longing desire to be acquainted with other places,—I have considered home
rather as a theme for poets. But my opinion now is that love of
home is an affection that lives throughout existence,—an indelible
principle.

This affection was continually drawing Dr. Earle back to
Leicester, though his life was most of it spent elsewhere.
And it rested, primarily, on a deep recognition of how much he
owed to his devoted father and mother, whose lives moved

there in a far narrower circle than his own.   Writing, in 1832, in anticipation of his father's death, which occurred in that year, he said : —

I have often thought that, in whatever situation we brothers and sisters may find ourselves,— whatever may be our characters or our success in the world,— we can never throw the least shadow of reproach upon our parents.   They have done everything in their power for our benefit; and, though they may have failed in one respect (which indeed is of trifling importance) to do so much as they wished, that failure was owing to events beyond individual human agency to control.   And are not those benefits we have received of far greater value than wealth?   If we compare the situation of our family with that of the great mass of people, shall we not find abundant cause to be thankful?

The unity of that large family circle, of which Dr. Earle was the last, was very little disturbed by the course of events, whether prosperous or adverse.   Like the prospect from their native hills, they took a broad and sunny view of life; or, if dark hours came, they supported each other till the clouds passed away.

CHAPTER II

Quiet as had been Dr. Earle's home life up to his eighteenth year, he had the inborn instinct to travel and know the world by sight, which was one of the traits of the New England man, as it has been of his English cousins. His short excursions around Leicester, in aid of the family business, had for him the stimulus of curiosity and novelty, as well as the sense of duty; and, when he became a schoolmaster, he gratified his inclination by longer journeys, of which he has left some record. In the complete change that has come over the Northern States in all matters of industry, locomotion, race-distribution, etc., within the past sixty years, these itineraries and observations have a quaint interest.

Trip to Fall River and Nantucket.

[1830.] *May* 16.— After leaving Worcester for Providence, in the stage-coach, the first place at which we stopped was Waters' Village, in Millbury, where, when I alighted, I was met by the son of Waters, who told me he had a fine horse and gig which he wished to send to Providence. Glad of the opportunity, I offered to drive it; and I could thus be at liberty to call upon my friends as I went. Soon I was transferred from the lumbering old stage to a light gig, with a horse that would easily carry me eight miles an hour. I therefore called on Uncle Thomas Buffum's family, whom I found pleasantly situated, then for a few minutes at Uncle William Arnold's, and next proceeded to Uncle William Buffum's, where I found them at dinner. Considering that I might not be so fortunate at any other place, I ventured to partake with them. I next called at Uncle Otis's, and then at Daniel Robinson's,— a very different journey from that by the stage-coach.

At Pawtucket I met with a student from the Deaf and Dumb Asylum at Hartford, just returned. He has been there but two years;

yet it was astonishing to see how much knowledge he had acquired. Almost any question I asked him was answered with much facility and accuracy. If he could not at once comprehend the question, a melancholy gloom came over his face; but, when the idea struck his mind, how quickly his features lightened with the glow of conscious intelligence! Debarred as such persons are from the power of speech, they acquire the power of expressing slight variations of passion and emotion by the countenance more readily than the rest of us.

I spent two days in Providence, and lodged at Uncle Sam's, where I met Cousin Rebecca Buffum, who was visiting Providence to attend the infant school,* and become more thoroughly acquainted with their system of instruction. I went with her to the school taught by Charlotte Bradley, which is yet quite small.

This was that period in the development of education in New England when infant schools, which had been rather neglected, were taken up with zeal by the friends of a better instruction. And it was to be concerned in such a Boston establishment that Bronson Alcott had removed from Connecticut to Boston a few years earlier. The Quakers took much interest in his school reforms, and it was by them that he was invited to Philadelphia in 1831.

Fifth Day [Thursday] I was tumbled over the road from Providence to Fall River,—a better prescription and more effectual remedy for gout than all the nostrums imposed upon the world since the god Æsculapius was invented. I took tea at William Newhall's, where I was met by Uncle Arnold [Buffum †], whom I accompanied home. Saturday morning I met Uncle Silas [Earle], and soon after began a morning's walk to Tiverton, three miles below Fall River. On the way I stopped where Mount Hope Bay lay stretched out before me, bounded by the land on the Rhode Island side where the mount itself rises with its cliff and crags against the western sky. I had long wished to visit that hill, once the abode of the Indian King Philip, grandson of Massasoit; and I therefore chartered a

* Afterwards Mrs. Marcus Spring, of New York, and now (1898) in California.

† This was the brother of Dr. Earle's mother, and the father of Mrs. Marcus Spring, Mrs. Elizabeth Chace, and other cousins mentioned in the letters. He had visited Europe for the first time a few years earlier, and was active in reforms.

boat, took an oarsman, and in an hour was landed on the opposite shore,

> Where Hope lifts up its craggy sides,

but not now, as in old times,

> Clothed with forests deep and dun.

A few minutes' walk brought me to the base of that rugged perpendicular crag where is the celebrated "seat" of King Philip,— a throne hewn by Nature's hand from the everlasting rock. I usurped the regal chair, and sat where that ruler of a savage nation once reclined. It is on the eastern declivity of the hill, at the foot of a precipice fifty feet high, and itself raised three or four feet above the ground. Immediately under it is the well, six or seven feet deep, from which, they say, Philip quenched his heroic thirst. The wild honeysuckle [columbine] grows in great profusion around; and I enclose a flower of it, which I plucked from the chair itself. One of the De Wolfs of Bristol built a fine summer-house on the summit of Mount Hope a few years since, but it is fast dropping in pieces. I recrossed the bay, and after a two-mile walk arrived at A. Barker's. Neither he nor his wife was at home; but, as it was two o'clock, and I was fatigued, I made myself at home by calling for some dinner.

I spent First Day here very pleasantly. Monday morning I was introduced to Dr. Foster Hooper of Fall River, and spent an hour or two with him. Then I took the stage for New Bedford, with the expectation of leaving there the succeeding day in the steamer "Marco Bozzaris," now plying between Nantucket and New Bedford. But, when I had made the journey through the rocks, briers, bogs, and fens of that uncultured country in no very easy manner, I discovered that the boat had gone down the bay that morning, and would not return from Nantucket and sail again till Fifth Day next, running only on Tuesdays and Thursdays. Therefore, the only alternative was to wait with William Eddy until the boat's next departure; and I went to his store, where I had the pleasure of meeting with perhaps the most weighty character in New Bedford. It was the hero of Padanaram. He was sitting on the counter in a profusion of perspiration, and looking as if he were just ready to adopt the words of Shakespeare, and exclaim,

> Oh, that this too, too solid flesh would melt!

I called on a New Bedford painter, and heard of another artist now
there,— a young lady, who bears the romantic names of "Marietta
Tintoretta Catharine Francesca Thompson." Another call was at
the infant school, which, in the number and proficiency of its
pupils, the capability of its instructress, the size of the building,
or the arrangement of apparatus, is the most perfect thing of the
kind that I have seen. Here, again, Friends are in the absurd
practice of keeping their children away from such schools, merely
because they are copying from everything which is going on in the
universe (even from Nature herself) by means of uniting their voices
in an audible harmony.

On the 13th of May, then, I left New Bedford on the good boat
"Marco Bozzaris," * Captain Barker, bound for Nantucket. With
this marine road you are acquainted, so I need not speak of the
Black Rock, the beauty of the Elizabeth Islands, the legend of
Naushawn, the rocks and ledges of Wood's Hole, the portentous
breakers on Tuckanuck shoal, and the other wonders of the great
deep. Our boat was named not so much in immediate honor of the
Suliote captain as in acknowledgment of the worth of Halleck's
poem, with its speaking numbers. We sped over the billows at the
rate of ten knots per hour, and enjoyed ourselves, notwithstanding
the rain. Saturday, the 15th, I rode with Timothy Hussey to the
city of Siasconset, where I examined a fine collection of shells, the
property of Mrs. Elkins, the landlady of one of the hotels. I have
since walked to the south shore, and ridden with Dr. Swift to the
western part of the island. One evening I was with Lieutenant Prescott, a scientific young man, sent by the government to excavate a
channel through the bar, in order to admit large vessels to the
wharves.

At this time, and for twenty years more, Nantucket and New
Bedford were the chief whaling ports of the world; and the
business was largely in the hands of Quakers. In 1830, Nantucket had 7,200 inhabitants, and New Bedford 7,500; while
Worcester had less than 4,200, and Fall River 4,158. Leices-

---

* The Greek chieftain, Bozzaris, killed seven years before at Karpenisi, near Missolonghi, had
been celebrated in verse by Fitz-Greene Halleck, and the poem beginning,

At midnight, in his guarded tent,

was for years the most popular American "piece," recited and spoken, in schools and parlors,
a thousand times every year. It is not yet quite forgotten. The German poem on Bozzaris by
W. Müller was as popular in Europe.

ter, which now has 3,300 inhabitants, then numbered less than 1800; and all Massachusetts had but few more than Boston has now. Providence, in 1830, had 16,832 people, but was then, as now, the second city in New England. Dr. Earle goes on : —

Captain Arthur has recently arrived from the Pacific, bringing the largest cargo of oil ever landed in this country. He also brought a remarkable stone. In appearance it resembles granite ; but is very slightly put together, and will readily float on the water. It was picked up by Captain Arthur's men in the Pacific, west of the Sandwich Islands, April 22, 1828 ; was thinly covered with sea-weed and shell-fish, and bore every appearance of having been a long time afloat. In size it is 3 ft. 2 1-2 inches long, 18 1-2 inches wide, and 5 1-2 inches thick. Its weight is 133 pounds. I succeeded in obtaining a small piece of it. Firmly pinched between the thumb and finger it will crumble into particles, and some of them, about the size of coarse sand, will scratch glass, as can be seen by rubbing the thumb, covered with these particles, heavily over a pane of window glass.

May 22, 1830.— I spent this evening in the Nantucket Museum, examining the implements and curiosities there collected from all quarters of the globe. Lieutenant Pinkham of our navy, recently returned from a Mediterranean cruise, employed an artist, while in the ports of Greece and Italy, to take sketches of different people, in order to preserve their various costumes and characteristics. Among them is one of the Greek admiral Canaris,* which the lieutenant avouches to be an extremely accurate likeness. But what a likeness ! At first view it would sooner be recognized as a Mahdi of Africa than a commodore of Grecia ; but examine it closely, and that unbending spirit of heroic valor for which he is celebrated is easily discovered

* Constantine Kanaris, born at the island of Ipsara, in 1790, was the latest survivor and the most distinguished of the four brilliant naval commanders of the island-Greek sailors in the Revolution,— the others being Miaulis (Andrea Vocos), Sakturis, and Tombazis. He was at first a captain under Miaulis (of whom there is an admirable account in the "Narrative of a Greek Soldier," by Petros Mengous, New York, 1830), afterwards a fleet commodore, and finally admiral. He long survived the war, was active in the expulsion of the Bavarian King of Greece, Otho, and was one of the deputation sent to invite the present King George to the throne in 1864. He died in 1877, at a great age. Dr. Howe had served under him in the Greek fleet, as well as under Miaulis. They both took much notice of the young American surgeon, who had been a land-soldier of the Greek army before going in the fleet. In his "History of the Greek Revolution" (now a rare book) Dr. Howe says little of Kanaris, but much of Miaulis, who was the older captain. The dress of Kanaris, above described, was that of the Greek islanders in actual service. On shore they wore much more gorgeous raiment, though they often went barefoot. An Italian sea captain, who lost a sailor, and wished to ship a Greek in his place, was told to go ashore at Hydra and find one. He did so, but came back, after seeing the stately Hydriotes stalking about, and said, "I saw no sailors,— nothing but captains."

in his countenance and the lofty pose of his head. His dress is simply a plain green coat and vest without collar,— no appearance of a shirt,— but a black handkerchief is carelessly tied around his neck, between which and the top of the coat the skin is visible. Upon his head is a cap which bears more resemblance to that applied by the hangman than that of a military officer.

Providence and its People in 1830–31.

The two chief educational establishments of Providence, when Pliny Earle went there as a pupil in 1826, were the Friends' School, which was removed to that city in 1819, and Brown University, founded in 1764, but very small and unimportant for the first half-century of its existence. Though controlled by the "denomination called Baptists or anti-Pædo-baptists," as its charter described the then dominant sect in Rhode Island, the same charter provided that five of its thirty-two trustees should always be Quakers, in recognition of their importance in the little State, and of the wealth some of them had bequeathed. Eminent men, like Horace Mann, the educational reformer of Massachusetts, and Dr. Samuel G. Howe, the chief philanthropist of a philanthropic age, had graduated there before Dr. Francis Wayland became its president, in 1827, and proceeded to reform its discipline and elevate its scholarship. One of his first steps was to remove the free ale-barrel, kept in one of the cellars, to which all undergraduates had access,— a form of "local option" not unusual before the temperance reformation of Dr. Wayland's period. The university in 1825, when Sarah Earle was an active teacher in the Friends' School, was often contrasted with the latter; and in one point, which bore witness to the diligence of her sex, Sarah Earle delighted to find her school preferred by visitors. From a lively letter to her sister Lucy, in August, 1825, I take this anecdote : —

We have had a good many visitors this summer, and in the last three days have had ladies from Montreal, New York, Virginia, and Washington, gentlemen from some of those places, Judge C.

from Maine, a young man from New Orleans, etc. These visitors are all to be conducted from the kitchen to the observatory, their remarks heard and their many questions answered. They generally appear well pleased, and pay us many compliments, particularly for our cleanliness. One man told the company that they saw here the effects of the best administration in the world,— a female administration. Then, turning to me, he said, "We have been over the other college, Brown University, where they have a male administration." Instantly I replied, "A mal-administration?" and, though I had not a thought of being very witty, they almost shouted their applause, so that I felt quite ashamed of myself. I did not admire the Virginian, she was very inquisitive and somewhat sneering; but the Canadian who was with her was an interesting creature. She said her education was in a nunnery, and this school seemed to her something like one. . . . There is a Sicilian in town about to establish himself as a teacher of Italian, and I wish either to attend myself or to have Eliza come and learn it. He has called at the Friends' School several times. He comes highly recommended both from Italy and Salem, where he has been teaching this year past. He is a gentleman. His estates were confiscated and he imprisoned on account of political difficulties, and he finally left the country to save his life.

At this time Moses Brown, for whose family the university was named, was still living in Providence, at the age of eighty-seven; and he lived on for six or seven years longer, for in August, 1831, Sarah Earle, then newly married, writes thus:—

Last Seventh Day, after sunset, Moses Brown had his carriage brought for the express purpose of coming to see me,— came and made his call, apologizing for not coming sooner, and returned home. Such a call from such a man, at the age of ninety-three, is not to be despised. The next Monday morning I took Benjamin Clark to see Moses Brown. We found him not very well and not quite so animated as usual, but mild, affable, and interesting. Benjamin said that visit crowned the whole, that would be something to treasure up and reflect upon.

At that time the university can have had scarcely more students than the Friends had pupils in their coeducational school; for they were wise enough to admit both girls and boys to the higher education, while the university excluded all girls until long after President Wayland's time. In the society of Providence the Quaker teachers and the college professors met on equal terms. And, when Pliny Earle went to New Haven on his way to Philadelphia, he carried letters of introduction to the Yale professors from his friends, the Brown professors. He thus wrote in 1830–31 : —

Nov. 25, 1830.— I am much pleased with my boarding-house; have a room and fire to myself, where I keep bachelor's hall as comfortably as need be. There are but nine regular boarders at present, among whom are Professor Elton, of Brown University, and J. Kingsbury. The professor is one of the finest men I have ever known. He is very learned, both in science and general knowledge, and also very sociable.* He has been a traveller, too: has stood on the Alps, if not on the Apennines; traversed the Highlands of Scotland and the Lowlands of Holland; has been a resident of Edinburgh, London, Paris, and Rome; is acquainted with Sir Walter Scott and the Grand Duke of Tuscany; has examined the ruins of Herculaneum and Pompeii, burned his fingers and toes within the crater of Vesuvius, and, "furzino," is acquainted with the father of Amelia Pottingen, for he spent some time

At the U-
niversity of Goettingen,

mentioned by Canning in the *Anti-Jacobin*. . . . Some excitement prevailed in Providence last week in consequence of Daniel Webster's presence in court here. The court-room was literally overwhelmed with ladies and gentlemen during the day when he spoke. John Whipple occupied the forenoon with his argument, and the company waited with a pretty good grace until he concluded. Then Webster rose, and a hush came over the audience as if the voice of

* This word "sociable," a characteristic New England expression, is often used by Dr. Earle, who long retained some of the dialectic peculiarities of rural New England. It signifies "affable," ready to meet others in social intercourse,— a trait which distinguished the doctor at all times, except when the peculiar melancholy, to be mentioned hereafter, came upon him. The odd phrase "furzino," just after, is the dialectic Yankee for "so far as I know," but really means, "I suspect, though you might not think it," with a slight shade of quiz or sarcasm, as in this instance. The verse quoted is from Canning's soliloquy of the suicidal German student who had loved "sweet, sweet Amelia Pottingen," a name which the English then fancied to rhyme with "Goettingen."

a spirit had stilled them. He spoke for nearly four hours, and I heard him for an hour; but it was not a case upon which he could show all his talents.

This was the period when Webster * stood at his highest point as a forensic orator. He had made his magnificent reply to Hayne of Carolina in the January preceding, and his splendid description of crime and remorse in his argument in the Salem murder case, in the early autumn; and, just before coming to Providence to argue against Whipple, the leader of the bar there, he had made a great tariff speech in Boston (Oct. 30 and 31, 1830), which extended over two evenings and nearly five hours. His earlier orations had made him widely known, particularly that on Adams and Jefferson in 1826, and the Plymouth oration of 1820, in which he had attacked Bristol, in Rhode Island, as the seat of the New England slave-trade, then carried on by the De Wolf family. Of that town Webster had said : —

Let that spot be purified, or let it cease to be New England! Let it be purified, or let it be set aside from the Christian world! Let it be put out of the circle of human sympathies and human regards, and let civilized man henceforth have no communion with it!

Not yet had the great orator separated himself from "the circle of human sympathies," and his appeal for generosity towards the struggling Greeks had commended him anew to the growing spirit of philanthropy. Nor had he identified himself, as he did a few years later, with the money power of the country, and accepted fees and favors from bankers.

December 5.— After making six calls last evening after tea, I spent the remainder of the evening at Uncle Samuel Shove's, where

* Daniel Webster, born in New Hampshire in 1782, died at Marshfield, in Massachusetts, in 1852, was, like Dr. Earle's friend in Paris some few years later, General Lewis Cass, the son of a Revolutionary captain, and educated under Dr. Abbott at the Exeter Academy. While Cass entered the army and distinguished himself in the War of 1812, and afterwards as Governor of Michigan, Webster graduated at Dartmouth College in 1801, and began practising law in his native State, which he represented in Congress in 1812-17. There he made himself known as an orator, but also as a bitter opponent of President Madison and his administration. He also won great distinction by his appeal in behalf of Dartmouth College in 1818, leading (with the efforts made by himself and others in the court vacation) to the famous decision in the Dartmouth case. In 1830 he was not only the leader of the Massachusetts and New England bar, but a conspicuous Presidential candidate.

I met a host of cousins. There were seven of us, all cousin to one another, and of six different families. For myself, that period is approaching (my twenty-first birthday) towards which the untried, enthusiastic heart of boyhood has looked with an impatient anticipation,—as a landmark beyond which all will be enjoyment, because I should then be free to act for myself. But how differently does the mind of maturer years regard that date! I am now to go forth and wrestle with a wrangling world alone. I am nearing the imaginary artificial line which separates the boy from the man, and a mistaken idea of thraldom from fancied liberty. To me there is no promise of greater freedom than I have felt for years, while I have the confirmed assurance that the title to parental dependence is void. Had I known the direction which seems now to be given to my path in life, these past years might have been employed, more than they were, in preparing myself. But even now there is a silent, powerful voice coming up from the deep recesses of my heart, telling me it is not too late,— urging me onward to gather from the broad fields of knowledge that which will tend to exalt the soul and carry it forward towards that goal of perfection which lies before us.

March 19, 1831.— I had the pleasure of dining the other day, at John Smith's, with John Bristed, who married a daughter of J. J. Astor of New York, studied divinity at the age of (nearly) fifty with Bishop Griswold, and has been for a year or two rector of an Episcopal church at Bristol. He is a jolly Englishman, educated at the old college of Winchester, in Hampshire, who studied law in London, practised it in New York, and is now a clergyman not far from Providence, as well as an author. But his volumes,* according to Halleck ("Resources of the United States," etc.), are "dear at half-price." We spoke of a satirical poem lately published in Boston, entitled "Truth; or, A New Year's Gift for Scribblers," full to overflowing with sarcastic venom against the American poets of the present day. Its author doubtless took Byron's "English Bards and Scotch Reviewers" as his prototype, but has come far short of that.

May, 1831.— I have recommenced botany, with the opening of the season for rambles and researches. We are to form a class as soon as we can procure books enough; and, by thus awakening an interest in the study, we shall soon have all the flowers of the neighbor-

---

* One of these, "Hints on the National Bankruptcy of Britain in the Present Contest with France" (New York, 1809), was given by Bristed to Gouverneur Morris.

hood brought in. Just now we are full of stenography. A young Englishman (about my age) professes the art in town, and "we teachers" are taking lessons of him. Our Yearly Meeting must look out now! Just take a specimen (to his sister Eliza at Leicester): —

Here follow the twelve lines with which Campbell's "Pleasures of Hope" commences, in a shorthand that phonography has antiquated.

We have been agreeably disappointed in finding it much easier than we anticipated. I have devoted my leisure moments to it for eight days, and can now write it faster than longhand, at my greatest speed.

Thus in early manhood we find him interested in poetry and poetic science, for such was botany then.

Pliny Earle had been preceded as a teacher in the Providence school by his sister Sarah, nine years older than himself; but, while he was teaching at Fall River and Providence or studying medicine at the latter place, Sarah Earle had returned to Leicester (May 15, 1827), and opened there her Mulberry Grove boarding-school for girls, which she gave over to her sister Eliza, at her own marriage with Charles Hadwen, of Providence, in August, 1831. Three years later, in July and August, 1834, a few months before her death, she took a journey with her husband from Worcester to Lowell, Lynn, Boston, and Providence, which she described in a letter to Eliza; and this description may serve to show how travel was managed before railroads were common. She says: —

Our journey lasted five days, Friday, Saturday, Sunday, Monday, and Tuesday, the last of July. Friday we left Worcester, and had much ado to drag through and arrive at Lowell in our chaise just at dusk. [The trip is now made in three or four hours, — forty-five miles, — and might be in two hours.] Strangers as we were, we feared it might take some time to find our place of destination [George Brownell's]. Several avenues to the town [of fourteen thousand people] and two or three bridges were presented to our view; and, having not the least clew, we so far left ourselves to the guidance of chance as to follow a carriage over one of the bridges.

Coming immediately upon a house which did not appear to be really
in town, we halted ; and Charles asked a man, who was just entering
the door, where G. Brownell lived. " He lives here," was the reply ;
and then I perceived that he was the man. This may seem nothing
wonderful ; but it struck me at the time as so remarkable, and at
the same time so joyful, that I thought much of it. The next morning (Saturday), which was one of our hottest, we went out with
George ; and, while the men were viewing the town, I stopped at
Dr. Elisha Bartlett's [he was the first mayor of Lowell, and a cousin
of the Earles], where I spent about three hours very pleasantly, and
engaged to take tea with them. We had intended to go to South
Reading [now Wakefield] that night, and to Lynn the next (Sunday)
morning ; but the heat and a shower prevented. We visited at
Elisha's ; and the next morning set off for Reading, which we
reached just as people were going to meeting. We stopped at a
public house, and, upon inquiring for John Clapp, were told that his
carriage was just coming ; and the man kindly offered to go and tell
them we were there. He did so, and John came over and engaged
us to go home with them after the meeting. We rested and refitted,
and rode home with them, about two miles. Susan Flint was there,
employed as organist in a small church at South Reading.* The
family attend a small meeting at Reading, being the only one of the
right kind very near. Their officiating minister, a son † of Thayer of
Lancaster, came home with them in the afternoon, and took tea.
When I observed the freedom of their conversation, I felt less like
an intruder on that day of the week than I feared. Still, we felt
ourselves on every account one day behindhand. Had we gone on
Fifth Day [Thursday, July 24, from Worcester], we should have had
a fine cool day, and should have been in Lynn on First Day [Sun-
day, July 27], which was very desirable. I do not recollect that I
ever spent a First Day out from amongst my own people [the
Quakers] before ; and I have no desire to again.‡ Still, we had an
excellent visit, were received and entertained with all the wonted
hospitality of our kind host and hostess.

* This was a daughter of Dr. Flint, of Northampton, aunt of Dr. Austin Flint, of New York, and
niece of the Sedgwicks, of Lenox. South Reading is now Wakefield.

† Dr. Thayer, of Lancaster, was the father of the wealthy brothers, Nathaniel and John E.
Thayer, of Boston, himself a classmate and intimate friend of Rev. W. Emerson, father of R. W.
Emerson. Rev. Dr. Thayer died in 1840. His son, Rev. Christopher Thayer, here mentioned as
preaching in a Unitarian parish at Reading, died in 1880.

‡ The secluded character of the Quaker families in their religious life is seen by Mrs. Hadwen's
remarks about spending Sunday anywhere but among Quakers.

Second Day morning we rode eight miles to Lynn, called at Avis Keene's, as we supposed, but found it was Josiah Keene's, he having recently returned. We would have spent the day there [Lynn], as there were many we wished to see; but of all times in the week to be calling on people in such a place as that! [It was washing-day; and Lynn being then a place of but seven thousand people, mostly engaged in shoemaking, the families were not expecting visitors on Mondays.] So, having dined, and having a good day, we proceeded to Charlestown, and visited the State's prison, with which we were much pleased, and left it with the conviction that, if we had a friend or relative worthy of the place, we should rejoice at his being there. The cleanliness and comfort of the apartments were admirable, as well as the convenience of all their arrangements. We then passed through Cambridgeport to Brighton,* Charles having a great desire to view the cattle market there. We also had Mount Auburn in view, and regretted to learn that we had missed the right turn, which was to have taken it on our way. As we were going to Boston, it would now be quite out of our way. So we gave it up.

We passed over the Mill-dam just in season to take a turn to the railroad, and witness the animating spectacle of the passage of the cars. Imagine a black giant seizing by force three or four huge coaches filled with passengers, and carrying them off at the top of his speed, hissing and bidding defiance to all opposition! And, before you have time to ask him what he means, he is gone! We stood and laughed like true Jonathan Doolittles, then entered the city, and passed the night with our friend Holden and her daughter, Charlotte Lander, who is a widow.

In the morning (July 29) we set off for home, which we reached without much incident at night, just in season for the meeting the next day. We have now been at home a week, one day monthly meeting, and two days committee at the school. Rebecca Buffum dined with us on First Day, and returned home yesterday afternoon with a member of the committee. Fall River folks will think certain now.† Dr. Tobey says it is highly important for mother to live

---

* The Brighton cattle market was then the largest in New England, the rural parts of which in 1834 furnished 100,000 sheep and more than 75,000 cattle and hogs for slaughter there.

† This cousin of Dr. Earle was the daughter of Arnold Buffum, who soon after married Marcus Spring, and long lived in New York; afterward in a sort of community at Perth Amboy, N. J., where Thoreau visited in 1856, and surveyed the estate of "Eagleswood," largely the property of Mr. Spring. Mrs. Spring is still living in California. Her older sister, Mrs. Chace, of Valley Falls, R. I., is also living, upward of ninety. The physical vigor of the Earles of this branch seems to have come from the Buffums.

on the Graham system; but, as her disease has become chronic, this will not probably be sufficient of itself to effect a cure. She must therefore, whenever attacked, use sweet oil copiously. He says every time she takes cicuta she undermines still more her constitution. It is strange, when it has been so strongly urged, that she should neglect so simple a remedy.

The railroad, which the Earles had never seen before, was that from Boston to Worcester, which was running trains of English coaches for short distances in 1834, though not opened to Worcester till 1835. The Mill-dam, of course, was that avenue, then a turnpike, which runs westward from Boston over the old dam which retained the tide-waters for the tide-mill, near Beacon Street. The trip of five days, here chronicled, could now be performed, if haste were requisite, in one, and with all the visits named, in two days. The remark about the regimen for Mrs. Earle shows that the use of coarse wheaten meal instead of fine flour, introduced by Dr. Sylvester Graham, was well known in 1834. Though a chronic invalid then, the mother lived fifteen years longer; while the vigorous daughter died a few weeks after this letter was written.

Short excursions, such as his sister could make, and with which he had once contented himself, had ceased to have much attraction for young Pliny, in whom, as in his Roman namesakes, the naturalist and the tourist were combined. Taking advantage of the temporary closing of the Friends' School in the summer of 1832, he took a companion August 5, and set out for the White Mountains of New Hampshire, by way of Portland. He writes: —

Trip to the White Mountains [1832].

S. L. Gummere* and I left Providence last Seventh Day morning, at eight o'clock, for Boston, and arrived after a pleasant ride of about seven hours. Our stop there was short, as the boat in which we were to take passage left for Portland, Me., at 4 P.M. At 3.30 we were on board the good steam-packet "Connecticut"; and at 4 we left the wharf with one hundred and seventy-five passengers, all

* Gum-me-re.

bound for Portland. It was a delightful afternoon; and our prospect, as we sailed out of Boston Harbor and along the northern coast, was very fine. The sun shone clear upon the scarcely ruffled ocean; and the broad expanse of deep blue water, studded in all directions with verdant islands, afforded as beautiful a (water) landscape as I have ever seen. We passed in sight of Lynn, Nahant, Salem, Marblehead, and Cape Ann in rapid succession. The Nahant Hotel appeared really like an old acquaintance, thanks to S. B. Stiles for an introduction to it. As we passed Cape Ann, the evening closed upon us, and the sky, which had been so cloudless, became overcast with light vapors; but there was a fine moon behind the clouds, and this, together with a balmy summer air, made a seat on deck desirable. The distance to Portland from Boston is one hundred and ten or one hundred and twenty miles. We were to be out all night, and for our one hundred and seventy-five passengers there were but fifty or sixty berths. Fatigued with our ride from Providence, we wanted sleep. The thing was where to get it. At 8.30 we found a mattress in the after-cabin, carried it up the stairs at the stern of the vessel, and took a refreshing nap on it directly before the cabin windows. At ten I rose, and walked the deck, where I was particularly interested in the man at the helm. He was a negro, six feet two, as I judged, and with a most dignified carriage. A single passenger, a seaman, and myself were the only persons on deck besides. We all entered into conversation; and, as I asked, "What time shall we arrive at Portland?" the passenger replied, "At 8 A.M." Upon this the giant negro, projecting his head forward to observe the light ahead, said very moderately, "I-beg-your-pardon-sir." That was all he said; but to me his words had a farther signification. In a moment it flashed through my mind that he had been in France. I questioned him, and found it was so. He had been a great traveller, and had gleaned much information. His acquisitions might have graced a higher sphere. I went to bed again, and at 5.30 in the morning found myself in Portland. It was First Day morning. We breakfasted at a public house, and at nine o'clock called upon Isaiah Jones (a Quaker).

His house is near the centre of the city, in the same block with N. Winslow's. Although the parlor was unoccupied when we entered, yet within five minutes a sociable circle was formed around us,—Isaiah, his wife and child, N. and J. Winslow, and E. Northey and his wife. We accompanied them to meeting, having engaged to return to dinner, and to go to N. Winslow's to tea. After meeting we were introduced to nearly all present, and soon engaged ourselves to breakfast the next day; and, had we concluded to stay another day, we should undoubtedly have been quite as itinerant in our eating then. Dined very pleasantly, and took tea equally so with N. W., and a very sociable family. Called in the evening at Rufus Horton's, and at nine returned to our lodgings. The Winslows are great admirers of the course pursued (about anti-slavery) by Uncle A. Buffum. The next day we breakfasted at Edward Cobb's, where we spent two or three hours agreeably. Dined with James Oliver, a brother of the great anti-Masonic Oliver at Lynn. He married a daughter of E. Cobb, and is cashier of a Portland bank. Took tea with a large party at Josiah Dow's, the father of H. and E. Dow.* During the day we visited the Observatory, Arsenal, Custom House, Court House, Town Hall, and two schools; walked through all the principal streets, and had an introduction to John Neal, with whom we spent a half-hour of rapid conversation. We left Portland at five o'clock, and arrived at Conway, N.H. (fifty-nine miles), in the evening, which we left at four the next morning, passing through the Notch by the valley of the Saco, past the Willey House, and arrived at Ethan Crawford's "White Mountain House" (thirty-five miles) at 1.30 P.M. Mount Washington, its lofty summit even now enveloped in an overhanging cloud, rests against our sky, while the peaks named in honor of Jefferson, Adams, etc., stand at distances from this more noble compeer, forming with Mount Pleasant a range of mountain scenery unequalled in the United States. On Thursday morning, August 9, a party of nine, including two of us, got horses and a guide, and began to ascend the mountain.

In our party, besides the guide (who had to go on foot, because we could find but eight horses), were a gentleman from Charleston, S.C., a Bowdoin student, a Harvard student, a young gentleman, something of a dandy, from Boston, a Unitarian minister from New Hampshire, a Mr. White, formerly of Worcester, but now on a journey from Indiana, via Montreal, to Massachusetts, with myself and

---

* Probably also of Neal Dow, the temperance reformer, who was of Portland, and died in 1897, at the age of ninety. John Neal, another distinguished citizen of Portland,— poet and essayist,— has long been dead. He wrote the poem of the "American Eagle," beginning,

There's a fierce gray bird with a bending beak,
An angry eye, and a startling shriek.

companion. It was amusing to look at our motley group,— our guide now mounted on a pillion,— as we went

> Full slowly pacing o'er the stones
> With caution and good heed,

now winding, Indian file, through narrow passes, and now fording the crooked Ammonoosuc River. We had laid our landlord under contribution for clothing; and now before me was seen our jolly Carolinian, furnishing by his jokes amusement for us all, mounted on a black steed, and behind his saddle the sober guide in a linsey-woolsey roundabout. Next went the student from Bowdoin, in a huge woollen coat of Crawford's, hanging about him like a meal-sack over an iron bar. Underneath that was a waistcoat of Crawford's, on the back of which the traces of a bear's paw were still visible, in a melancholy rent. The story is this: Ethan, having caught a bear in one of his traps, determined to carry him home alive. He therefore let him out of the trap, swung him over his shoulder, and took up the line of march homeward. The bear was rather pleased with his ride for the first mile, but after that became uneasy, and at the end of the second mile determined on hostilities. This led Crawford and the bear (to use his own words) "into a squabble," during which he tore the vest quite unhandsomely. At length the man of the woods, finding the resistance of his prisoner too unpleasant, gave up the idea of carrying him any farther alive, and slew him on the spot. Such is the story which Crawford tells.

To return to our party: The Bowdoiner was followed by something on a pale horse,— something that had gone to the mountain in the shape of a Boston dandy of 1832; but, alas! what a transfiguration! Though the Ethiopian cannot change his skin, nor the leopard his spots, yet the Boston dandy can lose himself under the flabby-brimmed *chapeau* and the enormous *manteau* of Ethan Allen Crawford.* This metempsychosis was followed by other figures, mostly clad in suits which they had brought from their homes purposely. However, I was enveloped in another coat of mine host;

---

* This was the brother of Tom Crawford, who long kept a mountain hotel at the great Notch, and a son of old Abel Crawford, with whom, in September, 1850, I rode from the Willey House to Tom Crawford's, questioning the veteran about bears and other game. Twenty years earlier an adventure such as Ethan described was not wholly improbable, and it may be credited. This pioneer family, of Scotch descent, who went up to the White Mountains from Connecticut, is now entirely extinct in the mountain region; and a railroad takes the visitor through the Notch, which had to be widened a little at its western end, to allow the trains to pass.

and, but for this, I should now have been without some forty pounds of minerals, which I translated from the summit of Mount Washington in its capacious pockets. Doubly surrounded with this, which was confined within hailing distance of my body by a bandanna handkerchief, and carrying weight in the shape of a pair of saddle-bags, filled with bread and cheese, I plodded on with the rest. Six miles over rocks and hills, among woods and raspberries, brought us to the end of equestrian navigation. Here we left our horses, and started to perform the remaining three miles to the summit on foot. Three-quarters of a mile brought us to a spring, of which the waters, issuing from the side of the mountain, were by far the coolest I ever drank. From this spring to the summit (two miles and a quarter) is a most wearisome journey, the acclivity in some places forming an angle of not less than forty-five degrees.

We arrived at the summit about one o'clock, having been almost four hours travelling three miles. But here, indeed, it seemed as if we

Looked from our throne of clouds o'er half the world.

Though the day was rather cloudy, we were on the mountain long enough to witness all the changes of scenery. One moment we were wrapped in clouds, and could see but a few rods ; the next the cloud rolled away in stately motion from the mountain side, and, floating off, gradually opened to view the landscape below, where hills, forests, and rivers dwindled into insignificance, stretched away and away into a hazy distance far as the eye could pierce. Snow was lying still upon the mountains in three spots,— a sight rarely seen in August, even on these summits. We found another spring as cold as that below, gushing from the rocks within a few rods of the highest point ; and there we sat down to eat and drink, with keen appetites,— all but the minister. He, unfortunately, had been bred so daintily that he "couldn't eat bread and cheese from a pair of saddle-bags." As if the delicacies and ceremonies of the parsonage tea-table could not be dispensed with for a few minutes on the summit of Mount Washington! The rest of us had no such qualms, and at two o'clock we were refreshed and ready to descend. I filled, not my pockets, but those of Ethan Crawford, with good specimens of mica and quartz, before following the others down. It took us but half as long to descend as to come up, and, after riding the six miles back, were glad to reach our inn after an absence of ten hours and a half.

Harriet Martineau, who visited Crawford's hostelry a few years later, has left a more lively description of it and him. She says : " Ethan Crawford cannot be said to live in solitude, inasmuch as there is another house in the valley ; but it is a virtual solitude, except for three months in the year. After a supper of fine lake trout the son of our host played to us on a nameless instrument, made by the joiners who put the house together, and creditable to their ingenuity. It was something like the harmonica in form and the bagpipes in tone ; but, well played as it was by the boy, it was highly agreeable. Then Mr. Crawford danced an American jig to the fiddling of a relation of his,— the dancing somewhat solemn, but its good faith made up for any want of mirth. He had other resources for the amusement of guests,— a gun to startle the mountain echoes, and a horn which, blown on a calm day, brings a chorus of sweet responses from the far hillsides." In my time (1850) Fabyan, who kept a large hotel on the plain north of Crawford's, had the same devices of gun and horn to amuse his guests ; and it was then still possible to see the deer at night feeding on the plain, while the bears were now and then killed in the forest. Dr. Earle took the same course away from the mountain which I followed eighteen years after ; that is, to Littleton and Bath, and so down the Connecticut valley. His description of the scenery, and some mention of the New Hampshire Shakers, here follows :—

We left Crawford's Friday noon, and journeyed north-westerly eighteen miles to Littleton, a pretty village in a low valley on the banks of the Ammonoosuc, surrounded with lofty hills. Thence we followed the Ammonoosuc to Bath, and so into the valley of the Connecticut, just below the junction of the two rivers. Our ride was delightful. The fertile meadows on the Connecticut are worthy of all the praises so long bestowed on them. Verdant with grass or luxuriant with Indian corn, profuse with waving grain or heavily laden with fruit, they lie before us as we turn to the right in passing down the New Hampshire side of the stream, and stretch away in either a continued level or a gentle undulation, interspersed with neat dwellings, and with a noble river rolling on between them. We dined at Haverhill, a village about as large as Leicester, with a court-house and an academy in the same building. From there to Hanover, twenty-seven miles, our route still lay on the river bank; and we admired the varied yet always romantic and beautiful scenery through which we passed. At Orford, before reaching Hanover, we stopped to examine silkworms. Such a curiosity to me!* We spent the Sabbath at Hanover, and attended a Shaker meeting a few miles away. It consisted of about one hundred and twenty members and perhaps fifty spectators. Our friend Lazarus, the Southerner, who still favored us with his agreeable company, thought that "four out of five among those black-eyed girls would get away if they could." I could not feel that I was in a house of worship. Hanover is finely situated. Most of the dwellings are placed around a very large common, and are well shaded with ornamental trees. The east side of this square is occupied by the college (Dartmouth) and the other buildings thereunto belonging. The view of Dartmouth College upon the fireboard in the Leicester parlor is very good.

On Monday we rode fifty-four miles to Concord, the capital of New Hampshire, across a rough and rugged country, over high hills, and in sight of many mountains. I called on Stephen Breed, and concluded to go to the town of Weare the next morning. Accordingly, at that time, Samuel Gummere, Lazarus, and Prince,—a young man from Boston, who had been our constant companion since we left the mountain,— set out for Boston, and I for Weare. Arriving at noon, I called at Pelatiah Gove's in the afternoon. Thursday morning I left Weare, and, riding seventy miles through Amherst, Nashua, Lowell, Billerica, etc., I arrived at Boston in the evening; and Thursday we returned to Providence.

Fears of the cholera, which was then visiting America, had kept the Friends' School from opening at the usual time, and allowed Pliny Earle to make this comparatively long tour. It was finally opened in October; and, in mentioning the fact to his sister, he indulges in that odd jesting so characteristic of him in later life, saying :—

The school-house was opened on Sunday last, pursuant to notice. In course of the week ten girls were admitted, and three boys in the

* This is sarcastical. At Leicester the Earle family had long been raising silkworms, and losing money by it. An uncle of Dr. Earle lived at Weare, N.H.

Classical Department; while we (in the English Department) received so many that, were the number to double each succeeding
week till April 1 (twenty-two weeks), we should then have no less than
4,194,304 pupils, more than the whole population of New England
and New York combined. To save you the trouble of computation,
I may as well add that we have had just one solitary scholar, George
Taber, a little fellow from New Bedford, who has been crying because
he has been lonely, and picking potatoes for amusement.

Providence, Nov. 24, 1832.— Dr. Griscom has come to Providence,*
but is not expecting to remove his family until spring. He will be
in the school in a few days; and, after the close of our lectures on
" Natural Philosophy " (four have been given), he will give a course
upon " Chemistry," from which we expect much. We have one hundred and thirty scholars on both sides, with the prospect of enough
more to make us (un)comfortable. Among the one hundred and
thirty I count nearly a dozen cousins; namely, four of Uncle
Arnold Buffum's, four of Cousin David's, two of Uncle Otis's, and one
of Abraham Barker's children. I could sit under the clock each day,
and then not see each of my cousins oftener than once a fortnight.

May 2, 1833.— Dr. Griscom has returned from New York, after an
absence of three weeks, bringing three daughters and a son with him.
They have taken lodgings at Mary Easton's on Main Street, opposite
the Episcopal church. I have spent two or three evenings in company with the girls, and am very much pleased with them. The
youngest is fine-looking, sociable, and, if I am in any measure a disciple of Lavater, she is amiable. John Gummere has been spending
two or three days in Providence. He and Dr. Griscom have given
their presence to our sitting-room together once or twice. They are
doubtless the two most learned Quakers in America. A few days
ago I went one evening with two of the Miss Griscoms to the Mansion House, where we met the wife and three daughters of Rembrandt Peale, the artist. In a few minutes we were as sociable as
old acquaintances, and the clock struck ten before we thought of the
time. To praise the daughters would be a matter of course,— what

* This was the elder Dr. John Griscom, a New Jersey Quaker (born 1774, died 1852), who distinguished himself as a teacher in early life in New Jersey, then removed to New York in 1807, and
taught there for twenty-five years, besides being active in charitable and scientific work. He had
been "literary principal" in the Providence Friends' School for some years at this time, but resigned
in 1835, and returned to Burlington, N.J. His son, John H., was professor of chemistry at New York
for some years, and an active member of the New York Prison Association, as well as a copious
writer. Rembrandt Peale (born 1778, died 1860) was the son of C. W. Peale, studied with West, and
painted good portraits of Washington, as his father had done.

every one would feel bound to do,— but I was none the less pleased with Mrs. Peale.   She appears to be one of your good, kind, motherly women, one who acknowledges there is reality as well as romance in the world.   Her husband has been in England some seven months has decided to make that country his home, and she and her daughters are going to meet him in London some time next summer.

During this season, in a school so large as above mentioned, Dr. Earle's tasks were many and engrossing, especially as he was also studying medicine with Dr. Parsons, at the same time that he taught five and a half days, with an occasional evening lecture.   "Every day and every evening," he wrote, "has its particular exercise.   Even Sunday shines no Sabbath day to me."   He taught reading, writing, English grammar, algebra, and geometry, besides botanical lectures ; and it was now that he gave that particular attention to spelling which his autobiography mentions.   March 24, 1833, he writes : —

D. does pursue the method of having the words written for spelling ; but it was introduced by me.   I recommended it a long time before it was adopted, but could get none to encroach so far upon the "good old way" as to attempt this reformation.   Therefore, I asked my class one morning to take their slates for spelling, They did so, and were much pleased with the exercise.   Very soon the whole school were using their pencils so.

Dr. Earle came to the head of the Providence school in 1835, but did not long continue there ; for his preparatory medical studies were now so far advanced that he entered the Medical College at Philadelphia in the autumn of that year. His journey to Philadelphia was the occasion for many visits and observations, which he thus records, in a letter to his sister Eliza, at Mulberry Grove : —

Anno Mundi 6839, and Anno Plinii xxv, on the 21st of that month vulgarly called October, I arrived at the summit of the hill of all hills, Leicester Hill,* intending to take the stage-coach for Hart-

* From the ridge on which the Earles lived in 1835 it is a mile and a half to Leicester Hill, on which the village stands,— a "Yankee Perugia," as one of its residents calls it ; and there is a resemblance to that Italian town in the site, not the architecture or art.   "Mount Pleasant" is a hill farther westward, which was early occupied by a provincial magnate as a country seat.   Indeed, all the hills in this region are suited for rural magnificence.

ford. It soon arrived, not, as I had feared, crowded with passengers, but containing one journey-man and one journey-lady. And who should these be but the Honorable Leonard M. Parker and his daughter Elizabeth? The father very kindly and politely offered me a seat beside the daughter, which I did not hesitate to accept. It would have been crossing myself and very ungallant to refuse. "Crack went the whip, round went the wheels." We pleasantly mounted Mount Pleasant on our way to the capital of Quinnihtiquot. Brookfield, Brimfield, many a cornfield and potato-field, besides enormous quantities of pumpkins and bumpkins, were among the objects of our attention that forenoon. Ten days earlier the beauty of the scenery would have been increased by the autumn foliage of the forests; but now the thousand tints which had decked them were mostly melted into a sombre brown, and the eye was pained where it might have been delighted. We dined at Stafford, Ct.; and, while dinner was being put on, I went into the "cupola furnace" of the Hydes. The tremendous bellows were wheezing at an awful rate; and from the brilliancy of the flame one might well suppose that it

> was so hot, Josiah,
> That if you only was put in it,
> Then took out and laid on the fire,
> You'd freeze to death in a minute.

At Hartford we lodged at the City Hotel, with excellent accommodations. After tea I visited the Deaf and Dumb Asylum, where I found a daughter of John Macomber, of Westport, the only person in the institution with whom I had been before acquainted. She recognized me immediately, and we had an interesting *tête-à-tête*. Before breakfast on the 22d (Wednesday) I went to see the Charter Oak, which looks very much like other oaks equally old. After breakfast I went again to the asylum with Elizabeth Parker and her father; and we were conducted through the various departments,— school-rooms, kitchen, dormitories, workshops, etc. The school had been suspended for a few weeks, and some of the pupils were absent. However, nearly one hundred were present, all industriously employed during our visit, the girls with their needles, and the boys at the several trades there taught. After what has been said of Julia Brace,* I need say nothing except that I saw her thread a

---

* The American Asylum, mentioned above, was the first school for the deaf established in America, and then served for all New England. At present there are seven other schools for this class in

needle, which she did very expeditiously, and was presented with a piece of her patchwork sewed quite decently.

After we returned, A. S. Beckwith, whose family live in Hartford, took me to ride with him. We passed Washington College (now Trinity) and the beautiful residence of Mrs. Sigourney,* and stopped at the Retreat for the Insane. Its situation is remarkably pleasant, commanding a delightful prospect. It is conducted upon a plan very similar to that of the Lunatic Asylum at Worcester. While at the City Hotel, Rev. T. H. Gallaudet, who founded the Deaf and Dumb Asylum, came in; and I had the satisfaction of being introduced to him. He is a plain, modest man, about five feet five in height, with spectacles on nose, and a face that beams with benevolence.

New Haven, October 23. (Tontine Hotel.) — We reached here before nine last evening. Just after breakfast this morning I went to the house of Professor Olmsted, to deliver the letter with which Professor Elton, of Providence, had favored me. The professor had gone to Yale College to give a lecture. I followed, but the lecture had commenced. I was desirous to hear the person who had just become extensively known as a scientific man by publishing one of the best recent works on Natural Philosophy, and as the first person who saw the comet in America at its late approach. So I went to the door of the lecture-room, which I found in that position when it is not a door, — because it is ajar! The lecturer stood with his back towards me; talking to eighty or ninety young men about "nodes," "apsides," "perigees," and "apogees." He very soon turned, perceived me, came to the door, took my letter, and invited me in. After the instructive and well-delivered lecture closed, he took me to his room, and, upon some remark about the comet,† asked me into the observatory where he discovered it. His tele-

---

New England; and even Connecticut has a second school at Mystic, near New London, where the oral method is used, and signs discarded. Julia Brace was deaf, dumb, and blind.

* The once famous poet, Lydia Huntley, (born 1791, died 1865, married Charles Sigourney in 1819), to whom Dr. Earle, on his return from Europe in 1839, sent flowers and shells gathered by him in classic scenes. A statue of Dr. Gallaudet, the work of D. C. French, now stands in the asylum grounds. He died in 1851, at the age of sixty-four, having founded the asylum in 1817 when thirty years old.

† This was the comet upon which Dr. Holmes wrote his amusing verses, about the time Professor Olmsted discovered it. The latter was forty-four at this time, being born in 1791. He died in 1859. Professor Silliman was the elder of two Yale professors of that name (born 1779, died 1864). He travelled in Great Britain and Holland in 1805-6, and in 1812 secured for his college the collection of minerals made in Europe by Colonel Gibbs. In 1835 he was the most eminent geologist in America, though not the best.

scope is a refractor of ten feet focal distance, so fixed upon the
standard that every part of the heavens may be observed except
near the zenith. He said that the comet, when first seen, was like a
speck of smoke no bigger than a thumb-nail. The only proof that
it was a comet was the change of place apparent the next night.
After examining his apparatus, including the most powerful electri-
cal machine I had ever seen, we went to the cabinet of minerals,
where we found Professor Silliman about to lecture on mineralogy.
His special subject was quartz and its silicious companions. His
style was simple, and his manner easy and informal. He remarked
in conversation that "the New England Friends know not what they
have lost in allowing Dr. Griscom to leave their school at Providence."

In the afternoon I noticed in the burial-ground north-west of New
Haven the monument of Eli Whitney, inventor of the cotton-gin,—
of freestone, consisting of a parallelopipedon base, 8 feet by 4 and
3 feet high, surmounted by a beautiful entablature a foot high, termi-
nating at the ends in a scroll, like those in the capital of an Ionic
pillar. Returning to the city, I visited a collection of paintings left
to Yale College by Colonel Trumbull, the painter, and handsomely
arranged in a building erected for that special purpose.* Many additions have since been made to the gallery. I left it unwillingly, before examining half of the pictures, in order to take tea at Professor
Olmsted's, where I spent most of the evening. He is about forty,
in height five feet seven, with an activity of motion that would grace
a youth of sixteen. His complexion is dark; his hair, eyebrows,
and eyes, black as jet.

New York, October 25.—I walked in the north-east, or "new,"
part of the city. This modern American Babel increases astonish-
ingly. Arriving at Washington Square, my attention was attracted
by a building, the University of New York, of purely Gothic architecture, and a stately marble pile. It somewhat resembles Newstead
Abbey; but the towers and turrets are surmounted with blocks of
marble instead of spires,— rather a compound of Abbotsford and
Newstead.

These remarks on architecture in New York and New Haven
show that Dr. Earle had been studying that subject at the

_____

* The painter Trumbull did not die till 1843, but gave his pictures to Yale College for an annu-
ity of $1,000.

time when Greek and Gothic styles were getting introduced and mingled in America. His comments were founded on engravings; for he had not seen any ancient buildings, and photography was yet in its gloomy infancy. His interest in art was always marked, but his taste was far from severe. Continuing his journey, he reached Philadelphia by steamer on the 26th, and found friends there, as everywhere. The Vice-President, Martin Van Buren, soon to become President, was in Philadelphia at the time; and Dr. Earle, always ready to see notabilities, went to call on him at his hotel, but found him gone.

Philadelphia, October 27.— While at breakfast, Dr. Griscom called, in fine health and spirits. I went with him to call on John Farnum. Also, having sent my letters of introduction in advance, I called on Dr. Robert Hare, and found him fat and more than forty,— as jolly as he is fat, and as gray as he is forty. Add an inch or two to the stature of Alexander Gaspard Vottier, of the sugar-plums, give him an intellectual instead of a bacchanalian countenance, a little more expansion of forehead and enlargement of sinciput, and you have a model of the carnal portion of the American giant in chemistry. Even in their speech there is a very striking similarity.

In Philadelphia for the first time the student saw Christmas kept as it never was at that period in New England, where the Puritan Thanksgiving, a month earlier, had quite supplanted Christmas, which was not even a holiday in Massachusetts till many years after 1835. Writing home on Christmas evening in that year, Dr. Earle said : —

A Christmas among the people of this city of Penn puts to the blush all the blessed Thanksgiving Days that animate the comparatively sober inhabitants of the Bay State. It would be hard for Jonathan Doolittle to strike a note high enough to describe the "lots o' good livin'," the fun, frolic, flash, and fashion that characterize this day of festivity in Philadelphia. I say a day of festivity, for such it is with a large proportion of the citizens; although many (the Catholics, particularly) consecrate it to divine worship. If a man passed through the crowded market this week, it was at the expense of comfort, if not of a broken rib or a demolished or overturned huckster's tub.   Book-stores, toy-shops, confectioners,— in short, every place of retail trade,— are teeming with the rare and the beautiful.   Last evening Santa Claus did his prettiest, showering uncounted blessings in the shape of whistles, rocking-horses, wooden swords, counterfeit puppies, mice, and kittens, together with cakes and confections of all kinds, on the children.   The stocking of every manikin and womanikin overflowed this morning with the gifts of Saint Nicholas.   With honor be his name spoken!   After dinner I thought I would mingle with the rest of the fashionables, to see and be seen ; and I found the streets swarming with a joy-seeking population.   Boys ringing a grand chorus upon rackets, whistles, and would-be flageolets, crowds of young men at the street corners smoking cigars, and unnumbered ladies, eloquent with smiles and enveloped in capes with large cloaks attached to them, threading the streets,— all were as merry as Christmas.   So much for Sixth Street and Franklin Square.   In Race Street a long procession, in the deepest mourning, followed the remains of a departed friend.   Arch Street, of course, was thronged.   And there, again, as if to contrast the luxury of life with the pangs of death, an extensive cake and confectionery establishment was filled with eaters ; while above and around and before the next door, in large, staring capitals, was to be read, "Coffins ready-made."   An oyster-cellar came next, where the vulgar, the profane, the intemperate,— very offscourings and canaille, — were drinking and carousing.   The confused gibberish of a hundred tongues, the hollow laugh,— long, loud, and hysterical,— the horrid oath, the thumping of the toddy-stick, made not only the room, but the street before it, odious.   Then Chestnut Street,— whew! what a river of humanity! what a condensation of flesh and vesture, a flood of men, women, and children!

> With scores of ladies, whose bright eyes
> Rain influence.

But at this moment the clouds also began to rain, and put a damper on the general hilarity.

All this was a new scene to the serious-minded Quaker from Leicester and Providence, but his kindly heart inclined him to look on it with pleasure.   Not so the state of things in the

Medical College,— never a very quiet place,— and just then, in
1836–37, unusually disturbed by unmannerly students. Writing
at the end of February, 1836, Dr. Earle says : —

It appears that three hundred and ninety-eight medical students
have attended lectures the present term, nearly every one of the
twenty-four States being represented here, as well as Nova Scotia,
Canada, England, and South America.   These heterogeneous
materials have mingled during the last four months with as little
effervescence as could be expected.   Indeed, our preceptors say we
have been very good boys, "the kindest of classes," "the most
gentlemanly class that ever attended this school," etc.   Let us see :
(1) The son of a Governor of one of our Southern States caned
another "gentleman" at the theatre, who thereupon, believing that
"one good turn deserves another," repaid the caner with compound
interest.

> Behold how good a thing it is,
> And how exceeding well,
> Together, such as brethren are,
> In unity to dwell.

(2) Another gentleman stabbed one of the vulgar with his jack-knife ;
(3) another was kept in three or four weeks by wounds received
from the dirk of a fellow-laborer ; (4) another drew his dirk upon the
driver of an omnibus, but shed no blood ; (5) while a fifth benevolent
creature called on one of his classmates in the evening, invited him
to the door, and there, upon the steps, shot him in the legs with a
charge of buckshot.   He who received the wound was instantly
confined in Arch Street Prison, to prevent him from challenging his
friend ; while the one who gave the wound died a few weeks after
of typhus fever.   After these "gentlemanly" encounters, the minor
affairs of "cabbaging" cloaks, umbrellas, overshoes, etc., are unimportant,— they hardly begin to make a man a "gentleman" nowadays.   Heretofore the conduct of students has been such that
odium is cast upon the whole tribe of Æsculapian tyros.   The
term "medical student," with many citizens, is intimately associated
with "roguery," "impudence," "lawlessness," "delicate sense of
fashionable honor," etc. ; while another very large class (the Philadelphia negroes) add to this list "tyranny," "cruelty," "murderer,"
"thief," and a few other endearing epithets.   This last fact is fraught

with an advantage, however; for, of all the mothers in the twenty-five thousand colored population, I hardly think there is one who does not govern her children by threatening them with the medical students. Every disobedient urchin is told, "I'll give you to the students"; and by this magic of a name he is brought back to the path of rectitude. And yet, in spite of all this, a great majority of the four hundred students are gentlemen in the proper sense of the word,— men of kind, generous, and ardent feelings, with native talent, well cultivated, and of a spirit that scorns to commit acts by some thought necessary to support their "honor." It is the conduct of a few which has stigmatized the whole.

These remarks recall to the aged the state of things which the semi-civilization of certain slaveholding communities imposed upon much of our country sixty years ago, and which drew forth from foreign observers the censure that was found so provoking by Dr. Earle's contemporaries. In August, 1835, Mrs. Kemble-Butler, then living in Philadelphia, wrote to her publisher in London, Murray, this extreme statement:—

There are mobs in every part of this country, burning, tarring and feathering, hanging without jury, judge, or other warrant than their own sovereign pleasure. The slave question is becoming one of extreme excitement. The Northern folks push the emancipation plans with all the zeal of people who have nothing to lose by their philanthropy; and the Southerners hold fast by their slippery property, like so many tigers. The miserable blacks are restricted every day within narrower bounds of freedom; and the result of all is clear enough to my perception. The abuse is growing to its end; but it will not be done away with quietly. There will, I fear, be a season of awful retribution before right is done to these unfortunate wretches.

No young man brought up as Dr. Earle had been could fail to see where the poison of our social and political system lay; but it was hard to prescribe for an evil so deep-seated. Mrs. Butler was right in her general prognosis, as the event proved; but most Americans in 1837 hoped for an easier solution of the slave question. Dr. Earle was one of these. His attention was chiefly drawn to other topics, though he never neglected this one. Philadelphia interested him in many ways, and not merely as the place of his medical graduation. Its scientific and philanthropic eminence among American cities drew his attention; and the prominence of the Quakers attracted him and his relatives, of whom several settled there. From his letters of 1836 and 1837, this may be cited : —

Saturday evening Dr. Griscom had the kindness to introduce me into the rooms of the American Philosophical Society, — a little paradise upon earth to a scientific man. The library contains twenty thousand volumes, chiefly scientific works, ranged about the room in cases ; while those parts of the walls not so occupied are hung with portraits of worthies eminent in the annals of science. Dr. Franklin was its first president and one of its first members. The present librarian, an active octogenarian, still adheres to the practice of whitening with powder that hair which the snows of age have blanched. He was one of the earliest members, and long an intimate friend of Franklin.* I am to breakfast with him on Tuesday morning.

Feb. 6, 1837.— The Abolitionists in Philadelphia are about to have a large hall erected for their especial accommodation. It will be the largest in the city. Charles C. Burleigh has lately been speaking here, and was very much liked. J. G. Whittier also has been spending some time here, but not on business connected with the Anti-slavery Society. While here, he added another link to the prolix chain of marvellous things said to have been performed as animal magnetism at Boston and Providence. He was present, it seems, when Poyen performed experiments upon the damsel from Pawtucket, before Drs. Walter Channing and Ware, Rev. Dr. Channing, and some members of the State legislature.† Dr. Ware acknowledged

---

* This was Mr. John Vaughan, born 1755, died Dec. 30, 1841. At the date of his death he had been treasurer of the society more than fifty years, or since 1790. He lived in the building of the Philosophical Society, which is on the west side of Fifth Street, just below Chestnut, and appears to be in Independence Square, but really is older than the square, standing in a plot of ground given by the city before the square was formed. Mr. Vaughan had a famous custom of giving breakfasts to distinguished visitors to Philadelphia in his rooms there. Mr. B. S. Lyman, one of the present curators, says, " The old meeting-room had a charming, old-fashioned look of quiet elegance, but was wholly changed at the time the building was enlarged and altered, about 1890."

† Whittier was chosen a member of the Massachusetts legislature from Haverhill two years in succession,—1835 and 1836. He was one of the members present at these experiments in Boston, no doubt, though he does not seem to have taken much part in legislative proceedings in 1837. He

himself a proselyte ; and Rev. Dr. Channing declared his meta-
physics to be confounded. Dr. Tobey (of Providence) informs me
that M. B. Lockwood has become an adept in the science.

There were disturbances among the Philadelphia medical
students in the winter of 1836–37, which came to the public
notice through articles in the *Ledger* and other newspapers ;
but, amid all the troubles of the class, Dr. Earle pursued his
studies calmly, and took his degree early in March, with
some distinction. He made a brief visit to Washington at
the inauguration of Van Buren as President ; made his arrangements with deliberation and good judgment for his proposed year of medical study in Europe ; visited Leicester and
bade farewell to his mother,— his father having died in 1832,—
his sisters and brothers ; promised to correspond from Europe
for the Worcester *Spy*, which his brother Milton was then editing ; and, on the 25th of March, 1837, sailed from New York
for Liverpool on the packet ship "Virginian," a sailing-vessel.
The first use he made of his nautical observations was to correct a false opinion which he had formed at Providence as to
sea-distances ; and the remark in his diary is so characteristic
that this chapter may well close with it.

March 27, 1837, *Lat.* 41° 6', *Long.* 68° 30'.— The Havre packet
"Albany," which sailed at the same hour with the "Virginian," is
still in sight. My previous impressions with regard to the distance
at which small bodies at sea are visible have been erroneous. They
need not have been, had I reflected ; but, having drawn my conclusions from observation at the Providence School, I believed they
might be seen much farther than is possible. From the height on

did not go to live in Philadelphia until late in that year ; and the new hall mentioned above was not
completed till 1838, when Dr. Earle was in Paris. It was destroyed by a mob in the same year. The
excitement in New England over mesmerism or animal magnetism followed close upon that ardent
pursuit of the pseudo-science of phrenology which was stimulated by the popularity in Boston of Dr.
Spurzheim, who, with the eminent anatomist, Gall, was its zealous propagandist, and died in Boston
(November, 1832) while lecturing on phrenology. Dr. Earle no doubt heard Spurzheim, and
became more than half a believer in the science, as did also Dr. S. G. Howe and other Massachusetts
physicians. Some allusion to this will occur hereafter. Indeed, Gall and Spurzheim, though ridi-
culed for making a chart of the human skull to correspond with certain inward functions of the
brain, did lay the foundation of the present doctrine concerning the brain as the organ of the mind ;
and this part of their theory continued to interest Dr. Earle through life. His brother Thomas was
a mesmerist, and often had experiments at his Philadelphia house, but long after 1837.

which that building stands, it is evident that vessels would be wholly visible at Newport or even far beyond, were there no intervening objects; but, situated as we are now, no portion of the hull of a ship can be seen farther off than ten or fifteen miles. Hence the vessels that we meet, though they heave in sight directly ahead, are very soon (from three to six hours or more, according to the force of the wind) all invisible, having passed out of sight in the opposite direction.

This candor of mind, this love and research of the exact truth, whatever his own predilection might be, was my friend's distinguishing trait. It made him welcome wherever he went, and it gave to his well-considered opinions almost the force of natural fact.

CHAPTER III.

It happened fortunately for the young physician on his first tour in Europe that the railway and the steamship had not annihilated distances and made it possible to see a great country in a week. Dr. Earle found himself in England in the very culminating period of the English stage-coach, described by Dickens with so much zest, and therefore familiar to all who have read that popular novelist. He journeyed from one end of the island to the other in 1837 in such coaches, and lived at such inns as Dickens and the earlier novelists set before us in every chapter. He crossed the Atlantic from New York in the spring of that year, sailing on the 25th of March and landing in Liverpool the middle of May. Among his fellow-passengers, fourteen in all, was Joseph Sturge, of Birmingham, an English Quaker, just returning from a visit to Jamaica and the other British West Indies to report on the effects of the then recent policy of slave-emancipation. This fact, and the many introductions to English Quakers which had been given him in America, opened to young Earle at once the rich and philanthropic circle of Quakerism in Great Britain and Ireland. He met on the most friendly terms the Gurneys, of Earlham, the Allens, of London, Sir Fowell Buxton, Mrs. Opie, Samuel Lloyd, the great banker, the Forsters, Becks, and other members of that well-known society. His sketches of these persons are interesting : —

Sir T. F. Buxton is a plain, familiar man, six feet two inches in height, not prepossessing in appearance, but interesting in conversation. He has just succeeded [June, 1837] in obtaining the acceptance by the House of Commons of a report in relation to the cruelties and acts of injustice practised by the British upon the aborigines

of their various dependencies, and hopes soon to have an act passed
by which those barbarities will be stopped. . . . At the quarterly
meeting, Elizabeth Fry, Hannah Backhouse, Anna Braithwaite, and
Elizabeth Dudley sat at the head of the women's department of the
meeting; and all of them appeared either in testimony or supplication
[that is, either preached or prayed]. A quaternion of ministers
such as are not met at every place! Elizabeth Fry has more dignity in the gallery than any other woman I ever saw. This, with
fluency and elegance of language, and a voice rich, melodious, and
of great compass, renders her a most impressive speaker. . . . The
English women Friends who are elderly seem less anxious to conceal
the footsteps of Time than do those in America,— I mean, those
traces left by the lapse of years on their persons. However gray the
hair may be, it is not concealed, but frequently more exposed by
bringing it forward upon the forehead, as Anna Braithwaite does.
Mrs. Fry has a sandy complexion and hair corresponding, now con-
·siderably changed by years. However, she dresses it in the manner
named, having a portion cut short and brought from beneath the
cap-border through the whole expanse of the forehead. She has a
more natural dignity of manner than Amelia Opie, particularly during her public communications. I shall never forget the silence and
solemnity of the last meeting held by J. J. Gurney (her brother) in
London, while she was speaking. As she closed her sermon with
the appealing exhortation contained in the seventeenth verse of the
last chapter of Revelation, "And the Spirit and the Bride say,
Come," etc., an almost palpable stillness prevailed throughout that
immense assembly. . . . I have met her at the meeting-house during
Yearly Meeting, at S. Gurney's (both in London and Upton), at
her own house two or three times, and also at Newgate Prison. She
still continues to attend that abode of sinners once a week; but,
others having become enlisted in the cause, she is very much released
from the onerous duties formerly attendant on her work there, and
is left at liberty to exert herself in other forms of benevolence. In
her associations she approaches the English throne. She showed me
two long letters received by her, immediately after the death of the
king [William IV.], from his two sisters, the Princess of Gloucester
and another; and she gave me as autographs two or three letters,
one of them from these ladies. . . . I accidentally learned that Mrs.
Opie had rooms in the same London house where I was lodging,

and I sent at once a letter of introduction which Uncle Arnold Buffum had furnished me. The following morning I met her at her
breakfast table, in company with Eliza Kirkbride. [This lady was
from Philadelphia, and afterwards married J. J. Gurney.] Although
several years a member of our society, Amelia Opie has not effaced
all traces of her fashionable life. Her dress, though quite plain in
its shape, is put on with a showiness of manner not so conspicuous
in those who have birthright membership. This effect is heightened
by her gold watch, and is perfected by a peculiar grace of manner.
To her I am indebted for an introduction to Samuel Gurney, at
whose table, in company with her, I first met Elizabeth Fry. This
was the last day I saw Mrs. Opie. She bade me farewell with the
remark, " I hope I have launched thee well."

Reginald Heber, afterwards Bishop of Calcutta, when he went
to hear Mrs. Fry in Newgate in 1820, described her as "a
Quaker, the wife of a merchant in the city who some two
years ago obtained with difficulty permission to attempt the
reformation of the female prisoners." Her brother-in-law, Sir
Fowell Buxton (who did not receive his baronetcy until after
Dr. Earle's first tour in Europe), had occasion, twenty years
after Bishop Heber's visit, to call on the same day upon the
Secretary of State in Downing Street and upon the Gurneys in
their counting-houses; and, finding the ministry niggardly in
fitting out the Niger expedition, which his Quaker kinsmen
liberally aided, he exclaimed : —

Well, I go into the City, and I see brokers who behave like princes.
I come back to Downing Street, and see princes who behave like
brokers.

The Gurneys, of Normandy, under the name of De Gournay,
were indeed princes in the time of William the Conqueror, and
sent several of their name to assist him in his victory at
Hastings, after which they established the English barony of
Gournay, and left their name at Barrow-Gurney in Somerset
and several other English places. But, in the time of George
Fox, one of their descendants, John Gurney, citizen and cord-
wainer of Norwich, was sent to prison for three years (1683) for

espousing Fox's Quaker principles.   His son John, in Sir
Robert Walpole's day, "by his celebrated extempore speeches,
February, 1720, before the Honorable House of Commons,
turned the scale of the convention between the woollen and
linen manufacturers, being the weavers' advocate." He was
himself a woollen manufacturer; and his eloquence was commemorated by an engraved portrait, over which Addison's
"Britannia" leans, smiling, and points to the Latin motto,
"*Concedat Laurea Linguæ.*"

A grandson of the prisoner, and nephew of the woollen
merchant, John Gurney, of Keswick, had a son John, who
married a descendant of Penn's friend Robert Barclay of Uri
(Catharine Bell), and became the owner of the estate of Earlham Hall, near Norwich, where the Gurneys were born or
brought up whom Dr. Earle knew.   They were connected by
blood or marriage with the Barclays, who succeeded to the
great brewery of Dr. Johnson's friend Thrale; with the Pease
family of Darlington, and the Backhouse family of the same
Yorkshire town (Hannah Backhouse, often named by Dr. Earle,
being a cousin of Mrs. Fry); and with others of the wealthy
and politically powerful Quakers of London and the provinces.
Mary Anne Galton (afterwards Mrs. Schimmelpenninck) was
another cousin; and Opie, the painter, who married the daughter
of Dr. Alderson, the popular physician of Norwich, belonged to
the Quaker circle, though neither he nor Mrs. Opie was at first
a Quaker.   Elizabeth (Mrs. Fry) was the eldest of the Gurney
sisters of Earlham; and Samuel was the youngest brother, born
in 1786, and early admitted into the banking house of his
brother-in-law, Joseph Fry, who married Elizabeth Gurney in
1800.   He was a "plain Quaker," not very attractive in person
or manners, but well educated, and with a talent for making
money, which nearly all the Quaker circle had.   His father,
William Fry, had a fine house at Plashet, near London; but
Joseph and his wife long lived at St. Mildred's Court in London,
where Samuel lived with them until his marriage with another
cousin, Elizabeth Shepherd, of Ham House, near Plashet, which
in time became his own property.   Fowell Buxton, not yet a
Quaker, had married Hannah Gurney, the sister of Samuel and

Joseph John, in 1807, Samuel married in 1808, and Joseph John (who also married a second cousin) in 1817.

In the mean time, while Louisa Gurney had married a London banker, Samuel Hoare (distantly related to the Hoar family of Concord, Mass.), and while Joseph John had been studying Greek and Hebrew with a private tutor, Samuel, hardly of age, had become an important member of the rising firm of Overend, Gurney & Co. in Lombard Street. As the children of these various marriages grew up, they formed other connections. Some of the Quaker circle entered Parliament, others went on missions to different countries, and Mrs. Fry, the most distinguished of them all, had made herself known throughout the world by her labors in prisons. It will be interesting to see how she was viewed by Bishop Heber, then rector of his native parish of Hodnet in Shropshire, when she first began this work at Newgate : —

She is now [June, 1820] assisted by a numerous committee of ladies, and governs the women's side of Newgate with full authority. We found her in a room where she was expecting her flock to come together for prayers, and I was greatly struck both by her and them. She is a tall, well-looking woman of forty-five, has no pretensions to eloquence, but is the best reader I ever heard, with a voice of perfect music. She read the parable of the Prodigal Son and one of the penitential psalms, and then said a few words of advice to the poor women before her, who listened with deep attention and some of them with tears. . . . You will ask to what I attribute Mrs. Fry's great power over such beings as these. Partly, I conceive, it arises from the contrast between her and any human being whom these poor wretches have ever seen before, partly from the immediate temporal advantages which she has it in her power to bestow, the clothes and comforts of which she is the dispenser, and the mitigation of punishments which she has in some instances obtained for them from Lord Sidmouth. Still, much must be ascribed to her own calmness, good sense, and perseverance, her freedom from all enthusiasm or vanity, and her not expecting too much at first from either convicts or magistrates. Yet there are a set of men who cannot bear that anybody should do good in a new way, who absolutely hate Mrs. Fry; and, when I was at Oxford, I had to fight her battles repeatedly with persons whom that arch-bigot, Sir William Scott, had been filling with all possible prejudice against her.*

Persecution and ridicule had been the lot of the Quakers in England during the first century and a half of their existence as a sect; but with the opening of the nineteenth century a better era had dawned. Dr. Fothergill, the good physician, the friend of Franklin and of all mankind, who died in 1780, and many other Quakers had shown such a talent for success (which the English value above most men), as well as so many of the national virtues, that it was impossible not to respect them. Even in the humbler callings their piety and benevolence had won the good will of persons who could not understand either their doctrines, their modesty, or their scruples. Wordsworth's Westmoreland friend, Thomas Wilkinson, who tilled his own farm with the spade which the poet celebrated in verse, and who walked the three hundred miles from the Lakes to London (calling on "Edmund and Jane Burke" at Beaconsfield, on the way) to attend the Yearly Meeting, was one of these. Charles Lamb, whose humorous eye caught both the charming and the laughable traits of the society, said of this yearly gathering: —

Every Quakeress is a lily; and when they come up in bands to their Whitsun conferences, whitening the easterly streets of the metropolis, from all parts of the United Kingdom, they show like troops of the Shining Ones.

When Esther Maud, the wife of William Tuke, of York, the founder of rational care for the insane in England, knocked at the door of the London Yearly Meeting in 1784, and with her feminine comrade made the first appearance of women in these London gatherings, the exalted clerk, who presided, said in his heart: "What wilt thou, Queen Esther, and what is thy request? It shall be even given thee to the half of the kingdom." Her request was for a "Women's Yearly Meeting," and it was at once granted: hence the throng of Quakeresses whom Lamb

*From "Bishop Heber, Poet and Chief Missionary," etc., by George Smith (London, John Murray, 1895.) The passage cited is on pages 73, 74. Heber was the half-brother of Walter Scott's friend Richard Heber, of Hodnet. His sister Mary married Rev. Charles Cholmondeley, father of Thoreau's friend, Thomas Cholmondeley.

noticed, and among whom the susceptible young American now found himself,— sometimes rambling with them in the gardens at Upton, which Dr. Fothergill had planted, or visiting the great Ackworth School, which the same benevolent physician had endowed.

Luke Howard had been a London chemist, and the partner at Plough Court of William Allen, the philanthropist. Both were Fellows of the Royal Society, at that time a great distinction. Howard was a meteorologist, as Dr. Fothergill had been. He wrote a book on the climate of London, in which Fothergill had been the first to publish a record of the weather. Howard's country home was at the villa, near Ackworth, fresco-painted by an Italian artist, and hospitably served by Maria Bella, an Italian cook, who ten years before, in 1828, had served the fever patients at the Friends' School with delicacies from her kitchen. At the same period Luke Howard broke up the week-day religious meeting at the school with the remark, "Under present circumstances I think the children ought to have shorter meetings and more generous diet." This made him very popular at the school. When Dr. Earle, in 1837, visited Ackworth, Hannah Richardson, of York, who had long lived with the New York Quaker, Lindley Murray, at Holdgate, near York, had been for two years governess of the girls' department. "She was the most unselfish, disinterested character I ever knew," wrote one who was a schoolmistress under her. "She is before me now, with her kindly, smiling face, in her Friendly attire, with her erect form and somewhat measured step. Wherever we were, even if going out to dinner at a quarterly meeting" (perhaps at S. Gurney's), "to houses where footmen stood behind our chairs (so different from our school life), we were sheltered behind her, our pioneer, to whom we looked up with unmixed confidence and respect, mingled with deep love. She once told me that, if she could have but two books, they must be the Bible and Thomas à Kempis." She was ever active. "I will just step over to Pontefract," she would say, before setting off four miles to that old town, where another Quaker grew licorice to manufacture into "Pomfret Cakes" for colds and coughs.

A general meeting was held at Ackworth for a week in July each year, and was a yearly holiday. Dr. Earle was present at this meeting in 1837, near the close of July, and assisted as a member of the committee to examine the boys, the girls being examined only by a committee of women. The treasurer of the school was then, and for long after, Samuel Gurney; and thither came the other Gurneys and their connection, also the Tukes, of York, the Pease brothers, John and Joseph (the latter the first Quaker M.P.), and that fiery young Quaker, John Bright, whom Dr. Earle afterwards met. Dr. Earle was struck with the simplicity, even to rudeness, of the boarding-school arrangements. Writing before the modernization of the school, in consequence of the efforts of James Tuke and others, he said to his sister Eliza, herself a successful teacher : —

The examination here is not so interesting as that in Providence, since the higher branches are not much studied, from the fact that none are permitted to stay after the age of fifteen. The present number is about three hundred; and there are more girls than boys, I think. They dress almost exclusively in uniform, the clothing being made by a tailor and a seamstress, who are here constantly employed. The food of the scholars is much more simple than that in American schools, and the table is set in a style that would hardly be tolerated by our republican pupils. Wooden trenchers and tin cups, which appeared as if taken from the ruins of Noah's ark, and from each of which cups four persons drink at meals, form the chief table furniture. Yet the scholars look as robust as a regiment of Green Mountain boys. The other accommodations are very good, and the discipline apparently mild and efficient.* The buildings are arranged on three sides of a square. The court, or green, thus partially enclosed is divided by a flagged walk, the eastern half of the yard being occupied by the boys, and the western by the girls as their playground. Brothers and sisters, also cousins, have the privilege of

---

* It was not always thus. When Thomas Pumphrey, who was in charge of the boys from 1835 onward, was in his first week at Ackworth, he made this entry in his diary: "Examined the records of caning,— a very humiliating volume. It carries its own refutation with it as to the good effects of such punishments,— two hundred and thirty-five inflictions in a year, of which half the number have been upon eight boys, varying from three to twenty-four times in the year. My mind is greatly pained by the perusal." The records of other schools, including the most famous in England, would have pained the good Thomas still more, as may be seen by the memoirs of the period, and for long afterwards. There was less of this discipline in the American Friends' schools.

meeting at any time upon the dividing walk. It is remarked as a
curious fact that nearly all the scholars are related to each other.

Dr. Earle did not visit Ackworth when again in England in
1849, so far as his letters show. He met Samuel Gurney and
many of his old Quaker friends; but Joseph John Gurney had
died in 1847, and Samuel Gurney did not remember him.
John Bright had by this time become an active politician, conspicuous for the part taken by him in the Corn-law repeal, in
which, at first, the wealthy Quakers did not much sympathize.
Speaking of the Ackworth General Meeting of 1846, Mrs. Ann
Ogden Boyce says :—

The presence of John Bright was not always a source of un-
mingled gratification. What had they done,— those gentle, soft-
voiced people,— who never imputed a motive, passed a hasty judgment, or made a rash promise,— who wrapped up their censure, even,
in elaborate sentences of long Latinized words, who were, above all
things, peacemakers,— that from their midst should come a young
man whose short words smote like sledge-hammers? who never
"believed" nor "hoped" nor "trusted," but was always quite sure
he was in the right, who treated some leading Friends with no more
reverence than he would have treated a bishop, and who spoke of
some Quaker institutions with little more respect than of the House
of Lords! The young "Tribune's" physique, his resolute carriage,
the head thrown defiantly back, the sensitive mouth set firmly, may
have resembled Friends of the seventeenth century, but not those of
the nineteenth.

How well Mrs. Opie, novelist and late-made Quakeress, had
launched the attractive young American, may be judged by
these notes from his English diary of 1837, revealing a continual round of dinners, teas, and Quaker meetings in the first
month of his residence in the island, where he had planned to
tarry but two weeks on his way to Paris, and where he lingered
four months : —

May 27, 1837.— Dined with Richard Beck. J. J. Lister present.
May 28.— Meeting at Stoke Newington. Dined with Richard
Beck at his country seat.

June 4.— At the meeting in Plaistow, Essex. Dined at Samuel Gurney's. Evening meeting at Devonshire House, Bishopsgate, London (the Quaker headquarters in the city). Returned, and spent the night at S. Gurney's.

June 5.— To town (from Upton) in the gig with S. Gurney. Yesterday, at the Plaistow meeting, Elizabeth Robson preached. The evening meeting at Devonshire House was appointed by J. J. Gurney, who was soon going to America. Opened with prayer by E. Fry, followed by a sermon of J. J. Gurney, then prayer by W. Ball, and sermon by Hannah Backhouse, closing with prayer by J. J. G.

Samuel Gurney lives at Ham House, formerly occupied by Dr. Fothergill, the gardens of which were set under the direction of that celebrated physician. It is five miles from town. Many rare and curious exotic shrubs are in the gardens, still flourishing among the trees.

June 6.— Last week, as I was walking through Houndsditch, a tap on the shoulder caused me to look round. I recognized a person whom I had met at dinner a few days before (at Richard Beck's). "I understand you are an American." "Yes." "Well, if you'll come to my house at Isleworth, and spend a week, with such accommodations as I can furnish, I shall be glad of your company." I thanked him. "No, no, no thanks. I shall only be paying old debts. I know what it is to receive hospitality in a foreign country. I am an old sailor, and my habits stick to me. I do things and say things in a straightforward manner. I live in a little cottage,— a widower with one son, a little boy. Now you know what to expect when you come." So to-day I took an omnibus ; and, going through Brentford to Islesworth (a village on the Thames near Richmond Hill, about fifteen miles above London Bridge), I found my friend, a brother of Richard Beck, living in a house large enough to supply a parlor, sitting-room, library, wash-room, kitchen, etc., on the ground floor, with a view of the gardens,— one of the prettiest places of the kind I have seen. And here Edward Beck lives, in what he calls very humble style, spending an income of $6,000 a year. Here I passed a week or, more exactly, eight days, during which I drank tea and spent an evening with Charles Allen, a Friend retired from business, with a family of five boys and girls.

June 14.— A monthly meeting to-day about a mile from Edward Beck's. At dinner his table was filled with friends belonging to the meeting, but living at some distance, among them John Hull, author of a philanthropic work on the poor and a zealous advocate of total abstinence. He was about to attend a temperance meeting at Windsor, fifteen miles further west, and requested me to go with him. When I declined on account of previous arrangements, he added the inducement of promising to take me to the grave of William Penn, at Stoke Park. I finally accepted.

June 15.— At the Windsor meeting a Mr. Greenbank, who had spent twelve years in America, held forth; and also another gentleman from Lancashire, who spoke Englishly, but is uneducated. He "'oped and troosted that hall would koom forward and join the temperance society." In Mr. G. I recognized the gentleman opposite whom I rode from Manchester to Birmingham, who suspected me to be an American from the crooked handle of my umbrella, and asked if my name was not Earle, from my resemblance to brother Thomas, whom he knew in Philadelphia.

June 16.— At John Hull's, who gave me some autographs, among them a letter from Lady Byron.

June 19.— I rode to Croydon, ten miles south of London, on the road to Brighton (Brighthelmstone), dining there with Peter Bedford. After dinner we visited the Croydon boarding-school for boys and girls, one of several such Friends' schools in Great Britain. It is pleasantly situated, with highly cultivated gardens, divided by some of the hedges which make England, in its most luxurious districts, seem a paradise. The idea of gravel walks at this school seems not to have excited so much ridicule as it did at the Friends' School in Providence, when John Griscom suggested one in the front grove. This Croydon school is limited to eighty boys and seventy girls, and is always full, mainly with those unable to pay for an expensive education, and patronized by the wealthy only so far as to prevent the children from feeling that our society separates the "precious" from the "vile," and that they are among the latter. We called at two other places, and met at one of them John Barclay, descended from Barclay of the "Apology," and himself an author of some note. Took tea with William Frith, another old bachelor, like Peter Bedford, retired from business, and living with a sister and two nieces in one of those thousand villas, near London, that bloom under a perfect cultivation.

June 23, *Friday*.— Met Elizabeth Fry at Newgate Prison.

June 24.— Took the coach to Upton, five miles from London. Called at Joseph Fry's (husband of Elizabeth), and saw him, but not his wife. Dined at Ham House. After dinner walked through the grounds of S. Gurney, with him and his family and the wife and two daughters of J. J. Lister. Mr. Gurney has one hundred tons of hay now cut and out. Many men and women were making it. Day after to-morrow (June 26) the children are to give a haymaking party. Spent this Saturday night at Ham House.

June 25, *Sabbath.*— The Gurney family assembled this morning. Three of the younger children read, and so did S. Gurney. The children repeated poetry. At the Plaistow meeting, not far away, there was prayer by Mrs. Fry, and sermon by Hannah Backhouse. At dinner, with her and her brother and Eliza Kirkbride (at S. Gurney's), I met Sir T. F. Buxton and his son. In the evening I supped with J. Fry. At table were his wife, a daughter, and two sons. Before supper we walked in the garden and grounds, examining the flowers, the Jersey cows, and an old pony. After supper Mrs. F. read the chapter in Luke about the Pharisee and publican.

Mrs. Opie, in one of her letters of 1838, gives a fuller description of life at Ham House and in Upton Lane, near by, where Mrs. Fry then lived. She says :—

Monday I reached a dark-looking house in Lombard Street — Mr. Gurney's house of business — at 3.30 P.M.* Going upstairs, I found in a back room Mr. Gurney, two young ladies, and an old gentleman, rather crooked and odd-looking, with two or three others. "Truly glad to see thee, my dear," said Mr. Gurney. An hour's drive brought us to Upton (Ham House). "How does my little gal do?" said he to a little child that ran out to meet us at the door. "How glad I am to see thee are home, Sam!" exclaimed a tall lady with white hair, coming out ; while a very tall gentleman in a blue coat with gilt buttons (Fowell Buxton) called from behind, "And how's the king of London and all the princesses this morning?" One would have thought Mr. Gurney had been out for a year, by all the greetings; but they are a very affectionate family. At 5.30 we assembled in the drawing-room, and I was introduced to the five daughters and son and several guests. I went in to dinner with Mr.

---

* This was the business house of Overend, Gurney & Co., the largest discounting house in the world then. It had grown out of the Norwich business of Joseph Smith in 1806-7, whose clerk Overend was.

Gurney, who placed everybody before he took his own seat: "Fowell, sit by my wife; Catherine next; Prissy, my sweet, by Charles; the little gal by me," etc. The evening was finished by a supply of wine-glasses of gruel.

Tuesday morning we were all summoned into the dining-room at 8.30 by the ringing of a great bell, when Mr. Gurney read a chapter in the Bible. Directly after a tall clergyman, rather lame, made his appearance, having come, rather to the surprise of everybody, by one of the mails. The only introduction I had was, "Francis, thee knows Amelia,"— a mistake, but a common mode of introduction at Upton. Though it was a damp, drizzly morning, we all went to the end of a terrace walk in the garden,— their usual practice before breakfast. "Francis," said Mr. Gurney at breakfast, "I'll give thee five pounds for Chenda's schools, if thee likes." Meantime it was being arranged who was to be asked to that day's dinner; and at least three notes of invitation were despatched, and the answers received, before Mr. Gurney left the breakfast table, which he did ten minutes before the rest, to start for town. They seem to think nothing of giving short notice at Upton. After breakfast, to my surprise, one of the girls ushered me into my bedroom with: "We generally separate for the morning, but meet at twelve to read with John (the invalid brother). Perhaps thee'd like to join us." I assented, and was left to my meditations in my pleasant room over-looking the front door, where the numerous departures and arrivals amused me exceedingly. I came down at twelve, when some of the party settled to drawing, others to working, while their brother read to them. Luncheon — a famous hot meal, at one — put a final end to further literary pursuits. All the afternoon arrangements, most various, were made then.

After luncheon Mrs. Opie was taken to Mrs. Fry's, Upton Lane.

I found her, like the party at Ham House, quite full of business. There were already two persons to speak to her; but she kindly came forward to speak to me, and introduced me to one of the persons as master of a coast-guard station, and to the other as a matron going out to some establishment in New South Wales. She was so taken up with this matron that I saw little of her till the carriage came with Mr. Gurney, who called out: "Oh, I must go speak to

Betsy. Betsy, here are these letters. Thee must do so and so with them: do thee understand?" ... At half-past-five the dinner-party assembled at Upton,—a seven-leaf table. ... At dessert the little girl was despatched to fetch a little boy, who was soon perched on grandpapa's knee, and before long was on his way to grandmamma, walking along the table, amid exclamations of, "Take care! take him off!" which were perfectly unheeded; and he arrived at his destination safely. In the drawing-room three kittens are generally playing. A parrot named Thomas lives on a tree near the house; and there are, besides, dogs, doves, and canaries without end. Nobody who has not been at Upton can understand its pleasures and peculiarities.

Dr. Fothergill, who had laid out the grounds of Ham House, was a celebrated physician, contemporary with Dr. Erasmus Darwin, but older, and, like him, fond of rare plants and trees; a Quaker also, and one who practised medicine as much from philanthropy as for gain. Plashet House, where the Frys lived before their loss of property, was near Ham House, both being in Upton, and not far from the Quaker meeting of Plaistow. The old home of the Gurneys at Earlham was occupied, after his father's decease, by Joseph John Gurney, the scholar of the family; and George Borrow, in "Lavengro," has given a picture of it and of its owner, as the strolling author saw him, when fishing one day on his grounds. The misfortunes which overtook the banking house of Overend* & Gurney did not come until after the death of Samuel Gurney, in 1865.

Of Joseph John Gurney many notices and anecdotes are given. Mrs. Ann Ogden Boyce, a kinswoman of the Richardsons of Cleveland, England, in her "Records of a Quaker Family" (London, 1889), says: "One of a family of brothers and sisters (children of John Gurney of Earlham) remarkable for their gifts of mind and person, cultured, prosperous, and

---

* One of the founders of the house of Overend & Gurney was Thomas Richardson, of a remarkable Quaker family in the county of Durham, whose sister married John Overend (born 1769, died 1832). Overend was the inventor of the plan of charging but one commission on bills, and converted John Gurney to the plan, who soon sent his son Samuel to join the new firm of discount and bill brokers. Overend and Richardson were both clerks in banking houses at the time, early in the present century.

generous, Joseph John Gurney was a man of great influence
in his generation. His sweetness of nature exhibited itself in
a manner full of the most winning courtesy and consideration
for the feelings of the humblest and youngest person. He
walked about the Ackworth school garden like a prince, surrounded by his loyal subjects. When it was announced that
Joseph John Gurney had reached the school, the girls gathered
with one accord upon the green, clustering round him like a
swarm of bees." Mention has been made of this Ackworth
school when Dr. Earle records his visit there. It had been a
provincial branch of the London Foundling Hospital, but was
given up as such, and was purchased, with its farm and fine
stone buildings, by Dr. Fothergill in 1777. He and his friends
paid $35,000 for what had cost $85,000. It was the model of
other Friends' schools in England and America, and is still a
flourishing establishment.

Of Dr. Fothergill (born 1712, died 1780) Dr. Franklin said,
in a letter to another Quaker physician, Isaac Lettsom, written
from Paris while Franklin was American ambassador there,
after his friend's death, " If we may estimate the goodness of
a man by his disposition to do good, and his constant endeavors and success in doing it, I can hardly conceive that a better
man than Fothergill has ever existed." His portrait was painted
by Hogarth at a time when Quakers were averse to sitting for
pictures.

Among all these English Friends, so hospitable and so
interesting, there was one, Joseph John Gurney, of whom Dr.
Earle makes little mention, because he had been moved of the
spirit to visit America, a little after the young American's arrival in England. He remained on our continent, visiting the
United States, Canada, and the West Indies, until after Dr.
Earle's return to Philadelphia in 1839, and they met there in
1840; but, when Dr. Earle made his second visit to Europe, in
1849, J. J. Gurney was dead. He was the most learned of the
whole Quaker Society in England, and one of the most orthodox, so that the secession of Elias Hicks and his followers
in 1828 had given him great concern; and his visit to the
United States had for its objects to oppose the Hicksite

Quakers, and to do what he could for the enfranchisement of
the slaves. It seems that nearly or quite a third of the American Quakers had separated from their brethren, following the
views of Elias Hicks,—chiefly in New York, Pennsylvania,
and Maryland; in New England there was no open secession,
though the opinions of Elias were probably held by some of the
Quakers there; in Virginia and North Carolina also, no secession occurred. Of the troubles in Philadelphia, mention has
been made in the first chapter. Dr. Earle in his English diary,
presently to be cited, speaks of the departure of J. J. Gurney
for America; and the jocose verses circulated at the Yearly
Meeting (ascribed by some, but incorrectly, to Dr. Earle as
their author) make allusion to J. J. Gurney, and the English disputes in which he took an active part. The diary
goes on :—

June 26, 1837.— Rode to London with S. Gurney, after spending
the night at his house. Visited at Jonathan Backhouse's. The illness of his sister has long detained them near London. They will
leave to-morrow for Liverpool, whence, July 8, Eliza Kirkbride and
J. J. Gurney will sail for Philadelphia. Rode in the afternoon with
J. J. Lister, his wife, and three children, to his house at Upton.
He lives near S. Gurney's. We sat up till midnight, viewing objects
through his microscope.

June 27.— Quarterly meeting at Plaistow. At 2 P.M. the meeting
adjourned for dinner, and met again at five. I dined at Plough
Court with a son-in-law of William Allen, who was present, and also
Robert and Josiah Forster.

June 28.— Called at J. Fry's, where Mrs. Fry gave me some
autographs, one of them from a royal princess. To London with
J. J. Lister.

June 30.— To the British Museum. My stay in England has been
unexpectedly prolonged.*

---

* Dr. Earle, late in life, told me the circumstance which enabled him to spend so much time
travelling in the three kingdoms, when he had formed a Spartan resolution to devote himself and his
small property to the completing of his medical education in Paris. He was dining one day with a
party at the house of a wealthy English Friend, and was asked by one of the company how long his
stay in England would be. Dr. Earle named some brief space, adding that he must go on to Paris
and take up his studies there. "But," said his friend, "you are not seeing enough of England and
Scotland: you ought to spend the summer here." "I should be glad to do so," said the young
American, "if I could afford it; but I came to Europe to study, and must deny myself the pleasure."

July 1.— I go to **Tottenham** to spend Sunday with Josiah and **Robert Forster. Dine** there this evening.

July 2.— At the Tottenham meeting, where **Anna** Braithwaite preached from the text, "Be not overcome of evil, but overcome **evil with good." Dined in company** with her and her daughter at **Josiah Forster's.** Caroline B. is very *spirituelle* and **quick in repartee. I have** often been tortured by **the** arrows of her wit.

July 3.— **To** town with Robert **Forster, where** I supped last **night.**

July 5, 6.— Supped, lodged, **and breakfasted with** George **Stacy** at Tottenham. He married **a daughter of S. Lloyd, the** banker. Dined at John Hodgkin's with **Sir Augustus D'Este, a son** of the Duke of Sussex. G. Stacy **resembles President Van Buren. I told** him so, thinking, of course, it would be a compliment; but, *misericordia !* he came as near being offended as would answer for a disciple of George Fox. At what? At the idea of being even physically analogous to a man of such heterodox opinions on the slave question as Van Buren is. His wife is about **the age of sister Sarah** Hadwen, and, like her, retains the appearance of "sweet seventeen." **Beside her sits a daughter who** might be mistaken for **a younger sister.**

July 11.— Anti-slavery meeting at Exeter **Hall. The Duke of** Sussex presided, led in by William **Allen. Joseph Sturge spoke at** much length.

July 13.— Dined with **Robert Howard at** Tottenham, who married **another daughter of S. Lloyd. Rode with** him to Chingford church. **Took tea and passed the night at Robert** Forster's.

July 14.— **Breakfasted with Josiah Forster in the city, and** back at night to stay at R. **Forster's.**

The next day Dr. Earle started **northward on the** Birmingham Railway, after six **weeks of this genial Quaker** hospitality. The character of **his entertainers is disclosed by their** names.

Nothing further passed at the moment; but, when they rose from the table, this Friend took Dr. Earle **aside,** and said, 'I have a sum of money which is at thy disposal for a tour in England, and I shall be glad to have thee take it." "But I cannot repay thee at present, probably not for some years." "Never **mind,"** was the answer: "I will trust thee until thou canst pay." The offer was so kindly made, **and the thing** to be done — to make the acquaintance, not only of English scenery and life, but of the attractive and hospitable English Quakers, who invited him so cordially to their houses — was so eminently desirable, that it was accepted; and some years after this the loan was repaid. **The** incident seems to me a delightful illustration of character in both lender and borrower. As **Emerson** said of his **brother Edward,**—

> Prosperous Age held forth his hand,
> And freely his large future planned.

They were the most wealthy and prominent of the Friends
about London, and at that time becoming powerful in the affairs of Parliament and the nation. This was due in part to
their riches, but much more to the active share taken by them
as a sect in the discontinuance of the slave-trade and the abolition of slavery in the British colonies; in part, also, to those
personal traits which made William Penn and some of his contemporaries influential at the court of the Stuart kings. The
Gurneys and some others of the leading Quakers of England —
notably, William Allen and Mrs. Fry (herself one of the Earlham Gurneys)— had that charm of manners, along with sincerity
of conviction, which never fails to please an aristocratic circle.
This is evident enough from what Dr. Earle says of them, both
in England and afterwards in France, where he met Mrs. Fry
and some of her friends in the following winter. He was a
close observer, not without humor ; and many of his descriptions and anecdotes may still be read with amusement. Speaking of the stage-coaches and taverns, he says : —

The public coach of the English is a model of compactness, neatness, and lightness, drawn by large horses, elegant in form, and
handsomely caparisoned, the brass trimmings of their harness
glistening in the sun, when that happens to shine. The coachman
is a portly creature, in genteel dress, wearing white-topped boots and
white gloves. He seldom touches his whip while driving. *Au con-
traire*, the French diligence is driven by a small man in a blue frock,
over which in cold or wet weather he wears a curious goatskin garment, dressed with the hair on ; and, what with his whip and his
mouth, he keeps up a continual crack and chirrup from Calais to
Marseilles and from Bordeaux to Strasbourg. His diligence is a
lumbering vehicle, weighing of itself from one to two tons, and sometimes carrying on its top, at least a ton of merchandise. It is drawn
by small horses, harnessed with ropes, and driven three or four
abreast. All the inns in England of any importance, and some that
are unimportant, are dignified with titles, and seldom known by the
name of the landlord, as in America. I saw "The Star and Garter,"
" The White Horse," the " Cock and Castle," and " The Jolly Butch-
ers." One near Sheffield is called " The Fiery Dragon," and its
landlord is a " Tempest." The " Bell at Edmonton " famous in John

Gilpin's day, still exists; and on its front is a picture of Gilpin's race, taken at the moment when

> The dogs did bark, the children screamed,
>   Up flew the windows all,
> And every soul cried out, " Well done ! "
>   As loud as they could bawl.

In the stage-coach in Derbyshire I found myself in company with two very intelligent men, a Whig and a Tory. Party politics were running high ; for it was on the eve of the election of members to the first Parliament of the youthful Victoria, whose coronation I witnessed the next year. In the discussion I made a remark which implied me to be a foreigner. " But, surely, you are an Englishman ? " said one of them. " No, I am an American." " Then you have always lived in England ? " " I have only been in your country six weeks." " But you must have been educated here." " This is the first time I have ever been out of the United States." " Indeed ! do all the Americans speak our language as well as you do ? " All are not such in England ; for one damp morning, as I was perambulating the streets of Penrith, wearing my camlet cloak and overshoes, and gazing like a country gawky at the objects about me, a huckster-woman, coming up to me with a courtesy, said, " Pray, sir, are ye an American ? " " Yes." " Is your name X——? " " No : why do you ask, and why think me from America ? " " Why, I seed ye wears a cloak, and there's American missionaries in Westmoreland that wears cloaks, too ; an' I didna know but ye was one o' them." After a pause : " I hope ye'll excuse me for speakin' to ye. I didna know but ye was one o' them missionaries, and wanted a place to board. I hope the missionaries will succeed, for I think there's more moral darkness in Westm'r'l'n' than in the Indies."

After Edward Beck had invited me (in the streets of London) to make him a visit at Islesworth, he went home and told his sister,— for he has no wife,— " Well, I have invited an American to come and spend a week with us." " O dear brother, how could thee ? " " Because I think it will be pleasant to both him and myself." " But," — and she spoke as if ruin were likely to come upon their furniture,— " but *we have no spittoons in the house !* Really, I hope he won't be spitting about everywhere." There is certainly a great difference between the English and the Americans in regard to this habit. Absolutely, I have no recollection of having seen a man spit since I came to England, unless he were smoking. Neither have I observed any chewing tobacco. There is a vast amount of pipe-smoking among the lower classes; but cigars, from their high price, are used only by politicians. They are the Tories of Nicotiana.

The English understand the true philosophy of living better than we Americans, although perhaps they drink a little more porter and wine than is best. But a change in that habit is rapidly taking place. Proselytes to the doctrine of the "teetotalers," as they are called here, are made almost as fast as to the anti-slavery cause in the United States. There was a discussion on the subject at the Yearly Meeting in May. Many remarks had been made, both pro and con, when one of the assistant clerks of the meeting, a leading member of the society, arose. He said he must acknowledge that he was not ready to unite with the sentiments of some who had spoken. He was fully satisfied that, after the labors of the day, he had often experienced great invigoration from a glass of porter, and been thereby better prepared for the duties of the evening. No sooner had his coat-skirts touched the bench than a Friend, still higher in the "rising seats" than himself, rose to clinch the nail which the brother had driven. Imagine a Friend of seventy years standing in the gallery, covered by a real primitive tri-cocked hat, and leaning upon a cane to plead the cause of the juice of the grape, with an earnestness that would do credit to some of the young men on the other side of the question. Wine is set upon the table by a much greater proportion of our society members than I had supposed. However, they rarely drink more than two glasses, and generally but one.

It has been my pleasant lot (Sept. 9, 1837) to see a great deal of our Society of Friends, considering the short time I have been in England, and much of the best society among them. They bring about them all those little (as well as great) conveniences and comforts which so much conduce to the luxury of living. Their social affections are cultivated, if possible, to an objectionable extreme. I speak not from my personal observation alone, but from the testimony of some English Friends themselves. I lately passed an evening with Samuel Tuke (of the York Lunatic Retreat), who is now in London. Our conversation turned upon lunatic asylums, insanity in general, the predominance of that disease among the Friends, and

the cause of such preponderance. Among other influences tending
that way, he mentioned the extreme cultivation of the ties of consan-
guinity, the parental and fraternal affections.

This is the first intimation given in the young doctor's letters that he was specially considering what was to be his life-
work in America and the occasion of several future visits to
Europe. But, before he returned home in 1839, he had inspected many of the European asylums then existing; and he
reported on their condition, soon after his return, in a work
which first drew general attention to the European specialty.
Crossing over to Ireland in the summer of 1837, he visited an
asylum in Dublin, and relates this incident : —

I have a strong inclination to wear a mask. My plain Quaker
coat, although in a land of Friends, attracts too much attention.
September 8, while near the "Bell at Edmonton," I was accosted
thus : "Excuse me, sir, for the intrusion ; but I am a poor man with
a family, and can get no work, else I would not beg. If you will
give me a few pence, I shall be very much obliged to you. Pray,
sir, let me *turn down the collar of your coat.*" He suited the action
to the word, before I could say Jack Robinson. Passing along the
wards of the lunatic asylum at Dublin, we met a patient apparently
very happy. "Well, Tom," said the keeper with me, "how are you
to-day?" "Oh, illigant, illigant," replied the maniac. Then, stepping up to me, he asked, "Are you an Englishman, sir?" "I came
from England." "Well, I like the English. Why? Because they
give a fellow a bit of something to ate. Let me fix your coat-col-
lar," and accordingly gave it a turn. I thanked him, and pursued
my way.

A concise review of his first English experiences was given
by Dr. Earle in this letter to Mrs. Spring, of Sept. 1, 1837,
written from the Isle of Wight : —

Dear Cousin Rebecca,— Even at the present late period, I have
not yet seen the coast of *la belle France.* The English people
and the English scenery, the English antiquities and institutions,
have presented attractions powerful enough thus long to protract my

stay among them, in this thrice-blessed yet doubly cursed land. I could not have selected a more desirable season to be in Great Britain. The weather has been uncommonly warm and dry (though there has not been a day that I should call very warm), and vegetation remarkably luxuriant. The many changes which have occurred in the royal family, and the consequent dissolution of the old Parliament and election of the new one, have furnished constant subjects of excitement among the people, and enabled me to see more of a monarchial government as it exists here than would have been possible under ordinary circumstances. I have seen the queen three or four times, but had the best opportunity of studying her face while she was on her way to the House of Lords for the purpose of dissolving Parliament. The royal procession on that occasion was one of the most magnificent displays of regal splendor ever exhibited in England. And the head and heart and soul of the whole of it was that little girl just turned of eighteen. Young as she is, she played her part very well.

I arrived here this morning, after a tour of more than fifteen hundred miles through England, Scotland, Ireland, and Wales. Loch Katrine and Loch Lomond (a larger and, in my opinion, a more beautiful lake) were the places farthest north that I visited. I landed and spent some time on the island where the Lady of the Lake landed before me. Since then I have been among the lakes in England, visiting Windermere, Derwent, Ullswater, Thirlmere, Grasmere, Rydal Water, and Esthwaite Lakes; passed some time in rich yet poverty-stricken Dublin and its vicinity; ascended Mt. Snowdon in North Wales, and have come thence to the Isle of Wight. I have been in London, Liverpool, Birmingham, Manchester, Leeds, Sheffield, Wakefield, York, Edinburgh, Glasgow, Bristol, Bath, Oxford, and Cambridge, besides numerous places of minor importance.

I found in Joseph Sturge a very agreeable fellow-passenger. He sat at my right hand during the whole passage over. When in Birmingham, I visited very agreeably at his house, and have since met him several times. Since his return, with the mighty lever of horrid truth which he brought from the tropics, he has moved the whole British nation. You will have heard of the breakfast given him by the inhabitants of Birmingham, and the exposition which he made at that time; also you will have read of the great anti-slavery meeting at Exeter Hall, at which the Duke of Sussex presided, and J. Sturge, among others, addressed the audience. I had the pleasure of being present then, my friend, Robert Forster, having given me a ticket to the platform. The form of a petition on behalf of the West India Apprentices, to be addressed by the women of Great Britain to their queen, was adopted at that time, and is now among the people for signatures. The numbers obtained exceed the most sanguine expectation of the friends of the negro. It will, in all probability, exceed the renowned petition presented to Parliament by T. Fowell Buxton, before the passage of the Apprenticeship Bill, and which required four men to carry it. That contained but about two hundred thousand names. It is hoped that in this there will be five hundred thousand. In the city of Bristol alone, upwards of thirty thousand (equal to about one-third of the population) have already been obtained.

In Darlington I became acquainted with Elizabeth Pease, a Friend who is much interested in anti-slavery, and, I think, a correspondent of either Sarah or Angelina Grimké. . . . I sincerely regret that A. E. Grimké should have introduced the resolution which awakened the discussion upon "the rights of women." It was uncalled for and unnecessary. I expect to return to London in two or three days.

As this letter shows, by the 1st of September Dr. Earle had visited Edinburgh, the Scotch Highlands, Glasgow, Dublin, Dumfries, Hawthornden of the Drummonds, Gretna Green, Carlisle, Windermere, and other places of note in Wordsworth's country, and had not only ascended Snowdon, but

Climbed the dark brow of the mighty Hellvellyn.

Then, returning to London, he sailed down the Thames on his way to Boulogne September 12, and in two days more was in Paris for the winter. But even in that gay and studious capital he was not yet out of the Quaker circle of England. In October the family of Samuel Gurney were in Paris for some days; and in February, 1838, Mrs. Fry and her husband, with other English Friends, held meetings in Paris, which were largely attended by English, American, and French people of both sexes. Dr. Earle (February 18) went in the evening to

the rooms of Joseph and Elizabeth Fry, after hearing her give
elsewhere "the best sermon I have ever heard from her." He
then says : —

I introduced Dr. Mott and his daughter to Mrs. Fry, who spoke
of receiving a letter from Richard Mott, twenty years before, invit-
ing her to America. I said I hoped she would still accept the invitation. Joseph Fry: "I hope she'll consult her husband about it."
I replied that I had not finished my remark,— I was going to say,
"and her husband, too." He said, "In London, if you buy a span
of horses, you generally get one very good horse, the other only ordinary." I replied, "And sometimes two very good ones." "Generally," he repeated, "an ordinary one harnessed with a good one to
get him off." Among the audience at the sermon, which was in
English, was a Frenchwoman, of whom Mr. Fry asked if she understood what had been uttered. "Non," was her answer, "Je n'ai
pas compris les mots; mais il y avait quelque chose que j'ai senti,
beaucoup, dans mon cœur." ("Nay, I did not comprehend the
words; but there was something which I deeply felt in my heart.")

A month later Robert Ware Fox, of Falmouth, the father of
Caroline Fox, was in Paris with his daughters; and Dr. Earle
met them frequently. In May and June, 1838, he was again in
England, and renewed his acquaintance with them and with
his other friends among the English Quakers. Dr. Earle wrote
home that he was "enchanted" with the Foxes; and Caroline
(whose journals were published not long after her death) seems
to have been the most attractive member of a singularly gifted
family. On leaving Paris, he made this entry concerning the
final result of the labors of Mrs. Fry, Anne Knight, and other
English Quakers for the improvement of the French prisons
and for other social ameliorations : —

While Elizabeth Fry was here, a committee was appointed to visit
prisons, composed in part of Catholics and in part of Protestants.
Religious difficulties soon arose, and all the Protestant members resigned and withdrew. There is ground for the belief that the Archbishop of Paris will endeavor to undo all that was done by Mrs. Fry,
except what was done among the English in Paris.

On his return to England (Feb. 20, 1838), Dr. Earle took lodgings on Queen's Square, near the British Museum, the Royal College of Surgeons, and the London University, all which he visited. But his chief interest was still with the members of the Society of Friends, a few sketches of whom may be given, with the events therewith connected : —

Feb. 23, 1838.— Called at John Burrt's. John is a good-hearted, benevolent man, who is always doing something,— if not otherwise occupied, he talks ; and, if you wish it, he will do all the talking. Like many of the English Friends, he dresses in drab small-clothes and gaiters. Dined with the mother of Albert Savory, the party consisting of his mother, sister, two brothers, and James and William Tuke, sons of Samuel Tuke, of York. The Savorys live at Stamford Hill, between London and Tottenham ; but, like all Friends' families who live some miles away and have business in the city, they have a table at their place of business, where they dine,— at least during Yearly Meeting.

February 23.— Dined and passed the night with Edward Beck, at Islesworth, with whom I spent eight days last spring. He has since married Susan Lucas, a highly educated young woman. It was pleasant again to meet him. He is a man of little reserve, and speaks frankly what he thinks,— can perceive the faults of the English as well as of the Americans or any other people, and mentions them as freely. We have thoroughly canvassed the manners and customs of our compatriots, and always good-humoredly. He was never displeased by any of my remarks, but once he showed a little irritation at something I did or failed to do. He always has a variety of excellent wines on the dinner table. This day the dessert consisted in part of wedding cake. When it was brought in, I had already taken as much wine as I ought ; but with this cake it was verily needful to take a little more. So I poured a half-glass, saying, " Excuse me: I have already drunk more than I need." Instantly I perceived the irritation I have mentioned (I ought, according to common courtesy here, to have filled the glass). But he only said, " Certainly: thou well knows I have always given permission to do as thou pleases."

February 25.— Returned to London and called on Joseph Sturge to get a ticket of entrance to Exeter Hall, to a meeting of such as

favor the immediate abolition of the apprenticeship of the emancipated negroes in the colonies. At the meeting I met many acquaintances,—James Webb, at whose house I dined in Dublin,
George Thompson, who gave me items of news from America,—the
marriage of Angelina Grimké to Theodore Weld, for example,—
Frederick Tucket, an extensive traveller, William Smeat, with whom
I breakfasted in Glasgow, etc. Among them was Elizabeth Pease,
of Darlington, and a daughter of Isaac Braithwaite, the most
beautiful, be it said in passing, of all the young Quakeresses I have
met in England. But she is no longer a true Quaker in principle,
though still a member of our society. She is a Tory, regarding the
national Church, the hereditary peerage, and all the relics of feudal
times as the greatest blessings of her country. (I shall long remember a discussion of those subjects which we had in a twilight walk
to the ruins of the ancient palace near Kendal.) I also met Anna
Maria and Caroline Fox, the two daughters of R. W. Fox, who were
in Paris, and a brother of theirs, who reminds me of brother William.
The two young ladies are amiable and full of vivacity, not handsome (their complexion having the Spanish tint), but with that
which is better than beauty of face,—a wealth of mind, *richesse de
l'esprit.* Caroline is very *spirituelle* and quick in repartee.

Exeter Hall was my dinner this day,—beefsteak, well covered with
pepper, brought from the kitchen of Lord Brougham, a ragout
cooked by George Thompson, turtle soup served by Daniel O'Connell, and *entremets*, salads, and dessert from the cookeries of
several celebrated members of the *bourgeoisie.* I find that O'Connell
is not liked by all Friends, although they are very glad to have his
powerful assistance in the cause of emancipation. Against the
Roman Catholics the Irish Friends appear to have an almost impla-
cable hatred.

Sunday, 27*th.*—At the meeting in Plaistow we had sermons from
the two Elizabeth Frys, mother and daughter. I dined at Samuel
Gurney's, the other guests being Sir T. F. Buxton, with his beautiful
daughter Lucy, Anna and Caroline Fox, Thomas Pim, of Bristol,
William (Edward) Forster, Edward Backhouse, Jr., with his brother
and sister Lucy,—nephews and niece of Hannah B. The party
was so large that there were two tables, large and small, the latter
for the younger guests. In course of the dinner they became quite
turbulent, with loud talk and laughter. T. F. Buxton called to them

in a very loud voice, "A little silence there! a little silence!" The Stentor made things quiet for a few minutes. Sir T. F. Buxton is *hors de combat* on the apprenticeship question, having been persuaded to act against his own convictions when he gave his voice in favor of apprenticing, and for the payment to the masters of £20,000,000. Since then he has been silent on the subject; but he is still himself,— still the same benevolent man,— his philanthropic spirit always occupied with projects for the good of mankind. For some months he has been investigating the slave-trade; and he finds that the number of negroes carried from Africa to America is now twice as large as when the trade was abolished in England. The number of men killed in the wars to obtain these slaves averages one thousand a day.

The custom of English ladies to leave the table before the men is still kept up, even among some Friends. When they rose to-day, S. Gurney said, "It is our practice to let every person go where he will and do what he will until three o'clock, when all will assemble in the parlor to read the Scriptures," it being between meetings, and hence the early dinner hour. We remained at table but a few minutes; and then nearly all went into the garden, where we found the young ladies, with whom we promenaded, and went to the deer park, containing but twelve or fifteen deer.

I took tea with Joseph Jackson Lister, who last year showed me wonders with the microscope. There were present, besides the children, William Aldham, of Leeds, his wife, and five or six other guests. I was obliged to answer for the hundredth time such questions as this: "Is it true that you Americans do not call your domestics servants? I have heard that your servants do not ask leave when they go out, is that so?" We walked some time in the garden, where are two magnificent cedars of Lebanon, took tea, and then went to the afternoon meeting, which begins at 6 P.M. After meeting I went home with Joseph and Elizabeth Fry, passed half an hour there, and then rode to London with W. Aldham and family. His son was educated at one of the two universities, and has since travelled in Southern Europe and in Asia.

May 28.— I dined to-day with Edward Backhouse. The other guests were W. E. Forster and two or three strangers (to me). A daughter of E. B. is very intelligent, and converses with much ease and fluency. She was one of the first of my acquaintants among young English ladies ; and I was then much struck with her manners, —natural, but somewhat *brusque*. There is something of the kind in nearly all the young ladies I have met in society. Their movements are not so artificial and mechanical as those of American *demoiselles*. The principal topics at the table were Switzerland and whether it is proper for a member of our society to accept the office of a magistrate, Edward being a justice of the peace. [The Yearly Meeting afterwards adopted a minute in which members are advised not to accept that or any similar office.]

May 30.— Dined with James Tuke and his aunt at their lodgings, the "Four Swans." Samuel Tuke, of York, is not here this year. Doubtless the sole cause of his absence is the wish not to act as clerk of the Yearly Meeting. The last day of the meeting a pamphlet entitled "Quakerieties for 1838" found its way among some of the Friends, written in rhyme, and containing twenty-eight verses, each of which alludes to some member of the society. That concerning S. Tuke was as follows : —

> Samuel Tuke, Samuel Tuke,
> I have read thy rebuke
> Of Wilkins's strange resignation.
> I own thou hast tracked
> With astonishing tact
> The cause of his alienation.

The other verses were sometimes more sarcastic, as thus : —

> Joseph John, Joseph John,*
> Thou *sine qua non*
> Of a certain religious society,
> Thy bolts thou hast hurled
> On a sceptical world,
> And won what thou loved,— notoriety.

> Luke Howard, Luke Howard,
> Why fretful and froward ?
> Why leave us ? we miss thee and thine now ;
> And then, what is worse,
> We miss thy long purse,
> For Friends have an eye to the *rhino*.

* Gurney.

Friend Forster, Friend Forster,
Thou foe to imposture
And knight of the yearly epistle,
Fame's a very fine thing,
If it happiness bring,
And we "pay not too dear for the whistle."

Betsy Fry, Betsy Fry,
Where the fatherless lie,
And the widow, we find thee.   'Tis there
In the prison-house cell
That thy soft accents dwell,
And the culprit exults in thy prayer.

May 31.— At a meeting appointed by Sarah Grubb I met James, Sally, and Elizabeth Arnold (of New Bedford, in New England). They had left Paris a few days earlier than I, and came by way of Havre, Southampton, and Salisbury, whereas I came by Boulogne, and thence direct to London.   In the evening I called upon the Arnolds.   James's daughter Elizabeth is without exception the most highly educated young lady I have met on this side of the Atlantic.   She is not handsome; but one is charmed by the fluency and polish of her conversation, in which she draws from the resources of a mind largely stored with literary and scientific knowledge.   She speaks French well.   The family will soon leave London for Holland, where they will remain two or three weeks, and return to England for a tour through the southern counties before sailing for the United States.

June 1.— Dined with William Leatham, of Wakefield, in Yorkshire, who is at the Yearly Meeting with a son and two daughters,* John Hodgkin, a lawyer of Tottenham, and two daughters of J. J. Lister being of the party.   J. Hodgkin has eminence in his profession, with a practice of from \$10,000 to \$12,000 annually.   He is in law the oracle of the Friends.

June 2.— At the dinner table of J. Backhouse I met Alexander Cruikshank, with whom I supped and breakfasted in Edinburgh last summer.   Isaac Hadwen and Mrs. Richardson and her two

---

* The elder of these daughters of W. Leatham afterwards married the celebrated John Bright, himself a Quaker.   Her brother was chosen to Parliament, but unseated.   William Edward Forster and William Aldham, Jr., sat much in Parliament; and Mr. Forster was a zealous champion of the Union cause there in our Civil War.

sons from Belfast were present. While at the table, I. H. made a
short religious communication, and Hannah Backhouse a prayer.
How profound a travail of spirit when this woman prays! It is as
if the soul had forgotten the body which it inhabits. I took tea at
Isaac Braithwaite's, Jr., in company with his sisters, two brothers,
and some others, among them Assaad Yakoob Kayat, the Oriental
convert to Christianity. To-day the Yearly Meeting closed.

June 3.—At the Tottenham meeting I met W. E. Forster, R. W.
Fox and his daughters, William Leatham (whose son married Pris-
cilla Gurney, daughter of Samuel), and others. Dined at Robert
Forster's, and called at Robert Howard's. I stayed at Robert
Forster's, where I met also Joseph Price and John and Martha
Yeardley, whose travels in Greece were published in *The Friend*.
They speak German, French, Italian, and modern Greek. When a
young man, John Yeardley joined our society from conviction, and
went to reside among the Friends in Germany. About the same
time Martha, in obedience to a sense of religious duty, went to
Southern France to live for a while among the Friends there. The
two first met on the Continent, and were not long afterwards married.
At R. Howard's, at tea, I met Joseph Sturge and his sister, the
Foxes, and several other Friends. It was a few days after the
defeat in the House of Commons of the Abolitionists, on the apprenticeship question. J. Sturge was cheerful, notwithstanding the
defeat.

June 4.— Breakfasted with R. W. Fox, and went with his son and
Anna and Caroline Fox to King's College, London. Dined at
S. Gurney's. I breakfasted with Robert Ware Fox, who has apartments at 63 Burton Crescent. He showed me an ingenious instrument for determining the dip of the magnetic needle, invented by
him ; and I remembered to have assisted John Griscom at Providence, years ago, in taking the dip with a similar instrument sent to
him by R. W. Fox. Caroline showed me a book of the Proceedings
of a philosophical society in their town (Falmouth) in which her
father had a large share.

June 22.— Elizabeth Pease tells me she has recently received a
letter from William Lloyd Garrison, in which he said he had entirely
relinquished the idea that slavery will ever be abolished in the
United States by means of moral suasion. I am sorry to hear it. . . .
When I saw in the newspapers that Abby Kelly has come forward

as a practical contender for the rights of woman,— or, rather, as an
illustrator of the practice of those rights,— I was seized with a contrary opinion; and it appeared to me more suitable that women
should still guide the distaff and direct the loom, arrange the kitchen,
and grace the parlor rather than take so prominent a situation.
And yet I have ever contended for the propriety of their taking an
active part in public questions. If they can do more good in this
way than otherwise, let them go on; and I bid them God-speed.

June 25.— Went to the London University, to a lecture by Dr.
A. S. Thompson on Medical Jurisprudence, specially relating to
persons drowned; then to the University Hospital, where I followed
Dr. T. in his visit to the patients; and afterwards saw in the amphitheatre one of the most important operations in surgery (lithotomy)
performed by Lister, who, as an operator, stands at the head of the
profession in London, excepting, perhaps, Sir Astley Cooper, who
has much withdrawn from practice. Dr. J. Mason Warren, of
Boston, was present. In the evening called on the Arnolds, who
have just returned from Holland.

On the 28th of June Dr. Earle saw the coronation of the
Princess Victoria as Queen of England, and was so near her
that he could witness the whole ceremony. The year before
he had been at the funeral of William IV., and in the early part
of 1839 he saw the Queen Dowager Adelaide at a public function in Malta. But, as the passages cited amply show, his chief
opportunities in England were among the active members of
his own sect, from whom he received the most cordial welcome
and unstinted hospitality. The familiar combination of religious earnestness and practical shrewdness in Quakers did
not escape his notice, and was by no means absent from his
own nature. Of this earnestness, directed towards surgical
problems, a good example is found in this letter of Mrs. Anne
Forster, the grandmother of the parliamentarian and statesman,
W. E. Forster, already mentioned. It was sent to Dr. Earle in
June, 1837, before he went to Paris for his medical studies.

SIXTH MONTH, 1837.

Dear Friend,— In requesting thy kind consideration of the enclosed, I wish to express the sorrow I have for years at times felt

in hearing of Magendie's (of Paris) excessive cruelty, both there and when on a visit to this country, and my earnest desire that serious and honorable men of the same profession may not give encouragement to such proceedings.

I earnestly desire that those of the medical profession who are endeavoring to act up to the high standard of righteousness — that all earthly engagements should be in the fear and love of God — may very seriously consider whether, in actively promoting or passively allowing experiments on living animals (in fact, living dissections), with other acts of excessive cruelty, they have his holy countenance on their labors, and the trust that they tend to his glory, and whether such treatment can be consistently allowed by those who feel that they are but stewards over the creatures formed by Him whose "tender mercies are over all his works." However specious may be the pleadings as to some service thereby rendered to their fellow-creatures, will sanctified knowledge be acquired by such means?

Allow me, and that with true respect, to entreat such afresh to take the subject into their serious consideration, not only on account of the exquisitely tortured animals, but also on account of the hardening effect on the youthful pupils. I wish to call their attention to a statement at the sixth meeting of the British Association for the Advancement of Science, held at Bristol in 1836 : —

"*Anatomy and Medicine.*

"Dr. O'Berne read the following report of the Dublin Committee on the Pathology of the Nervous System. . . . They are of opinion, however, that more extended observations on this branch of their subject are required to be made; and they would also submit the necessity of repeating those experiments on animals, upon which so many authorities rely as a foundation for their doctrine."

I trust that using the word "necessity" implies a degree of caution on the subject; and I earnestly and reverently pray that this *necessity* may be solemnly looked at, and considered under the enlightening influence of His Holy Spirit who said, "Blessed are the merciful, for they shall obtain mercy."

It would be very pleasant to me to have more of thy company; but, as I am likely to go this week into Dorsetshire, I can hardly expect this, unless I may have the gratification of welcoming thee at our house near Bridport. My husband and son are likely to return to Norwich.*

With kind regards, thy friend,

ANNE FORSTER.

The duties of life were always taken up by Dr. Earle in this serious spirit ; and, whatever he may have thought afterwards of vivisection (then a new question in England and America), his opinion would be formed as this good and courteous lady desired, upon full and prayerful consideration. Cheerful as his temper was, and seldom averse to merriment, he had, even in youth, the sobriety that his religious profession required.

---

* On this letter Dr. Earle indorsed, "This was sent to me, while in London, by Anne Forster, wife of William Forster of Norwich, and mother of William Forster, who was father of William E. Forster, now (May, 1880) one of the ministers of the British government."

CHAPTER IV.

DR. EARLE IN FRANCE, SWITZERLAND, AND ITALY.

IN the latter part of the eighteenth and the first quarter of the nineteenth centuries, Americans, desiring to complete a medical or other scientific education, generally went to Edinburgh. But by 1830 the eminence of the French in almost all the fields of science drew our young countrymen to Paris, where Dr. Holmes studied medicine from 1833 to 1835. It was at this time that Pliny Earle was engaged in his early medical studies with the brother-in-law of Dr. Holmes, Dr. Usher Parsons, of Providence; and it may have been this circumstance which directed his attention to the advantages of attending the lectures of Louis, Broussais, Magendie, Ricord, Velpeau, and the other men of world-wide renown who were then practising or teaching medicine and surgery in the French capital. I incline to think, however, that it was rather the suggestion of a cousin of the Earle family, Dr. Elisha Bartlett of Lowell, who had heard Louis, and thought him the prince of instructors, as indeed he was. Dr. Holmes in later years used to say he had devoted himself too exclusively to the teachings of Louis, but that was not Dr. Earle's case. He had, even in 1837, looked forward to the specialty in which he afterwards attained such distinction as an alienist; and he gave some time in Paris to the study of mental maladies and their treatment. I find a letter from Dr. Elisha Bartlett to his cousin, then in the medical school at Philadelphia, on the subject of European study and travel, dated at Lowell, Mass., early in 1837, from which a passage may be cited : —

First, as to the cost of twelve or fourteen months' absence on a trip to Europe, staying eight or nine months in Paris and travelling as far as Rome or Naples,— I suppose $1,000 or $1,200 will do very well. It cost me about $1,100, including everything,— clothes, books, etc. I have only regretted that it was worth so little to me professionally on account of my general and desultory studies while in Paris. If you go, attend to a *few things*. If you are preparing yourself for the practice of medicine particularly, put yourself under the care of Louis, and study disease as he teaches it. It is the only way. Take hold of the stethoscope, and of the scalpel for *post-mortem* study. Become a true Baconian disciple of the Bacon of medical philosophy, Louis, and you will learn more true medicine than you can in any other way.

This advice was well followed by Dr. Earle in Paris for a few months. He learned French enough in a month or two to make the lectures intelligible, and then applied himself to special studies, with Louis and others, till he felt himself sufficiently advanced to "come out of his professional shell," as he phrased it. He then gave many hours to society, to the theatre, to the study of Italian, and to other pursuits likely to further his present or his ultimate purpose. In the spring of 1838 he made visits to the great asylums for the insane at Paris (then but two, the Bicêtre and the Salpêtrière), and thus described his first visit : —

The insane department of the Bicêtre contains seven hundred and sixty men, besides about two hundred idiots. We found them under the medical care of Pinel the younger, Ferrus and Leuret. The latter accompanied us on our tour of inspection. Dr. Pinel, the son of him who first unchained the maniacs here, has written for the Academy of Sciences an account, no doubt correct, of that famous deed of his father, Philippe Pinel, early in the year 1793, when Couthon, the friend of Robespierre, finally consented that the chains should be removed from about fifty of the madmen then at the Bicêtre, when the whole number was somewhat less than I found there. It was not this son of Pinel (as incorrectly stated in my "Visit to Thirteen Asylums"), but his colleague, Dr. Leuret, who showed us the bathing-room, and explained his manner of using the douche for purposes of mental and moral discipline, which appeared to me injurious. The scene of this treatment contained about a dozen bath-tubs, over each of which was a douche-pipe with a capacity for a three-quarter-inch stream. In two tubs we saw patients,

each kept from leaving the tub by a board fitted to his neck where
he sat, as a man stands in the pillory. One was a robust man, subject to varying hallucinations, who now thought himself the husband
of the widowed Duchess of Berri, and had been permitted the day
before to have writing materials on condition that he would not
write such vagaries as that he was a favorite of the exiled Bourbons
and of Louis Philippe. He had written, however, his usual absurdities about the Duke of Bordeaux, Charles X., etc. Dr. Leuret,
with this letter in his hand, reminded the patient of his promise, read
him the nonsense he had written, and asked him if he still believed
that. "Oui, Monsieur." "Give him the douche," said Dr. Leuret
to the attendant, who at once turned the cock and discharged the
stream on the madman's head. He screamed and writhed, and
begged to have it stopped. It was checked; and he was asked,
"Do you still believe you are the intimate friend of Charles X.?"
"I think I do." "Let him have the douche." He again floundered,
shouted, and begged for mercy. "Well, are you the chum of
Charles X. and the Duke of Bordeaux?" "I — I presume so."
"Give him the douche once more." In this way, sometimes with
argument and sometimes with the cold stream, the doctor labored
for half an hour to break up his fantastic notions. At last the
patient gave in, and his tormentor gave him a lesson to be learned
for the next day.

Turning to the other man in his tub, Dr. Leuret said he had
yesterday refused to do a task assigned to him, leaving the work un-
touched. He then asked the man why he had neglected to work.
"To tell the truth, Monsieur, I did not feel any special desire to
work." This was said with a jocose leer which almost made us
laugh. "Well, will you work hereafter when you are told?" Re-
flecting an instant, with the same comic air he said, "*Parole d'honneur,*
I will *not* work." "Give him the douche," said Dr. L. The effect
of the stream was now instantaneous. Like a child who is whipped,
he cried, "I will, I will!" The douche was then stopped, and
orders given that he should do the task before night.*

Dr. Earle was shocked at this use of physical pain to coerce
or punish the insane, which in itself was no better, though the

---

* This singular treatment, long since given up, like Dr. Rush's panacea of bleeding the insane,
is described at greater length in the "visit" above mentioned. But Dr. Earle pointed out to me
numerous errors in the printed account, which I have here corrected.

motive was good, than the old abuse of chaining the men whom Pinel released.

Ordinarily, the young doctor, while in Paris, was each day at the Hôtel Dieu, the old general hospital of the city, where Louis, Velpeau, and sometimes Magendie lectured and gave clinical instruction; and it was Louis who gave him introductions to the three asylums. Esquirol himself, a worthy successor of Pinel, and better instructed in the specialty, was then at the head of the Charenton asylum, some miles outside the city. Here he found both men and women, under better conditions and receiving more enlightened care than either the men at the Bicêtre or the women at the Salpêtrière. In both the last-named asylums the sane and the insane poor were received in the same establishment, as in the Blockley Almshouse of Philadelphia, though kept in separate departments. Even the Hôtel Dieu, the great general hospital, was found by the medical reformer Chaptal, seven years after Pinel's noble act at the Bicêtre, occupied in part by noisy, chained maniacs. Chaptal says (1800) : —

A visit made by me as Minister of the Interior to the Hôtel Dieu decided me to begin my reforms there, — the most important and the worst kept of all our Paris charities. Sixty maniacs, tied by the feet and hands to the four posts of their beds, occupied the upper rooms. Their outcries, which were heard almost all over the building, kept the sick men in the neighboring wards from going to sleep. These unfortunate insane persons received the public charity only amid torments which nothing but death could end. The other wards contained about two thousand patients of all sexes and ages, lying almost everywhere two in the same bed; and I saw that the bed linen was insufficient and in very bad condition, while the food was all of poor quality. I summoned the then chief of the hospitals and other charities, and told him my determination, in three particulars : (1) to remove the very next day all the insane to the asylums of Charenton and Bicêtre, where the other insane were cared for; (2) to establish at once a special hospital for sick children exclusively, and to assemble and treat such there; (3) to admit to the Hôtel Dieu thereafter only the adult sick of both sexes, and not to admit those until their physical condition had been carefully deter-

mined. Will it be credited that the chief, a very reasonable and
well-informed man, opposed these measures? He told me that I
was acting contrary to the fundamental principle of the Hôtel Dieu,
which by its constitution was ordered to receive the sick of all
kinds, whatever the disease, without distinction of age or sex; that
I was perverting such establishments, and that the families of the
founders would make protests against the failure to carry out the
will of their ancestors. But the next day the maniacs were sent to
Charenton and the Bicêtre.*

I have cited this fact, probably known to Dr. Earle, though
taken from a volume printed since his death, in order to show
how slow is the process, even in the more advanced communities, of improvements such as Pinel, Chaptal, Dr. Howe, and
Dr. Earle have suggested or initiated in the care of the insane
and the general reformation of a traditional system. From the
outset of his special studies Dr. Earle seems to have been
guided by his good sense, his logical, inductive turn of mind,
and his benevolent heart to those simple, judicious, and useful
methods of treatment which have not yet established themselves firmly even in his native State, though gradually super-
seding the old fanciful, routinary usages.

Accustomed in America to the rather languid and perfunc-
tory performance of the duties of medical instruction and care
which then prevailed, Dr. Earle was surprised at the arduous
activity of his Parisian professors. He says in one of his letters of 1838 : —

Although the most volatile of Europeans, the French furnish a
very large number of the most learned men. No nation has produced more profound students in the abstract sciences, and their
professional men are paragons of industry. To visit in the hospitals
from fifty to one hundred patients, and prescribe for them by candle-
light in the morning ; then to give a lecture of an hour before breakfast ; between breakfast and dinner to visit an extensive circle of
patients in private practice, and perhaps attend the meeting of a
medical society ; after dinner (at 6 P.M.) to pass the evening in por-

---

* "Mes Souvenirs de Napoléon, par le Comte Chaptal," Paris, 1893. This interesting book
contains not only what its name implies, anecdotes of Napoleon I., but also Chaptal's autobiography,
and other facts concerning this greatest of French chemists, and one of the best organizers even in
hat most organizing of nations, the French.

ing over professional books or in writing some original essay,— such
is the life of any one of the more eminent physicians of Paris. The
honors and emoluments of the profession scarcely will recompense
this unremitting toil.

His observations extended to very minute and curious particulars of the French modes of life. He says : —

No class of persons are more healthy in appearance than the most
respectable of the laboring women of Paris; yet they are seen in
the coldest weather threading the streets with nothing on their heads
but a muslin cap. They act upon the old maxim,—" Keep the feet
warm and the head cool." You will find that over woollen stockings
and thick shoes they not unfrequently wear socks lined with wool,
and sometimes over these the wooden shoes. In thus preserving by
dress the natural heat of the body, they can do without much artificial heat. Last winter was colder in Paris than any previous one
for more than a century, the mercury several times standing at zero.
Yet a Frenchman in an apartment adjoining mine in the Place
Odéon, and who spent most of his evenings at home, had no fire in
his room the whole winter. In the spring of 1839 I returned from
Havre to New York in that dubious season when it is too warm to
keep up a fire and yet too cold for comfort. However, we had none.
On the coldest days, when the American ladies shivered in the
cabin, in bonnet and shawl, there were Frenchwomen sitting on deck
and sewing, with neither shawls nor bonnets.

In Paris, as in Edinburgh, Leyden, and Florence, the anatomical
museums are open to the general public, and are visited by large
numbers of ladies; while in America they are almost held sacred to
the use of the medical profession. At the University of Leyden I
was shown through by a woman, who called my attention particularly to some of the most revolting preparations as the most curious
in the collection. In Paris the show-windows of the shops for the
sale of natural history specimens are ornamented (shall I say?) with
children's skeletons,— some of them infants,— a practice which I do
not mention for imitation. In contrast with the hesitation of our
countrywomen in 1839 to take up the useful study of anatomy, I may
say that Miss Leatham, of Wakefield, in Yorkshire, who afterwards
married John Bright, the statesman, but who was then studying with
a private tutor, showed me the work on anatomy which she and her

sister were studying, and said it was one of the requisites of a good education for Englishwomen.

In Paris (February, 1838) I made my first acquaintance with European homœopathy. It was at a *soirée* of Joseph and Elizabeth Fry, at which were Lady Fitz-James and Lady Bethune, from Scotland. I was standing by the fire, conversing with Josiah Forster, when Anne Knight* came to me to ask what the word was which she had just heard me apply to the doctrine of the homœopathists. I told her 'twas "infinitesimal." She stepped back to the two ladies with whom she had been talking. I followed her, saying, "I hope neither of you favors that doctrine." "*Voilà* the professor of the doctrine," said Anne Knight, pointing to one of the two ladies from Britain. We then entered upon a learned discussion, in which my opponent showed her knowledge of the profession by the readiness with which she employed its technical terms. She related several cases of wonderful cures by the treatment,— cases, too, which had been given up as hopeless by the regular practitioners. When she had done, in steps the other lady (who was no other and no less than Lady Bethune) as an ally, and asserted that she once had a child entirely cured of "convulsions," and another of quite as formidable a disease, by the homœopathic treatment. Then the first (the lady physician), a young Englishwoman with a profusion of golden curls, Miss Ferrier, drew from her reticule a box about five inches by four and an inch thick, looking externally like a miniature case. It did contain a miniature, sure enough; but of what? Of a druggist's shop, or the whole magazine of Æsculapius! There were no less than one hundred and twenty bottles of pills in it, besides many powders ; and, moreover, in each bottle there were from one hundred to two hundred pills ! There were as many different medicines as bottles, the pills, however, all alike in appearance, being white, and the size of a grain of mustard-seed. All are made of the same neutral substance, and derive their virtues from being dipped into a solution of each medicine. So it may be imagined how large a quantity of the medicament one of these little pills coated with a solution can contain. Well, after getting an idea of this quantity fairly fixed in your mind, mark the following : Lady Bethune is herself taking one of these medicines. She dissolves *one* pill in five

* This was an English Quakeress, temporarily residing at Paris in order to bring influence from England to bear on the French government and Chambers in favor of abolishing slavery in the colonies.

tablespoonfuls of water, and then takes *ten drops* of that water each morning! She was ordered to take a teaspoonful every morning, but she found it was too much for her! I asked her ladyship, since the physicians of both schools employ the same medicines, how it was possible that in one case so minute a quantity should have an effect greater than one hundred or one thousand times as much in another case. Her answer was that the virtues of the specifics are brought out by friction." *

Dr. Earle himself, however, was rather surprised at the small quantity of medicine given by his instructors in their hospital practice, which he followed with great interest every day that he went through with them. He says : —

Since I left America, I have not seen an emetic given, nor heard of one ordered to be administered. Louis never gives them, unless, perhaps, in cases of poisoning where there is no stomach-pump at hand. In small-pox no medicine is given ; and in three-fourths of the cases of typhoid fever the patient is merely put upon " absolute diet," with a bottle of seltzer water daily. There is a great differ-ence between the French and the American practice in this respect.

April, 1838.— I have now " followed," as the French say, the hospi-tals for more than six months, and have taken down in French more than two hundred pages of good histories of cases of disease, to say nothing of an earlier hundred pages,— imperfect, because they were written before I well understood the language. I can now write French (as you perceive), and read Italian with nearly the same facility that I could read French when I left home.

At this time, and for some months before, he had been at the hospital from 7 to 10 A.M. and from 3 to 5 or 5.30 P.M. But this did not prevent him from seeing company. He says : —

Feb. 8, 1838.— At 9 P.M. I took the omnibus to go to the *soirée* of the American minister, General Lewis Cass, who lives near Anne Knight's, two miles from my Hôtel de la Place de l'Odéon. When we had gone about two-thirds of the way, an elderly man got into the

---

* Although homœopathy was introduced in America by 1821, and in England somewhat earlier, this is the first mention I have found of women practising it in either country. At present many women practise medicine in England, as well as in the United States. The Maternité Hospital, for the instruction of women in midwifery, was opened by Chaptal in Paris early in the century. See his " Souvenirs."

'bus, and told the conductor to let him down at the end of the Rue Matignon, in which General Cass lives. I suspected he was going to the same *soirée;* and, on looking at him, I perceived he wore the badge of the Legion of Honor,— a red ribbon, worn usually in the upper buttonhole but one on the left side of the coat. As we alighted together, I ventured to say to him, in view of the mud in the street, "Il y a beaucoup de boue," which served as an opening for conversation. He asked my country, profession, name, etc. (in this order), and said he had himself travelled in Egypt and Great Britain, and hoped to go to America; mentioning the names of several American societies of which he is an honorary member, among them the Academy of Natural Sciences and the American Philosophical Society of Philadelphia. I then asked his name, which was Jullien de Paris, he said. In the house of General Cass we had further conversation ; and he handed me a note, which I found to read thus : "Encyclopedic Dinners. These banquets, at which habitually assemble a certain number of the friends of science and of the public good, and many honorable men of all countries,— where fortuitous meetings have often led to lasting relations, reciprocally agreeable and useful,— were established in 1815, and have continued, without interruption, ever since." (Then followed an invitation for me to the next dinner, February 13, signed "Jullien de Paris.") I returned an acceptance.

At General Cass's the servants were in small-clothes, and wore a gilt eagle on the end of the upright coat collar on each side. Going from the anteroom, in which our overcoats were left, we passed through a billiard-room, where women as well as men played during the evening, and entered an elegant drawing-room, as our names were pronounced in a loud voice by the usher. Except this announcement there were no introductions; but any guest is quite free to address any other without an introduction. General Cass and his youngest daughter (of three) were present, Mrs. Cass being indisposed. This officiating daughter, a genteel girl of perhaps eighteen, with dark hair and dark blue eyes, performed her duties *comme il faut.* About twenty American and French guests were present when we arrived, and twenty or thirty succeeded us. We were treated to tea and cake and ice-cream several times during the evening. The gentlemen at such *soirées* carry their hats the whole evening, some, to save labor, suspending them from a button on the left side. Upon the whole the gathering was a little too stiff, conversation not being so general or continual as if more French people had been present. At 11.30 my friend and I took a *citadine* (a small hackney coach), and drove back to the Place de l'Odéon.

February 13.— I went at 6 P.M., the appointed hour, to meet M. Jullien's company at the encyclopedic dinner, or *réunion des nations*. Before seven fifty-five guests had assembled, among whom were the president (M. Jullien), Sir Sydney Smith of the siege of Acre, Counts Orsoni and Ugoni of Italy, Joseph M. White, a member of our Congress, Professor Menai of Rome, Professor Schotley of Breslau, Rev. Edward N. Kirk of Albany, Dr. Evans of Philadelphia, a young Mr. Harrison of Baltimore, one or two members of the Chamber of Deputies, several notables from Spain and Portugal, others from England, Scotland, Denmark, etc. We sat down to dinner at seven, around a table with three extensions. At the head of the centre and connecting table sat M. Jullien, with Sir Sydney at his left. I had a seat beside Count Orsoni, who was exceedingly sociable, and promised to give me letters to the Roman princes, when I should go to Italy. Another Italian offered to give me a letter to Silvio Pellico, with whom he is acquainted. The courses at dinner were about fifteen, with *vin ordinaire* and champagne, at discretion. When about to open the champagne, M. Jullien rose to make a speech, in which he gave an account of the origin and progress of the society, recited the names of distinguished men who had previously dined there and of those then present. He had a compliment for each of those, as well as for the country each represented, which, of course, were received with much hand-clapping and drumming upon the tables. He was followed by Sir Sydney in a speech. When he had ended and the whole room was ringing with applause, M. Jullien rose; and the two kissed each other as fervently as if they had been sisters.

A Portuguese gentleman then spoke, with the evident purpose of lauding France and the French with all the fulsome compliments in his vocabulary, and to set England and the English in bold contrast. At this the English present began to look sour; and soon the speaker was called to order by a Frenchman sitting near, who declared that in such a place, where persons from so many countries were assembled, there ought to be no invidious comparisons. The Portugee sat down in silence; but, when the room resounded with cries of " Parlez, parlez!" he rose again, said a few civil words, and took his seat again. He was followed by another from Portugal, and then by

one or two Frenchmen, after which our Congressman White made a
very good speech in English, apologizing at first for not speaking
French. He dwelt on the pleasure he felt in being present, and proceeded to compare this "reunion of nations" around the table to the
United States, which of itself is a reunion of nations. At this the
applause was loud and long, perhaps more so than if his remarks had
been understood by half the company. M. Jullien, in closing, passed
a high eulogium upon the United States for having made great and
successful exertions in the cause of temperance, and said, "Honor
to the country which, though so remote, has sent us an agent"
(Robert Baird, then present) "to establish temperance societies in
France and on the Continent!" During the dinner Count Ugoni had
an epileptic seizure, and was carried from the table. He soon recovered, and was taken home.

It was in this same winter of 1837–38 that Mrs. Fry, who in
a former visit to France had observed the unsatisfactory state
of the prisons, made herself an agent in Paris to effect an amelioration in this respect. She was accompanied by her husband
and other English and American Quakers, and made a deep
impression. Dr. Earle, as already mentioned (p. 84), was
often present at her meetings, and at the private gatherings of
her own circle, and has recorded many incidents. Twenty
years before, when not yet forty, she had begun those visits to
Newgate that have made her so famous. She was now nearly
sixty, and her life was to be continued but a few years more.
She reached Paris, not in the spring, as Mr. Hare says in "The
Gurneys of Earlham," but late in January, 1838, and on the 5th
of February held a meeting which Dr. Earle thus describes : —

This evening I went to a gathering of English, Americans, and
French at the rooms of an Englishman named Kemp, in Rue Mt.
Thabor. Perhaps fifty were there when I arrived, and took a seat
beside a lady from New York. They were passing tea and cake as
at an evening party, having no license from the police for a public
meeting. The London Friends soon came in, and, as I had a comfortable fauteuil, I yielded it to Elizabeth Fry, and took a chair
near. Mrs. Fry was very sociable. She had a word for each one
present, speaking to all who were within speaking distance. On

my left was a young lady I had not seen before. Elizabeth Fry
asked her and a young man beside her whether they were Americans or English. They said, "Americans." "From what part?"
"Boston." "Ah! a beautiful city. I understand some relations of
mine, the Backhouses,— thou knows them" (turning to me),— "were
very much pleased with it. May I not ask your names?" "Salisbury, cousins of the Salisburies of Worcester." After the tea-cups
had been collected, an Englishman, who has lived many years in
Paris, advanced to the middle of the room, and began questioning
Mrs. Fry, asking her how long she had been in Paris, if she had
been there before ("Yes, in Normandy last year, and then in
Paris"), how she liked Paris, what was the moral state of the people,
etc. She answered much as she afterwards wrote to her sister,
"Such a nation! such a numerous and superior people, filling such
a place in the world! and Satan appearing in no common degree to
be seeking to destroy them." She then returned the compliment by
asking him the same questions. He said there had been great
improvement in the French people during the fifteen years since
1823. Bibles are more read, religious meetings more attended,
schools better organized, etc. Josiah Forster then rose, and related
the methods of the British and Foreign Bible Society. He next
spoke of the belief of Friends with regard to women appearing in
the ministry, and of the motives of Elizabeth Fry in coming to
Paris; and he finished by reading her certificates from the monthly
and quarterly meetings and that from the meeting of ministers and
elders. After a short silence Mrs. Fry addressed the audience at
length, chiefly upon the state of the Parisians and French generally,
of the means by which all English and American residents or travellers might do good, and of their duty to do it. She spoke also of
the benefit she believed to arise in every family from a daily assem-
bling of its members to read the Scriptures, and she urged the
importance of a period of silence after such reading. As to her
membership in the Society of Friends, she said that, although convinced she was in the proper course for herself, she believed she felt
no sectarianism, but was ready to give the right hand of fellowship
to those of any faith who loved the Lord with sincerity. She afterwards appeared in supplication [prayed], and the meeting was closed.
Most of the audience remained half an hour in conversation, and a
large number of tracts thrown on the table for distribution were
taken away by them. The wives of three or four of the French

nobility were present, and a month later (March 5) Mrs. Fry called on the king and queen by invitation. She thinks the queen a very agreeable and even interesting woman, and the Duchess of Orleans an uncommon person.

Indeed, Mrs. Fry went so far in her communications to her family as to call the mother of the present Comte de Paris a very valuable young person, which was greater praise than perhaps it sounds to those not used to the Quaker moderation of statement.

At a friend's house Dr. Earle saw a strange sight : —

"At I. Sargent's in the Champs Élysées, before sitting down to dinner, we heard a great rumbling in the street; and, stepping to the window, what should we see but a locomotive rolling in cloudy majesty along the Allée d'Antar directly in front of the house ? It was a very heavy engine, having six large, broad wheels, the hindermost apparently six feet in diameter. Attached to it was a tender, and one of the largest-sized diligences, the latter filled inside with passengers, and covered with them outside, somewhat as the branch of a tree is covered with bees when a swarm has lighted there. This odd train was going from eight to ten miles an hour. Some horses in the street were much frightened at it, and one so much so that he fell, throwing his rider headlong, but on the greensward under the trees beside the Allée, so that he received little injury.

Feb. 21, 1838.— A French gentleman (M. St. Antoine, a chevalier of the Legion of Honor), who is an active member of the French Society for the Abolition of Slavery, gave me an invitation to attend a meeting of one of its committees to-day. Accordingly, I went with him from his house in the Place Vendôme to the palace of the Chamber of Deputies in which the meeting was held. Among those present were the Comte d'Harcourt, the Marquis of Rochefoucauld, and several deputies. M. de Lamartine, the poet and author, was to have been there, but was kept away by illness. He is a member of the committee. Query.— Would the meeting of such a society be tolerated in the Capitol at Washington ? *

---

* Certainly not in 1838, nor for many years after. Professor Daubeny, an Oxford professor, then travelling in this country, heard Mr. Calhoun declare (Jan. 4, 1838) in the Senate at Washington that, to advocate the abolition of slavery as immoral, would be "a direct and dangerous attack on the institutions of all the slaveholding states."

Upon his introduction to General Cass, who was then American minister at Paris, Dr. Earle found that statesman ready to
converse on the slavery question, and perhaps with more freedom than he would have done a few years later or even at that
date (Feb. 5, 1838), had he been in America.   The diary says:

At noon, after a morning spent at the hospital clinic, I went to deliver my letter of introduction from Dr. Griscom to General Cass.   I
found him in his office or study.   Perhaps it might be called the
latter, since he devoteth two hours each morning to the study of
French.   I know not when I have been made to feel immediately
so much at ease when first introduced to one of the powerful of the
earth.*   He was in his *robe de chambre*, a very comfortable garment,
much worn in Paris.   He took off his turtle-shell-frame spectacles,
adjusted his sandy wig, and went to talking, first about the Canadian
question and then upon abolition.   He thinks the burning of the
steamer "Caroline"† will not cause a rupture between England and
the United States, and quoted the conduct of General Jackson in
Florida and of Commodore Porter in the West Indies as being cases
of even greater infringement of the rights and the peace of other
nations than was the act now in question.   As to slavery, he says he
has been astonished to find so general an abhorrence of that system
by Europeans.   In his exact words, "It is impossible to convince
them of the justice of holding the negroes in bondage a single
moment."   He made no exceptions.   I asked him what he thought
of the prospect of a dissolution of the Union.   "A man may as well
talk of committing suicide," was his reply, "as the South to talk of
dissolving the Union.   She has the elements of death within herself;
and, the moment the separation should be effected, those elements
would begin to operate.   The slaves would rise, and there would be

---

* Lewis Cass (born in Exeter, N.H., Oct. 9, 1782, died in Detroit June 17, 1866) was the son of
Major Jonathan Cass of the Revolutionary army, and was himself an officer in the United States
army in the War of 1812, rising to the rank of general in 1813.   He soon became governor of Michigan Territory, and held that position with credit and profit to himself until President Jackson made
him Secretary of War in 1831.   Jackson sent him minister to France in 1836, where he remained until
1842, and was an important personage.   He was in the Senate from 1845 to 1848, when he was defeated by General Taylor as candidate for President in consequence of the formation of the Free-soil
party and the nomination of Van Buren and Adams at Buffalo.   Under Buchanan he was Secretary of
State from 1857 to December, 1860, when he resigned because Buchanan refused to re-enforce Major
Anderson in Fort Sumter.   He supported the Union against the South, and survived the Civil War.

† The burning of the "Caroline" by the Canadian forces in the rebellion of 1837 was long a griev-
ance against England, but was settled by Webster's treaty of 1842.

no military force to repress their insurrection. Besides" (and here I got a new idea), "the Western States would not go with the South, because the control of the waters of the Mississippi would then belong to both nations. This Indiana, Illinois, and probably Kentucky would not suffer. They would not let Mississippi and Tennessee go with the South, if so disposed; for those three States would not yield the control of the mouth of the great river." That is very plausible. He regrets the course of the Abolitionists, thinks the condition of the slaves has been made worse by it, and that in Virginia the abolition of slavery has been retarded by it. (He does not remember that Moses was near when Pharaoh oppressed the children of Israel.) While conversing on Canada, I mentioned the remark of an Englishman with whom I had been talking lately about the patriotism of the Canadian rebels; and he quoted the definition of "patriotism" by Dr. Johnson,—"the last refuge of a scoundrel." Whereupon General Cass quoted the remark of Horace Walpole (I think), who said, "If you only reject some imperious and impudent demand, up jumps a patriot."

The slave question was much agitated all over the world at that time; and Dr. Earle in Paris often came upon incidents of its discussion. He says:—

Feb. 10, 1838, *Sunday.*—Took the omnibus at 11 A.M. to go to Anne Knight's meeting. There was a young man inside, to whom, as he had the New York *Commercial Advertiser* in his hand, I ventured to speak. He was a native of Georgia, he said, and had spent four years in Massachusetts. He wished John Quincy Adams was dead. "No, I don't wish any person dead; but I should like something to occur to throw him out of Congress." A moment after he said, "Garrison ought to be hung or else imprisoned for life." He admitted that the answer of Mr. Adams to Waddy Thompson, of South Carolina, after the introduction of the resolution to expel Mr. Adams from the House of Representatives last winter, was the best thing of the kind he ever read.* I asked him to go to the meeting, and hear Elizabeth Fry. He went with me, and said he liked her

* In February, 1837, Mr. Adams (born July 11, 1767, died Feb. 23, 1848), who had been a member of Congress from Massachusetts, after leaving the Presidency in 1829, was successful in defeating a vote of expulsion offered in consequence of his presenting anti-slavery petitions. His eloquence and courage were remarkable, and he had frequent occasion for their exercise in the long contest for the right of petition which he kept up against the Southern slave-owners and their Northern allies.

preaching very well. About twenty-five were at this meeting; and Mrs. Fry began her sermon with the texts, "Say to the North, Give up, and to the South, Hold not back," and "Come unto me, all ye who labor, etc." I afterwards dined and spent the evening with Isaac Sargent and family in company with Anne Knight. She thinks Lord Brougham a traitor to the cause of the Abolitionists, and says that by their means he climbed the ladder of fame, and, having reached the top, forgot his former zeal. She further quoted some one who was present in the House of Lords when he presented the famous Ladies' Petition some four years ago, and who said he did it with very much the air of a school-boy going to be whipped. This is the first time I have heard that noble lord spoken of in such terms. Late in the evening Dr. Godfrey, of London, invited me to meeting on the 12th at the house of a Wesleyan clergyman, who lives here as superintendent of missionary stations in France.

February 12.— I accompanied Dr. Godfrey to the meeting, where about forty were present, among them several young physicians of my acquaintance. After the cake and tea had been passed, during which there was the sociability of a tea-party, Mrs. Fry gave an account of her visits to five of the Parisian prisons, where she had been the preceding week. She had found but little wanting in them, so far as personal comfort is concerned, but a total destitution of the means of moral and religious instruction. They are thus superior to the English prisons in comfort, but inferior in moral culture. Josiah Forster spoke at considerable length upon slavery and the slave-trade, giving a particular account of the existing state of the trade and of the horrors of the middle passage.

March 28.— Last First Day I attended the meeting at Anne Knight's, and was agreeably surprised in finding there some English Friends, with whom I became acquainted in London. They are Robert Ware Fox, his wife, two young Foxes, their daughters, —— Fox, brother of Robert, his wife, and a grand-daughter. They reside at Penjerrick, near Falmouth, where R. W. Fox is the American consul. After a sojourn of a few days in Paris they go to Switzerland, after a tour in France.

April.— The Foxes have gone to Southern France. Robert Fox has much celebrity as a man of scientific acquirements. His brother is less known in the same line. I am enchanted (to use a word altogether French) with their families. They are all very intelligent.

My friend Sargent and I accompanied them one day to Notre Dame and the manufactory of the Gobelin tapestry.

In Paris Dr. Earle met a lady from New Bedford, with whom he soon became intimate. Why they never married is not perfectly known; the acquaintance continued for years; and the recollection of Elizabeth Arnold may have prevented any subsequent engagement. He says:—

Paris, April 21, 1838.— A few days ago I met at Anne Knight's a lady whom I had several times seen at the reunions while Elizabeth Fry was here. We had even conversed, each remaining ignorant of the other's name, and each supposing the other to be English. This day A. Knight said to me, "This lady is from thy country." That was enough, and we began to talk. She said she was from New England. I said I was. She then declared she was from Massachusetts. "That is my native State." "I know well by reputation persons of your name," said she, having learned my name from A. Knight; "and my father is acquainted with them." "Who?" I asked. "Oh, there was a Pliny Earle and a Silas Earle." "Just so. I am the son of Pliny and the nephew of Silas." "From what place are you?" "From New Bedford. Are you acquainted with Thomas Greene, who lives there?" "Yes, very well. I have often heard him speak of a Mr. Earle who is a conchologist." "That is my brother Milton; but your name, if you please?" "It is Arnold." (She is the wife of James Arnold, who returned to New Bedford in the fall; while she and her daughter Elizabeth have passed the winter in Paris.)

This acquaintance thus begun was kept up in England in June, whither the Arnolds went in May, and Dr. Earle soon after, as already mentioned.

The Arnolds early in June went from London to Holland for a few weeks, then came back to England for a tour through the southern counties, and soon afterwards returned to New Bedford; while the young physician, freed from his medical pursuits in France, went also to Holland, and then to Switzerland and Italy. In communicating this plan of travel to his sisters Lucy and Eliza at Leicester, he said:—

For some months I have regarded a journey through the south of Europe as a *labor* little to be desired, and yet I have a *penchant* to go. I wish to see the Eternal City: it would gratify me to stand on the Acropolis. But, to travel through Holland, Switzerland, Italy, and Greece, time will be required. To see those countries well, I should have at least a year. You will perceive, then, that I cannot return to America next autumn. But it is my intention to return early in the spring of 1839.

This plan he began to carry out by a visit to Holland and Belgium in July, 1838. He says, writing in August : —

James Arnold gave me a letter to John S. Mollet, a Friend who resides in Amsterdam, the only member of our society in that city. I found him without occupation, a man of leisure ; and he accompanied me to the public institutions and the curiosities of Amsterdam. It was particularly agreeable thus to find a friend in a country where I did not understand the language. I also made there the acquaintance of Ramon de la Sagra, a Spaniard of celebrity, who travelled in the United States in the summer of 1835, and published an account of his journey in a book of five hundred pages. He was twice in Worcester, where he visited the hall of the American Antiquarian Society and the State Lunatic Hospital. He was enchanted with America, and speaks complimentarily of Dr. Woodward, the hospital superintendent. I had intended to go up the Rhine to Switzerland, but was ill in Belgium, and remained several days in Antwerp in the hope of full recovery, but at length decided to return to Paris, where I am not yet (August 15) entirely well.

Aug. 26, 1838. — I have been occupying myself in illness by reading the French " History of the Revolution," by M. Thiers, the journalist turned statesman. It is in eight volumes, and I am now in the third. Interesting, but rather too minute in detail. Several of my Paris friends call, too, and thus help to relieve the ennui of the sick-room. Dr. Kean, of Providence, who lives very near, comes in two or three times a day. He is *un bon enfant*, as the Savoyard says, who has the care of my chamber. Then I have a young Irish friend, a physician, who first came to Paris three years ago, before he studied medicine, to withdraw himself from painful associations, after the death of a young lady to whom he was affianced. Time, that potent physician, seems to have brought him solace. He was with me yesterday nearly five hours, relating many anecdotes of O'Connell, the great agitator, and giving me much information about the manners and customs of his countrymen. To-day he has been here an hour and a half, in high spirits, and kept me laughing, sometimes to tears, almost the whole time. He told many anecdotes of Dean Swift, of Curran, and of his own Irish acquaintance. A third friend is another Irish physician, Dr. Newenham, who was educated in German schools. Handsome in person, in intellect highly cultivated, and endowed with all the moral virtues, he is physically small, somewhat effeminate, and of a very mild disposition. But he is an enthusiast; and his conversation, enlivened by all the gesticulation of the French people, is particularly attractive. A fourth friend is an English physician, young, highly gifted, enthusiastic, and somewhat chimerical. I first met him in this Hotel de la Place de l'Odéon, the second day after I took these rooms last year. Since that time (little more than a year) he has shown me the titles of four or five books which he is going to write. One is to be a large medical work in several volumes; another upon *l'état populaire*, or the lower classes of the people of Paris; a third, in opposition to the national church of England; fourth, a code of laws or system of government, under which nobody would be oppressed or unhappy. While generally pursuing his studies in the hospitals, he also has had his thoughts upon the future. At one time he is going to serve in the army, at another in the navy. Sometimes he meditates the life of a recluse, in which he can study, write, become renowned, and render great service to science and mankind. Sometimes he intends to marry, and live a country life in England; and again he is going to start off, with some friends, immediately for New Holland, there to found a colony under the beneficent system just mentioned. Such a medley bespeaks the lunatic, or the man of brilliant imagination, or else a particularly active and vivacious mind, or, finally, a *lover*. I think that in this case there is a little of the last.

August 31.— The Parisians are now making a great noise over the birth of the high and mighty Louis Philippe Albert, Count of Paris, and son of the Duke of Orleans. On the 28th the king and the royal family attended a "Te Deum" at Notre Dame; and the next day there was a grand fête, similar to those of May 1 and July 29.

The "Acte de Naissance," which is published in the journals, signed by members of the royal family and the ministers who were

present at the birth, is a curiosity. The municipal government of
Paris has presented the baby with a sword costing 35,000 francs
($7,000). The little fellow would make a droll figure wearing it.

Sept. 14, 1838. — Since I returned to Paris in July I have
read "Belgium and Germany," in two volumes, and " Paris and the
Parisians," in three, both by Mrs. Trollope, " Homeward Bound," by
Cooper, and five volumes of Thiers's " French Revolution," to say
nothing of Galignani's *Messenger, Le Siècle,* and other daily newspapers, or of two volumes of the *London Keepsake,* brought in by
my good friend, Dr. Newenham. My friends continue their frequent
visits, some in the morning, some in the afternoon, others in the
evening. Indeed, my chamber has become an evening rendezvous,
where are generally three or four persons. Dr. Spencer has missed
but one evening in the last ten days.

Paris, October 26. — It is now past 11 P.M., and I am expecting to leave Paris in the diligence at seven to-morrow morning. My
place is taken, my trunks packed, for a three days' journey day and
night in succession. . . . I have given up the idea of going further
east than Venice and further south than Naples and Paestum. I
devote three months to Italy, and three here in the spring, and mean
to sail from Havre about the 1st of May, 1839; that is, six months
from now.

This plan was much altered, as will be seen; and before
Christmas Dr. Earle was in Constantinople, where, he says,
"my eyes rested on St. Sophia and her sister mosques in the
city of Mahound, and I wandered through the streets of Stamboul, among congregated thousands of the nations of the East,
where everything is novel,— now admiring, now deploring."
His diary thus continues : —

Nov. 1, 1838. — After three and a half days' travel by way of Dijon
and over the Jura, day and night, I arrived here October 30 (at
Geneva), situated not only upon the blue and rushing Rhone, but
also on

> Clear placid Leman, thy contrasted lake
> With the wild world I dwelt in,

as you remember Byron says in " Childe Harold's Pilgrimage," where
also he mentions Ferney, the residence of Voltaire, which I have

visited. Did I speak in my letters from England of a Dr. Fauconnet, who boarded at John Burtt's when I did last year? Well, after travels in Scotland, Ireland, Germany, and Austria, he has returned to his home near Geneva, where I found him yesterday; and he has the kindness to act as *cicerone* for me. His father died recently; but he still lives with his mother and sister (the handsomest girl in Switzerland) in a pretty little cottage among the environs of Geneva. I have taken tea and spent the evening with him and them. Their house is surrounded by an ample garden of flowers and fruits, and overlooks the lake, whose waters dash but a dozen rods away.

St. Maurice, November 4.— Leaving Geneva by steamboat, I went up the lake by Lausanne, Clarens, Montreux, etc., to Villeneuve, at the place where the Rhone enters the lake, and thence went back a short distance to the Castle of Chillon. I was conducted through that by a French-speaking woman, whose tongue ran as fast as a locomotive, going two ways at once. She told me the history of a young man who was imprisoned there at the same time with Bonnivard (who was Byron's "Prisoner of Chillon"), making a tale which, in the hands of Byron, might have equalled any of his poems. She added that the person who showed Byron and Shelley through Chillon neglected to tell them this.

From Villeneuve I came to this place, a most romantically wild and picturesque situation in the valley of the upper Rhone. Suppose the village church, with its steeple as tall as that of Worcester Old South, with a huge rock rising perpendicular beside it and towering high above the steeple,— a rock which would put any of ours in Worcester County to the blush,— and yet small enough to wish to hide itself when placed beside those I shall see in crossing the Simplon. St. Maurice is all at the foot of this rock; and here the two routes from Geneva to the Simplon intersect, the one passing round the lake and up the Rhone valley, as I came, the other, constructed in part by Napoleon in his passage from Geneva to Milan, over the Simplon, running through Douvaine, Thonon, and Bouveret, and thence up the Rhone valley to St. Maurice. From here I follow Napoleon's route to Milan.

Milan, November, 1838.— My companions from St. Maurice in the diligence were a young Swiss merchant going to Milan and a young Italian widow from Udine, on the north shore of the Adriatic, returning from Geneva to her native town. We filled the coupé of the

vehicle until we arrived at the frontier of Sardinia, where the young
Swiss was stopped, likely to be detained fifteen days because his passport was not *en règle*,—a specimen of the beauties of monarchical
government. At Domo d' Ossola, the next town where we stayed after
passing the frontier, his place was taken by two young Catholic
priests, seventeen years old (we now had an Italian diligence which
holds six passengers, as did that English one mentioned in the *Anti-
Jacobin,*—

> So down thy hill, romantic Ashbourne, glides,
> The Derby dilly, carrying six insides),

one of whom resembled our ideas of a priest as much as chalk does
cheese. He was one of the handsomest youths I ever saw, with a
noble head, and features in which manly firmness and dignity were
admirably mingled with effeminate beauty. He was in the sacerdotal
robe, with a hat as large as that formerly worn by Friend Ichabod
Sylvester, and differing from that only in being cocked *tricorne*. Of
French birth, but educated in Italy, he spoke the two languages with
the greatest fluency; and, what with talking, laughing, and taking
snuff, he succeeded in occupying every moment. He was none of
your delicate snuff-takers, either, who must have the black maccoboy.
On the contrary, he used the common yellow, taken in such quantities
that his upper lip was the color of a pumpkin, and seemingly permanently stained; for, when wiped with his handkerchief, it was not
changed in color.

At the tavern, in the village of Simplon, which stands at a height
(4,856 feet) 1,500 feet higher than the top of Monadnoc, we saw an
English family of six persons who had been detained there a week
because their passport had not been properly signed. Descending
from here, I once felt greatly in danger. In most places this road
over the Alps has no fence upon the dangerous side, even where the
precipice is of the greatest height, with a yawning gulf on one side
and an overshadowing mountain cliff on the other. There are only
stone posts, two feet high and twelve or fifteen feet asunder, forming
a very imperfect barrier; and in places the road turns very short and
at less than a right angle. We were going at a brisk trot, the road
steep, when we came to one of these short turns. The German
postilion pulled the rein of his horse, when snap! went the strap
which tied the heads of the two horses together. With such a
harness as we had (it would disgrace the plough-horse of a good

New England farmer), this was the failing of an important part. The off-horse was left perfectly beyond control, and, instead of turning as he ought, he took Davy Crockett's advice,* and went straight ahead. I never shall forget that moment. Having taken a seat with our German guide, I could see all that passed, as well as the horrid gulf below us. The blood rushed to my heart, my sight became dim, and my limbs as feeble as an infant's. The risk was enough to rouse our phlegmatic guide ; and, by dint of his swearing, and the mastery by the postilion of the horse he was bestriding, we succeeded in turning just in time to shun the guard-posts.

I know of no view more lovely than that from the top of the central spire of the great marble cathedral of Milan, which I ascended one day. While enjoying it, I was joined by a party of Italian ladies and gentlemen, one of whom at once asked me, in French, if I was a Russian. " No, I am an American." " O, O, O ! ella è Americano " (third person feminine instead of masculine for " He is," agreeably to Italian usage) burst from the mouths of two or three at once. One of the men spoke English, and had been in England. He said they took me for a Russian because many from that country are now in Milan, in the suite of the crown prince of Russia. Had I been a brother, I could not have expected so much attention as I received from this Italian party. They were going to the imperial palace to see the apartments, and invited me to go with them. I went with them through the richest suite of rooms I have yet seen ; and then one of the party, a physician, invited me home with him. I accepted, and the next day he went with me to the hospital, etc. (Query.— Would an Italian, encountered for the first time by a party of Bostonians in the cupola of the State House, receive similar attentions ?)

It will sufficiently appear already that the young American, with all his modesty, and really by virtue of it, was a charming person to the Europeans whom he encountered, since he was everywhere welcomed and made at home. At that time the number of his countrymen travelling in Europe was not large; and the rapid growth of liberal political sentiment, by reaction from the repression and police surveillance which followed the

---

*The Tennessee marksman, whose legendary sayings were once common in America; among others, " First make sure you're right, then go ahead."

Napoleonic wars and the Greek Revolution, had made the republicanism of the United States much in favor among the educated men of the Continent.   Nor would it have been easy to find a better representative of the republican simplicity which America was then thought to favor than was this Massachusetts Quaker, fresh from the home of Franklin in Philadelphia.

Venice, Dec. 1, 1838.— The Italian widow, who joined our travelling party at St. Maurice, came in company with me as far as Venice; and, upon parting, she gave me a handsome bead purse in return for my kindness,— "*per la vostra bontà.*"   She speaks French well; but I requested her to talk Italian with me, so that, from conversing with her and other passengers, I became enabled, not *parlare molto bene*, but *un poco*, before reaching this seat of the Queen of the Adriatic.   Before arriving here, I had not sufficiently learned one truth,— that reading poetry, or poetical descriptions of places, or looking at engravings (flattered views, as they are nowadays), is one thing, but visiting the reality is quite another.   I had expected, not withstanding the assertion of Byron,—

> In Venice Tasso's echoes are no more,
> And silent rows the songless gondolier,—

to find the Venetian boatmen altogether composed of poetry.   But the kaleidoscope has turned : the picture is changed, and I behold it now in all the sublimity of truth.   I do not recollect to have felt actually in danger but twice since I left Leicester,— on the Alps, as already described, and here just before I was setting forth for Greece.   I had some difficulty with a gondolier, about sunset, because I would not pay him twice as much as he had agreed to work for.   He had threatened me severely, and, finally, on leaving, told me I should have trouble in getting to the steamboat, which, as in nine-tenths of the European ports, lay at anchor some distance from the shore.   In order to avoid danger, I asked my landlord to get me another gondolier from another part of the city, which he did. I still feared a coalition with other gondoliers, but go I must.   The price was agreed upon (being twice as much as an Italian would have paid), and I got into his gondola.   It was ten o'clock, the moon not risen ; and, consequently, it was dark.   Off we set, the gondolier

rowing through a series of canals about ten feet wide, unlighted, and
bordered on both sides with stone houses rising directly from the
water, five or six stories high. Not a lighted window was to be seen,
and nothing heard but the rippling water. My luggage might have
been temptation enough, I thought, particularly after what had
passed that day, to place me where the waters would leave no
record. I never breathed more freely than when we emerged from
these narrow canals into the Grand Canal, near its junction with the
Giudecca. The gondolier now stopped his boat, came to the window
of the little cabin in which I sat, and said, " If you will pay me two
zwantzigers [twice what I had agreed], I'll row you to the steamer
by way of the Grand Canal." I knew more of the location than the
fellow thought; for he could not row me any other way, except by
going back and rowing four or five miles round. I told him to row
along, I should not give it. " But it will take an hour to row there."
This " raised my Ebenezer," for I knew it would not take more than
five minutes of good rowing. So I mustered what Italian I had, and
reeled it off to him. He took away his head, muttering; but in
a few minutes I was on board the steamer.

The visit to Naples and Rome was postponed until Dr.
Earle should have returned from Greece and Turkey, for which
he sailed in the steamer which he thus boarded in the dark
waters of Venice. He reached Malta on his return in January,
left it in February for Syracuse, Catania, and Messina, touching briefly at those ports, and sailing between Scylla and
Charybdis, and very near the perpetually burning volcanic
island of Stromboli, the " Faro," or lighthouse, of Italy, reached
Naples before March. A letter written in Italian to his sisters
at Leicester gives these few particulars of his journey through
Western Italy and France, back to Paris, where he arrived
early in April, 1839: —

I was ten days in Naples and its vicinity, visiting the chief places
of interest, in company with three Englishmen. We ascended
Vesuvius together on a magnificently beautiful day, and next made
a journey of archæological interest to Herculaneum, Pompeii, and
Paestum. From Naples I went to Rome in thirty-six hours; and the
journey from Rome to Florence, visiting the cataract of Terni on the

way, occupied six days. My stay in Rome was so brief, and there were so many churches, ruins, statues, pictures, and other things to be seen in that wonderful city that I was constantly occupied. From Florence my route was down the Arno Valley to Pisa and Leghorn, and thence by steamer to Marseilles. Upon the whole, I think that in each important city of Italy I enjoyed about as much as in boyhood, when going to the High Rock, to Bumskit, or to the Mill, to "go in swimming."

From Marseilles my route was by way of Avignon, Lyons, and Châlons, to Paris; and here I am (April 12) in the same hotel (Place de l'Odéon) which was my home last year. Elizabeth Fry is again in the city, but I have not seen her yet. So busy am I in attending the hospitals, taking a course of practical lessons in surgery, and in much else that I want to do before leaving for America that hitherto I have not called on Dr. Mott or Anne Knight.

It is worth mentioning that, although Charles Sumner arrived in Paris early in 1838, and remained there four months, there is no record in his letters or those of Dr. Earle that they ever met. They must have done so at the receptions of General Cass, which both attended, and of which both gave striking accounts. But the pursuits and associations of the two young Americans * were then so unlike that they can have had little in common. Afterwards they were good friends, and often met in Washington. In a few weeks after reaching Paris from Italy, Dr. Earle sailed for America.

* Sumner, writing from Paris, Feb. 27, 1838, to Longfellow, the poet, says: "Mrs. Fry has been at Paris, exciting some attention on the subject of prisons. The French, by the way, are just waking up on that subject, and also on that of railroads." So little did he then concern himself with a matter that afterwards engaged his earnest efforts that this is the only allusion to Mrs. Fry in his published letters from France and England in 1838-39. But he heard Louis and Magendie lecture in Paris; and of the latter he says (Feb. 9, 1838): "He is a man apparently about fifty" (in fact, fifty-five), "rather short and stout, with a countenance marked by the small-pox. He is renowned for killing cats and dogs: there were no less than three murdered dogs brought upon the table while I was there,—at the Collège Royal,—in order to illustrate the different appearance of the blood at certain times after death." Sumner also followed Velpeau one day through the wards of the Charité, and heard him lecture clinically. Magendie died in 1855, but Velpeau lived till 1867. The latter was born in 1795, and was twelve years younger than Magendie.

CHAPTER V.

In November, 1838, after travelling through Switzerland and Northern Italy, Dr. Earle sailed from Venice to Patras, on the Gulf of Lepanto, at the western entrance of the Gulf of Corinth, and thence proceeded to Athens and Marathon. From Athens he sailed to Constantinople, and returned thence to Western Europe by way of Malta, where he was compelled to spend three weeks in quarantine in January, 1839. Many adventures befell him in this rather adventurous journey; for at that time Greece was not the quiet and civilized region which the tourist now sees in visiting only those places reached by our young physician. He says:—

At Patras I landed, a perfect stranger, ignorant of the modern Greek tongue, but knowing there was an American missionary there, I walked into the market-place of the town, where I saw a man who, I felt convinced, was an American, and asked him if he spoke English. "Yes, sir." "Do you know an American missionary here?" "I am the man," said he; and he went with me to the schools and other places of interest in the town. His name is Cephas Pasco, and he came from Stafford, in Connecticut. I dined with him, and he gave me letters of introduction for Athens. I witnessed here the packing of the small grapes which we call Zante currants, and which grow in large quantities along the Corinthian Gulf, from Patras to Corinth, as well as in the southern parts of the Peloponnesus. It is said that, if you are to dine at a tavern, you should never look into the kitchen; and a like remark might be made about the packing and lading of currants. I will only say that, while one man stands among them as they lie in a large pen or vault, another, with his naked feet well greased, gets into the cask and treads them down. Such as fall out of the shovel, cask, or boxes upon the dusty pier, where they are loaded into boats, are carefully swept up and put in with the others.

At Athens I made many acquaintances. The American missionaries there were then Rev. J. H. Hill of New York, Rev. Jonas King
of Windsor, Mass., and Rev. Nathan Benjamin, also from Western
Massachusetts. Dr. Roeser, the Bavarian physician of the Bavarian
King of Greece, was my good friend; and I was indebted to him for
my election into the Medical Society of Athens, of which I have
ever since been a member, and for which I wrote a thesis while detained in quarantine at Malta in January. In my first visit to the
antiquities of Athens, I went on horseback, though the distances
were small, accompanied by Messrs. John H. Hill and Benjamin.
From the neighborhood of Mr. Hill's school, near the gate of the new
Agora [the Stoa of Hadrian], we went eastward, and crossed the
Ilissus, where no water was then to be seen, to the Stadium of
Herodes Atticus.* Its oval form is nearly perfect, and the tunnel
through the hill at its eastern extremity, through which the Pana-
thenaic procession may have passed, remains; but the marble seats
with which its interior was furnished by the wealthy Herod of Attica
(who also had a great estate at Marathon and along by the sides of
Pentelicus) have all disappeared. The original Stadium was made
by Lycurgus,—not the mythical Spartan, but an eminent citizen of
Athens, in the fourth century B.C. Returning, we entered a new
Protestant cemetery [where, thirty-seven years later, George Finlay
was buried], and thence to the terrace and ruins of the temple of
Jupiter Olympus, originally the most magnificent of Grecian temples,
550 feet long and 170 feet wide, and flanked on each of its two sides
with a double row of 20 Corinthian columns, while at each front was
a triple row of 10, in all 120 columns, each nearly 60 feet in height
and 5½ in diameter. Only 16 of them are now standing, and the
beauty of these is disfigured by large holes chiselled in them for
the purpose of extracting the leaden and iron clamps which bound
the marble drums together. Yet some of the flutings are still as
perfect as if they came but yesterday from the sculptor's hand.
Upon a small portion of the architrave which remains, supported
by some of the pillars, I saw a small building, of modern construction, which, report says, was once inhabited by a monk. Near by
is the Arch of Hadrian, through which we passed, and along by the

---

* This has lately (1896) been restored by a wealthy Greek, Mr. Averoff, to something like its
former magnificence; and his purpose is to replace the temporary wooden seats, from which tens of
thousands saw the Athenian games in the spring of 1896, by marble ones, hewn from the unexhausted
quarries of Pentelicus, whence Herodes supplied his chairs and benches.

military hospital to the so-called Prison of Socrates,— small caves
hewn in the rock on the declivity of a hill; thence by the crumbling
monument of unknown Philopappus to the Pnyx Hill, on which public meetings were held, and where Demosthenes and other orators
harangued their fellow-citizens. Standing there, the Athenian saw
the plain of Athens spread at his feet, the groves of Academus in
the northern distance, Hymettus with its lofty ridges on the right,
as he faced the Acropolis, with its costly magnificence in marble
and gold. On the left lay Salamis, and behind him the sea and
islands. This closed our first day's sight-seeing.

Modern Athens has recovered but slowly from the dilapidation
and depopulation in which the Turks left it in 1832. It then had
but about 2,000 inhabitants, though before the Revolution of 1821
it may have had 12,000. Christopher Wordsworth, nephew of the
poet whose Lake region I visited in 1837, was here in October, 1832 ;
and his account is dismal enough. "The town of Athens," he say,
"is now lying in ruins. The streets are almost deserted : nearly
all the houses are without roofs. The churches are reduced to bare
walls and heaps of stone and mortar. There is but one church in
which service is performed. A few new wooden houses, one or
two more solid structures, and the two lines of planked sheds which
form the bazaar are the inhabited dwellings of which Athens can
boast."

Things had changed much for the better in the six years before
my visit. The whole population of Greece was less than 800,000,
but of these some 20,000 were in Athens. The king, Otho, made
it his residence in 1834, with his court and the foreign ministers ;
and a royal palace was going up on a great square, which the
frugal Greeks viewed with a rueful eye, because costing them
millions of their drachmas. I saw many comfortable houses, and
some which are even elegant. The finest building in the city,
however, was a hospital. The most densely peopled part of Athens,
on the north side of the Acropolis, was a mass of wretched buildings,
most of them but one story and none more than two stories. From
one corner of this quarter ran the street of Æolus,— the Wall Street
of the city. There on the sidewalks, had there been any, were men
and women seated on the ground or on low benches, some selling
oranges, others chestnuts, roast or boiled ; while behind small tables,
piled with stamped paper money or bags of specie, sat the money-

changer, as in the temple at Jerusalem. The awnings in front of
the shops were fastened, not to posts or supporting braces, but by
cords stretched across the street, and tied to the opposite buildings;
while other cords spanned the same street, on which clothes were
hung to dry,— the chief street being thus a laundry-yard. Many of
the shops have the whole front thrown open to the street; and in
them the occupants, particularly the tailors and tobacco-workers, sit
on the floor at their trades. None of the streets were paved, and
most of them were filthy. To insure safety from the vile condition
of the streets and also from robbery or assassination, every one who
goes out in the evening is required by law to carry a lantern, as in
the days of Diogenes.

This custom once led my friend, Dr. Roeser, into a ludicrous
situation. Though the most learned man in Athens, he was absent-
minded, and accustomed to have his evening lantern carried before
him by a servant. Being about to leave an evening party, he came
to the door with hat and cane, and stepped into the dark street, just
as a stranger with his lantern was passing. Mistaking this for his
man's lantern, Dr. Roeser followed it trustfully. The two had gone
some distance when the stranger, perceiving that he was followed by
a man without a light, quickened his step. So did the doctor. He
then walked slower. The doctor did the same. Finding, after a
while, that his pursuer kept about the same distance behind, the man
grew alarmed and started to run. So did Dr. Roeser, and more
than kept up. Street after street was quickly passed, and they were
already in the suburbs. The open fields or some place of refuge
were the only alternatives for the shadowed and enlightening
stranger. He chose the latter. A large door stood open. He ran
within, and in the twinkling of his own lantern closed it upon the
doctor, creaking as it turned on rusty hinges. Thus aroused to con-
sciousness that something was wrong, Dr. Roeser looked about him,
and found himself beneath the lofty portico of the old temple of
Theseus. When I questioned him on the subject, he said that he
ran because he supposed his man was taking him to some patient
whose case was urgent.

Those who had lived long among the Greeks united in giving them
a bad name. One of them said to me, "I cannot trust a Greek with
my back turned." As a people, they seem to be quick-witted, shrewd,
but suspicious, fickle, and treacherous. Like most mountaineers,

they are hardy, bold, and independent; and, taking advantage of their facilities for retreat beyond detection, no wonder, when poverty presses hard on a proud spirit, that they sometimes resort to robbery. And perhaps there was never a time when the country was more infested with brigands than while I was there. I had been in Athens but a few days when a policeman was killed and another wounded in an ineffectual attempt to capture a band of them on the road to Marathon. Soon after two of their leaders voluntarily gave themselves up, vainly hoping for pardon by such a surrender,— a custom which prevailed under the Turks. I was one day riding up a street, when I saw before me, and near where my street crosses Æolus Street, a dense crowd of people; while others were rushing up. I alighted, pushed into the crowd, and soon saw what caused the excitement. Amidst a motley assemblage of red caps, black hats, turbans, fezzes, mustaches, long beards, and ferocious faces, were four men mounted on donkeys, their arms pinioned, their faces covered with blood, and one of them giving evidence of a wound by rude dressings, red with blood. They were brigands, just captured near the Marathon road; and in the skirmish with soldiers and peasants one of the robbers had been killed and several wounded.

Life is rarely taken by the bandits, who are satisfied with the spoils without murder. But woe to the unlucky traveller whose purse is not garnished! His life may be granted, but he may expect the bastinado. An English gentleman and artist, Edward Noel, a cousin of Lady Byron, has an estate in Eubœa (Achmet Aga), bought from the confiscated lands of the Turks when they left the island in 1834. Being about to visit his property, and knowing the dangers of the road, he left most of his money in Athens. On the way he was beset by brigands, who, finding so little in his purse, advised him to carry more the next journey, and, lest he should forget to do so, gave him a sound whipping.*

In spite of the brigands I determined to visit Marathon, for which purpose I got a guide and a pair of horses. My route took me through Kephissia, at the foot of Pentelicus, and was good at first; but the last few miles it was a mere bridle-path, over steep and lofty

---

* Mr. Noel was also interested, in 1870, in obtaining the release of the Englishmen seized by brigands at Pikermi, a ravine on another and shorter road to Marathon than that described by Dr. Earle. In spite of his well-meant efforts and those of his son, Mr. Francis Noel, who now (1898) owns the Achmet Aga estate, the Englishmen were shot by the brigands; but this led to such vigorous action by the Greek authorities that for a quarter of a century the roads to Marathon have been as safe as that from Worcester to Leicester. I have tried them.— F. B. S.

hills, through deep, rocky ravines, and in some places as difficult for a horse as an ordinary flight of stone stairs. Yet this was called by the Greek authorities a "carrossable" road, though you never met a carriage on it. Now and then we encountered men or women, sometimes riding and sometimes driving laden beasts, on their way to market; sometimes only a man with a gun slung across his shoulder, going to Athens or Kephissia.

The country through which our route lay may thus be described to a Leicester citizen: Let all the stone fences and other enclosures be removed from the three townships of Leicester, Paxton, and Holden; cover the hills and valleys with low whortleberry bushes or the "high-bush blueberry"; let the cows be the only path-makers — not a single stone being removed by man — from our house at Mulberry Grove over the top of the Indian hill Asnebumskit, in a nearly straight line,— and you will get some conception of the region and the road by which my guide and I travelled on our steeds. However, in some places it was as much worse than that as that would be worse than a good English road; and this is no exaggeration. I took with me as guide a Greek who was recommended as being honest; but at one point I felt some misgivings, in view of the fact that five brigands had either been captured or surrendered to the Chorophýlakes, or gens-d'armes, since I had reached Athens from Corfu and Patras. We were near the foot of Mount Pentelicus * when this guide pretended to have taken the wrong path, and made off through the bushes towards the mountain. From some things which had occurred earlier I felt a little suspicious, and now I began to consider myself in danger. After suffering from fears for a while, I said to myself, "Well, I'll see it through," and was perfectly easy from that time on. We soon came into another path, and reached Marathon before night. I spent the night at the village of Lower Souli, two miles from the battle-mound, and returned safely to Athens the next day. But within forty-eight hours after my return the three brigands already mentioned were brought

---

* Dr. Earle was taking the old route to Marathon (there are three), leading through Kephissia, Stamata, and over Aphorismós. His guide's perplexity evidently arose from his wish to take the steep Vraná road, which branches off from the Marathona road, a little west of Stamata. Apparently, he went finally down the gorge in which lay the ancient deme of Thespis, "Icaria," where the American School at Athens in 1888 excavated the remains of a small temple, and identified the home of Thespis, in whose traditional honor the region is still called "Dionyso," his dramas having grown up around the festival of Dionysus, the Grecian Bacchus, whose legends connect him with this Marathonian region. Dr. Earle's immunity from brigands was probably due to this choice of roads by his guide, safer than that by Pikermi.

in by the gens-d'armes from the route to Marathon, where they were
captured after a struggle in which they were wounded, one of their
comrades killed, and several of the Chorophylakes killed or wounded.

The field of Marathon is a plain six miles long and two or three
miles wide, and nearly as level as the surface of a quiet sea.   On its
eastern side is the Bay of Marathon, beyond which rise the high
mountains of Negropont.   Its other sides are shut in by the Attic
mountains of Argaláki, Aphorismós (a spur of Pentelicus), Kotroni,
Koraki, and on the north-east the hills of Apano-Souli, which separate
Marathon from Rhamnus.   When I saw the battlefield, a very small
part of it was rudely cultivated, the rest covered with short grass,
except in a few marshy places, where grew a profusion of rushes.
Rude shepherds guided us to the southern extremity of the plain,
where are the remains of a few marble columns, which are mentioned
by Dr. E. D. Clarke in his account of the plain, visited by him in
the beginning of the century.   But the tumulus (Soros) is the most
striking object, a little south of the centre of the plain, broad at the
base, conical in form, and from thirty to forty feet high.   Some
shrubbery and flowers grow near its summit, on which, as I sat,
these lines depict the quiet of the place : —

> Here, as upon this rising mound
> I sit and cast my vision round,
> 'Tis silence all, save when a note
> Comes, on the creeping breeze afloat,
> From yonder rugged mountain rock,
> Where the rude shepherd guards his flock.*

Twilight was already yielding to the deeper shades of night when
we left this mound, and pursued our way to the village, two miles to
the north, where we were to pass the night.   Arriving at the only
house open to travellers, we ascended a flight of stone steps leading
(outside) to the second story, where I remained in the open air for
some minutes, while my dragoman went in to ask for lodging.   He
was absent some time, being obliged to tell who we were, whence

---

* From "Marathon, and Other Poems," by Pliny Earle, M.D., published by Henry Perkins at
Philadelphia in 1841, and containing many of the verses the young schoolmaster and physician had
been writing and printing in newspapers and magazines since 1830. They have little merit as poetry,
but preserve the memory of places and persons that impressed themselves on Dr. Earle's mind in
youth.   The smooth and varied metres show the influence of Byron, Scott, Willis, Whittier, and
Bryant; but there is little originality of thought, though much calm depth of feeling. A diffuse prose
style also marks the writings of the same period, which I have often shortened in quoting.

we came, etc. Finally, he came out and asked me to walk in.   By
the sole light of some dying embers on the hearth I saw beside the
fireplace in one corner of the room two boys and a man of say
forty-five years, lying on blankets spread upon the floor; while two
women, one of them advanced in years, sat on low stools, such as
that on which

Immortal Alfred sat,
Who swayed, the sceptre of his infant realms.

The other woman was younger; and there were two seated men, apparently under thirty.   The elder woman lighted a candle, and showed
me to an apartment seven feet by ten, with but one window and no
glass, two old chairs, the frame of a looking-glass, and a small pine
table, on which was a goodly pile of coarse wheaten loaves, recently
from the oven.   There was no bed: a mattress laid on the floor was
to serve.   My guide brought in a chicken, provided by him at
Athens, our landlady furnished a knife, some salt, a piece of goat's-
milk cheese, and cut for us one of the said loaves. I called for a
tumbler of water.   It was brought; but, while I drank it, the landlady looked at me in blank astonishment, desiring the dragoman to
tell me that it would certainly make me ill, and that wine was the
only thing fit for a man's stomach.   .

I gathered many flowers at Marathon, either at the village in the
morning or on the plain,— the anemone, which I had already found on
the Areopagus, and which blooms in Attica all winter, the autumn
crocus, the rock rose, etc.   In spring the jonquil blooms abundantly
near the battlefield. While returning to Athens along the rapid
river that flows beside Marathona, and forms the marsh near the sea,
in which so many of the Persians were slain, and over the rocks of
Kotroni and Aphorismós, we stopped at a *kapheneion* (café) in
Kephissia, and took coffee, *à la Turque*, without milk.   The room
was thronged with men, most of them smoking, and many appearing
to be under the influence of the resin-wine of the country, which
they had drunk in honor of the patron saint of the day.   There was
no floor; but upon one of the tables standing on the earth I spread
my herbarium, and, taking some flowers which had been placed
in the crown of my hat as I came along, I began to prepare them for
preservation.   One of the men came up, and looked over my
shoulder. He was followed by another, he by a third, and so on
until my table was surrounded by a group of beings most ferocious in

aspect, but chattering, laughing, and looking astonished that any
such flowers should be thought valuable.* They took up some of
them, turned them over and over, and examined them sharply, as if to
find something remarkable they had never seen before in these
flowers with which they had been familiar from childhood. My
dragoman then told them a story of the wonderful medicinal proper-
ties of such flowers, and the great cures they might effect. Thereupon the men laid down the *loulouthia* (posies, the common word for
all flowers in Greece), and began to converse in lower tones and
with a mysterious air. Those who were nearest me withdrew a step
or two, and all gazed with their bloodshot eyes, in still greater
wonder.

Dr. Earle was particularly struck, as most tourists have
been, with the great attention paid to education in Greece. He
thought the Lancastrian school at Patras and a girls' school
there, which he visited, were very satisfactory; and he much
admired the private school for girls established by Rev. J. H.
Hill and his wife at Athens. In 1838 he described it thus: —

This school is divided into five departments, and contains about
four hundred pupils, in a large building near the gate of the new
Agora. That department called the "Troy Seminary," under the
care of Mrs. Hill, is very flourishing, and is the best school for girls
in Greece. It cannot fail to exert a powerful influence for good in
both Greece and Turkey by sending forth so many highly educated
young women where a prejudice against female education has long
prevailed.†

The Greek religion, with its pictured saints, its genuflexions,
ceremonies, and antiquated ritual, naturally did not please the

* The collections of plants and flowers made by Dr. Earle in Greece and elsewhere in Europe
gave him opportunity to send dried specimens to many of his female friends in America and
England, particularly to the literary ladies of America, Miss H. F. Gould, Mrs. Sigourney, Mrs.
S. J. Hale, Mrs. Amelia Welby, of Kentucky, and others, who acknowledged the graceful attention in
pleasant notes and sometimes in poems. The trait of childish curiosity here remarked among the
Greeks, and their general ignorance of the botany of their own ever-blooming land, is familiar to all
who travel in rural Greece. I had occasion to pass the night at the village of Marathona forty-five years
after Dr. Earle. It had much grown and improved in the interval, and the battle-plain is now
well cultivated in vineyards.

† This anticipation has been fulfilled; and now the education of girls is carried as far in Greece at
public expense as in most nations, though only a portion of them partake of it. They have even
gained entrance to some classes at the University of Athens; while excellent private and endowed

young Massachusetts Quaker; but the native liberality of his soul led him to see good in these forms, so repugnant to his own simple service.   He says : —

In Corfu, then under English control, where I landed on the voyage from Trieste to Patras, I accompanied a young Greek to a church, an ancient structure, miserable in its externals, but internally rich and beautiful.   On the walls were pictures of the saints, with tapers burning before them.   The ceiling was wrought with the most elaborate carving, adorned with gold and paintings or mosaics ; while chandeliers of massive silver hung suspended, with lighted tapers at evening and on saints' days.   On either side of the high altar was a small chapel, entered from the church by a doorway. The body of the church was filled with such a medley of beings as I had never before seen in a place of worship.   There, mingled together in unspeakable confusion, were riches and poverty, youth and age, beauty and deformity, the apparently devout and the evidently indifferent, those who flaunt in rags and those who flutter in brocade,

The snowy camese and the shaggy capote

of the Albanian and the Greek, the Turkish robe and turban, and the stiff costume of Western Europe.   While the priest performed the service at the altar, on the steps beside it sat a young mother, whose infant was lying before her at the feet of the image of Jesus. Crowds of people continually entered during the service, approached and kissed the images of the saints, and then retired.   Such as remained long stood on either side of the church, with their faces towards the altar.   Nobody sat.   Many also entered the side chapel on the right, a room so nearly dark that to me, standing almost in front of the door, nothing could be distinguished within except a full-length figure of the Savior, covered with burnished silver.   This picture shone in the feeble rays of the one small taper with which the chapel was lighted.   I joined the throng and entered the door, a grateful odor of roses and of incense meeting me as I drew near, and increasing as we entered.   I stepped aside from the doorway to make room for those who followed me ; but, though inside and breathing the delightful fragrance, I could at first see nothing dis-

schools for girls exist in that city of 130,000 people, besides the successors of Mrs. Hill's school. Those devoted missionaries and their assistants have long been dead.

tinctly but the image of the Savior. Gradually the few surrounding objects became discernible. Before me in the centre of the
chapel, and so large as to fill a third part of its area, was a sarcophagus of massive silver, containing the body of a saint, and covered
with figures and allegorical devices, curiously wrought. Old men
and young, matron and maid, drew near, and kissed it with all the
fervor of apparent devotion. Immediately beside me, and at the
foot of the sarcophagus, two women, in convent garb, were kneeling,
and as motionless as if they were marble statues. I had never
been in a situation where external surroundings were better arranged
to waken a feeling of devotion.

Returning to the church, I took my former position, but found the
building thronged with beggars. The old and infirm, the youthful
and deformed, the cripple, the madman, the moping idiot, — in short,
all that one ever meets of distortion in shape and wretchedness in
condition, among mendicants, was there. They formed themselves
into a row, which reached the whole distance round the interior of
the church, and thus they passed along, in pitiable succession, im-
ploring alms, "*per l' amore di Dio*," for the love of God; and many
an obole or mezzo-obole (the minute coins of the Ionian Islands)
was dropped into hat or hand, to aid the supplicants. And thus, I
thought, for once in my life have I seen, within a Christian church,
some close approximation to that pure democracy which is a dominant ideal in the teachings of the New Testament.

After touching at Smyrna, where he visited the traditional
spot of Polycarp's martyrdom, near that Asian city, Dr. Earle
proceeded to Constantinople. His mention of the saint's hold
on Mahometans, as well as Christians, is curious : —

Upon a declivity of the mountainous ridge which bounds the city
of Smyrna to the east, at a place near the ancient walls commanding an extensive and lovely view of the bay, the town, and its
environs, there is a solitary cypress. Beneath it, on one side, is a
sepulchral monument; on the other, a large stone, before which faithful Moslem are accustomed to kneel in prayer, with faces directed
towards Mecca, the "city of the Prophet." It was here that Polycarp, bishop of the church at Smyrna and a disciple of Saint John,
the apostle, suffered martyrdom. It is further said, either by this
tradition or by authentic history, that the people who were present

ran down the hill to procure fagots with which to burn the body. And in December, 1838, when I was there, a magazine of fagots, near the base of the ridge, was to be seen, which had existed from time immemorial. If it seems inconsistent for the Mahometans to pray at the tomb of Polycarp, it should be remembered that many of those whom Mahomet wished to proselyte were Christians, accustomed to worship their martyrs; and it is a proof of his sagacity that he encouraged what he could not hope wholly to eradicate.

It was just after leaving Smyrna in the French steamer "Dante," on his return to France, that a view and a colloquy occurred which left a strong impression on the voyager's mind, from the beauty of the one and the oddity of the other. Those who have sailed in those seas in such magical weather will appreciate Dr. Earle's raptures.

On the afternoon of Dec. 31, 1838, we were sailing between Scio and Asia Minor. The summits of the Chian Mountains lifted themselves to the heavens, covered with snow; and, as evening drew near, though we had passed the island, its mountains were still in view, like a blue cloud, snow-topped, resting on the horizon. The last glimmering rays of the sun lighted them, as he went down behind the dark, western waters of the Archipelago. The time and the place were adapted to a thousand pleasing associations. Olympus, Smyrna, and Scio were behind us; and before us was Greece, with its exhaustless store of memories. We were carried back, in reverie, to the days, in this clime, when poesy was young,—when among those sunlit mountains Homer was tuning his harp or instructing his pupils in the art of song.* As the twilight shadows deepened, the moon, round as the battle-shield of the ancestors of Ossian,—" O thou that rollest in heaven, round as the shield of my fathers! whence hast thou thy beams, O Sun? whence thy everlasting light?"—was rising in the cloudless sky. And when the last vestige of day had departed, and heaven was illuminated as for a festival by her milder beams, the waters of the Ægean gave them brilliantly back from a surface unruffled by the lightest breeze. The air was bland; and the night, though the last of the year, might have been mistaken for one

* It is on this island, the ancient Chios, that tradition places the "School of Homer"; and the place (a kind of theatre) is still shown.

of those which give beauty to our earlier autumn. The passengers came up from the cabin to enjoy the bright scene from the deck,— a motley assemblage, such as may usually be seen on the steam-vessels that traverse the Eastern Mediterranean. Turks, Greeks, Armenians, Jews, English, French, Italians, and Germans were among them, even Egyptians, Arabs, and Algerines.

Among them was a Jewish rabbi, from Muscovy, on his way to Italy, with a venerable, gray-bearded servant. He was quite the finest-looking Hebrew and one of the handsomest men I ever saw. His eyes, brows, hair, and profuse beard were black as jet, his skin light and transparent, his face full, and his head noble. His small, soft, white hand indicated an exemption from toil, of which his octogenarian servant must have been aware from sad experience. As I paused in walking the deck to look upwards and fix the points of the compass by the North Star, the rabbi advanced, and inquired if I had studied astronomy, then put the same question concerning algebra, geometry, and astrology, and went on to point out the mysteries of those sciences, in which he said he was profoundly interested. Thence he advanced to the topic of religion, and declaimed in no measured terms against the Protestants, who, as he believed, were seeking to revolutionize the religious world. Having uttered his anathemas, he asked me whether I was a Jew, a Catholic, or a Protestant. Being answered, he said no more upon religion; but, as if to show that, though he detested Protestants as a class, he had no hostility to me as an individual, he called his servant, and ordered a peace-offering,— not salt, but coffee. That venerable man soon returned, bringing two tumblers of the beverage. As I took from him the one meant for me, I asked him a question about one of the subjects we had been discussing. "No, no," cried the rabbi, "don't ask him any question: he is an old fool." The rejected servant walked off in silence, as if he took for granted all his master said; while the rabbi sipped his coffee. Then, looking cautiously about, to see that no one was near, he took my hand, led me to the side of the vessel, and, as we leaned against the taffrail, said, "Ah! I have a great secret to tell you,— a very great secret."

"And what may it be?"

"'Tis a most sublime and mysterious thing" (here his countenance kindled with a smile, and his dark eyes turned towards the heavens): "I have discovered what the wise men of all ages have been seeking in vain. I have found the means of changing the baser metals into gold. Oh, it's a most wonderful thing."

In the long conversation that followed, I learned that he professed to have discovered the magic power once ascribed to the chimerical philosopher's stone. It actually resides in a vegetable growing near Mecca. The stalk of this plant, according to him, is of a golden color. Its flowers have the odor of musk. It will operate (thus far) only upon brass, lead, silver, and mercury. Iron has withstood its operation,— a fortunate circumstance, I thought, since we should be quite too luxurious, riding on rails and driving ploughshares made of shining gold.

There are few records of Dr. Earle's visit to Constantinople, except those which relate to the insane asylum there,— the Timar-hané, then adjacent to the mosque of Suleiman. His companions in the city of the sultan were Rev. William Goodell and two other American missionaries, Henry A. Homes, afterwards State Librarian of New York at Albany, and William Schofler; Dr. Millingen (the friend of Byron, and of George Finlay, who was long the Sultan's physician), and Foster Rhodes, also in the Sultan's employ. Dr. Millingen was an Englishman, of Dutch ancestry, who had been with Byron in his last illness at Missolonghi, afterwards in the Greek Revolutionary army with Finlay, and, when captured with the Greeks, at the taking of Navarino in 1825, was induced or forced to enter the service of Ibrahim Pasha, who devastated the Morea; from which, after an interval, he passed into the employ of Mahmoud at Constantinople. He was an archæologist, like his father and his descendants, some of whom still remain at Constantinople, where I saw them in 1893. At the time of Dr. Earle's brief visit (December, 1838) Dr. Millingen had resided in Turkey more than ten years; and it was through his good offices that the young American was admitted, during the feast of Bairam, to the dismal corridors where the maniacs were chained. Mr. Goodell and Mr. Rhodes seem to have gone with him. What he saw there is concisely related in his first book, "A Visit to Thirteen Asylums for the Insane in Europe," which he published as a sort of certificate of his fitness to write on the subject that afterwards chiefly employed his pen. But he has left on record a few of those pleasant anecdotes which have been cited so freely in previous chapters.

Mr. Goodell, one of the American missionaries at Constantinople, told me there that a very intelligent and pious Greek lady, who had been converted to Protestantism, and enjoyed the services at the missionary meetings, once remarked to him that, though she had no acquaintance with the English language, she yet liked to hear it spoken. " It sounds so finely," she said, " when uttered by those who, in conversation, frequently use the phrase, ' God d—n your soul,' " which the new convert seems to have thought some form of blessing. Mr. Goodell explained to her the real meaning of the phrase ; and, as may be supposed, she was greatly shocked at her mistaking an oath for the chief beauty of our language. This reminded me of what happened on my trip from Athens to Marathon, when my guide told me he knew Greek, Italian, French, and German, but no English. What was my surprise, then, as we were riding at a brisk trot through the valley that borders the northern base of Pentelicus,* to hear from him the same startling curse which had deceived the ear of the convert of Constantinople. It rang through the clear and silent air with fearful distinctness. I turned round to ascertain whence it proceeded, and saw that, my guide's horse having become unruly, he was attempting to calm him with whips, spurs, and English imprecations. " Ah," said I, " people generally learn the worst things first."

The relations of Dr. Millingen with Dr. Earle in 1838 did not permit him to learn in detail the events of his life among the Turks, which had begun in 1825 at the capture of Navarino, though he did not become official court physician until a year or more after Dr. Earle's visit. With the exception of Byron's friend, Trelawny, Millingen was the only Englishman remaining in the Greek revolutionary service for some little time after Byron's death, in April, 1824, as he says himself in an account from which I now quote. Dr. Millingen remained in Greece (1824) where, after recovering from the typhoid fever then

---

* This was between Kephissia and Stamata, before reaching where the path turns off to the right for Icaria.

prevalent at Missolonghi, and which attacked **him** soon after Lord Byron's death (probably a disease of the same nature **as** that which **proved fatal to** the noble poet), he entered again into active service.

I **was** then appointed officially **to join** the forces encamped **at Ligovitzi in** Acarnania, under **the command of** Mavrocordato, **and remained there** until the termination **of that** campaign. In **1825, Navarino** being closely besieged **by the Egyptian army (under Ibra-** him Pasha), and its garrison **having repeatedly, yet ineffectually,** solicited medical assistance in **behalf of the daily increasing sick and** wounded,— none of the medical **officers in the Greek service proving** willing to undertake **so arduous a mission,—** George Conduriottis, then president, **invited me to do so.** I accepted his proposal, and, after **eluding the enemy's** vigilance, **succeeded in** entering that fortress in **Mavrocordato's** company. **From that day, in** the midst of the dangers of an uninterrupted **bombardment by** land and sea, I **continued, unassisted** and unpaid, **to perform the duties incumbent on the physician and surgeon, until, reduced to extrem-** ities, the garrison capitulated, and, after surrendering its arms, **embarked for Kalamata.** I **was** detained by Ibrahim Pasha, when **on my way to the** place of embarkation. Nor did I volunteer into his service, as **my detractors have said, as** if, for the sake of better **pay, I had** basely deserted the banner of the Cross to follow the **standard** of the Crescent. I was then fully aware that by accepting **the Egyptian** service I might **in a few** years have realized **as con-** siderable a fortune as other physicians have done.* **But, far** from being influenced by this **consideration, I no sooner reached** Modon than I wrote (12th **and 19th of June, 1825)** to a friend at Cepha- lonia, requesting him to **apply to the British** authorities for a pass- port, without which **no vessel would receive me,** it being my intention to embark secretly. **On the 8th** of September following **Lord** Howard de Walden **wrote to my friends as** follows: "Mr. **Canning directs me** to **acquaint you that the fact** (admitted in Dr. **Millingen's letters) of his having been** found in the service of the **Greeks, must preclude Mr.** Canning from recommending his case to His **Majesty's Embassy at the** Porte for interference, as the protec- tion **of government** cannot be extended to British subjects engaging in foreign service **against an act of** Parliament." It was not before

*Sir Henry Holland, the son-in-law of Sydney **Smith, had been physician to Ali** Pasha.

November, 1826, that I was allowed to go to Smyrna, and not till fourteen years after that the reigning Sultan appointed me one of his court physicians.

The feast of Bairam, in course of which Dr. Earle made his visit both to Smyrna and Constantinople, continues thirty days, and corresponds roughly to our Christmas holidays. As observed by him, the details are curious : —

The poor work on these days as usual; but the rich close their shops, though many of them are willing to do business. Only the large-tailed breed of sheep are used in sacrifices then, at least in Asia Minor, where they are bred. They are killed at two or three years old, and cost about two dollars. Each good Mussulman is expected to sacrifice a sheep every year; and the superstition is that, if he should die before the next feast, that sheep will carry him into Paradise. For the three bridges over the rivers of milk, honey, and butter, which encircle Paradise, are so narrow that only a sheep can cross them; and the departed, on arriving at these streams, must bestride a sheep they have sacrificed. The rich often kill several sheep, for precaution, and give the mutton to the poor. Flocks of these sacred animals now and then are seen at pasture near Smyrna, where the numerous Greeks are not allowed to own them, no Greek being wanted in the Moslem heaven.

Constantinople is built on an angular point of land, something like New York, which it resembles in several other ways. Pera, where the Franks live, is situated as Brooklyn is to New York, though the stream between is narrower. The streets are narrow and filthy, abounding in dogs and lined with tall wooden houses. The old Roman city was on Seraglio Point and the high land behind it. And here is the mosque of St. Sophia and that of Suleiman, near which I found the insane lodged in a one-story building, arranged round a central court, like the caravanseries of Turkey and Asia Minor. A corridor runs on the outer side of this court, and gives access to the rooms and the wards. Within the court-yard we found many persons, mostly youths or boys, who had come out of curiosity or to bring gifts to their insane friends. Outside of the few asylums the insane are regarded by the Mahometans as sacred creatures, and their incoherent language as divinely given. Dr. Millingen says he has known the wandering lunatic to be entertained for weeks by

strangers, who treated him with distinguished consideration. But
the treatment in the Timar-hané was far from hospitable. In the
first room we saw an inmate fastened by the neck with a chain six
feet long, itself made fast through an unglazed window to the external wall. Two other patients were in the same room, chained in
the same manner. Indeed, of the forty or fifty patients found there,
but one was unchained. The length of the chains was so graduated
as just to allow the inmate to lie down on a rude bed of boards and
blankets.* The unchained man was secluded in a room, having several times broken his chain. He had been confined there fifteen
years, and was a chronic maniac, raving and noisy, but not probably
homicidal (though he threatens to kill those who gaze at him), were he
properly treated, as Pinel treated the maniacs at the Bicêtre in 1793.
Yet the patients appeared in good health, are frequently seen by a
physician, and were talking with their visitors while we were present,
who gave them tobacco, lighted their pipes for them, and supplied
them with food of various kinds, and even money.

Dr. Earle was impressed, as all travellers are, with the Turkish cemeteries, especially that at Scutari, on the Asiatic side of
the Bosphorus. He says : —

The almost boundless cemeteries of Constantinople and Scutari
have long been objects of admiration. The noble cypresses constitute their chief beauty, apart from their situation on the picturesque
shores of the Bosphorus. In many of them the grounds are not enclosed, the graves are neglected, and the turban-crowned headstones
are either falling or actually lying on the ground. The passing
breeze — and in that region the breeze is almost always passing,
so steadily does it blow down the Bosphorus — makes a low and
plaintive murmur in the evergreen branchlets of the cypress, and
reaches the heart with an eloquence unknown to lecture or to
homily.

* At that early date chaining the maniacal or wandering insane was customary all over the world,
with the exception of a few communities, where the teachings of Pinel, Tuke, Horace Mann, and
others, had shown the needless barbarity of it. But it has not yet entirely been "dismissed to the
moon," as Emerson said of some similar absurdity. In visiting the new county almshouse of Hills-
borough at Grasmere, a few miles from Manchester, N.H., in November, 1896, I found three patients
wearing chains, and those women. I was obliged to tell the keeper, who seemed to see no impropriety
in it, that it was twenty-five years since I had seen an insane man wearing a chain, although I must
have visited fifty thousand lunatics, in all parts of the world, in that interval of time. A little more
than twenty years before I had caused the release from seclusion of a woman at the Tewksbury Almshouse of Massachusetts, whose condition, except the chain, was much like that of the Turkish men
seen by Dr. Earle.

Leaving these scenes, the young voyager returned by
Smyrna and Athens to Malta, where he was forced to a longer
stay than in any of the more famous places of his tour. He
took advantage of this to give his friends fuller details of
his life there than at either Athens and Constantinople.

I had pleasant companions from Smyrna (one of them the Jewish
transmuter of metals), but the sea was tremendously rough after the
calm evening between Scio and Syra. We were six days from that
island to Malta. Syra is one of the Cyclades; and, though we
left it and the other "sick ladies" behind, we had sick gentlemen
enough before we arrived here, on the 7th of January, 1839. We
were making the same voyage (in rather shorter time) that Saint
Paul made when they beat up and down so many days; and I have
since seen the spot where he landed, and where "there came a viper
out of the heat and fastened upon his hand." You know that com-
mentators and others differ in regard to this landing, some maintaining that it was upon Meleda, in the Adriatic, and not this Melita,
that the shipwrecked apostle to the Gentiles found refuge. This
sea is not commonly called "Adria," nor are there venomous
serpents here now; nor were the residents in Paul's time strictly
barbarians, as he calls them. But he may have styled all men "bar-
barous" (jargoning) who did not speak Greek, like himself; and the
poisonous vipers may all have been killed in eighteen hundred years.
At any rate, the weight of argument is in favor of Malta. So I went
to see the pretty, rocky little gulf called St. Paul's Bay. It is on the
northern coast, six or seven miles from the capital, Valetta, the whole
island being but twenty miles long, twelve wide, and sixty in circuit.
A tower and several small houses are at the head of the bay, and a
small stone church stands where the fire and the viper are said to
have been. Its interior is but ordinary. A large but inferior painting of the shipwreck hangs behind the altar, and two others on the
same subject on the side walls. A small image of Christ, crowned
with thorns, stood on one side, in a glazed case, before which a
taper was burning; and engravings of events in his life hung here
and there in the church.

The needful miracle ascribed to saintly presence is shown at
another church of Saint Paul, in Città Notabile, where the sacristan
lighted torches and led the way, downstairs and through a dark alley,

into the Grotto of Saint Paul, a circular cave hewn in the island rock, twenty-five or thirty feet in diameter, and, in the centre, eight feet high. A marble statue of Paul stands there ; and tradition says that he and Saint Luke, with Trophimius, lived here for three months. Consequently, the sacristan told us, though whole ship-loads of the rock have been carried away from this cave, its dimensions remain unchanged, the rock supplying by growth the loss of its surface. He then beat off a few pieces with his pickaxe, and gave them to us, saying that they would cure the bite of a viper or other venomous thing, if rubbed on the bite at once, "provided you only have sufficient faith."   Another grotto where miracles of an earlier faith were wrought is that of Calypso, at the foot of a hill in which are many other small grots, mostly now used as houses or store-houses by peasants. I visited it, and found a spring of clear water running through this cave of Calypso (Homer speaks of four fountains) and thence into a large basin, from which it is drawn out to fertilize a beautiful garden below. Yet some say Gozo, a few miles away from Malta, was really Calypso's island ; and her grotto is also shown there, which I did not see.   But a recent tourist says it is in a rock overhanging the Bay of Ramla, with a very narrow entrance, quite too small for a goddess, and, in his opinion, "a very safe retreat for a company of foxes." I must therefore believe that the Maltese cavern was that which the old Greek fox, Ulysses, inhabited for a time.   Byron thought so, too, and places here the scene of that leap which Telemachus took, at the suggestion of Mentor and Féne-lon ; but he lets us choose either island : —

> But not in silence pass Calypso's isles,
>   The sister tenants of the middle deep :
> There for the weary still a haven smiles,
>   Though the fair goddess long hath ceased to weep,
>   And o'er her cliffs a fruitless watch to keep'
> For him who dared prefer a mortal bride. ·
>   Here, too, his boy essayed the dreadful leap
> Stern Mentor urged from high to yonder tide,—
> While, thus of both bereft, the nymph-queen doubly sighed.*

It is supposed that Malta furnishes 700 species of indigenous plants.   Dr. Zerafa in his botanical treatise names 644.   Were

---

* Childe Harold, Canto II. xxix.   In the verse following this Byron bestows the name of Calypso on Lady Spencer, under the designation of "Fair Florence" ; and this episode in his voyage up the Mediterranean was perhaps his only reason for placing Calypso in Malta. Homer's geography, as we all know, was strictly poetical and ideal ; but a recent writer (S. Butler) puts Calypso west of Sicily.

it not that the earth produces two or three crops in a year, so large a population as 120,000 could not be supported here. Frost is never seen, and, though there are hail-storms, snow never falls. In summer it rarely rains. The sirocco, which blows most in early autumn, is oppressive to foreigners, especially the consumptive, who often come here from England. John Hookham Frere, the poet and translator, has lived here for his health since 1816. The language of the Maltese is, like the Albanian, unwritten. Some Greek asked an Albanian the history of his alphabet. "It was written on a cabbage-leaf," was the answer; "and an ass came by, and ate it up." Italian is used in the courts; and English, which was introduced in 1800, when the island was captured from the French, is in the schools, and becoming more and more universal. The costumes are peculiar; and the top-hat is in disfavor, as generally in the Orient. When the English hat first went to Damascus, the people disliked it so much that they have since spoken of an Englishman as "Aboo-tanjara," "the father of a pot." The poorer peasants seldom wear shoes: if they have a pair, they keep them for great occasions. A woman was overheard the other day to ask her companion how long she had owned her shoes. "Since the year of the plague," was the answer; that is, 1813!

There are more than one thousand ordained priests and friars in Malta, and nearly three thousand *abbati* are preparing for ordination. When we visited Città Vecchia (the same as Notabile), it is no exaggeration to say that a majority of those we met in the streets were either priests or beggars. Several monasteries are here, the most remarkable being that of the Capuchins, in which, when a monk dies, he is dried, dressed up in his robes, and set in a niche until his bones fall apart, the skulls being afterwards ranged in rows along the ceiling of the Carneria, or charnel-house.

At our lazzaretto the three weeks of quarantine * passed off rapidly. We had accommodations in a splendid fortress. My room-mate was a Swiss merchant, several years resident in Naples,—a man of thirty-

---

* It is to be remarked that the rules of quarantine had long been observed at Malta; for, when George Sandys, traveller and poet, was there in 1610, he came near encountering the same seclusion which Dr. Earle underwent in 1839. It was in June that this early voyager put into the harbor of Valetta, and, not being allowed to land in the city, for fear of infection, had this adventure: "I was left alone on a naked promontory, right against the city, remote from the concourse of people, without provision, and not knowing how to dispose of myself. At length a little boat made towards me, rowed by an officer appointed to attend on strangers that had no *pratique*, lest others should receive infection, who carried me into the hollow hanging of a rock, where I was for the night to take up my lodging, and the day following to be conveyed by him into the Lazzaretto, there to remain

five, and a pleasant companion. We talked and read and wrote, and
walked and laughed and smoked *à la Turque*, and told stories and
conundrums and enigmas and anagrams, and picked flowers and
collected shells, and ate oranges at four cents a dozen, and glorious
musk-melons, as cheap as need be; and thus the time slipped by
swiftly and pleasantly. Nor did we play it all away, as you might
infer from the above. For, aside from some reading, my comrade
wrote letters in such abundance that I find paper is more than twice
as dear here as in Paris, and made figures without number; while
I, besides a medical essay for Dr. Roeser to present in my name to
the Medical Society of Athens, translated and wrote out the translation of two hundred and eighty pages of a medical work, which I in-
tend to have published, if some one does not get the start of me.
There are more than nine hundred pages in all, and I mean to
finish it before reaching America.

Nor were we two alone in our prison enjoyments. (I say prison
because we were limited to a part of the space enclosed by the
fortress walls, about an acre of ground; and yet on that acre I
found no less than sixteen species of wild flowers in blossom in this
month of January.) Among our companions were a Greek merchant
and his wife, on their way to the island of Gerby on the coast of
Biledulgerid, where he has a sponge-fishery, with forty divers engaged
in plunging after sponges, as they do at Kalymnos near Syria. The
best sponge-fishers can stay three minutes under water. Then we
had a young Greek, going to Toulon by order of King Otho, to learn
in the navy-yard there what Peter the Great did at Saardam. The
five persons named, including me, clubbed together, hired a man-
servant, cooking utensils, etc., and lived *chez nous* as snugly as need
be. At any early hour in the morning the servant brought us, each
one in his chamber, a cup of black coffee,— a luxury which the
Americans have yet to learn to appreciate. At ten A.M. we all

thirty or forty days, before I could be admitted into the city. But the Great Master the next morning,
as he sate in council, granted me *pratique*. So I came into the city, and was kindly entertained for
three weeks' space, where with much contentment I remained."

What Sandys saw of the inhabitants and their then rulers, the Knights of St. John, may be quoted
in contrast with Dr. Earle's observations. He found but some twenty thousand people on the island,
and says: "The Maltese are little less tawny than the Moors, especially those of the country, who go
half-clad, and are indeed a miserable people; but the citizens are altogether Frenchified, the Great
Master and major part of the knights being Frenchmen. Their markets they keep on Sundays.
They stir early and late, in regard of the immoderate heat, and sleep at noonday. Their country is no
other than a rock covered over with earth, but two feet deep where deepest. The soil produceth
no grain but barley. Bread made of it, with olives, is the villagers' ordinary diet. The inhabitants
die more with age than diseases."

assembled in the apartment of the Greek, and breakfasted on bread
and butter and *café au lait*. (This, by the way, our countrymen
never will make good until they *brown* the coffee instead of burning
it, boil the milk, and sweeten with loaf-sugar.) I took tea with our
former consul in Malta yesterday. They had brown sugar on the
table, the first time I have seen any since I left New York.

At four P.M. we dined in quarantine, always having four changes,—
(1) soup, (2 and 3) two different kinds of meat, and (4) dessert,
consisting of cheese, oranges, raisins, melons, almonds, etc. Poor
Life Harrud [Eliphalet Harwood, of Leicester], when he said, " I hain't
come to broth yit," had yet to learn that soup is as needful at the
dinner of a European as potatoes to an Irishman, I might say to
an American. After finishing our meal, we went upstairs, and ended
by smoking a pipe, drinking a cup of Turkish coffee, etc. I will
give you a recipe for making coffee *à la Turque*. Take your own
coffee-pot when you have done breakfast, and nothing will run from
the spout but grounds mixed with a little liquid. Then seek the
smallest earthen salt-cellar you can find or, what is nearer the thing,
a cup in an infant's set of miniature dishes. Pour the cup or salt-
cellar two-thirds full of said liquid, and it is ready for use. Only be
very careful not to put in any sugar.*

We came out of quarantine January 27, five days ago ; and I have
been working a great part of the time since,— writing, reading,
translating, and packing shells. Mr. Eynard, our former consul
here, with whom I took tea, lives in a house where there is as much
space, I think, as in our whole Leicester house in a single room.
It is certainly as high,— an old palace, built by a member of the celebrated order of the Knights of St. John of Jerusalem, who were ex-
pelled from Malta by Napoleon in 1798. Mr. Eynard has introduced
me at an extensive library and reading-room of the English, where I
have brought myself up even with the times, having fallen a month
or two behind in crossing the line between Western and Eastern
Europe. A vessel arrived January 31 from Boston in thirty-six days,
having left that city the day I left Constantinople (December 26).
It brought files of several Boston papers to our present consul, a

---

* This is scarcely just to the present mode of making that favorite beverage of the Greeks and
Armenians as well as the Turks. Indeed, Turkish coffee is now served at the best hotels in South-
eastern Europe, and is sipped by the tourists of all nations with gusto, except, possibly, by the
French. The young physician had lived so long in Paris, to which he was now returning for a month,
that he was impatient of any but the French cookery. Much sugar is now served with these tiny
cups of Turkish coffee, and the making of it is a part of the economy of the humblest Greek cabin.

Mr. Andrews; and I have been looking them over to-day. It is quite reviving to get news so fresh from a place so near home. I send you from here a half-barrel filled with straw and other natural curiosities. All the shells not marked are from Smyrna. You will perceive there are some from Marathon, the Acropolis, etc., valuable, from their locality, as mementos.

Dr. Earle's tour in the Levant ended at Malta. It had occupied less than four months, and was never repeated. Yet no portion of his extensive travels seems to have given him greater pleasure. It was one of the dreams of his later life to go round the world from California, and approach Egypt, Syria, and Greece from the Orient; but this plan was given up in consequence of the death of his proposed companion.

The Insane in Malta.

After visiting asylums for the insane in Milan, Venice, and Constantinople, Dr. Earle gave some attention to the insane in Malta, where in 1839 he reported 130 lunatics in a population of 120,000. "The asylum for their reception and treatment," he says, "is at Floriana, in the suburbs of Valetta. The building is old and very incommodious. Baths have recently been constructed. In 1812 the use of chains — those implements of confinement and torture, fit only for wild beasts — was entirely abolished. The patients have ever been, and still are, mingled together, irrespective of stage or intensity of disease. A division of the incurable from the curable is about to be made. Most of the patients are remarkably quiet. Many died of Asiatic cholera in the summer of 1837. The superintendent could not tell me the precise proportion of cures effected here, but thinks it exceeds 50 per cent. The number seen was 90, — 40 men and 50 women, — the proportion of women to men insane in Malta being usually as 3 to 2. A very large proportion perform manual labor. The principal employments are gardening, sewing, knitting, spinning, and domestic affairs. Of three yards adjacent to the building, one is planted with orange-trees, another is a kitchen garden cultivated by the patients." It is doubtful if any other American physician ever inspected the Valetta Asylum in the sixty years since elapsed.

CHAPTER VI

DR. EARLE had now completed his medical studies begun at Providence six years earlier, and finished by a few weeks at Paris after his return from Malta and Italy in the spring of 1839. He was in his thirtieth year, had made the grand tour in a fashion of his own, and had begun those special studies concerning insanity which were to occupy the next half-century of his professional life. With these qualifications and experiences, he returned from Europe; and, after a visit to his mother, sisters, and brothers at Leicester and Worcester, he established himself as a physician in Philadelphia, where his brother Thomas had long been in practice as a lawyer. From an essay published some years later, we may learn something of the general average of medical knowledge and practice where Dr. Earle began his professional career, and in the years from 1837 to 1844.

My medical education was received at the school in which Dr. Benjamin Rush had been a professor; and, along with respect, esteem, and affection for the professors at whose feet I sat, I imbibed reverence for Dr. Rush. But his theories of the pathology and his principles of the therapeutics of insanity, and the inconsistencies into which these led him, did not die with their originator. His " Medical Enquiries and Observations" has had a circulation among American physicians more extensive than that of the works of all other authors upon mental disorders. These theories and principles, and the method of treatment recommended by him (frequent and copious bleeding), are still to a very considerable extent in vogue over a vast extent of inland territory in America; and the professor of the practice of medicine in our largest medical school inculcates that method of treatment and its supporting theories. It is not a fact, therefore, that in America Dr. Rush is "almost without

a follower," nor that his arguments have lost their force and authority. When physicians having the care of the insane began to de-
nounce venesection, they were confronted by what was considered
the paramount authority of Dr. Rush. They were told, "You crazy
doctors ride hobbies," as if Dr. Rush were not as liable to hobby-
riding as Dr. Ray or Dr. Bell. No individual authority could overcome the far-prevailing (but, happily, not, as formerly, the all-per-
vading) influence of Rush in the United States. Even in England
his theories still live, according to Dr. Munro, who in 1856 said:
"The term 'mania' has become inveterately associated, among practitioners of the old school (many of whom still exist), with a strength
to be pulled down,— a disease requiring antiphlogistic treatment.
He bleeds, he blisters, he purges, and finds the fury mitigated for a
time. Therefore, this practitioner says again, 'Mania must result
from excess of power.'" I believe that Dr. Rush's theories are annually consigning hundreds prematurely to the grave, and hundreds
more to premature insanity; while the book which inculcates them is
not only extant, but probably to be found in more libraries than all
other books on the same subject."

Although these remarks, made in 1857, relate to one special
form of disease with which Dr. Earle had then become very
familiar by long observation, it is almost equally true that
"heroic" treatment was the rule in ordinary practice. We
have seen with what surprise Dr. Earle noted the small amount
of drugs given in doses by the French hospital physicians.
This was because medical science — never very complete —
was exceedingly imperfect sixty years ago in America as compared with its present state. In 1839, when he opened a general office in Philadelphia, a considerable revolt had broken out
in New England and other parts of the country against the
extreme use of mercury, then very common; and the homœopathists, of whom Dr. Earle heard for the first time in a practical way at Paris, soon made their crusade throughout the
Northern States against the use of large doses in general. Dr.
Earle was never the first to innovate on the professional practice of his day; but, on the other hand, he was firm and conscientious in the support of what he believed to be for the good

of patients. And it is probable that he was drawn from general practice into the specialty in which he became so distinguished by his perception of the good field it offered for improving the traditional usages, without shocking too much the professional body of which he was a young and unknown member. At any rate, he had not long been at work in Philadelphia before he was asked to take a place as physician in the small hospital for the insane maintained by the Quakers of that vicinity, and known as "The Friends' Retreat," at Frankford, now a part of the great city of Penn and Franklin. He began his service there in the summer of 1840; and one of his first experiences led him to a cardinal principle in the care of the insane,— not to deceive them nor allow others to do so. Writing to his Leicester family (Sept. 30, 1840), he says : —

We have a C. E. here from Maryland, who, in homely phrase, is "crazy as a loon," but improving rapidly. When she arrived, her husband, a brother, and two sisters came with her. After a while we walked out into the garden, C. walking with me. While I amused her, these relatives slipped away, and were off before she was aware of it. For a month afterwards she believed that I had ordered her friends to be murdered, and, having assumed the name of her husband, was making pretensions to her hand. Finally, this delusion was removed by the receipt of letters (written at my request) from all those who came with her. Never again shall I insist on detaining a patient by deception or stratagem. It shall be straightforward work.

It was fortunate for the young alienist that he could begin his real life-work in a small asylum like that of his own religious society and among persons naturally inclined to favor his efforts. Frankford was thus to him a preparatory school, in which he learned, without too much controversy or publicity, what to do and what to avoid. Nor was his time too fully occupied to forbid his lecturing on scientific, literary, and general topics. This he did often and to general acceptance. He won some local applause also as a poet and a contributor to the magazines of that early day, the *Knickerbocker* of New

York, and the venture which that brilliant, erratic genius,
Edgar Poe, was then first making in Philadelphia.   Oct. 15,
1840, Dr. Earle says : —

I have written several pieces this summer, which I would send to
thee [his sister Eliza] if I had time to copy them in an easy position.
[He was ill from blood-poisoning in consequence of an autopsy at
the Retreat.]   I will copy one, which I think a little posterior to the
others, the "Soliloquy of an Octogenarian." * . . .

> 'Tis nearly past, this fitful dream
> Whose phantoms gladden to deceive, etc.

Edgar A. Poe, formerly editor of the *Southern Literary Messenger*,
is about to commence a journal similar to the *Knickerbocker* in
Philadelphia.   I have sent this piece to him, and have received an
answer, in which he says the lines are "beautiful," and "shall
certainly appear in the first number."   Another of the cast-off scoriæ
of my brain is an "Address to a Flower," brought from Mars' Hill,
in this measure : —

> Bright flower of the Orient, bathed in the dyes
> That crimson the vault of Hellenean skies,
> Fanned by zephyrs which over Pentelicus blew,
> And nurtured by drops of Hymettean dew,
> Or by vapors, perchance, on the breeze wafted o'er
> From the Hieron Helian of old Epidaure.†

I have forwarded it to the *Knickerbocker*.

This poem came out in the volume printed by Dr. Earle in
1841, entitled "Marathon, and Other Poems," where it begins
page 104.   The verses "To my Mother," at page 86 of the
same volume, were those which appeared in the *Knickerbocker*
of July, 1840, and were written at Passignanò in Italy, in 1839.
Poe wrote to Dr. Earle, Oct. 10, 1840, from Philadelphia, in a
beautiful hand, thus : —

Dear Sir,— Your kind letter dated the 2d inst. was postmarked
the 8th, and I have only this morning received it.   I hasten to thank

---

* Published in "Marathon, and Other Poems," Philadelphia, 1841.

† These Grecian place-names are brought in to give the right Attic flavor to the lines; and the fact
that Pentelicus is east-north-east from the Areopagus would not hinder the south-west wind (zephyr)

you for the interest you have taken in my contemplated magazine, and for the beautiful lines "By an Octogenarian." They shall certainly appear in the first number. You must allow me to consider such offerings, however, as anything but "unsubstantial encouragement." Believe me that good poetry is far rarer, and therefore far more acceptable to the publisher of a journal, than even that *rara avis*, money itself.

Should you be able to aid my cause in Frankford by a good word with your neighbors, I hope that you will be inclined to do so. Much depends upon the list I may have before the first of December. I send you a prospectus, believing that the objects set forth in it are, upon the whole, such as your candor will approve.

Very truly and respectfully,

Yr. ob. st.,

Dr. Pliny Earle.   EDGAR A. POE.

The name of this long-expected journal, whose first number never appeared, was to be *The Penn Magazine.* It was first announced June 13, 1840, as to come out the next January, then deferred to March 1, 1841, and then given up entirely, Poe taking charge of *Graham's Magazine* instead. The *Penn* was to be monthly, to publish a thousand pages a year, in two volumes; and its price was five dollars a year. Its chief object was given as "an absolutely independent criticism," and this was to be something unique and not yet seen,—

Yielding no point either to the vanity of the author, or to the assumptions of antique prejudice, or to the involute and anonymous cant of the quarterlies, or to the arrogance of those organized cliques, which, hanging on like nightmares upon American literature, manufacture, at the nod of our principal booksellers, a pseudo-public opinion by wholesale.

These were brave words, and Dr. Earle waited for six months to see them fulfilled. Then he gathered up his early and later verses into a volume, as mentioned, and dealt no

---

from blowing "over Pentelicus" *after* fanning the poet's flower, which was a scarlet anemone. "Epidaure" is the French version of that Hieron of Æsculapius near the old town of Epidauros on the coast of Argolis, a short sail from Athens,—called "Helian," I fancy, from the commingling of Apollo and his mythical son, who was nursed by goats on the mountain overlooking the temple.

more with Mr. Poe.   His verses in the July *Knickerbocker*
(then edited by Lewis Gaylord Clarke) had brought him a new
acquaintance at the inopportune time of sickness, which had
delayed the posting of his "Soliloquy" to Poe.   He thus notes
the fact (Oct. 15, 1840) :--

Yesterday Thomas Wright, a Hicksite, formerly of New York
City, but now of Hudson, came to see me with a letter of introduction
from J. Turnpenny.   He found me *en déshabille parfaite*, with a
cotton shirt on, the left sleeve and side of which were saturated with
blood and lead-water, the bedclothes in very similar condition (my
bed not having been made, my hands and face not washed, nor even
my head combed for sixty hours), with two nurses working over me,
and forty leeches filling themselves at my arm.   He stayed a few
minutes, talked a little, seemed as kind and familiar as if we had
been acquainted forty years, and then left.   I wondered what the
man came for, and to-day have had an explanation from J. Turnpenny, who heard of my serious illness and called to see me.   Last
summer he was at the house of Wright, in Hudson, just after the
Knickerbocker with my verses came out.   Wright was "very much
taken" with the stanzas, and wondered who Pliny Earle was.
Turnpenny informed him.   And now, being this way on business, as
I presume, he took the opportunity of seeing me.   During our
interview he said nothing about poetry; but, after going back to
town, he told J. T. "to thank Pliny Earle for me for writing that
piece, and say to him that I have taken one verse of it,

> Thou whose locks are hoary, etc.,

to myself."   I wish the author were half as good as a perusal of that
piece would lead people to suspect.

This brief comment on an incident so flattering to an author's
vanity illustrates Dr. Earle's view of his literary work.   He
desired it to have an instructive and moral effect, or else he
wrote merely for the entertainment of readers easily amused.
His true vocation was something different; and, after a few
years, he gave up literature.   Phrenology went the same way,
but after a longer interval; for, as already intimated, Dr. Earle

had taken much interest in that queer half-science, now gone to decay. Early in 1842 he wrote : —

The examination of Stephen Earle's head and of mine, by L. N. Fowler did more to convince me of the practical utility of phrenology — not to say of its truth as a science — than anything else that I ever saw, read, or heard. Stephen was told what I believe he might have been rather than what he is. But, for myself, I doubt if any of my nearest relatives or most intimate friends could have given a more accurate synopsis of my character. Dr. Barber * could titillate the ears of his audience, and talk most eloquently of "the sensible fibres of the corporeal organization," "the infinitesimal corpuscles constituting the basis of the wonderful temple of the human economy," of the "transcendental, heaven-born, heaven-bound ethereal essence, which, under the diverse modifications of the superior sentiments, elevates man above the brutes that perish"; he can recite

> Roll on, thou deep and dark blue Ocean,— roll!

and "Ha-a-a-ail ho-o-o-oly Light!" but, as for the power of appreciating character by the craniological developments, he had hardly a tittle.

In describing one of Dr. Earle's confused patients at Frankford, phrenology comes in : —

He is unsettled, restless, and constantly worrying about something. His Conscientiousness thinks that the buttons of his vest, which are covered with plain black "lasting," are too gay. His Reverence is in an inexplicable quandary in regard to a copy of Scott's Family Bible, which it and Acquisitiveness procured. After the purchase, Reverence, reading the commentary, became dissatisfied, and openly promulgated dissatisfaction. Hereupon Destructiveness advised to burn the book. "That would be a wise expedient for the commentary," remarked Reverence; "but for the text it would be sacrilegious, and to separate them is impossible." Benevolence, hearing this colloquy, proposed to give the book away. "And contaminate

---

* This was a rhetorical Briton, who made a figure in Boston and Cambridge, for a time, by his recitations, readings, and, finally, by lecturing on phrenology. The brothers Fowler were very different persons,— shrewd and gifted in Hogarth's art, "to see the manners in the face."

somebody else, eh?" cried Reverence, holding up both hands in astonishment. At this point Secretiveness whispered that, if he had the management, he would box the book up, and hide it among the lumber of the garret. "And thus contaminate posterity," exclaimed Reverence and Philoprogenitiveness, simultaneously. Here the consultation ended, and poor Reverence can see no way out of the dilemma. Acquisitiveness and Conscientiousness have long been in combat. The former came into possession of some notes of hand, and, on the day they were to be renewed, sat down composedly to cast compound interest on the several sums. At this moment Conscientiousness came in, declaring that Acquisitiveness was doing wrong. "Bigot!" cried Acquisitiveness: "you are always meddling with other people's affairs." "But you outrage justice," said Conscientiousness, in a tone that showed he was spurred on by his neighbor, Firmness. "Grumble and growl away," retorted Acquisitiveness. "I shall stick to my text, and pocket the compound interest." The field was won by the last speaker. Conscientiousness retreated, but has kept up a kind of predatory warfare ever since.

This is a good account, in the jargon of that day, of the divided mind of many insane persons. As for the intricate problems of mind and matter, which even the casual study of insanity calls up for solution, we find this utterance of Dr. Earle, after the preliminary years of his life in asylums: —

The longer I live, the more am I impressed with a belief in the all-controlling supremacy of mind over matter, of the far-reaching, mysterious power of the divine intelligence within, and of the limited bounds of present knowledge, compared with what is to be known when mind shall have thrown off its fetters of clay. Science is proud, even presumptuous; but how much cause for humility in the fact that it cannot trace one particle of its knowledge upward, through effects, to the original cause and centre of all things! Science is lost at once in the mazes of uncertainty and ignorance, whenever it attempts to fathom mind itself.

Early in 1844 Dr. Earle gave up his prefatory work in Philadelphia, and entered on his more public career by taking charge for five years of the New York Asylum for the Insane

at Bloomingdale, a large and wealthy foundation for the care
and cure of insanity, which had been receiving patients ever
since 1821. In course of his life there he had much to do with
settling the family affairs at Leicester, which are mentioned in
the following letter from his mother. She wrote him from
Mulberry Grove on his thirty-sixth birthday, when she was
seventy-five years old.

LEICESTER, 12 mo., 31, 1845.

Dear Son,— "Procrastination is the thief of time." I have neglected answering thy agreeable and obliging letter for no other
reason than what is contained in the above often quoted adage, and
my seeming inability to write, arising from such a total disuse of a
pen, and want of energy sufficient to make a beginning.

We are all in about our usual state of health. Jonah, I think, is
better this winter than he has been for the same length of time for
several years. He makes himself quite useful at the barn, is going
to-night to help the Methodists watch the old year out and the new
one in. Thy Uncle Jonah is quite sick, has been pretty much confined to his bed for two weeks; and there seems little probability of
his recovery at his advanced age.

With regard to the business thou wrote about, I should be exceedingly glad to have it settled; and I see no prospect of any other way
but for thee to do it, and for myself it matters but very little how.
I feel entirely willing it should be done in a way that thou would
not be much of a loser, and, if thou couldst come and attend to it
thyself, should be very glad to see thee, and shall be perfectly willing to arrange the business in a way that appears to be right, and
that will be satisfactory to thee. We have paid out a great deal for
repairs, etc., besides the debt to Waldo. But I feel very desirous to
see it settled, and shall consider it a great favor for thee to do it.

There are some other things that I want to consult about; and I
feel as though they ought to be seen to before it is too late, and very
sensibly feel that whatever I do must of necessity be done soon. So
that, if thou canst make it at all consistent with thy employment to
come, I should feel very glad and greatly obliged; and I think we
may get our matters satisfactorily arranged, and so as to be a great
relief to my mind.

Since writing the above, I have received thy letter, and think

the way thou proposes may likely be the best. I have long
thought that there might be a part of the land sold off, to good
advantage, at some future time. If thou should conclude to come,
please to let us know when.

We are in hopes thy Uncle Jonah is getting better, though he is
very weak, and it will be hard for him to regain his strength.

They have been making a survey for a railroad from Worcester to
Barre, and past between Amos's factory and William's. Please to
write soon.   Thy affectionate mother,

                                        PATIENCE EARLE.

This epistle verifies the character given of Mrs. Earle by her
son,—affectionate, sensible, and patient, with no remarkable
gift of expression, but much perception and practical faculty.
Her son Jonah, here mentioned, was the youngest of her nine
children, and, except Sarah Hadwen, the earliest to die. He
was odd and not brilliant, but noted for occasional turns of wit,
and with the family admiration for beauty.

CHAPTER VII

SELDOM has a specialist in the care of the insane been more carefully and gradually trained for that difficult work than was Dr. Earle. His graduating thesis at Philadelphia in 1837 was on the general subject of Insanity, in regard to which he had been frequently an observer of the treatment of patients by Dr. S. B. Woodward at the Massachusetts Lunatic Hospital in Worcester. This gentleman, "whose affable manners and enthusiasm in his work," says Dr. Earle, "were well calculated to fascinate a neophyte in the profession," was long at the head of the Worcester Hospital, and ranks high among the earlier specialists of America. A part of Dr. Earle's thesis was published in the *American Journal of the Medical Sciences*, (to which he contributed for nearly half a century) in August, 1838, under the too comprehensive title of "The Causes, Duration, Termination, and Moral Treatment of Insanity," neither of which divisions of the subject could be very well known to the medical student at that early date; but the statistics involved in the treatise were then more numerous than any collection of them before published in the United States. In this, the peculiar field of Dr. Earle as a theorizer on Insanity, he was thus at work betimes; and he was one of the first to see that any useful theory must have careful statistics for its basis. He showed this demonstratively in his "History of the Bloomingdale Asylum," published in 1848,—a volume containing statistical records of all the cases received there from the opening of that New York asylum in 1821 to the close of 1844. These were thoroughly analyzed, and so presented as to lead easily to general conclusions, towards which Dr. Earle was working his way by close and systematic observation of his patients.

Examples of his method and results may be given. When he

took charge of patients at Frankford, the great authority of
Dr. Rush, as before intimated, had begun to wane after half
a century, and there were sceptics who questioned the Rush
specific of bleeding the insane ; but this practice was still much
in vogue at Frankford, though not so universally as Rush had
urged.   Head-shaving, blistering, or liberal cupping of the
scalp were also often prescribed by the visiting physicians,
whose authority was greater than that of the young resident.
Dr. Earle soon convinced himself that such treatment did more
harm than good, and never prescribed it.   At Bloomingdale he
followed the same safe course, rarely using venesection there,
and never cupping the scalp.   When, finally, he wrote an essay
on the subject, his own observations confirmed the great
authorities he cited against bleeding.   His studies of the
rapidity of pulse in the insane were pursued for years at Frankford and Bloomingdale, and his essays, when published, carried
conviction.   At that time (before 1846) an extract of *Conium
maculatum* was very extensively used upon the insane, but its
precise results were in doubt.   In order to learn, by actual
experiment, both the effect of this drug and the comparative
strength of the American and English preparations of it, Dr.
Earle himself took a succession of constantly enlarging doses,
and thus learned experimentally that it did not have the effect
generally ascribed to it.   From the first he had relied on moral
treatment rather than on drugs and mechanical aids ; and,
though he found that invention of professional indolence, the
"tranquillizing chair," in use both at Frankford and Bloomingdale,— together with muffs, wristers, and other leathern inducements to quiet, which the attendants employed freely in order
to remain quiet themselves,— he soon diminished their use
or entirely abolished them.   Of course, those abominations
of water-torture which he had seen used in Paris * he never
employed, any more than the primitive restraining apparatus of
Constantinople.   But he addressed himself to the mind and
moral sense of his patients, introducing lectures and scientific
experiments (for the first time in America) and soon a school
of instruction for the patients.   This he established at Bloom-

* See pages 94 and 137; also the Appendix.

ingdale in the autumn of 1845, and found it of much value in
many ways. His invention has since been rediscovered in many
asylums, and sometimes vaunted by more recent experts as
their own invention.

Of the impression made by Dr. Earle on his associates in the
slow and difficult task of improving the treatment of the insane,
whether rich or poor, in America, I find a striking evidence in
a letter from Dr. Edward Jarvis, of Concord, who took the first
census of the insane and idiotic in Massachusetts (and up to
this time the most complete one) in 1854. A few years later
(April, 1857) he thus wrote to Dr. Earle, then living in retirement at Leicester, and giving some aid to Judge Washburn in
his preparation of a history of that town : —

You have never been forgotten or ignored by me since I first had
the pleasure of meeting you at your asylum (Frankford) in August,
1842. Your reception of me was then very cordial, and left a very
happy and abiding impression on my mind. I had been long living
beyond the mountains in Louisville, Ky. Homesick and disheart-
ened, I returned, hoping to meet those who cared for the things that
had interested me in Massachusetts. Fortunately, I went to Philadelphia on my way, and saw you. Your greetings and Dr. Kirkbride's revived me. You were both strangers to my eye, but not to
my sympathies ; for you gave me that cordial sympathy that I had
been longing for through the five years of my dwelling in the West.
From that moment I felt restored to my Eastern home. You gave
me a copy of your "Visit to Thirteen Asylums," and I read and enjoyed it. It opened my eyes to a larger field, for which I had been
yearning.

Dr. Earle was indeed fitted by nature and experience to introduce new methods, and recall men from tradition and routine
to the teachings of kindly observation and plain good sense.
Never too forward in seeking innovation, he based it on his
own observation and the authority of men who had tested their
own work ; and he never fell back from experience thus gained,
whatever might be the popular or the professional delusion of
the moment. Coming to a profession much devoted to those
false objects of worship named by Bacon "idols of the cave"

and "idols of the forum," he had the advantage of entering late, when his judgment was matured and his knowledge of practical affairs (as we have seen) was much greater than that of the city-bred medical student. He belonged to a body of Christians, also, who looked with cool and searching eyes at most of the shams and hypocrisies of modern life, and sought their guidance from within rather than from without. Yet this freedom of mind was tempered by a moderation that seldom gave offence to prejudice, and by a real respect for the thoughts and feelings of others. As Burke said of Fox, "To his great understanding he joined the utmost degree of moderation, was of the most artless, candid, open, and benevolent disposition, and without one drop of gall in his composition." He also deserved that term and that definition given by Hazlitt to one of his characters : "He was by nature a gentleman, by which I mean that he had a certain deference and respect for the person of every man."

How foreign this often is to the New England nature need not here be insisted on ; nor how often, even when beset by ill-health and misconstrued in his action and motive, Dr. Earle rose above the influence of his locality. Seldom, indeed, do we see the child of nature and the man of the world, simplicity, experience, and urbanity, so mingled as they were in him. If this laid him open to attack and to those wounds which selfishness inflicts on sensibility, his fund of benevolence and good sense soon healed the hurts which arrogance and exposed imposture might make. Nor is it common to find persons so capable of keen mental vision both at long and short range — so telescopic and so microscopic — as he was. Both kinds of vision are needed in the patient investigation of truth, especially in the care of the insane.

When Dr. Earle took charge of the Bloomingdale Asylum in the city of New York, it had existed for nearly twenty-three years, and contained little more than 100 patients. It had received in that period about 2,150 patients, at the rate of about 90 a year ; but these had been admitted 2,937 times,— that is, there were nearly 800 more cases than persons under treatment. This fact early called Dr. Earle's attention to the

fallacy which he afterwards so thoroughly exposed,— founding
a percentage of recoveries on the *cases* rather than the *persons*.
He also saw the necessity of sifting out the inebriates from the
actually insane, and of not confounding, as so many of his colleagues did, temporary sobriety with restored sanity.   Among
the 2,150 persons who had been received at Bloomingdale, 322,
or more than one-seventh, came as inebriates, and had 594 admissions, or more than one-fifth of all admissions.   They also
made more than 500 "recoveries," and some of them were
received a dozen times in the twenty-three years.   Of 1,841
persons really insane when admitted (2,308 cases), the recoveries were, in all but 726, at the asylum, though 18 more
recovered after discharge, so that the percentage of actual
recovery in twenty-six years, based on persons, not cases, was
but 40, while of these more than 105 relapsed, many of whom
died insane.   The permanent recoveries, therefore, were less
than 34 per cent. (about one-third of all admitted); and even
this small proportion has not been maintained in the State of
New York — and probably not elsewhere — in the half-century
that has since elapsed.   At the beginning of 1844, when New
York (the State) had a population of about 2,500,000, and the
city had about 350,000, there were but 751 patients in all the
insane asylums then existing.   Three years later they had
increased to 1,125.   There are now (January, 1898) nearly
22,000, though the population has only increased to about
7,000,000.   Permanent recoveries in the mass of the New York
City insane are now less than 15 per cent., and in the State at
large not above 20 per cent., so that the recovery rate has
greatly declined in the half-century following Dr. Earle's retirement from the Bloomingdale Asylum, which took place
early in 1849.

For this decline in the recoveries many causes have been
alleged, and many have doubtless existed.   But it was Dr.
Earle's opinion — resulting from his personal experience in
small hospitals and in larger ones — that one great cause was
the increasing size of such establishments, which practically
forbade that best form of treatment which he and his earlier
colleagues, Brigham of Utica, Ray of Providence, Bell at the

McLean Asylum near Boston, Todd and Butler at Hartford,
and Kirkbride at Philadelphia (all in small asylums), could give
with favorable results.   He never abandoned this opinion,
which led him, in his later years, into some controversy with
those of his specialty who had yielded to the apparent demand
for huge asylums under the name of "hospitals," reaching
now in some American instances the monstrous total of 2,300
inmates, and in the London County Asylum of more than
4,000.   Speaking at Boston in 1868 before the Massachusetts
Medical Society, he said : —

I desire here to quote from myself an opinion published in 1852,
after an examination of the German hospitals and a perusal of
much that had been written in Germanic countries: "It appears to
me that the true method in regard to lunatic asylums is this: let no
institution have more than two hundred patients, and let all receive
both curables and incurables in their natural proportion from their
respective districts."   The only modification which I would now
make is an extension of the limit to two hundred and fifty patients,
and this only because of the large proportion of incurables among
the existing insane.   In no other way can the insane be so well and
so effectively treated, and the greatest probability of their restoration
assured.   The superintendent can obtain a sufficiently thorough
knowledge of every patient.   Inspection by him may be frequent, all
details of treatment, medical and moral, may be known to him, and
hence the greatest efficiency secured.   All the labor of which the
patients are capable may be obtained, and a large part of it devoted
to the care of the curable, the sick, and the excited, thus diminishing
the necessity for paid employees.

All these advantages were in fact obtained by Dr. Earle at
Bloomingdale, so far as the social condition of his patients
(mainly from wealthy families, in his time) would permit their
manual employment, in regard to which he held equally positive opinions.   These he was able to carry out at the Northampton Hospital, where he spent the last third of his life,
having spent the first third in preparing himself, by study and
practice of many kinds, to take the best care of the insane.
Just before going to Northampton as superintendent, he de-

livered before the Berkshire Medical School in Pittsfield an
address on "Psychologic Medicine," in which he said:—

Manual labor is universally eulogized as among the most potent
curative means, and yet it is as universally intimated that it is never
required of a patient without his cheerful volition. But there are
some patients — a class of patients — who can be cured by labor,
and apparently by nothing else. If they do not resort to it, they
become apathetic and incurable. Very many have thus died who
might have been cured by labor. In these cases, why is the only
medicament which will effect a cure not prescribed and administered?
If the patient required an emetic, would it not be administered? If
he refused to eat, would he not be fed, if necessary, under coercion?
Yes, drugs and medicine may be forced upon a patient till he becomes a perfect apothecary's shop, and all is right; but an attempt
to force him to the genial, wholesome, and curative exercise of
manual labor is an outrage upon humanity.

No such nonsense disfigured the medical record of Dr. Earle,
and he did not allow a supposed public opinion (probably non-
existent) to prevent him from administering labor as a remedy
and a means of discipline. Whether this had aught to do with
his short term of office at New York I have never heard, but
it is conceivable. By the time he was offered the position at
Northampton, this squeamishness about labor had been overcome, at least for that hospital, the inmates of which were
mostly paupers of foreign parentage then; and he was allowed
to employ them on the large farm to such advantage that, after
the first year, the work done by patients materially reduced the
cost of their support, while it also furnished them with a better
dietary of vegetables, milk, fruit, etc., than most of the other
Massachusetts hospitals enjoyed. To such an extent was this
economy carried, with no stinting of the patients, that this
hospital, which he found in debt, and for which it had been
needful often to ask State appropriations, did, under his long
administration, save from its board-price (fixed by law for the
poor at $3.25 and $3.50 a week) enough to pay extraordinary
expenses in land, buildings, repairs, etc., amounting to some

$200,000. Thus he demonstrated in practice what he taught
in theory at Pittsfield and that of which he was convinced at
Bloomingdale.

Had his five years in Bloomingdale done nothing more than
enable Dr. Earle to publish his account of that asylum's statistical history since 1821, it would have been time well spent;
for in that work he pointed the way to the proper collection
and use of statistics of the insane, in which he has been tardily
followed by other experts, and by whole States and countries.
His standard book on the "Curability of the Insane" was but
the development, for a special purpose, of his system in the
narrower field of the small asylum he was then directing. The
average number of his patients, while at New York, was but
125, and they were more largely of native American parentage
than can now be found in any hospital near a large American
city; nor had the variety of diseases now included under the
loose general term "insanity" become common even in New
York. The first case of paresis (now so painfully common
even in rural asylums) ever described in the United States was
examined and described by Dr. Earle in 1847 at his asylum;
and subsequent observations on this disease were contributed
by him to the *Journal of the Medical Sciences* in 1849 and
1857, his first paper having appeared there in April, 1847.
With his accustomed precision he proposed to call this malady
(known to the French who discovered it as *paralysie générale*)
by the more exact name of "partio-general paralysis"; but
the short Greek term "paresis," generally mispronounced, has
supplanted both names, and the English have even carried
abbreviation so far as to speak of it as "G. P." In after years
Dr. Earle had occasion to see many examples of this disease,
but his first diagnosis is believed to have been in the main confirmed by all his later observation. And this general remark
may hold good of both his periods of executive management
in small asylums, at Frankford and Bloomingdale,—that he
learned therein, at comparative leisure, what he afterwards had
occasion to teach and practise on the much more extensive
arena where he found himself after his second visit to Europe
in 1849. In connection with his duties and his acquired repu-

tation at Bloomingdale, he was in 1847 appointed, without previous notice to himself, one of a board of physicians to visit the
City Lunatic Asylum on Blackwell's Island, which then contained something more than four hundred pauper patients.
The governors of Bloomingdale, however, thought this outside
duty an interference with his regular work in their asylum,
and he made but one official visit to this pauper asylum.
Could he have continued in the position, it is probable that
this fast-growing and usually ill-managed island establishment
would have made a better record for itself. The insane asylums of New York City, and those in Kings County, now
included in Greater New York, have had great need of the
practical sense, the courageous humanity, and the consider-
ate frugality of men like Dr. Earle. After a long period of
neglect and abuse, often exposed, but never sufficiently corrected, they have finally passed under the experienced control
of Dr. P. M. Wise, of the State Lunacy Commission of New
York; and it is hoped that they will now attain a character
worthy of the great city which sends its unfortunates to fill
and overcrowd their wards.

Pliny Earle.

CHAPTER VIII

THE GERMAN ASYLUMS.

NEXT to his later book on Curability, Dr. Earle's chief single work was that which he published in 1853, entitled "Institutions for the Insane in Prussia, Austria, and Germany." It grew out of his observations during a second tour in Europe, in 1849, of which mention has already been made. But he took infinite pains to enlarge and correct those observations by a study of the history, statistics, and general character of each establishment inspected, and as many more which he did not see. In all, during the summer and autumn of 1849 he visited thirty-five establishments in Europe, eight in Great Britain, five in Belgium (including Gheel, not yet reformed by government inspection and control), six in France, seven in Prussian Germany, six in other German States, two in Austria, and finally one in the imperial free city of Frankfort. Few subsequent visitors from America have seen so many, and none, except Mr. William P. Letchworth of New York, has published such valuable and impartial accounts of the European asylums. Nearly fifty years have since passed, and many have been the changes, social, economical, and political, affecting the countries visited and the whole subject of insanity; but Dr. Earle's book of 230 octavo pages has still much value, both from its historical information and the tone of candor and practicality which pervades it. Before its publication German was little studied in the United States. Few young men went to the German universities, and very little was known here of the insane and their treatment in any country where German was the vernacular. Consequently, an important part of human experience on this subject was either wholly unknown or very imperfectly understood; and a wide range was given to that natural and almost national foible of our countrymen,—the fancy that we surpass all the world in enlightenment and

humanity.   Travel and study and the immigration, since
1849, of millions of Germans, have modified all this ; but it is
even now too common for experts in " psychiatry," as the
Germans call the specialty, to neglect the varied and often
admirable German asylums, and the literature of the science,
various, profound, and often most practical in its teachings,
which comes to us from the German-speaking countries, including Austria and Switzerland.   Even in 1849, as Dr. Earle
himself remarked, he found in those countries "a long list of
men eminent in the specialty, who had produced a surprisingly
large amount of published matter, both of speculative research
into the origin and essential nature of insanity and of treatises
on its practical care and recovery."   His personal acquaintances
among the men then eminent included Jacobi, at Siegburg near
Bonn, Damerow, and Laehr at Halle (near which, at Alt-Scherbitz, is now the best of all the German asylums, under the
charge, for nearly twenty years, of Dr. Paetz), Roller at Illenau in Baden, Spurzheim (a cousin of the founder of the
pseudo-science of phrenology, who died in Boston and is buried
at Mt. Auburn), then at Vienna, and Martini at Leubus in Silesia,— all in active service as asylum superintendents, and comparing favorably in knowledge and practical fitness for their
positions with the then prominent alienists of Great Britain and
France.   Indeed, he was himself surprised to find in Germany
" a larger number of institutions, and those in a condition more
advanced, than had been suspected."   Up to that time neither
England, France, nor the United States took much account of
German " psychiatry."   The name was puzzling.   The Germans
were viewed as chiefly idle metaphysicians, verging on infidelity,
and little notice was taken by the self-satisfied Briton or the
roving American of what might be going on among them.   Dr.
Earle observed at the outset of his work :—

With a knowledge of the labors of Pinel and Tuke, we Americans
had pursued our way without the endeavor to push researches
beyond Great Britain and France.   We had the excellent work of
Dr. Jacobi ; * but he was upon the very borders of France, less distant

* Translated into English at the suggestion of Samuel Tuke.

from Paris than Marseilles is. Some volumes of Heinroth, the spiritual Heinroth, leader of the " Psychics " and pupil of Pinel, had found their way, in French, across the Atlantic. Institutions at Schleswig, Pirna, Vienna, and Prague, were incidentally mentioned in English and French publications received here. Dr. Ray has visited Siegburg and Illenau. Further than this we knew but little of the German establishments, had no idea of their condition, and knew not even the existence of most of them, and some of those among their very best.

Dr. Earle seems struck with the fact (which he communicates here and there in his book) that the Saxons were the first reformers of insane asylums in Germany; and they continue in the lead, in spite of the fame of Vienna. Heinroth was a Saxon (born at Leipzig in 1773, died there in 1843). Reil was a Saxon, and established at Halle in 1805 the first periodical devoted to mental disease; and it was in Halle, in 1845, that Dr. Damerow, a Saxon, established and printed the well-known *Journal of Psychiatry and Psycho-legal Medicine*, though for convenience it was published at Berlin by Hirschwald. Two years earlier the Provincial Asylum at Nietleben, near Halle, had been opened under Dr. Damerow (1843), from which in July, 1876, was developed the beginning of the asylum at Alt-Scherbitz. The history of this, the latest development of the Saxon spirit of progress in the care of the insane, has been well set forth by the director of Alt-Scherbitz, Dr. Albrecht Paetz, in his volume of 1893, "The Colonization of the Insane in Connection with the Open-door System." The parent asylum, a mile or two out of Halle, which, when visited by Dr. Earle, six years after its opening, had but 262 patients, had become so overcrowded in 1874 that a hundred of its patients were in the spare room of a prison near by; and when I visited Saxony in 1893, half a century after the opening of Nietleben, the two asylums there and at Alt-Scherbitz contained more than 1,300 inmates, or five times as many as at Dr. Earle's visit. There was no talk in 1849 of the "Open-door System"; and Damerow employed as means of restraint camisoles, muffs, and leathern straps. "But I saw no strong chairs," adds the com-

passionate American.   Even then much work was done on the
large farm by the men, and in the kitchen and sewing-room by
the women.   There were several shops for artisans (" but I did
not go into them "); and the farm "produces all the vegetables
consumed in the establishment, besides many for market."
This good custom of labor, as has been said, Dr. Earle afterwards introduced most effectively at Northampton.   More than
a third part of the cost of the Alt-Scherbitz asylum for its inmates is now borne by the product of the labor of its 850
patients.

Dr. Earle entered Germany by the lower Rhine, and made
his first visit to Dr. Maximilian Jacobi at the small asylum of
Siegburg, on the river Sieg, just above its confluence with the
Rhine, north of Bonn.   It was an old Benedictine monastery,
founded in the eleventh century, and diverted to the use of
persons more insane than monks in 1825.   It was the first of
curative hospitals for insanity in Prussia, and long had a high
reputation there and abroad.   Its capacity was for two hundred,
and the cost of adapting it to its alienist uses was less than
$100,000.   Its annual cost in 1849, for less than two hundred
patients, did not exceed $30,000.   It reported about 30 per
cent. of its patients as "cured," but one-fifth of them relapsed.
The number of deaths was singularly small.   Dr. Jacobi was
thought by his visitor to bear a strong resemblance to that
handsome old American alienist, Dr. Woodward, first superintendent of the Worcester Hospital,—"his presence commanding, his manners unpretending and affable, yet with manly
dignity."   His opinions were sound and frankly expressed : —

Of every hundred recoveries in the hospital, he thinks that no
more than twenty are affected by medical treatment.   The rest he
attributes to hygienic, disciplinary, and moral means.   Manual labor
he considers the most effective means for cure, under the head of
" moral treatment."   A large part of his patients work.   They are
given to understand, soon after admission, that this is expected of
them as a matter of course.   The higher-class patients keep the
walks in the gardens and grounds clear, and have various light
agricultural employments.   Patients are also instructed in literary
knowledge and in music.

Nevertheless, the medical means and the mechanical re-
straints used by this veteran of the Rhine Province would make
a modern alienist " stare and gasp."   " He has employed opium
with benefit in melancholia, not in mania.   He sometimes uses
setons.   A more favorite external remedy is tartar emetic.   The
vertex of the head being shaved, antimonial ointment is applied
until it produces ulceration.   He also hails with pleasure the
appearance of intermittent fever among his patients, since it
generally results in the permanent cure of several from insanity.
The camisole and 'tranquillizing chair' are the principal means
of restraint.   The patient subjected to the shower-bath, involun-
tarily, is confined in a strong chair beneath it."

Dr Earle noted at Siegburg and elsewhere that German
physicians studied mental disease very thoroughly and minutely.
" A consultation of all the physicians is held upon every case
soon after admission, and frequently afterwards," — a custom of
quite recent introduction in most American asylums, if practised at all.   Dr. F. at Siegburg " has not only visited all the
principal hospitals for the insane wherever the German language is spoken, but has passed five months in some of the
best hospitals in Great Britain, and speaks English fluently."
Though quite young, he had contributed to the *Zeitschrift
für Psychiatrie* articles on " Typical Insanity " and "How to
determine Incurability."   At Andernach, near Coblenz, and
at Düsseldorf, Dr. Earle visited small asylums for the incurable, some of whom, as coming from Siegburg, Dr. F. had
passed upon.   In Andernach were one hundred and twenty
patients, at Düsseldorf one hundred and ten.   At both the
women seemed to do more work than the men, while about
equal in number.   Dr. F. gave him a letter of introduction to
Dr. Snell, of the Nassau Asylum, then at Eberbach, in an old
monastery, but soon transferred to new buildings on the Eichberg, near the more famous Johannisberg, on the Rhine, whence
comes the wine of the Metternichs.   Visiting this combination
of ducal prison and insane hospital, Dr. Earle walked from
Erbach, by Elfeld, passing the vineyards of the Steinberg as
well as Johannisberg, and found Eberbach, as its name —
" boar's brook " — implies, in a valley among hills instead of

at the top of the near ridge of Eichberg, to which its insane inmates were soon removed.   He found only one hundred and fifty-one patients, but in its vicinity was an "After-care Society," the first on record, which had been established by Mr. Lindpaintner (described by Dr. Damerow as the last non-medical director of a German institution for the insane) as early as 1829.   From that date until 1844 it had aided eighty-one discharged patients, and, before Lindpaintner's death, in 1848, many more.   The little duchy of Nassau, which in 1849 had but four hundred thousand people, thus took the lead in caring for its insane, under the guidance of a layman,— a lesson not lost on Dr. Earle.

At Eberbach, as elsewhere in Germany, "industry" was the watchword of the hospital.   At times the wards were almost empty of men, most of whom were at work in the garden or at the grounds of the new hospital on the Eichberg near by, to which all the patients moved a few months later.   The chapel of the monks had become a wine-press, and their refectory a sewing-room for the women ; while some of the men were busy at tailoring and other trades.   In the high-vaulted and frescoed sewing-room women were spinning as well as sewing and knit-ting.   On a hillside not far off the private patients of rank were gardening with hoes and rakes, or weeding the flower-beds.   Dr. Snell said that the friends of his patients always wished them to labor, if the medical officer thought it best. Indeed, he thought the fact that general paralysis was almost unknown in the hospital was due to the exercise of so many of his patients in the open air,— a conclusion which Dr. Earle did not accept any more than later alienists would.   "The cause must be sought in their habits of life before admission," he thought.

From Eberbach our tourist proceeded to Frankfort, the home of Goethe, even in whose time there was a small insane hospital.   Indeed, it is recorded that in 1728, twenty-one years before the birth of Goethe, funds were raised to improve this Frankfort mad-house.   At Dr. Earle's visit the city asylum, managed by Dr. Varrentrapp,—father and son,— contained 83 inmates, chiefly paupers, with ten attendants, the city at that

time containing some 50,000 people. There was no farm, and
the work done was mechanical. Evidently, the whole establishment impressed the visitor unfavorably. At present Frankfort
has 180,000 people, and is one of the richest cities in the world
for its size. Its insane are much better provided for.

Returning down the Rhine to Düsseldorf, the next visit was
made to Hildesheim, in Hanover, another old Benedictine monastery, dating from 1001, converted to an asylum in 1827, and
containing in 1849 200 patients, under Dr. Bergmann. Here
for the first time Dr. Earle found much use of baths as a part
of the medical treatment.

He also found there two establishments, one for the curable
and the other for the incurable, separated only by their gardens
and under the same control; and the curative hospital was in
two separate buildings, one for each sex. Consequently, fewer
were discharged from the establishment than in cases where
no asylum for incurables made part of the plant; and, of those
discharged, the greater part were supposed to be cured. Yet
out of 540 cases in four years the cures were but 141; while
the deaths and removals to the incurable asylum were together
161, only 6 out of 257 being entered as "improved." This
seemed to Dr. Earle "inconsistent with Dr. Bergmann's character for minuteness and accuracy of investigation." But his
baths aroused attention in the American, for such a method,
now common, was then little practised here.

Baths both simple and medicated are used. Here for the first
time in an asylum I saw the vapor bath. Cold water is employed
in the neuroses of headache, tic-douloureux, sciatica, sleeplessness,
hypochondria, hysteria, and general atony. The flexible hose is also
used, as I saw it afterwards at Berlin, Illenau, and other places, for
applying either the douche or shower affusions upon the head, when
the patient is in the warm or the tepid bath.

Proceeding from Hanover to Halle and Berlin, Dr. Earle
noticed that clinical lectures to medical students had long been
given in Dr. Ideler's Charity Hospital at Berlin and for a few
years at Halle. He afterwards found clinics at Prague, but

not in Vienna, where, however, they were introduced soon after
by Dr. Riedel, of Prague, when transferred to the new hospital
in Vienna, among the lilacs and shrubbery of the suburb, where
I visited it in 1893. At Berlin he missed seeing Dr. Ideler,
but went through the Charity Hospital with the assistant physicians, and was impressed with the truly Prussian discipline,
the men-patients all wearing uniform,— a morning gown and
striped trousers,— and all rising to salute the staff as they
entered the ward. Great stress was laid on baths, and great
use made of straps for restraint, particularly bed-straps. Chloroform had become a frequent soporific; and tartar emetic was
used for an external irritant, as at Dr. Jacobi's in Siegburg.

It was not till he reached Sonnenstein, in the kingdom of
Saxony, ten miles above Dresden, on the Elbe, that Dr. Earle
became really enthusiastic in praise of a German asylum.
This one was opened in 1811, and was the first of the well-
organized curative hospitals in any German land; so success-
fully conducted, too, that its reputation rose high, and it served
as a model for other States and countries. Its buildings were
antiquated, and in some respects inconvenient, but the spirit
and discipline of the establishment very satisfactory. Dr. Earle
says : —

I have rarely passed four hours more agreeably and usefully than
when I accompanied Dr. Klotz in his morning walk through the
establishment. Everything was in good order, bearing unmistakable
evidence of industry, system, discipline, and an ever-watchful supervision. The patients, if seated, rose as we entered the room. They
were all well dressed. This has been the case in all the German
asylums I have visited,— this was the ninth,— for I have not seen even
one patient whose clothes were ragged or patched. At Sonnenstein
a high estimate is placed on the curative influence of labor. Some
of the men work on the grounds of the institution; others, with an
attendant, upon the neighboring farms. There are workshops for
tailors, shoemakers, and some other artisans. Absolute coercion is
never resorted to; but the deprivation and granting of privileges,
and even pecuniary recompense, are inducements. Something more
than $50 is annually appropriated for these rewards. The purely
medical treatment is restricted, as much as possible, to a few simple

remedies, as rhubarb, senna, and saline cathartics. The hope of cure is based on suitable diet, regularity of hours, discipline, exercise, amusements, and the other means of moral treatment. Some use is made of baths. In ordinary forms of insanity venesection is never practised. Even local bleeding is rarely prescribed. Ether and chloroform have been tried, but without beneficial results. For 262 patients there are 3 medical officers,— Dr. Pienitz, the director (a pupil of Pinel), Dr. Klotz, and Dr. Lessing. Dr. Pienitz has had a number of young physicians under his tuition at Pirna (Sonnenstein), among them Dr. Martini, now at Leubus; Dr. Roller, at Illenau; Dr. Flemming, of Mecklenburg-Schwerin; Dr. Jessen, of Schleswig; and Dr. Marcher, of the Royal Danish Asylum at Copenhagen. Dr. Pienitz has been knighted and made Aulic Counsellor; Dr. Martini, Health Counsellor; and Drs. Flemming and Roller, Medical Counsellors,— all titles of much honor. In this kingdom of Saxony the directors of asylums are not merely experts, but judge and jury, so far as insanity is concerned. Their opinion given to the supreme courts is decisive.

Here, then, the American visitor had found a state of things long desired by him, but never yet attained in the United States. On the other hand, he had never found the asylum buildings satisfactory. They were mostly old and ill-adapted to their final use, though of good example, sometimes, for spaciousness. At Illenau, opened in 1842 under Dr. Roller, the pupil of Pienitz, Dr. Earle found buildings specially designed for the insane, as most of our asylums had been. This asylum is in quite another part of Germany from Sonnenstein, near the village of Achern, in the Rhine valley, between Baden-Baden and Strasbourg, and was built for 400 patients. It takes its name from the river Ill, a tributary of the Rhine, and was built upon plans of Dr. Roller, to receive the patients of Baden from the old and inadequate asylums of Heidelberg and Pforzheim. Consequently, it received from those two asylums more than 250 incurables, so that it could show, at the end of four years, only 111 cures among nearly 700 patients, while the deaths had been 77. Its classification of patients was very good, for its period, having been so constructed as to receive ten classes of each sex,— as many as the Danvers Hospital was built for,

a whole generation later.   It had in 1849 one attendant to
every five patients, and a medical officer for every 108 patients.
Its farm was small (43 acres), and less stress was put upon work
than in several of the German asylums.

Much smaller was the asylum at Leubus, in Silesia, where
Dr. Earle found another pupil of Dr. Pienitz, Dr. Moritz
Martini, who had been in charge from the opening of the
asylum in 1830.   In that time he had treated more than 1,500
patients; but, of 1,390 of them who had been discharged up to
1847, less than half (650) were cured, while more than a sixth
(237) had died.   Among 150 patients found there by Dr.
Earle, 120 were paupers; but for these eighteen attendants and
supervisors were employed,— more than one to every seven
patients,— a larger proportion of sane persons than is usually
found among the insane poor in our modern asylums.   These
paupers were clad in uniform, and did much work, both on the
little farm of thirty acres and in workshops for weaving, tailoring, cabinet-making, carpentry, and shoemaking.   One lesson
was there learned, which Dr. Earle afterwards put in strict
practice at Northampton, where there had been great need of
such economy:—

No supplies, even of a handkerchief, a shoe-string, a broom, or an
ounce of salt, can be obtained without an order from the proper
officer.   If a garment be torn or worn so as to make a new one
necessary, or if any article has become unfit for use, these must be
produced as evidences.   A regular account of debits and credits is
kept between the various departments; and thus unnecessary con-
sumption, carelessness, and "sequestration" are guarded against.
No institution can ever attain that perfection of good order which is
a chief beauty in a public or a private establishment without such a
system.*

---

* Upon his third visit to Europe, in 1871, Dr. Earle made an effort to find Dr. Martini, who was
still active in the specialty, though it was forty-one years since he began his labors at Leubus, and
almost half a century since he was the pupil of Dr. Pienitz, at Sonnenstein. They failed to meet for
a reason which is given in the following most interesting letter from the old alienist:—

"DRESDEN, July 29, 1871.

"*My very dear Colleague,*— I reached Dresden with my wife the very day that you had set out
for Prague; and your letter, dated the 25th, which you had sent to Leubus, only reached me this day.
I hasten to thank you for it. It is a precious souvenir for us all, which makes us regret all the more
that we could not meet you again, and express to you the affectionate feeling we all cherish for you in

At Brieg and Plagowitz there were asylums for the incurables
of Silesia, the former of which Dr. Earle visited, without admiring its arrangements. In the three provincial establishments
fifty years ago there were about 400 patients, and at Breslau
some 30 more; that is, in four establishments 430 inmates, or
less than are now usually kept in one of our American public
asylums. Silesia at the time had some 3,000 insane, and a
total population of perhaps 2,500,000, or about the same as
Massachusetts in 1895.

Finding himself so near Austria, Dr. Earle proceeded next
to the gay capital of that empire, and visited the unique Narrenthurm ("Maniacs' Tower"), built in 1783-84 by Joseph II.
for a mad-house of the old order. Dr. Viszanik, its director,
told his visitor it was the first institution in Europe which,
from its foundation, was intended exclusively for the insane;
most of the older mad-houses being originally either hospitals
for the sick, like the English Bedlam, or poorhouses diverted

our hearts. Since your visit to Leubus a score of years has slipped away." (In fact, twenty-two
years.) "In that period, characterized by every sort of revolution, political, moral, and religious, in
the midst of fearful events, and directed by ideas that have overturned the old order of things and of
principles, I have withdrawn into the circle of my family, and the solitude which I have dwelt in for
five-and-forty years; and I practise there the duties imposed on me by humanity's service, but aided
by my dear wife, my auxiliary angel, who has made me forget that text of Matthew's Gospel, 'Arcta
via est quæ ducit ad vitam.'

"Fanny married a Herr von Klitzing, proprietor of the estate of Lobetinz (Kreis Neumarkt,
Schlesien). She has five children, two sons and three daughters. The eldest, named John, is seventeen, and sits already in the second class at the high school of Tasser. Three girls come next,—Ella,
sixteen; Fanny, fourteen; and Catharine, twelve. The younger son, nine years old, bears the name
of his grandfather, Moritz. He is a fine lad, full of talents, and with much *esprit*. May the good God
hold over him a protecting hand!"

(Up to this point the letter is in fairly good French; but Dr. Moritz Martini here says, "The
French language bothers me (*me gêne*). Permit me to finish this letter making use of my mother
tongue," and continues in German.)

"Fanny, my only child, has brought up her children admirably. She has the good fortune that
all her children are healthy, strong, and well formed, mentally gifted, and good-natured. This com-
pensates her for many deprivations which life on a country estate brings with it. Her short distance
from us (four miles) makes it possible that we see her often. This now is a favor of fortune for
which, at my age of seventy-six years, I cannot thank God enough. The coming May I celebrate
my fifty years' jubilee as Doctor Medicus. Should I live beyond that, it is my thought to retire to
private life then, and to revise and arrange my Memorabilia.

"So much about us, who wish you the best fortune for your journey, and with the heartiest
greeting commend ourselves to your future remembrance.

"In true friendship,

                        Your respectful Colleague,   Dr. Martini.

"My wife desires the warmest regards."

This touch of German sentiment indicates the affection which the kind-hearted American tourist
inspired wherever he went. He was as welcome to the German alienists as to the English Quakers
and the people of Southern Europe.

to the special restraint of the dangerous insane. The Vienna tower was five stories high, cylindrical, but enclosing a central area, and containing twenty-eight rooms on each floor, except the lower one, which had twenty-seven. The rooms for the insane were along the external wall, entered through a keeper's room, which was the only one on each floor that opened on the stair-landing. The rooms were large; and many of them had rings and staples, as in the old prisons, for chaining the inmates. In these 139 tower-rooms were formerly kept more than 200 insane persons; and, as described by an English visitor in 1843, it resembled the ancient bedlam more than the modern asylum. He portrayed it as

A wretched, filthy prison, close and ill-ventilated, its smell over-powering, and the sight of its patients — frantic, chained, and many of them naked — disgusting to the visitor. ... A crowd of country-folk, many of them women, were conducted through the corridors along with me, as a mere matter of curiosity, or as one would go to see a collection of wild beasts.

Some such spectacle was that seen by Dr. Earle at Constantinople, ten years before; but, when he reached Vienna, this state of things had ceased. Other buildings had been used for the overflow of patients; and, though the faults of construction in the old tower were evident, something had been done to correct them.

The apartments were decently clean, most of them commendably so; and the patients were neither ragged, filthy, nor in chains. In the upper stories partitions had been removed, so as to unite several rooms in one, for associated dormitories. There was a workshop for making chair-seats and straw mats, and another for paper or paste-board boxes, a large assortment of these being ready for market. But many defects still existed. At dinner time no table was spread, for the very good reason that there was none to spread, and no room for one large enough. The food was brought into the corridor and distributed. Each patient then made himself as comfortable as he could, standing, sitting, or lying, with his dish in his hand, in his lap, or on the floor.

To this description Dr. Earle adds that Dr. Viszanik reported the most brilliant results from trying the cold-water cure on his patients since 1841, "one-third of the patients having been treated with no other medication than cold water, even in the most difficult and complicated cases." As there were 360 patients in 1849, and nearly 500 in course of a year, this must have meant that 150 a year had been treated by hydropathy, then in its greatest favor; and Dr. Viszanik boasted as many cures as other superintendents. Indeed, the statistics of the Narrenthurm for sixty years seemed to show as many recoveries as have been made in much better surroundings. Thus from 1784 to 1843, 14,761 cases were admitted, more than 13,000 of them in this Babel-tower, as Dr. Earle styles it; and the number of cures was reported as 6,949, nearly one-half of all the cases, while only 3,468 had died. In the rooms of the Vienna General Hospital, where, since 1828, 1,485 insane persons were registered (included in the total count above), a still more gratifying recovery rate was reported; for 1,058, or 71 per cent., had recovered in fifteen years, and only 142, or less than 10 per cent., had died. Unfortunately, Dr. Earle adds in a note, "Dr. Flemming asserts that the great number of cures chiefly arose from the fact that all cases of delirium tremens and many of febrile delirium admitted into the General Hospital were immediately transferred to the insane asylum." Upon these a cold-water treatment would naturally produce a speedy cure.*

The population of Vienna in 1849 was 422,000. In 1893, when I visited its insane asylums, there were more than 850,000; that is, the inhabitants had doubled in forty-four years. But there was a still greater change in the insane enumeration. Dr. Viszanik then received some 500 new admissions a year, and closed the year with about 350 patients. His successors began the year 1892 with nearly 900 patients, received during the year more than 1,000, and among all these cases made but 300 recoveries, with more than 200 deaths. That is, the recovery rate had fallen from 48 per cent. to about 16; while

* Dr. Earle had information similar to this from one of the successors of an American superintendent, who had this same suspicious abundance of recoveries in a hospital serving a great city,— delirium tremens figuring in hundreds of his cases entered as "insane."

the death-rate, computed on the whole number, was less than 10 per cent. From 1784 to 1843, according to the figures, the death-rate, reckoned in the same way, exceeded 20 per cent. The Narrenthurm had long since disappeared or been converted to better uses; and the halls of the present asylum, though overcrowded, like most of the Viennese charities, have witnessed some of the most skilful scientific treatment of insanity, and the most enlightened clinical exposition of its nature and varieties. As the recovery rate has fallen in about the same ratio that scientific knowledge of the malady has risen, we must suppose that much formerly deemed cure was fallacious, and either wholly imaginary or followed by speedy relapses.

Dr. Riedel, of Prague, who soon took charge of the newer asylum at Vienna (about 1852), was not visited in his Bohemian asylum by Dr. Earle, who reported it favorably by the testimony of others. But he went on from Vienna to the Tyrol, and there, near Innspruck, was received at Hall by Dr. Tschallener, who had been director of a small Tyrolese asylum in a disused monastery for fifteen years. Hall is six miles below Innspruck, on the river Inn; and the asylum was on the foot-hills of the Salzberg Alps, 7,000 feet in height. It overlooked from its lower elevation "fertile meadows luxuriant with grain, grass, and Indian corn, and interspersed with peasant houses of a Swiss-like architecture, which add a charm of novelty, with a tincture of romance, to the scene." The valley is indeed an extension of Switzerland.

Hall itself is a small city, not much larger than Concord in Massachusetts; and the whole of Austrian Tyrol has less than 900,000 inhabitants,—served in 1849–50 by two small asylums for the insane, that in Hall containing 100, and that in Trient, near Italy, less than 50. Thus a population larger than that of New Hampshire and Vermont had less than 150 insane in asylums; while those two New England States at the same date (having then 600,000 people) had more than 400 insane in their two asylums. Indeed, Dr. Tschallener had treated in his asylum in fifteen years less than 400 patients, or no more than Dr. Rockwell at Brattleboro, Vt., was then treating in a single

year. His cures in that time among the Tyrolese were about
130, while the deaths exceeded 60.   In this small asylum there
were schools for the patients and pecuniary rewards for labor
done by them.   Suicides were treated in a peculiar manner : a
large sack containing the patient who was suicidal was hoisted
nearly to the ceiling, so that he could neither escape nor do
himself harm.   The director gave this account of his discipline :
"To the good-humored patients I am good-humored, to the
rude unceremonious, to the proud haughty, to the submissive
affable, to the peaceable yielding, to the quarrelsome repellent,
and to the well-mannered indulgent.   Of the simple I am
watchful, and of the crafty cautious.   He who does not obey
voluntarily must be made to obey."   Dr. Earle adds :—

With the disobedient he is patient and long-suffering ; but he
assumes that, with rare exceptions, the insane can behave properly
if they will.   Obedience granted, he then spares no trouble in minis-
tering to their enjoyment.   He grants all appropriate privileges,
assists in their instruction, accompanies them to parties, gives musical *soirées* for them in his own apartments, and encourages them in
labor by pecuniary recompense.   Some patients have gone away
with as much as $15 thus acquired.

At Hall Dr. Earle saw the German *Zwangstuhl*, or "tranquillizing chair"; and, returning northward to Munich, he
found a still worse form of this instrument of torture in use at
Giesing, the city asylum of Munich, with but 40 patients, the
whole number in all the asylums of Bavaria being then some
700.   The population of the kingdom was about 4,500,000.   It
is now 6,000,000 ; and Munich has grown into a large city, with
a much larger asylum, built in 1859, and containing, when I
visited it in 1893, 600 patients, or *fifteen* times as many as Dr.
Earle found there.   Only some 350 of them, however, belonged
to the city of Munich, which then contained 260,000 people as
against 100,000 in 1850.   There are now ten public asylums in
Bavaria and several private ones, the whole number of patients
in them now exceeding 5,000, of which number more than
1,000 are in Upper Bavaria, with its two public asylums of

Munich and Gabersee. But to return to Dr. Earle. Of Giesing he says : —

The implements of restraint for Munich are the strait-jacket and the chair. It is of strong plank, put together in the simplest possible form. The sides project farther forward than the patient's body, when seated; and, from the knees downward, they extend beyond the feet. Being seated, a door is closed in front of his feet and legs, a lid closed over the thighs, and a board, fitted into grooves, is slipped down in front of the head and body, the head alone being visible to the bystander. To complete his felicity, two blocks of strong wood project over his shoulders, and prevent any attempt to rise. I have seen the insane of the Timar-hané at Constantinople in chains, and I have seen patients in various countries confined in the "tranquillizing chair"; and I assert that, so far as restraint is concerned, the condition of the Turks was the most comfortable, or, rather, the least fearful, the most desirable.

Time, which has so much multiplied the poor insane of Munich, has long since relieved them of the tortures of this detestable chair; and I found the condition of the 600 patients at Munich's Kreis-Irren-Anstalt fairly good in May, 1893. A much better asylum was that of Gabersee, in the Bavarian Oberland, some sixty miles north-east of Munich, with 300 patients in detached houses,— something after the plan of Alt-Scherbitz in Saxony. But one painful circumstance should be mentioned at the Munich asylum,— its enormous number of paretics. When Dr. Earle was in Germany, general paralysis was a new disease in America, and almost unknown in Ireland and other rural regions. As he went from asylum to asylum, he usually asked if any paretics had been treated there, and if any recovered. The answers were various, but the whole number of cases was small in all Germany. But the intelligent young assistant physician who escorted me through the long corridors at Munich told me that, of his 600 patients, 150, or a fourth, were paretics (120 men and 30 women); and, of the 270 patients admitted the year before, 61, or more than 20 per cent., were paretics. I do not recall so large a proportion anywhere else.

Dr. Earle's latest visits were made to Winnenthal, near Stuttgard, Illenau (already described), and Stephansfeld, in Alsace, near Strasbourg,— the last named not in Germany in 1849, but added by reconquest in 1870. At Winnenthal he met Dr. Zeller, from whom he quotes freely, and saw less restraint there than in any German asylum. It was then a small establishment, with but few more than 100 inmates; and its system of labor and amusement was very similar to that elsewhere, with larger numbers. At Stephansfeld, however, as at Sonnenstein, Dr. Earle allows himself the luxury of praising what he sees. It was a large asylum, comparatively, for there were 377 patients; and its industries were well organized. Several of its peculiarities were striking at that time, and he says : —

A remarkable feature is that none of the windows, except in the small department for the furious (and there they are not glazed), are in any way protected internally or externally. They differ from the ordinary French window only in having the turn-latch, when closed, moved by a tube-key carried by the attendant, and that a few of the sashes are iron. Of more than fifty public institutions for the insane which I have visited, no other is so exempt from what is generally considered necessary.

Further on he says : —

Manual labor has here a development surpassing anything of the kind known. Besides the numerous workshops where the patients can be useful, and exercise the trades of cabinet-making, shoemaking, weaving, painting, trough-making, coopering, book-binding, etc., the farm has been extended by bringing a hundred acres of land under cultivation.* The asylum bears the aspect of a farm colony rather than a hospital, the women even being at work weeding the fields, as well as spinning, sewing, laundry work, etc. The number of patients daily employed generally exceeds 180, or almost half the total number. A daily record of this labor has been kept for years, and in

* Dr. Paetz, in his volume of 1893, already cited, says that in 1878 the Stephansfeld asylum, having added a department at Hoerdt, extended still farther the open-door and colony system, thus indicating that the essential character of the establishment remained unchanged by the German occupation of Alsace in 1870. Indeed, this was from the first of a German rather than a French nature; for the improvements specified began in Germany.

1844 the money payments to patients for work were nearly 8,000 francs ($1,600). A portion of this is given to them, the rest reserved till they recover or are otherwise discharged. Since 1842 schools are established for men and for women, the latter under a Sister of Charity. The number of patients in both is sometimes almost 100, or a fourth of the population. Their tranquillity, diligence, and good behavior in the schools is praised by Dr. Roederer, the director. They are taught the common branches, and also history, translation, drawing, and music. Five years ago (May 1, 1844) 220 patients, or more than two-thirds of all, made an excursion to a neighboring wood, lasting more than three hours, in great order and quiet.

Although he visited but 17 German asylums in 1849, Dr. Earle briefly described in his book 39 more, making up his account of them from their reports, from German volumes, and from articles in the German *Zeitschrift für Psychiatrie* and the French *Annales Médico-Psychologiques*. He also gave a general historical sketch of the German asylums, and quoted freely from the writings of eminent German alienists. Hardly had his book come out, in 1853, when he received a work of Dr. Heinrich Laehr, one of Dr. Damerow's assistants, in which a list was given of all the German asylums in 1852 to the number of 91 public asylums and 20 private ones. This list Dr. Earle inserted in his volume at the end. It is incorrect in some particulars and defective in others, but was then by far the fullest statistical account of the German asylums which had appeared in America. Dr. Laehr republished his list in 1891, bringing it down to include the year 1890; and at that time the German asylums had increased to 222,— most of them much larger than in 1852,— and contained 56,234 patients,— an average of 253 in each. In 1852 the whole number of patients in 111 asylums was about 11,000,— an average in each of less than 100. The Austrian asylums were included in Laehr's first list, and perhaps in that of 1891; but in Austria alone there are more asylum inmates now than were found in all the German-speaking countries in 1852,— that is, more than 12,000. This may serve to show how insanity has been increasing in the regions visited by Dr. Earle — as in all civilized countries —

far beyond the gain in population, which has also been considerable, especially in the German Empire of to-day.

Dr. Earle did not enter Hungary in 1849, for it was still in a state of war; but it then had few asylums. In May, 1893, I visited the largest of the Hungarian asylums, at the old capital of Buda, across the Danube from Pesth, which now, united with Buda under the joint name of Buda-Pesth, is the capital of the Austrian emperor's kingdom of Hungary. The Buda-Pesth asylum was opened in 1850, at the close of the civil war. It stands on a high hill, far above the old fortress-ridge of Buda, beside the Danube, and is surrounded by pleasant hills and valleys, which on the 11th of May, the date of my visit, were blooming with spring flowers or covered with verdant trees and shrubs. The farm is large and well cultivated by the labor of the patients, who then numbered 800, including 50 of the criminal insane sent there for treatment. The director was Dr. Niedermann, first appointed in 1870, with seven medical assistants, giving one medical officer for every hundred patients. The inmates were equally divided as to sex; but the old building was crowded and architecturally faulty, so that a new asylum for the more violent cases — here quite numerous — was then building elsewhere. The asylum is intended for the whole *Comitat* of Buda, including the city of Pesth and much surrounding country. There is another Hungarian asylum at Presbourg, where in 1893 abuses had been discovered and were under investigation, in consequence of the death of a patient in his bath.

In accord with the practice of Dr. Earle, I inquired of Dr. Niedermann the number of his paretic cases, and was rather surprised at his answers. He then had 176 such cases among his 800 patients, more than one-fifth of the whole count. Of these, 160 were men and 16 women,— a fact which perhaps accounts for the excess of deaths over recoveries in a year,— 130 recoveries and 200 deaths. Reminding Dr. Niedermann that his Austrian and German colleagues were inclined to attribute general paralysis in all cases to syphilis, I was told by him that such a theory was baseless, that in his asylum not half the paretic cases could be ascribed to that cause, even as co-operative.

As the reports of his institution are only printed in Hungarian
(not in German, as formerly), I could not review his statistics
historically; but he must have been receiving some 400 patients annually, and the increase of insanity in Hungary, with
its population of 16,000,000, must be nearly as fast as in the
German parts of the Austrian Empire, though perhaps not so
fast as among the Bohemians.

It is evident that between 1838, when Dr. Earle inspected
some of the English, French, Dutch, and Italian asylums, and
1849, when he made his careful study of those in Germany and
Austria, his faith in the "cures" of the insane reported by his
professional brethren had lessened perceptibly; and the careful statistics of Dr. Jacobi, at Siegburg, must have had something to do with this scepticism, which later developed into
a complete disbelief of the much-paraded figures of American
asylums.   Of the 661 patients reported cured at Siegburg
from 1825 to 1845 (nearly half of the whole number), 322 had
not relapsed in the twenty years, and were still living; but
259 had relapsed, several more than once, and only 68 had died
without a relapse.   As the number who had died in a relapse
was almost as many (57), it was plain to Dr. Earle that the
state of "cure" was a very unstable one; and the subsequent
researches of many experts have confirmed this view.   But,
when he visited the Utrecht asylum in Holland (July, 1838),
then under the visitation of Van der Kolk, the Dutch reformer
of asylums, he was quite ready to accept the estimate of its
physician, that 40 per cent. of the admissions recovered.   It
was small (94 inmates in 1838), and had not much enlarged
fifteen years later, when Dr. Earle's friend, Dr. Hack Tuke,
inspected it, while on his wedding tour, in the autumn of 1853;
for he found but 127 inmates.   In reporting its statistics then,
Dr. Tuke observed (after quoting the 40 per cent. of recoveries before 1838), "It is singular that from 1844 to 1851 the
proportion of cures to admissions is considerably less than
from 1832 to 1837 inclusive."   In fact, the percentage had
fallen to 30, and no doubt has grown smaller since.*

* See a rare pamphlet, "The Asylums of Holland, their Past and Present Condition.   By Daniel
H. Tuke, M.D.   From the *Psychological Journal*, July 1, 1854."   When I last saw Dr. Tuke, in

The great question of separation between the curable and incurable insane naturally springs from a discovery of the fact (which Dr. Earle seems to have fully learned only in Germany) that less than half the insane can be cured, so as to remain well, and that, consequently, the uncured, and practically incurable, will accumulate in asylums to the detriment of the curable. Hence, as the result of all his observations, Dr. Earle said in this volume of 1853, what he afterwards repeated, that the true method for hospitals, such as we were then beginning to have in America, as distinguished from mere asylums, is this : —

Let no institution have more than 200 patients, and let all receive both curables and incurables, in the natural proportion for the admission of the two classes, from the respective districts in which they are located.

From this position he never varied, and only yielded to a supposed necessity in allowing that larger hospitals might serve some useful purpose; but, of course, he foresaw that what he had witnessed in Siegburg and other curative establishments in Germany would sooner or later occur in the American hospitals,— that is, that the uncured would accumulate, and must either be sent to another place or allowed to hamper the proper work of a hospital. He therefore summarized the argument of Dr. Zeller, of Winnenthal, in favor of separate asylums for the older incurables ; and this is one of the most instructive parts of the volume. He says :—

It is true that two separate establishments are more expensive than one large enough to accommodate the same number of patients ; but this cost, being subordinate to the welfare of the insane, should be overlooked, since the advantages of institutions independent of each other are more than sufficient to counterbalance the extra expense.

July, 1893, he lent me this brochure, saying it was his only loose copy, and he might wish to reclaim it. In case he did not, I was to keep it. He also then informed me it was the result of observations made in Holland when on his bridal journey. I had just come from the great asylum of Meerenberg, which had grown from the 400 inmates whom he found there forty years before to the 1,300 seen by me; and he was much interested in my account of the improvements there, the latest being the care of the male patients by women nurses, under the oversight of Mrs. Van Deventer, the able wife of the director, Dr. Van Deventer. As Dr. Tuke died without reclaiming his pamphlet, I keep it among my valuable possessions.

The spheres of the two institutions (asylum and hospital) are very different. They are specialties, and can be better conducted by two persons than one. The accumulation of many insane in one establishment, or in the same vicinity, has an unfavorable influence. In asylums for the incurable, various handicrafts may be regularly and systematically pursued. These cannot be prosecuted among curables, because, almost as soon as the patients begin to work, they are discharged. The sight of so many incurables would act unfavorably upon the curable patients. With a patient who, after long residence in one establishment, has been pronounced incurable, a change of scene by his removal to another, the placing of him under care of another physician, and all the new relations, etc., will be the most likely, of all possible means, to effect a cure. If the two institutions be separate, many will be taken from their homes to the curative hospital who might otherwise go to the asylum for incurables.

Another point in which Dr. Earle learned much, and sought to improve his countrymen by imparting what he had learned, regards the instruction of medical students in mental disorders. Here he was very clear and emphatic; yet, after the lapse of nearly fifty years, we are still as far from perfection (to use his own phrase) as the Germans were in 1849. They were then, as they are now, far in advance of us and of most nations in this matter. Dr. Earle said : —

It is safe to say that not one in forty of the graduates of our medical schools has ever read a treatise upon diseases of the mind. The subject of insanity does not enter into the programme of lectures in any of our leading medical schools. In Germany it has long been otherwise. Reil, so long ago as 1803, advised that suitable persons should be selected from the medical students and placed in the asylums, where, while learning the peculiar art, they might assist in treating the patients. Dr. Roller proposes to take six physicians, immediately after they have completed their other medical studies, into the Illenau asylum as internes, and, after they have remained a certain time, exchange them for six more, until all the medical graduates in Baden shall have had this opportunity. A similar practice is pursued at the Charity Hospital in Berlin. A professorship of " psychiatry " (the first) was established in the

University of Leipzig in 1811, and long filled by Heinroth. Others
have since been founded, and clinical instruction is given at Berlin
by Dr. Ideler, at Prague by Dr. Riedel, now at Vienna, and by
Damerow at Halle, and others.

It is only within the last few years, and by no means universally, that the American medical schools have followed the
example of these German leaders in teaching the treatment of
insanity to medical students.   A singular indifference, even
aversion, exists in some learned minds still to taking the needful means for giving this indispensable instruction.   In the
year 1879, when the late Governor Talbot of Massachusetts
signalized his single year of State administration by securing
more reforms in the charitable establishments than have been
carried in any three years before or since, I had occasion to
call on the late Dr. O. W. Holmes, medical lecturer and poet,
to consult him about the feasibility of instructing his medical
students at the Harvard School in Boston in mental maladies,
and particularly as to clinical lectures in some insane hospital
in or near Boston.   Dr. Holmes was genial and witty, as always,
— agreed that instruction was much needed, and wished it might
be given,— but had nothing special to suggest by which it could
be bettered.   When I suggested clinical lectures, he demurred :
they might be indispensable, but think of the effect on the
patients ! and he quoted Martial's epigram,—

> Languebam ; sed tu comitatus protinus ad me
>   Venisti centum, Symmache, discipulis ;
> Centum me tetigere manus, Aquilone gelatae.
>   Non habui febrem, Symmache : nunc habeo.

> I ailed : 'twas naught ; but, Doctor, *you* came at me,
>   A hundred students clattering in your train ;
> A hundred hands, colder than ice, did pat me.
>   I *had* no fever : now I feel its pain.

He left me to draw my own inference, after making my own
translation, which I have done above.

Nor has instruction in mental maladies yet been better
organized anywhere in Massachusetts than in the comparatively

recent Homœopathic Hospital for the Insane at Westboro, thirty-three miles from Boston, to which a class of students make the long journey weekly in the winter months; unless it be in the old and wealthy Worcester Hospital, where for medical graduates, four in number, clinical and class instruction as internes is given by an accomplished Swiss alienist, Dr. Adolf Meyer. This is carrying out on a smaller scale what Dr. Roller planned for the duchy of Baden so many years ago.

Dr. Earle's account of the German asylums, after appearing serially in the *American Journal of Insanity* at Utica, N.Y. (which he aided in founding), had some circulation as a separate work; but it was not widely read, and probably brought the author more renown in Europe than at home. It was in advance of the times; and the paradox was seen, as so often before and since, of the physician best fitted to carry on a hospital for the insane, unable to obtain preferment in his own land, before younger and less gifted but more pushing men, to whose unscientific direction many of the new and costly American asylums fell, in the decade following Dr. Earle's return from his second European tour.

CHAPTER IX

On the day that Dr. Earle landed in New York from his German tour, his mother died at the old home at Leicester, where the settlement of the family estate and other matters detained him until the latter part of 1852,— not always in the firmest health, but performing much intellectual labor in his chosen field. He had begun for the *American Journal of the Medical Sciences*, in 1842, a series of short reviews of the annual reports of institutions for the insane, at home and abroad, which came to him in great number and sometimes found in him almost their only intelligent reader. He continued this useful work during his whole retirement at Leicester, both from 1849 to 1852, and again from 1854 to 1864,—varying this rural retirement with excursions to Providence, Washington, Carolina, Cuba, etc., as he had occasion. It was probably the study of the irregular and often absurd statistical array of figures and percentages in these reports that convinced him how fruitless the existing methods of statistical showing for insanity then were; and, in particular, how far they were from indicating the real facts concerning the curability of the wide-spread and fast-increasing disease, which he had so long been examining, both in detached cases and in the general aggregates of asylums, States, and races. All this was preparation for his discovery and demonstration of the true ratio of curability, and also for his quarter-century of active asylum work at Northampton. But it was weary waiting in some of these inactive years before 1864 ; and Dr. Earle bided his time with some impatience and not without days and months of despondency. He lived at Leicester, in a small house, with no display, and amid humble duties of one sort or another. His age was greater than that of Montaigne when that Gascon sage retired to his château to spend a calm life among his books ; nor was he so resigned to quiet and solitude as Montaigne, who had, for all that, as great a love for travel and observation as Dr. Earle, though he never journeyed so far. When he came out from this retirement at the end of 1852, he returned to New York, opened an office there for consultation, and soon became a member of the Board of Visiting Physicians to the City Lunatic Asylum, then at Blackwell's Island, and containing comparatively few inmates. He continued to serve on this board while resident in New York, and thus became more familiar with the pauper insane of a large city than his previous hospital experience had required him to be. This fact renewed his observations on cases of general paralysis, which he had carefully studied and early reported while at the Bloomingdale Asylum, before going abroad in 1849. One of his Bloomingdale cases, after a period of years, appeared to have recovered,— a fact that surprised M. Calmeil, when communicated by Dr. Earle to him at Charenton, in 1849. At that time Calmeil (the first extensive writer on this disease in France) had been for about twenty years at the head of the asylum of Charenton, and had there treated and observed hundreds of cases ; and he assured Dr. Earle that he had never known an instance of complete recovery. Occasionally his patients had improved enough to go home, and now and then to resume their occupations ; but in every such case the malady had resumed its fatal course. Dr. Earle published a record of this recovered case in 1857, having then observed it for nine years ; and it is of sufficient interest to be given here in a shortened form.

Mr. X. was native and resident in one of the inland counties of New York (born in 1806), of strong constitution and intellect above mediocrity. He went through college and studied law, rising to some eminence in that profession. He married at thirty-four, lived well, and, though not intemperate, indulged freely in the luxuries of the table. One of his paternal uncles had been insane, and a maternal aunt melancholiac. At the age of forty-one, after the decease of a child and some pecuniary troubles, he became depressed, and early in 1848 had a succession of epileptiform fits. These had been preceded by some indications of local paralysis. His mental disease progressing, he was taken to Bloomingdale in July, 1848, then forty-two years old, and much excited, restless, garrulous, incoherent, and talking of pecuniary speculations which he wished to make in Wall Street. His utterance was rapid, but uncertain, his pulse quickened, his condition costive. This being remedied by cathartics, his excitement subsided; but the paralysis increased, so that in a fortnight he could not walk without support. His "delusions of grandeur" became excessive, and continued for months; his general sensations obtuse, his memory of recent events almost destroyed, his speech variable, and much more imperfect on some days than on others; his hand unsteady, so that he wrote his name with difficulty, the pupils of his eyes contracted, and one somewhat larger than the other. By the end of September his pulse was regular at 124, and he had all the usual indication of paresis, which continued through October. In November, 1848, he was removed to a private asylum in Flushing, where he began to amend after some months; and during the earlier half of 1849 he was discharged, recovered. Dr. Macdonald, the physician, said that no special treatment had been pursued, and that his recovery was due to an effort of nature. In 1857, ten years after his first mental symptoms were observed, he was living in excellent health, physical and mental, pursuing an extensive and successful business; and some years after I learned that he was well, and had accumulated a good fortune. This is the last intelligence received concerning him.

In 1853 Dr. Earle gave a course of lectures on insanity at the New York College of Physicians and Surgeons, and in 1854 published his treatise on "Blood-letting in Mental Disorders," from which quotations have already been made. Belief in the sanguinary doctrines of Rush had slowly become less general; but blood-letting by the lancet was still continued at some asylums, and local superficial bleeding at more. In Dr. Earle's pamphlet were condensed and classified, for analysis, comparison, or contrast, the opinions of many authors, American, British, and Continental, on the value of venesection in mental disease; and to this array of authority Dr. Earle added his own extensive observation and practice. Though controverted angrily rather than forcibly, the treatise had an important effect in confirming the sound opinion and converting the doubtful and even the unsound to his own view of the matter. The lancet soon fell into utter disuse, and the scarifying and cupping substitutes then followed. But in the mean time his own health required him to give up active practice. He left New York as a residence in 1854, and returned to Leicester, where his domicile continued to be until he was chosen super-intendent of the hospital at Northampton in 1864. He went forth from this retirement often, to testify as an expert in cases of insanity and for journeys here and there; and for a con-siderable time he visited in Washington, where he was engaged as an expert editor of the "Census Statistics of Insanity," taken in 1860. His chief task in that was the writing of an introduc-tory chapter on the causes, treatment, and curability of insanity, with a special history of the amelioration of the treatment of the American insane up to 1860. No such historical statement had previously been made; and it is doubtful if any since has so fully and accurately treated the twenty-five years from 1835 to 1860, during which Dr. Earle had personal knowledge, by visits, correspondence, and conversation, of what was doing in his chosen specialty.

Early in the period between 1850 and 1864, Dr. Earle visited the Carolinas and Cuba (February, 1852) in company with his cousin, Mrs. Marcus Spring, and her husband; and his letters of that date give interesting notes of a state of society now almost as completely passed away as if centuries had intervened instead of less than fifty years. Writing from Charleston, S.C., Feb. 1, 1852, to his sister Lucy at Leicester, he said : —

Time, 9.30 A.M.; place, the Charleston Hotel, room 156; both windows open, though the room is on the north side of the house, and I am just delightfully comfortable, sitting in front of one of them, where the soft air comes upon me in a gentle breeze. The doors and windows seen from my position are many of them open ; and, did I not know to the contrary, I should suppose the season to be late May or early June. I wrote you on January 28, from the store of Howland & Taft, the latter the son of Bezaleel Taft, of Uxbridge, near Worcester. He is in the cotton trade, and appears to have made a fortune. His wife is a beautiful Irish woman, and,

like many of the educated women of her country, speaks English
with an elegance of enunciation rarely acquired by Americans.
Being acquainted with Dr. Dickson, formerly a professor in a New
York medical school, and now in a similar school here, I went to
his college towards night, in the hope of meeting him. The regular
lectures of the day were over; but Professor Louis Agassiz was
about to begin one upon comparative anatomy, which I attended,
and afterwards had a conversation with him and Dr. Dickson. That
evening Marcus, Rebecca, Mr. Taft, and I went to the concert of
Catharine Hayes, the Irish singer. The rooms were crowded with
the *élite* of Charleston. She sang " Auld Robin Gray " better than
I ever heard a ballad sung before, also the "Last Rose of Summer," and took the audience by storm,— or, rather, by zephyr.

Next day Mrs. Taft called with a coach, and took us to drive.
We went several miles out of town near the banks of the Cooper
River, then crossed to those of the Ashley, between which two
streams Charleston stands on a point of land, as Philadelphia does
between the Delaware and Schuylkill. The country is level, the
soil sandy, the main roads made of plank. The principal trees are
pine, of several species, the willow, magnolia, palmetto, and the
wild orange. In many places the pines are covered with much of
a beautiful kind of moss, hanging from the limbs in dense clusters,
varying from a foot to six feet long. If the tree has not too much,
it looks very beautiful; but some are so completely covered as to
have a dreary aspect, the vitality of the tree being generally destroyed by this parasite. Negroes, both men and women, were at
work in many places, digging and manuring for planting. The
weather was so warm we rode without overcoats, with hats off, and
the carriage-windows open. Coming back, we rode through the
principal parts of the city, where ladies in large numbers were
promenading in King Street, the fashionable resort, with parasols
and spring dresses.

January 30, in the forenoon, I took a stroll through the market,
in a building similar to that of Philadelphia, and extending in length
five or six squares. The venders, with very rare exceptions, were
negroes; and the same is true of the purchasers. Chief among the
vendibles were great quantities of sweet potatoes, and two edible
roots I had never seen before,— the yam and the *kanyau*,— besides
enormous turnips. Next I went to a slave-auction, where two men,

two women, and three children were sold in four lots. While we were lounging about afterwards, Marcus called at the store of one of his customers, who, upon seeing me, knew me at once. He had been at Bloomingdale two or three times while I was there. He told me that the Friends' meeting-house that formerly existed here had been torn down, the lot remaining vacant. It stood on King Street at a place which is now really the centre of the city. When evening came, we went to another lecture on comparative anatomy by Agassiz, at 5 P.M., and at 7 a lecture on geology by him. The hall was crowded, and many had to stand; the lecture one of the most interesting I ever heard. At ten the same evening Marcus, Rebecca (Mrs. Spring), Mr. Taft, and I went to a ball at Dr. Bellinger's. There were about two hundred guests, and we had a fine opportunity of seeing "the beauty and chivalry" of the city. It is the most fashionable season of the year; and there are many strangers in town, attracted by the season, and perhaps more by the races, which commence next Wednesday, and are patronized by the *élite* of the land. The belle of the evening was a Miss Caldwell, of North Carolina, a blonde in blue, of sweet eighteen. A band of music, and dancing in two rooms and on the piazza. Four physicians came and spoke to me, having met me at Bloomingdale and other places, but whom I had forgotten as being from Charleston. The supper table was some seventy feet long, plentifully supplied with an almost endless variety of meats, cakes, etc., to say nothing of brandy, sherry, Madeira, and champagne. Marcus and Rebecca left at half-past twelve, and Mr. Taft and I at half-past one. I had expected to see darker complexions in the women, but in that respect I should not have known that we were not in New York or Philadelphia.

January 31, at eleven o'clock, Marcus and I went to a celebration, in the hall of the Charleston College, of the opening of a Museum of Natural History, in which Professor Agassiz had an important part. The hall was densely filled, and many were going away, unable to find even standing room; but we wedged ourselves along, and a seat was given me upon the platform, along with the orator (Agassiz) and the college trustees. About four hundred seats on the floor were occupied by ladies; and, but for the fact that I had once before seen a woman, I might have been embarrassed in meeting the gaze of so many. The chaplain read a prayer; and then Agassiz

gave an extemporaneous address for about forty minutes,—a most decided failure. The Museum was then thrown open, and for an hour
or two the audience entertained themselves with the curiosities and
with each other. Agassiz receives several hundred dollars more for
four months' services here than from his professorship at Harvard
College, and he is said to have engaged here for four winters.
After dinner (at three o'clock) we went to see the statue of Calhoun
at the City Hall, where is also a portrait of Washington by Trumbull.

To-day, Sunday, we have been to the Unitarian church to hear Dr.
Samuel Gilman, a Northern man, a graduate of Harvard, and author
of the college song, "Fair Harvard," who is the husband of Caroline Gilman, of literary fame. The Sabbath appears to be observed
here quite as strictly as in the Northern cities. In the evening Marcus, Rebecca, and I went, upon invitation, to Dr. Gilman's, and
passed two hours there very pleasantly. Later we accompanied
them to a meeting of the negroes belonging to his church. Their
number was not large, the belief and the ceremonies of the Unitarians being less attractive than those of Baptists and Methodists.

February 3.—This forenoon attended the auction-sale of about
thirty negroes. Dined at Augustus Taft's, in whose garden the daffo-
dils are in bloom and the rose-bushes have leaves out of the bud.
At 7 P.M. we went to another of Agassiz's lectures, this time on the
classification of animals. His manner of treating it was admirable.
He illustrates his topics as clearly as any lecturer I ever heard in
America or Europe. The hall was crowded, and many of the audience were ladies. He is paid by a subscription, and the lectures
are free to the public. At 11 P.M. I went to the "St. Cecilia's" ball,
having received a ticket from Dr. Monefeld, whom I met at Dr.
Bellinger's yesterday. The Cecilians are an old society or club,
conservative and exclusive, who give three balls each winter, to
which strangers may be invited, but which cannot be attended by
residents who are not members. About one hundred of each sex
were present, with a great display of dress and feminine beauty.
As it is now about Smithfield quarterly meeting in Rhode Island,
I will mention, in order that the Friends may answer the queries relating to me, "Clear, as far as appears," that I only danced twice,
and that, being with Miss Howland (two of them), a name prominent
in our society, it must have been all right. Besides, I kept good

hours, coming home as early as two o'clock. Yesterday evening I was at a *Soirée musicale, chez M. Gainbault, marchand Français*, who has lived in Charleston several years, between forty and fifty ladies and gentlemen being present, among them the two Miss Howlands aforesaid, daughters of a Northern man in business here. The evening passed mostly in conversation, occasionally interrupted by music, the pianists being Mrs. Gainbault, the Howlands, and a Mrs. West. As a matter of course, we topped off with a supper of oysters, game, cakes, ices, confections, and wine, in bountiful supply. I returned at 1 A.M.

February 4.— Marcus, Rebecca, Augustus Taft, and I rode out of Charleston about two miles to a large enclosure, within which, for some reason or other, a considerable company had assembled. Augustus, as member of an association bearing the patriarchal name of "Jockey Club," had a red ribbon tied in a button-hole of his coat; while Marcus and I, as strangers, had a white ribbon thus attached. These seemed to admit us into a high building, open at one side, and familiarly termed "a stand." Augustus did not tell us what he took us there for; and so, after remaining a little more than three hours to find out, we returned. But a remarkable thing happened in that time. A horse, which seemed to be travelling in company with others, went ahead of them all, and passed over a space of four miles quicker than any other horse ever did in the whole State of South Carolina.

I had dined at Dr. Gaillard's, in company with other physicians; and I spent the evening at Dr. Dickson's, where I met a physician recently returned from Turkey, who informed me of the whereabouts of several persons with whom I got acquainted in 1838–39, at Athens, Smyrna, and Constantinople. The next day, in company with Drs. Gaillard, Moulton, Holbrook, Wragg, a Mr. Lassaigne, and Marcus Spring, I went to Sullivan's Island, six miles from town, on which is old Fort Moultrie; but our object was not to see the Revolutionary battle-ground, only to visit Agassiz and his wonders of the deep there collected,— polyps, jelly-fishes, star-fish, sea-urchins, crabs, etc.,— many creatures quite new and interesting to me. We last saw him on the 6th, before sailing for Havana, at his lecture that evening on "the same subject continued."

The evening of February 5 we spent with friends at Mr. Howland's, father of the ladies twice mentioned. His two eldest daughters were four years in Europe. The elder speaks German, Italian, and French with much fluency. Among the company was a niece of the artist, Washington Allston, a beautiful young woman, answering to my idea of Marie Antoinette. The evening of the 6th we went at ten o'clock to a meeting popularly known as the "Jockey Club Ball," a yearly meeting which always assembles here in Charleston, not at the Friends' meeting-house, for that, as I told you, has been destroyed, but in a large hall appropriate to such gatherings. I did not dance with any one except the Miss Howlands, Miss Carter, and Mrs. Beach; and this meeting (like the St. Cecilia's) was closed with a supper of several things besides bread and butter. It was only a little past two when I got back to the hotel. This was our last day in Charleston. I am greatly in hopes that the quiet life, the regular hours, and the abstemious diet of my sojourn here will materially contribute to my health. If not, it is not my intention to try them again here.

Charleston was in 1852 the most cultivated and one of the most prosperous of the cities in the slave-holding States; not large in population, but with long-accumulated wealth in a few families of planters and merchants, and with a small class of professional men who stood high in law and medicine, and had that turn for control in politics which marked the long domination of the slaveholding States in Congress and the administration of government. Calhoun, the one leading statesman of the Carolinas, had lately died (1850). His great compromising opponent, Clay, was still living, as was Webster; but both died in this year, 1852, after Webster had made an unsuccessful campaign for the Presidency in the Whig nominating convention. These three old statesmen had united in 1850 in a vain effort to postpone the conflict over negro slavery by adopting the pro-slavery compromises of that year; and, when Dr. Earle visited Carolina, the fanatical advocacy of slavery by the leaders of opinion at the South had reached almost its highest point. They declared that "cotton was king," and that only slave labor could profitably raise cotton; and they dictated, later in the spring of 1852, the nomination of General Pierce, of New Hampshire, for President, as the most subservient of the

Northern Democrats to their slave-masters' domination. He
was elected by a great majority over General Scott, Webster
himself favoring Pierce's election; and the policy of South
Carolina seemed likely to prevail for long years in the country,
bringing with it the annexation of Cuba as slave territory and
the extension of slavery over the new States won from Mexico
or built up from the western borders of Jefferson's Louisiana
purchase.   It was in this heyday of slavery extension and
cotton-growing prosperity that Dr. Earle visited Carolina; and
it was as friend or a scientific neutral that the pro-slavery
citizens of Charleston had the year before made Louis Agassiz
a professor in the medical college where Dr. Earle heard his
enchanting lectures.   His establishment on Sullivan's Island
was in a cottage lent him by Mrs. Rutledge as a laboratory, at
the head of a long beach, where he could easily collect the
marine animals which he was using in his researches and
demonstrations.   Dr. Holbrook, who went with Dr. Earle and
other physicians to visit this laboratory, as above mentioned,
had married into the Rutledge family, one of the most distinguished in Carolina; and it was at Mrs. Holbrook's country
house, "The Hollow Tree," near Charleston, that Professor
Agassiz and his family spent much time during this year.   He
had first begun to lecture at Charleston in 1851, and it was
understood that his engagement was for four years; but at
Christmas, following this visit of Dr. Earle, he was attacked
with a violent fever at Dr. Holbrook's house, and was compelled to give up his engagement in the third year.

For an early Abolitionist, as Dr. Earle was, and never an ad-
mirer of the peculiarities of Southern society, his letters from
Charleston show very little study of slavery upon its own
ground; but, in fact, the hold of that evil institution on the
country in 1852 seemed so assured that scientific men, like
Agassiz and Earle, might be excused for doubting if their
active opposition to it could avail to shorten its days.   They
were received by slaveholders with flattering courtesy.   The
graceful and pleasure-loving society in which they found themselves was agreeable to both; and, though Dr. Earle's Quaker
scruples appear humorously in his letters, he was too much a

philosopher and student of human nature not to enjoy for a few days this Epicurean life of Charleston. The city itself had a peculiar history. Its two rivers were named for the family of the first Lord Shaftesbury, Anthony Ashley Cooper, the ancestor of the lunacy reformer of England, Lord Ashley, and the friend of Locke, who had drawn up for Carolina its first inoperative philosophical constitution. It was besieged and captured by the British during the Revolution; and the adjacent region became the scene of the bitterest strife between the patriots and the Tories of Carolina, in which Marion and Tarleton figured on the American and the British sides. It had threatened rebellion under the name of "nullification" and the lead of Calhoun twenty years before Dr. Earle visited there; and in that crisis, which the firmness of Jackson terminated without danger to the Union, Trelawny, the lawless friend of Shelley and Byron, who had fought beside Odysseus in the Greek Revolution, came over to join the Carolina insurgents. Only nine years after Dr. Earle's visit Charleston fired the first gun in the Civil War; and under the unexpected result of that cannonade the whole social system of Carolina, as it existed in 1852, was destroyed, and political power, even in their own State, passed away from the slaveholders for years.

On leaving Charleston in February, 1852, Dr. Earle and his cousins sailed for Key West and Cuba on a steamer bound for the Panama Isthmus, with many emigrants to California, then newly gold-producing and very attractive to the roving American young men. His description of the short voyage to Havana belongs in this chapter : —

We left Charleston Sunday, February 8, at 8 A.M., in the steamer "Isabel," with 60 cabin passengers and 328 more in the steerage, the latter bound for California, and mostly "Crackers," as the Charleston people call them, — persons from the interior of South Carolina and Georgia, of primitive habits and uncouth manners. Among them are about 60 negroes, — a few of them free, but chiefly slaves taken to California (though a nominally free State) under some special agreement. Not 1 in 20 of the steerage passengers had ever seen the ocean before; and a good many soon wished they never

had seen it. At eleven on Tuesday evening we touched at Key
West, which is a port on an island between Florida and Cuba. I
went ashore, and walked through a few silent streets in the twenty
minutes we stayed there,— among low cottages of queer construction, shaded in many places by cocoanut and other palm-trees.
Everything around me bespoke a tropical climate, and the novelty
of the scene at midnight was singularly impressive. The moon was
just rising, and even she told us of our change of latitude. She was
at the third quarter ; and, instead of being turned up, as we see it
in New England, the line between light and darkness was horizontal.
The north star was much nearer the horizon than I had ever seen
it, even in the Levant; and the "Dipper" dipped its long handle
into the sea. In other words, Ursa Major wet the extremity of her
tail.

On his return voyage Dr. Earle landed at Savannah, and
went, by way of Charleston and Richmond, to Philadelphia
early in March, 1852.

In contrast to these halcyon days among the slaveholders
and the slave-auctions of Carolina is a picture of the Northern
emancipationist circle, many of them Dr. Earle's kindred, and
two of them (Mrs. Weld and Sarah Grimké) natives of Charleston, but excluded from the society of their birthplace because
of their faith in emancipation, not only for colored men, but for
white women. On his return from a few months in Washington, late in April, 1856,— four years after he was with the
Spring family at Charleston,— Dr. Earle went to their new
home of Eagleswood, near Perth Amboy, N.J. (where Thoreau
visited and surveyed the lands of the estate in November of
the same year), and there met the same circle of Quakers and
radicals which Thoreau describes in a letter to his sister : * —

This is a queer place. There is one large, long stone building
which cost some $40,000, a few shops and offices, an old farm-house,
and Mr. Spring's perfectly private residence, within twenty rods of
the main building. The central fact here is evidently Mr. Theodore

---

* See " Familiar Letters of Henry David Thoreau," Boston, 1894, pp. 336-338. Mr. Birney had
been a slaveholder in Alabama, but had freed his slaves long before, and removed to the North. His
wife was a Miss Fitzhugh, related to the wife of Gerrit Smith; and that baronial democrat of Central
New York often visited Eagleswood.

Weld's school, recently established, around which various other
things revolve. One evening I went to the school-room, hall, or
what not, to see the children and their teachers and patrons dance.
Mr. Weld, a kind-looking man with a long white beard, danced with
them; and so did Mr. Spring and others. Sunday morning I attended a sort of Quaker meeting at the same place. Imagine them
sitting close to the wall, all around a hall, with old Quaker-looking
men and women here and there: Mrs. Weld and her sister, two
elderly gray-headed ladies, the former in extreme bloomer costume,
which was what you may call remarkable; Mr. Arnold Buffum, with
broad face and a great white beard, looking like a pier-head made of
the cork-tree with the bark on, as if he could buffet a considerable
wave; James G. Birney, formerly candidate for the Presidency, with
another particularly white head and beard, etc. . . . . Mrs. Kirkland
has just bought a lot here. . . . Mr. Alcott has just come down here
for the third Sunday.

And now for Dr. Earle's experiences in the preceding May.
He had tarried in Philadelphia on his way North, hearing
Thackeray lecture there to a small audience on Swift, and
listening to sharp debates in the Yearly Meeting of the Philadelphia Quakers, long divided on theological questions. Finally,
we have this: —

Wednesday, April 30, 1856.— I packed my luggage, and bade adieu
to Philadelphia, crossing the Delaware River to Camden, and coming
over the railroad from Camden to Amboy, where I found a boatman
who brought me with oars a mile and a half up the Raritan River to
Eagleswood, formerly a "phalanstery" called the "Raritan Bay
Union." So here I am at Marcus Spring's. Rebecca (Mrs. Spring)
is confined to her room from the effect of a fall, though sitting up
most of the day. Mrs. Pauline Wright Davis, of Providence, and
Mrs. Oliver Johnson are here on a visit. The "helps" in her household are a Frenchman, a French woman, a German girl,— well educated,— and an Irish woman, the object being to teach the children
to speak German and French (but not Irish). Uncle Arnold and
Aunt Rebecca (Buffum) are here, and well.

May 1.— All the old folks and young folks of Eagleswood, of
whom there are in all about fifty, had made great preparations for

celebrating May Day in the old English style here. There was to have been a picnic in the woods, and a Queen of the May to be crowned there. But the winds blew and the rain fell in torrents, and the young folks were sadly disappointed. Partial consolation was found in the evening festival,—a fancy-dress ball, at which about thirty danced, including myself. Time brings the unexpected; for example, Mrs. Davis and me dancing together, with Sarah Grimké, Angelina (Grimké) Weld, and James G. Birney as spectators. I omitted to say that on the evening of my arrival here I attended the weekly meeting of the Eagleswood Lyceum, at which papers were read by Mr. Birney and Charles Weld, son of Theodore.

May 3.—I went to New York to-day, and returned to Eagleswood in the evening, Mrs. Caroline Kirkland, the author, and her daughter accompanying us for a visit.

May 4.—On this very pleasant Sunday we had a meeting, at which a hymn was read, a chapter in the Bible read, and a sermon delivered. Afterwards we rambled all over the large premises of romantic Eagleswood, the property mainly of Marcus Spring, who was one of the owners when it was a community.

It was at Eagleswood, in the October and November of 1859, that Mrs. Spring received as her guest the wife of John Brown, of Kansas and Virginia, on her way to and from the prison of her husband at Charlestown, W. Va. Among the Northern women who gave sympathy, money, and admiration to that heroic family, none was more active or helpful than this cousin of Dr. Earle, with whom he had witnessed the flourishing state of the slaveholders of Carolina and of Cuba.

A few months before the tragedy of Harper's Ferry and Charlestown, Dr. Earle had again spent a few days at Eagleswood with his cousins, of which visit he thus speaks:—

I stayed in Eagleswood from the 13th to the 17th of January, 1859, and passed nearly half my time there, ;in Theodore Weld's school, which I think, on the whole, the best school I ever saw. It was a gratification, among others, to find a place where the letter *R* is recognized, practically, as an element of our language. His general system may be understood from an incident of the last day I was in his school. An assistant having charge of the common

school-room, Mr. Weld came in with his arms full of hammers, pin-
cers, shears, steelyards, etc., laid them, including a toy wheelbarrow,
on the table, and said to his class in Natural Philosophy: "Here
are various implements constructed upon the principle of the several
forms of the *lever*. They will be here two days, in which time I want
you all to examine them, and then be prepared, each of you, to
give a lecture on them, demonstrating the principle by which they
each act. And please remember that I wish each of you, in examining them, to depend on his own powers of observation, and not ask
explanations from others." That is the way to make good scholars.
In one class a pupil only nine years old, read a long original analysis of a play of Shakespeare's, giving his opinion of the several
characters. In the reading classes, if a pupil miscalled a word, the
others said, "wrong," and the reader tried again. If he failed the
second or the third time, his error was not pointed out; but he sat
down, and the next pupil read the sentence. Thus in every branch
the pupil is taught to rely upon himself, and does not fall into the
carelessness which always marks those whose teachers are constantly
assisting them. No better proof of the excellence of this system is
needed than the brilliant success of this Eagleswood school of
seventy pupils, boys and girls, educated together.

When I arrived, the river was frozen over. The next day Mr.
Weld and his assistant teachers, male and female, and nearly all
the children, after school hours, went to slide and skate on the ice.
Even Mrs. Weld — sober, staid, intellectual Angelina Grimké that
was — joined in the pastime. Alack and alas! what is the world
coming to?

Signor Mario, an Italian exile from Venice, with his English wife
(Jessie White formerly), who was seized and imprisoned in Genoa
two or three years ago on suspicion * that she was concerned with
Mazzini in his efforts to revolutionize Italy, passed a day at
Marcus Spring's while I was there, and addressed the pupils and
others upon the condition of Italy. At the close of the lecture a
contribution was taken up to assist a school for young Italians in
London. The donations amounted to $112.

* This lady still lives in Italy, and is one of the correspondents of the New York *Nation*. She
has written much, — among other things, a Life of Garibaldi, whom she knew well. It was true that
she was in the councils of Mazzini, who in 1859 was still under ban in Italy, but who is now honored,
with Garibaldi, as one of the noblest of his country's patriots.

CHAPTER X.

In these years of revolution and war in Cuba, following the emancipation of slavery in North and South America, the old order of things, when our slave-holding politicians hungered for annexing the rich island to add sugar planting to cotton-growing as two firm pillars of the system, has so completely passed away that Dr. Earle's description of his travels in Cuba reads like ancient history. He was in the gay mood of a tourist, as he had been many years before while traversing Southern Europe. He was now in his first tropical experiences; and his adventures, if not startling, as those of Americans in Cuba have lately been, were full of novelty and interest. His diary thus goes on : —

Havana, Feb. 14, 1852.—On Wednesday last, February 11, at 8 A.M., the high lands of Cuba appeared from the deck of the "Isabel," like a dim cloud on the southern horizon. Green fields soon became visible, with the groves of palms and other trees, and next the stately fortress of the Moro and part of the city of Havana. At ten we passed the castle, entered the harbor,— one of the largest and most secure from storms in the world,— and anchored near the wharves. In the two hours required for obtaining permission to land, we enjoyed from the deck the novel, interesting scene around us,— ships of many nations, the peculiar city houses, the fortresses, the distant country seats, and the groves of tropical trees. In the boats that came around us the people dressed in white linen, with Leghorn or Panama sombreros, two-thirds of them with cigars in their mouths, and the other third just going to smoke. Finally, we paid $2 each for a printed permit to land, came ashore in boats, and were whirled off in *volantes* to Mrs. Almy's hotel.

In all that I have seen of Europe there was nothing in nature so unlike New England scenery as this of Cuba, and nothing so different in manners and customs, this side of Greece, unless Venice be excepted. The original city of Havana is a fortress, surrounded by a high wall, and now contains perhaps 100,000 people. The streets are straight, few of them paved, and hardly more than eighteen feet wide,— some only sixteen,— mostly without sidewalks. Where there are any, they are but fifteen inches or two feet wide. The houses (all built of stone, covered with "rough cast") are often two or three stories high, each story from fourteen to twenty feet; but half are only one story, with flat roofs used as walks or for flowers or for drying clothes. The floors are of smooth, hard mortar, occasionally of marble; carpets rare, except small pieces of straw matting. The windows are most peculiar, very large (ten or twelve feet high by five or six wide), descending to the floor, and guarded outside with iron bars an inch thick. Inside they are furnished with blinds or close shutters. This is the whole window. I have traversed many streets, and not seen a dozen windows with sash or glass, the climate not requiring it. Every bed is high-posted, and with a gauze curtain quite enclosing it, to keep out mosquitoes. Neglecting to draw mine the first night, I found sixteen red spots on my hands in the morning, not to mention my face.

The last three weeks are said to have been as cold as the "oldest inhabitant" can remember, yet the people dress as thinly as our New Englanders do in summer. And, although barely past midwinter with us, summer vegetables are here plenty. At dinner we have lettuce, string beans, green peas and green corn, two kinds of sweet potatoes (one perfectly white), yams, the plantain fruit, bananas, oranges, and pineapples, the last much better than those exported,— softer, and retaining their peculiar flavor without that disagreeable acidity that often makes our tongues sore. But expenses are no joke here. We pay $3 a day each for board, and $1 an hour for a carriage when we drive out. The *volante* is generally used,— a queer concern with enormous wheels, and the horse a long way in front of the carriage, while the "body" is so far in front of the two wheels that the shaft-horse bears much of the weight of the passengers as well as the rider who mounts him, wearing seven-league boots to keep off the mud, and tremendous spurs. The horse's tail is long, braided, and tied to the back of the saddle. An awning keeps off the sun from you. The ladies sit without bonnets, but many with thin black veils thrown over their heads.

February 15.— It is First Day, but the change in Havana from the ordinary week-day is barely sufficient to be noticed by a stranger. I went out about seven this morning, and found that the shops were not generally opened so early as yesterday. The market, however, was more than usually crowded. As in most foreign countries, it is here a square building, enclosing a large court,— perhaps an acre,— and to-day thronged, building and court, by sellers and buyers. All kinds of vegetables that we have from April to October were there,— with many that we never have,— all fresh from the ground, the stem, the vine, or the tree. I went into several churches, the great Cathedral among them. The number of persons going to the churches was greater than on week-days, each family followed by a richly dressed negro, carrying a piece of carpet for them to kneel on. The señoras and señoritas were mostly on foot, in white or parti-colored dresses,— some ladies bareheaded, others with a black veil so thin as to impede the view very little, either of themselves or of those who look at them. In some of the churches there is a great deal of show; but it is tinsel and mortar rather than the gold, silver, and rich marbles I used to see in Italian churches. Beneath the Cathedral, they say, the bones of Columbus rest;[*] and within it is the only monument in Cuba to his memory, a marble slab inserted in the wall, near the high altar, with an *alto-rilievo* bust of the great navigator, and an inscription. As I entered, a priest was *performing* at a side altar; and there was a large audience. Half a dozen negroes were at work round the grand altar, supplying the many candelabra with wax tapers, six feet high, and making other preparations for high mass. I could not get within thirty feet of the monument without treading on the ground devoted to the priests and their servants; but, following a rule which I have found very useful to a traveller, "Go till you are stopped," I put on a bold face, walked straight up to the monument, took out note-book and pencil, and copied this inscription, in Spanish,—

> O Remains and Image of the Great Columbus!
> A thousand centuries shall ye be preserved in this Urn,
> And in the memory of our Nation.

[*] Although there is yet some doubt on the subject, it is probable that the bones of Columbus do rest, after almost as many journeys as his living body made, in this Cathedral of Havana. He died at Valladolid in Spain, May 20, 1506, was first buried there, but in 1509 was removed to Seville. About 1541 his remains were sent to Hispaniola, to lie in the grand new Cathedral of Santo Domingo, as they did, in accordance with his own wish, for two centuries and a half. But in 1795 the conquering French republicans got possession of the Spanish end of Hispaniola; and the Spaniards, acting in concert with the then Duke of Veragua, a descendant of Columbus, supposed they had removed the

At ten o'clock we took a barouche from a stable kept by a Yankee, and drove into the country. Farm labors were going on, as on week-days. Three miles out of Havana we halted at the Bishop's Garden, chiefly interesting for its many palms, mango-trees, and bamboos. The last grow like bulrushes, but are jointed, are from an inch to three inches in diameter near the ground, and from twenty to forty feet high. When swayed by the wind, they strike against each other with a clicking like castanets in the hands of a Spanish dancer. Among the visitors we saw a family of Creoles (native Cubans) sitting under a cluster of tall bamboos. They bid us good morning, and we stopped to admire a beautiful Italian greyhound belonging to them. The mother pointed to Jenny S., and said she was "a Spanish girl." One of the young ladies asked if she was my daughter. I told her no, that Marcus was her father. Then, putting on a very lackadaisical look, I added that I had no wife. At first she did not understand my bad Spanish; but, in a moment, assisted by one of the others, she caught the idea, and, with tropical vivacity, clasped her hands, laughed, and exclaimed, "Oh, Señor no tenga una sposa," and then blushed deeply as a brunette can blush from the top of her forehead to the top of her dress,— no little distance, to tell the truth. A mile farther from the town is the larger garden of the Conte Palatino, approached through a long avenue of royal palms, and with a much larger variety of tropical productions than in the Bishop's Garden, and kept in better order. It offers a fine view over the neighboring country. A negro cut for us a bouquet of roses, dahlias, the hibiscus, and flowers with names to me unknown. As we drove back to Havana, the road, on both sides, was bordered with roses and oleanders, all in blossom.

At 4 P.M. we again took the barouche, and drove first to the outskirts of the fortified part of the town. Here, in a street running next to the city wall, with houses on the opposite side, were many negroes,— men, women, and children,— assembled, according to their custom on this day of the week, for a half-holiday. In a short distance were a dozen rooms, opening by large doors and windows to the street, and used as dance-halls by these people. In all there was music of some sort, generally that of a rude drum, and a still

remains from Santo Domingo to Havana. But the bishop of that Cathedral has lately maintained that the bones then taken away were those of Diego, the son, not of Christopher, the sire. The Spanish authorities are sure that the bishop of Santo Domingo is mistaken, as presumably he is; but who shall decide when bishops disagree?

ruder instrument (seen by me for the first time here) formed of steel springs, vibrating as you press them down at the end, letting the fingers slip off. The dancing was as rude as such music,— no harmony in the one, no grace in the other,— such as one might expect in Central Africa, from which the slave-trade still brings many negroes. They engaged enthusiastically in the sport, and were uproariously happy. We next went to the Paseo, the fashionable promenade and driving-course, and now at its most fashionable hour of the week. Suppose from three to five thousand men, in their "Sabba'-day clothes," ranged along the sidewalks of Main Street, in Worcester, from the City Hall to the Court House (only this Cuban street was but half as wide), then take as many chaises, (mostly) half of them with the tops thrown back, as will form a close procession on both sides of the street, all the way. Dress all the pretty ladies in the carriages, and most of the homely ones, as for an evening party,— with a few gentlemen interspersed,— without head-dress or shawl, then set the carriages in motion at a walk. Let everybody look at everybody else, and make looking, with the natural comment, their sole business for two hours. Meantime the people on the sidewalks must stand still and stare, getting as close to the carriages as they can or as the police will let them,— say, within four feet. That is the way they do things on the Paseo, Sundays. We joined this procession as we might in the Bois de Boulogne of Paris, and enjoyed it much, until it grew so dark that "nobody couldn't see nobody" with satisfactory distinctness. Then everybody dispersed. Of course, the theatre was open in the evening,— the world-renowned Teatro de Tacon, larger than any other modern theatre in the world, except La Scala in Milan and one in Naples. This evening the house was full, the captain-general of Cuba, De la Concha, with two of his daughters, being present. I think this will do for one Sunday.

Yesterday (14th) I had walked for some hours in the country, going into the fields, the groves, and among the negro houses. It was all delightful, except the stepping on a big prickly pear, and getting three large thorns stuck through my thin shoe into my foot. A negro helped me to get them out, and was wonderfully pleased with the rubber springs of my Congress boot. I found the cocoanut palms very numerous, giving an African aspect to the country land-scape. The fruit, growing in clusters at the top of the tree, just beneath the leaves, was very abundant. On one tree I counted one hundred nuts, the lowest full grown, the highest as large as a hen's egg. Indian corn was growing in large fields for fodder, sown like grain, and cut when in tassel. Four crops a year are raised in the same field. It is brought into the city on horses and mules, the creatures so enveloped in corn-stalks that only the heads and legs are visible. Other things brought into the city or carried from it are transported in the same way, one man often taking charge of several animals. He leads the forward mule, and the rest come behind, Indian file, each tied to the tail of the other. Oxen are also yoked in an odd way, the yoke bound to their horns and to a cushion on their foreheads, without a bow, so that they draw by pushing with the horns and head, the head being almost as fixed as if in a pillory. Each ox has a rope in his nostril, while the driver in his ox-cart guides them by reins attached to the nostril-ropes. He carries a stick about the size and length of a rake-handle, with a sharp nail at one end. This is his goad. The ploughing is done much as in Greece. A plough with but one handle and a beam ten feet long, entering a ring of the yoke, has a long, narrow ploughshare of wood, tipped with an iron point.

February 18.— We came from Havana to-day by railroad to Guines (two syllables), a town almost fifty miles from Havana, inland, but nearer the southern than the northern coast, with some 2,500 people, an old stone church in its centre, surrounded by stone houses of one story, covered with brick tiling. The streets are wretchedly bad, rocky, uneven, and without drains ; but no such need exists for good streets as with us, for the transportation here, as in Havana, is on the backs of horses and mules. As we came, the country was almost an uninterrupted level, a ridge of high hills, around which the railroad curves to avoid grade, lying at a distance on our left. We came through forests of palms and other trees, often filled with an undergrowth of shrubs and clustering vines, in tropical profusion, and so dense that it would be almost impossible to get through them without a road. These alternated with fields of plantain and bananas, some of tobacco and pineapple, a few orange trees, crops of potatoes, corn, tomatoes, and other vegetables, some waste land, lots of wild flowers new to me, passing many *haciendas*, or farmhouses, invariably low, and with roofs thatched with palm-leaf. As showing the climate, I may say that we saw Indian corn in all stages

of its growth, from four inches high to the stalk of ripe ears. If a
Yankee farmer could come here, and preserve his habits of industry
and thrift, he might soon grow rich. His farm would yield from two
to four times as much as in Leicester, and most of it would need no
manure. Barns are almost unknown. No provision is needed for
cattle in winter. Clothing would cost little; for cotton may be worn
the year through, except an overcoat for cool mornings and nights.
The mercury this winter has been as low as 50° or even 48° Fah-
renheit, a degree of cold almost unprecedented. The average winter
temperature at Havana is 70°, the coldest about 60°. Carpets
would be a nuisance, unless of straw or. oilcloth; sackcloth, with
a folded blanket on it, and covered with a sheet, makes the bed;
and nine-tenths of the nights the sleeper needs nothing but a sheet
over him. No expense for fuel except to cook with. No chimneys or
fireplaces are needed save in the kitchen. Thus, while a farmer's
income is increased here, his expenses are much diminished; yet the
Cuban farmers have not half the conveniences of life that the New
England farmer has, and seem to be miserably poor. So I suppose,
if Yankees should come here, they would fall into the shiftless habits
of the people, and soon become as poor as they are.

In the afternoon we took a *volante*, and drove out two or three
miles to the famous Amistad sugar plantation. We hired the horse
of an old Frenchman, who had been one of Napoleon's *vieille garde*,
and is covered with wounds received in all parts of Europe, from
Spain to Moscow. He preserves his old arms as glorious me-
mentoes.* As we drove, the road for a long distance was through
great cane-fields on either side, farther than we could see, over-
topped in places by most beautiful groves of the royal palm. As we
approached the planter's house, we saw fifty negroes, more women
than men, cutting the cane with *machetes*, while a long train of carts
carried it to the sugar-mill. The knife used is like our bill-hook,
except that it is straight and is used with much dexterity. The

---

* In visiting Santo Domingo in 1871, with Dr. Howe and Frederick Douglass, Dr. A. D. White,
since ambassador to Germany and Russia, found there a still earlier French survivor of the Revolutionary and Napoleonic period, an aged "Theophilanthropist," who dated from the days of the
Directory, and could not endure to live under the Corsican despot. The West Indies have long been
the nursery or the retreat of French persons of odd types. It was at Martinique that Josephine
Bonaparte was born and first married. The Ceiba mentioned below as sung by Dr. Earle's friend
Whittier, the controversial Quaker poet, was introduced by him in his poem, written shortly before,—

As the serpent-like bejuco winds its spiral, fold on fold,
Round the tall and stately Ceiba, till it withers in its hold,
So a base and bestial nature round the vassal's manhood twines, etc.

stalk of the cane is cut close to the ground at one blow, and its top
lopped off by another. A second negro now takes it, stripping off
the leaves and throwing it on a pile. A third takes it to the cart,
while a fourth loads it,— all slaves, I suppose. A herd of oxen follow
the cane-cutters, eating the stripped leaves; but many remain on the
ground as manure for the new crop, which soon springs from the
roots of the cane. When cut, the stalk is one or two inches thick,
and from two to four feet long, rarely, five. Its whole interior is
saturated with juice, like a sponge with water. This is sweet as
syrup, very luscious for a time, but at length becomes nauseous.
The negroes like it, and often help themselves to it as they work.

The Amistad cane-mill is driven by water. It consists of three
iron cylinders, eight feet long by two thick, between which the cane
passes only once, the juice running almost in torrents between the
lower cylinders into a tank, from which it is forced into other tanks,
heated and clarified with lime. It then runs through charcoal filters,
is boiled to a certain density, filtered again, and then boiled till
sugar forms. The molasses is drained out by whirling it swiftly in
metallic tubs, perforated like the "centrifugal clothes-wringer," — a
recent improvement, which does in ten minutes what used to be the
work of ten days. Formerly it took nearly three weeks to convert
the cane into sugar for the market. This is done here in one day
now, and could be done in seven hours. The old story of Timothy
Dexter sending out warming-pans from Newburyport for the Cuban
winters, which the delighted planters used for sugar-pans, will no
longer apply. Mr. Dodd, of Newark, N.J., has just completed a
"pan" (as they call a boiler), which will save much labor, facilitate
sugar-making still more, and produce a much whiter, purer, and
more perfectly crystallized sugar. This pan is in use here at
Amistad's, and is the only sample yet made, producing lately seven
tons of sugar in one day. The day of warming-pans is well over,
and future Dexters will not make fortunes by similar blunders.

February 20, *Cardenas.*— A journey of sixty miles by rail, through
a country more fertile than any yet seen, brought us from Guines to
Cardenas. On this route we first saw coffee plantations and
frequent orange orchards. In the forests the gigantic Ceiba, celebrated by Friend Whittier, was abundant; and some species of the
palm were noted that we had not seen before.

Cardenas is a seaport on the northern coast, perhaps seventy miles east of Havana. A few years ago it was a small settlement, but now has a population of five or six thousand. Its growth has been rapid, and it may become a rival of Havana in time. The first expedition of Narciso Lopez landed here last year. The walls of the government house, burnt by him or his followers, still stand on the plaza; and there are bullet-marks on our hotel, kept by Mrs. Woodbury, a Portuguese lady from Buenos Ayres, whose husband was a cousin of Justice Levi Woodbury, of New Hampshire. In his second expedition, sailing from New Orleans in August last year, and landing at Bahia Honda, Colonel Crittenden, an American, with fifty of his captured men, was shot in Havana, near which he was captured, and Lopez himself was garroted.

We have been to-day nearly four miles out of town, to the house of Mr. Phinney, from Massachusetts, at which Miss Bremer, the Swedish novelist, passed two weeks, when she was in Cuba recently, and where she sat up after midnight to see the Southern Cross, a constellation invisible in our latitudes. His daughter, Miss Susan Phinney, educated in New England, told us she prefers a residence there, principally on account of the restrictions imposed on women by Spanish customs. She and a young lady, a visitor, entertained us in a parlor whose temperature was exquisitely comfortable and refreshing. We then walked in the garden, examined the coffee-fields and the process of hulling, cleansing, and putting up coffee for the market, and after two hours took to our *volante* again. Our half-drunken negro *calesero* (coachman), with his three braided-tailed, rib-showing-ready-for-the-crows-looking horses (as a German might say), harnessed abreast, the middle one in the shafts, and the others in long rope traces on each side, mounted the left-hand one, whipped them all, and drove us off. We returned to Mrs. Woodbury's over a road of red dust as fine as ashes, and as adhesive to the skin as wax, through groves of palms and fields of cane.

February 22, *Cardenas.*— *Las fiestas reales*, the royal festivities, ordered to be celebrated for three days, in honor of the birth of the Princess of Asturias, daughter of the Queen of Spain, begin to-day. The doors of many houses are bordered with palm-leaves; and arches of the same, wound about poles of bamboo, span the streets in places. Early this morning there was mass at the church for the benefit of the soldiers, at nine a grand "Te Deum" in honor of the princess. The governor of Cardenas and his military officers, with perhaps a hundred other men and two hundred women, were present, the women occupying nearly all the centre of the church,— a very pretty sight. The stone floor was covered with rugs of all colors, brought from private houses. On these were the two hundred women, some kneeling, many sitting Turkish fashion, and a very few in light chairs, brought by negro servants. The old, middle-aged, and young,— rich and poor, white, mulatto, and negro,— were mingled together for the time in a common equality; for they were in a house where — theoretically and so far practically — such distinctions are not recognized. None wore hats or bonnets. All had the transparent black veil, sometimes thrown back from the face. The greater part were wholly in black, some in white, a few in colors.

For an account of what followed this religious ceremony I am indebted to my barber, who was present. "About noon, accompanied by a gentleman of my acquaintance, I went to see the favorite sport of the Cubans, a cock-fight, without which scarcely a Sabbath passes, and which the law permits only on Sundays and religious feast days. The price of admission was 'two strong reals,' what you Yankees call a 'quarter.' We found the sport begun, in an amphitheatre, like that of a circus, occupied by four hundred men (boys are not admitted), most of them well dressed, and many belonging to the *élite* of Cardenas. One fight was nearly over, but another soon began. Two cocks, one black, the other variegated, were brought in, each having the feathers cut from his back and breast, and armed with natural spurs an inch or more long. The black cock is a renowned bird, never having been whipped, and now pitted by his owner, who brought him in, against any cock on the island. A rich citizen had sent to a distant town for the mottled cock which was to fight this champion, and betting now began. At times one hundred men were on their feet, crying out their bets, making a complete bedlam. Then the fight began, and never had I seen the passions so strongly depicted on the human countenance as there. For a while the combat was equal. Then the variegated bird seemed to have the advantage. His owner rose, and bawled out that he would bet a hundred 'ounces,' or doubloons ($1,700), of gold on his bird. Bedlam then broke loose worse than ever, but no one took his offer. Bets, however, were two to one on his bird. After a while the tide turned, and victory favored his antagonist. Black mustered all his strength, giving his opponent heavy blows till he slunk away to the side of the pit, hung his head, and would fight no longer. Thus Black was the winner."

Having finished his account, my barber leaned back in his rocking-chair, stroked his beard, and added, "This was the first cock-fight I ever attended, and I shall never go to another." I approved his determination, and there the matter ended.*

For a description of some of the proceedings at Cardenas, after dinner, I am indebted to an American physician now living in this city. He says: "About 5 P.M. I went up the principal street. The sidewalks were thronged, and there were many ladies in open *volantes*. As I looked up the street, hundreds of large, gay-colored Spanish flags met the eye,—almost one at every house. House-fronts were adorned with yellow and red drapery, and with pictur-esque devices for the coming illumination. Groups of persons, masked, with faces and forms so concealed by grotesque gar-ments that their familiar friends would not know them, were amusing each other in various ways. Near this street was a great open space (plaza), towards which the stream of people seemed to flow. Some two thousand had already assembled there. Near the centre of the plaza was a bull, his horns tied to a long rope, which was held fast at the other side of the square by a dozen men ; and the crowd was endeavoring, by blows, kicks, and red cloths, to enrage him. Sometimes they succeeded ; and he would charge upon them, but was so tethered that he did little harm, knocking one man down, butting another, etc. This sport was kept up until the bull was exhausted and fell. Then he received many kicks and stamps on his head and body, all this occasioning much hilarity and shouting among the spectators. In another part of the plaza stood a greased pole, thirty-five feet high, with a doubloon placed at its top, the prize of whoever could climb and take it. No one ventured till towards sunset, when some Catalan sailors came up from the harbor and tried for the prize. After nearly an hour, with many climbings and

---

* It may be observed here that Dr. Earle was his own barber, that he was the "American physi-cian now living," and also the mysterious "man who was in Europe when I was." This form of jest-,ing was a habit with him in his gayer moods, and was specially strong in this tour, as Mrs. Spring, yet living, at the age of eighty-eight, has written me. One day, she says, Dr. Earle was at the window, looking out, when he suddenly exclaimed, "Cousin Rebecca, here comes a friend in need!" She hastened to the window, only to see a poor club-footed, "in-kneed" man walking towards the door. Punning, indeed, in its many forms, was carried by him to an excess. It was one kind of the grammatical exercise in which he long delighted.

slidings down, amid great laughter of the multitude, they succeeded, by putting themselves *five high* upon each other's shoulders, each clinging to the pole."

A man who was in Europe when I was has enabled me to give a partial description of the evening entertainment. I could myself see from the hotel the illumination of the barracks and the church, and the lanterns, one or more, before each house in sight. But the man says: "The whole of the principal street and many others were brilliantly lighted by thousands of lamps. There were many inscriptions, — 'A la Reyna Isabella' and 'A la Princesa de Asturia.' Nearly everybody, to judge by the crowds, was in the streets. A great variety of maskers was seen, and all appeared to be enjoying themselves greatly. A masked ball at the theatre was attended by hundreds of persons, one-third of them in masks and fancy dress. One of the best characters was an aged gentleman 'of the old school,' in cocked hat and small-clothes, with big-buckled shoes. He never forgot his part, but carried it with the skill of an actor." So ended another Sabbath, and the record of it.

February 23, *Matanzas.*—This Monday morning we left Cardenas at sunrise, a dense fog enveloping us till eight o'clock, when the sun shone forth as clear, bright, and hot as on a first-rate Leicester hayday. We went back thirty miles towards Guines; and for the rest of our way to this town there was little worthy of mention, except some coffee plantations with the shrub in full bloom. The plants were four or five feet high, and as white to-day as a field of our buckwheat in blossom. At Matanzas we took rooms at the hotel of Madame Mortie, a French woman, on the wharf at the head of a magnificent bay. We front the east, and look out on the waters covered with vessels, the hills that bound the bay, and the many pelicans sailing now in air, now on the water, and ever and anon diving from the wing, with the speed of an arrow, upon their fishy prey. Oh, it is a beautiful country for a lazy man (with money enough) to spend the winter in! Glorious sunsets, balmy breezes, delicious temperature, flowery fields, nature's luxuriance, luxurious indolence, *dolce far niente, otium sine dignitate,*—make an *olla podrida* of these and other expressions of laziness, beauty, and romance; and the rich man has it all in Cuba.

North-west of Matanzas is a series of hills, to the top of which I went in the afternoon, and thence looked down on one side upon the

city and bay stretched out before us, like the lower lands of Paxton
and Leicester viewed from Asnebumskit; * while on the other side,
beneath a precipice several hundred feet high, lay Yumuri, the most
lovely valley in Cuba.   Our chief inducement to visit Matanzas was
to see this vale, which quite equals the expectation we had of it.
I remember nothing so fine, unless it were Edale in English Derbyshire, where I was in 1837.   Yumuri is four or five miles long and
one or two miles wide, nearly level, but encircled, except in a gap
just wide enough for a stream to flow out, by a ridge of hills varying
from two hundred to five hundred feet high.   Highly cultivated, it
was planted with the peculiar products of Cuba.

The royal festival was going on here as at Cardenas ; and, as
might be seen from the date, these *fiestas* were appointed for the
three days of carnival preceding Lent, in order to make the show
and the general hilarity greater.   In the afternoon we saw a sham
fight, in which six or eight hundred Spanish troops took part.   In
the evening the illumination was general and very brilliant ; and
everybody who was not at a ball, a music-party, or some other in-
door festivity, was outdoors, looking on.   All classes of society
mingled together in very orderly disorder.   More than five hundred
women were seated on the benches of the square ; and the broad
promenade, on one side bounded by those benches, contained every
moment, between eight and ten o'clock, twenty-five hundred or
three thousand people.   Here was an excellent opportunity to see
the beauty of Matanzas, where, it is said, there is more feminine
beauty than in Havana.   Many were masked, but probably not the
most beautiful ; for it is a remarkable fact in natural history that
very handsome women are the least disposed to wear masks.   Those
masked were mostly dressed in white, with no head-covering.   They
carried costly fans, which they so manage that they seem as much a
part of themselves as the wings are of a bird.   Maskers, both men
and women, are privileged persons.   They do what they please,
speak to whom they choose, and say what comes into their heads,

---

* This uncouth Indian name, as often mentioned, designates a fine hill near Leicester, which Dr.
Earle frequently used for purposes of comparison or description, when writing of foreign scenes, as he
did, for instance, in explaining the face of the country between Athens and Marathon, when he rode
through it, escaping the brigands, in 1838.   He seems to have left no detailed description of the lovely
Derbyshire vale which he saw in his first visit to England.   Marathon made a profound impression on
him, as on most who see that famous battle-plain ; and there is a good plan of it, and of Dr. Earle's
route over it, preserved in his collection of autographs, but evidently drawn by himself soon after he
spent the night at Souli, overlooking the plain from the side opposite Athens.

all speaking in a peculiar falsetto rather unpleasant to hear, but serving as an effectual disguise of the natural voice.   They tarry at the windows of even the best houses, chatting with the young ladies. Sometimes they go in and sit down ; and in one house we saw a genteel circle listening to their piano well played by a long-hooded white domino, looking as if the person inside were shrouded for the coffin.

February 24.— This is the last day of carnival and the *fiestas*. Parties of masked men, with some women, have been through the streets of Matanzas this afternoon ; and one party of them performed an imitation bull-fight with some wit and spirit, and without the cowardly cruelty of the bull-baiting at Cardenas.   Two youths had artificial horse-bodies so attached to them that, with short artificial legs, they looked much like boys on horseback. · These were picadors. Two others had similar bull-bodies, and several harlequins acted as matadors.   Very impressive was the singular contest waged between these doughty antagonists, with many comico-tragical incidents, ending in the destruction of one bull by knocking his brains out, which, however, did not prevent his fighting on as before.

Towards night a crowd assembled on a long wharf in front of our hotel to witness a game of climbing an upright pole, on which was a piece of gold to reward the successful climber.   The game was to walk out on a horizontal pole over the water, and thence climb a diagonal rope to the top of the upright pole without tumbling into the water, on which were hundreds of boats filled with people. Those who climbed got more ducks than gold.   Many fell into the water, amid tumultuous shouts and laughter ; and no one got the prize.   Elsewhere on the wharf was a trial of jumping for ducks,— this time real ones, tied to a rope with their heads hanging down, and both head and neck well greased, so that, unless grasped very firmly, the hand would slip.   Some jumped, and could not reach the bird.   Others would strike his bill, causing the duck to draw back the head.   Finally, a man grasped the head of one ; but his hold slipped, and he came down with nothing but a handful of grease. Finally, after many trials and some artifice, a big-boned man, six feet two in height, holds the duck's head fast, killing the bird, jerks himself up and down to break the string, and comes down at last with his next day's dinner in his hands, amid the shouting of the crowd.   Verily, man "is a rational animal, the only creature endowed with reason."

February 29.— We left Matanzas on the 26th, returning to Havana, where an irregularity in my passport, caused by the major-domo of Mrs. Almy's hotel, put me to some inconvenience as well as anxiety. But it enabled me to have an interview with Don José de la Concha, governor or captain-general of the island, and to see the inside of his palace, which would otherwise have been denied me. There appeared to be a very general apprehension of further invasion of Cuba from the United States, where, I was told, a force of seventeen hundred men was already collected on the coast of Alabama, expecting to sail for Cuba in April. Those Cubans opposed to annexation look forward with much anxiety to our Presidential election this year, hoping that Daniel Webster may be chosen, but fearing it may be General Cass or General Houston.* The South is determined to have Cuba, Spain equally determined we shall not have it, to say nothing of England and France.

We sailed from Havana for Savannah by way of Key West on this day, my passport having been satisfactorily arranged. Looking back, a few reflections occur to me. I came to the conclusion that life and property are more secure in Havana than in any of our American cities. The night police is very efficient, though peculiarly armed. Each man carries a long spear, a sword, a pistol, and a whistle, whose shrill sounds are heard at short intervals through the night. Perhaps the watchmen blow them to show they are not asleep. The government police are just now particularly watchful in regard to foreigners, especially Americans, since the Lopez raids. An American needs to be cautious, if he does not wish to be made to "walk Spanish." But the Cubans might teach us something of politeness. All the wheels and cogs and cranks and cams, and all other parts of the machinery of human intercourse, go there as smoothly as if they were constantly oiled. The graceful bow or wave of the hand, the *mille gracias* (thousand thanks), and many another thing as trifling, make a temporary residence among such people far more agreeable than it would be if they had the cold manners of some other nations. But there is a ludicrous side to it. Now, if two Worcester County men should meet in the main street of their county capital, one with a lighted cigar, and the other with an

* As we know now, there was never any chance for the election of Webster, who was then Secretary of State, and managed the Cuban filibusters very well. General Scott was nominated by Webster's party, but defeated by General Pierce, of New Hampshire. Webster died before the year closed.

unlighted one (always provided the law did not forbid smoking in Worcester streets), and if one should ask the other for a "light," and get one, and if, in doing all this, those two men should go through the evolutions of two Cubans doing the like in Havana, I shouldn't be surprised if the nearest constable were called to take them off as soon as possible to the Worcester Lunatic Hospital.

Publicity is the rule of life in Cuba. Many of the artisans work in shops flush with the street, so that, as you pass along the sidewalk, there are places where you can touch a half-dozen shoemakers or as many tailors with your cane. The women go shopping in their *volantes*, and, instead of getting out, make the clerks bring the goods to be examined to the carriage,— no great inconvenience, to be sure; for, what with the narrow sidewalk and the shallow shop, the counter is not often more than eight or ten feet from the *volante*. Although Spanish customs condemn women to a life of comparative seclusion (only allowing them to walk in the street at special times, and then accompanied either by brothers, husbands, or parents), yet nowhere else that I have travelled is their domestic life so much exposed to the public as in Cuba. Their parlors are always next the street, and the windows are so large and so readily looked in at (not being glazed) that every article of furniture and every person in the room is as plainly seen from the sidewalk as from the inside. The window shutters are mostly kept closed in the forenoon; but by 2 or 3 P.M., when the young ladies are all nicely dressed, and ready to see and be seen, they are opened. The ladies, if not more than two, sit or stand so near the windows that, as you pass them on the narrow sidewalk, you would brush against their clothes, were it not for the iron window bars. The chairs, mostly arm-chairs, are set in parallel rows each side of the window or windows. In the parlors of the poorer people there is often but one window; and in nine-tenths of them you will see six chairs thus placed, three on each side. When there are visitors, the people of the house sit in those nearest the wall, and their guests in the others. No matter how large the social party, they are all seated in this way. Each guest can thus look out of the window, and can be seen by all who pass along the street. Often, of an afternoon, I have seen the ladies of a family seated by one window, and their negro servants lounging at the other.

Among thousands of women whom I saw in these parlors, I do

not recall an instance in which one of them was either working or reading. They sit in idleness to gaze and be gazed at. A Cuban lady is about as useless as can be imagined. All *work* is derogatory, fit only for slaves, and hence is rejected. Eating, drinking, sleeping, dressing, and driving out are their methods of killing time. But some Yankees know how to make them pay for their idleness. An American mantua-maker, who did some work for Mrs. Spring, said that her net profits on the dresses made at her shop for a single party were $600.

March 2.— We reached Key West on the "Isabel" at 5 P.M. on the 29th, and remained four hours looking about the town, as well as over it, from the top of structures erected as lookouts for wrecked vessels. Our whole voyage from First Day morning to Third Day evening was the very perfection of sea travel; the temperature that of a New England July, modified by the sea-breezes; the sky almost without a cloud; the water calm as a mill-pond; the moon, almost at its first quarter, giving sufficient light for evenings; and last, though not least, an agreeable company of passengers. With all these, who could not make a pleasant voyage? I landed at Savannah, leaving my cousins, whom I rejoined at Charleston.

March 8, *Philadelphia.*— We spent one day in Charleston, and then came on to Richmond. There on the 6th (First Day evening) I took the cars for Washington, leaving Marcus and Rebecca at Richmond, and arrived here at noon. So end my notes on Cuba.

At the time of Dr. Earle's sojourn in Cuba, its 45,000 square miles contained about 1,200,000 inhabitants, of whom more than 300,000 were slaves. The slave-trade was in vigorous activity, in spite of treaties and armed squadrons; and nearly 5,000 slaves in a year were brought over from Africa. Its financial prosperity was great. It had doubled its population in thirty years, sugar was in demand, wealth was increasing, and there was no great wish for independence or for annexation to the United States, whose slaveholding rulers then desired to extend our national area of slavery by purchasing or conquering it. President Polk had offered Spain $100,000,000 for Cuba in 1848. In 1854 Mr. Buchanan, afterwards President, joined Mason, of Virginia, and Soulé, of Louisiana, in the

notorious Ostend manifesto, in which they declared that Cuba
ought to belong to the United States, and that, should Spain
be so wicked as to free the Cuban slaves, our country ought to
take the island by force.   Ten years later President Lincoln
freed the American slaves, and this led to legal though partial
emancipation in Cuba in 1870.   Since then the island has
been in insurrection half the time, and has now been largely
depopulated and financially ruined by the attempts of Spain to
put down the rebellion.   There could scarcely be a greater
contrast between the idle and gay Cuba of 1852 and the
tormented and decimated Cuba of 1898.

CHAPTER XI.

NEW YORK AND WASHINGTON.

FROM Cuba Dr. Earle returned to Leicester, where he had the care of an invalid brother, and where his housekeeper was his sister Lucy, for whom in her disappointed life he tenderly cared; but later in 1852, he established himself in New York for a time. There he was consulted in cases of insanity, and often gave expert evidence in the courts. His acquaintance with the City Lunatic Asylum and his official connection as visitor gave him a continuing interest in its fortunes, especially after its old "mad-house" (which he compared for unfitness with the Timar-hané of Stamboul and the Munich place of torture) had been replaced, under Dr. Moses Ranney, by a better building. In 1856, while collecting facts for his statistical work in the Philadelphia Quarterly, he got from Dr. Ranney figures showing how extreme had been the mortality at Blackwell's Island in the worst years,— a fact which he often mentioned afterwards, and particularly when in 1876 I was carrying on an inquiry into the neglect and death-rate of the insane poor in the Tewksbury State Almshouse, an affair in which he took great interest.*

---

* An abstract of these statistics used by Dr. Earle will be useful for contrast with the later figures of the much enlarged and dispersed insane asylums of New York City, now classed together as the Manhattan State Hospital, but lacking much of the hospital character from constant overcrowding. Dr. Ranney, who took charge in 1847, thus reports the years: —

Years.	Whole No. Patients.	Admitted.	Recovered.	Died.	Remaining.
1847	779	396	146	153	364
1848	855	491	163	116	437
1849	896	459	170	212	401
1850	792	391	154	77	464
1851	905	441	197	80	517
1852	1,012	495	234	130	527
1853	1,014	487	255	115	542
1854	1,028	486	180	190	555
1855	926	371	194	100	573
1856	939	366	174	66	597
10 years, average and totals .	915	4,383	1,867	1,239	481

Thus it seems that in ten years, with 4,766 cases (383 remaining from 1846), the average recoveries were 187, and the average of deaths 124,— a yearly excess of recoveries of 63; and even in the cholera years, 1849 and 1854, the deaths were but 52 more than the recoveries; while of late years the deaths

Dr. Earle's services as a medical expert in disputed cases of homicide, bequest, etc., were many and important, from 1852 onwards. In the trial of John M. Thurston for murder at Ithaca, N.Y., in 1853, he testified to the fact of insanity; and the defendant was finally acquitted on this ground. Thirty-five years later another trial for murder occurred in the same county, that of Richard Barber,—a very peculiar case, in which Dr. Earle took much interest, though he had then (in 1888) practically ceased to give evidence.* While he was thus called upon, he testified in New York, New Jersey, Massachusetts, and Connecticut, and was one of the many experts who gave their opinion at the trial of Guiteau for the assassination of President Garfield in 1881. In the case of Willard Clark, tried at New Haven in 1855 for the murder of R. W. Wight, the three experts who testified to his insanity were Dr. Earle and his two contemporaries, a little older than himself, Dr. Isaac Ray, then of Providence, and Dr. J. S. Butler, of Hartford. The verdict of acquittal, based on this testimony, was directly opposed to prevailing public opinion in New Haven; but its justice was proved by the event. Several years later his insanity was again tested in the Connecticut court. He was remanded to the Wethersfield prison, and thence sent to the Middletown Insane Hospital, where he died.

As illustrating the character of another expert, Dr. Brigham, of Utica, the following incident is related by Dr. Stephen Smith, of New York:—

I happened to be present, as a lad, at the trial of Freeman, a negro homicide, and sat among the audience in a sort of amphitheatre, with the court and bar below, when an extraordinary event occurred. John Van Buren, son of the President, was the attorney-general, and was prosecuting the case against Freeman, whom Governor Seward was defending on a plea of insanity. A chief witness

---

largely exceed recoveries. In seven years, 1890–97, the whole number averaging 7,362, and the admissions 1,600, the recoveries reported were but 1,269, while the deaths were 4,310,—more than threefold. This confirms Dr. Earle's preference for small asylums.

* Barber was a young Englishman from the little parish of Billingboro, in Lincolnshire, who came of an epileptic family, and, in the unconsciousness of the epileptic furor, killed one of his best friends, an aged English woman, at Trumansburg, near Cornell University.

for the defence was Dr. Brigham, of the Utica Asylum, then at the height of his reputation as an expert in lunacy. He had seen and examined Freeman, and testified that he was insane; and Van Buren was seeking to break down his evidence by cross-examination. "How did you decide that he was insane, doctor? Was it by looking at his face?" "That was one thing," said Dr. Brigham. "Did you think him insane by looking at his nose?" "No." "At his mouth?" "Not entirely." "At his eyes?" "The eye is a very expressive feature, indicative of the mind; but I did not judge altogether by that. I took all the features into consideration." "Do you mean to tell this jury that you can decide whether a man is crazy by looking at him?" "I have sometimes done so." "Will you, then, look through this large audience, and pick out some one as insane, from the looks of his face?" "That would be difficult." "From your testimony it would not be difficult for you, and I insist that you shall make the test." "Very well," said Dr. Brigham, quite composed, erect, and impressive; and he began to point his hand towards the benches, moving it as he passed from one section to another, and searching all our faces with his keen eye. My own heart beat fast as he came near me with his search, for fear he should pronounce me crazy; but he passed my section by, and had gone past the middle of the benches, when he suddenly stopped, raised his long arm, pointed his long finger at a man in one of the upper seats, and said very gravely, "That man is insane." Instantly the man sprang from his seat, angry and swearing, and rushed down towards the bench and bar, crying: "You lie! I am not crazy," with other manifestations of mania. The judge rose from the bench; Mr. Van Buren jumped on a chair; Dr. Brigham stood still, fixing his eye on the madman. The sheriffs rushed in, seized the shouting maniac, and the court adjourned in great agitation. The cross-examination of Dr. Brigham broke down, and Mr. Seward won his case. But Van Buren insinuated next day that Governor Seward had placed a madman in the audience for the purpose of having such a scene.

While Dr. Earle was in Carolina and Cuba, his friend and successor at the Bloomingdale Asylum became deeply interested in the establishment of a hospital for the insane at the seat of government; and in August, 1852, Congress made the first appropriation for a Government Hospital for the Insane in Washington. A few months later Dr. Nichols was appointed superintendent there, and early in 1855 a section of the buildings was opened under his charge. He naturally invited Dr. Earle to visit him, and profited by his experience. The first visit was late in February, 1856, during the administration of President Pierce, of New Hampshire, and when General Banks, of Massachusetts, was speaker of the House of Representatives, in a very agitated session of Congress. Dr. Earle, who had seen every President since Monroe, and had often visited the White House, took the first opportunity to pay his respects to the New Hampshire President. His diary says (Feb. 21, 1856) : —

I came to Washington from Philadelphia, where I had visited my sister and other kindred, and met many old friends. Was met at the station by Dr. Nichols, who took me to this hospital, two and a half miles from the Capitol, and gave me a very comfortable room, overlooking almost the whole of the city,—the Capitol, White House, Washington Monument, etc. He has less than 100 patients, a farm of 195 acres on the Potomac, south of the Capitol, on which last year grew 1,000 bushels of peaches. The river is still covered with ice. Among the animals kept are two Arabian horses, descended from the Arabian sent to President Van Buren, about the time of my return from Europe, a big and jolly Rocky Mountain bear, two monkeys, a deer, a wildcat, a fox, a raccoon, and two parrots.

February 22, *Washington's Birthday.*— This evening I went with Dr. Nichols to a reception at the White House. Shook hands with the President, bowed very low to Mrs. President, talked with Lieutenant Maury and a Congressman from Maine, looked up to General Houston, senator from Texas, six feet two in height, saw Speaker Banks, and should have been introduced to him, had he not been at the time gallanting a young lady round the East Room in the promenade. We were crowded by five hundred people, and gazed at many silks, satins, laces, flounces, low necks, and bare shoulderblades.

Saturday, February 23.— Drove to Washington with Dr. Nichols, to call on several Congressmen on business of the hospital; but, the day being fine, none were at home. We found the Secretary of the Navy, Mr. J. C. Dobbin,* of North Carolina, in his office,— a small, meagre, delicate-looking man, with a large head and a small, soft hand and a voice hoarse and feeble,— the effect of bronchitis. At the National Observatory we examined all the instruments, and had a long, interesting talk with Lieutenant Maury, the director, famous throughout the world for his discoveries in regard to the wind and the currents of the ocean, their laws, direction, etc. These discoveries are estimated to have saved $10,000,000 a year to the merchants and ship-owners of Great Britain alone. He gave me a chart he had just finished, of the winds and weather of the whole Atlantic, made from an analysis of observations covering 165,000 days, in all parts of that ocean. It seems that the atmosphere is more unstable in the Northern than in the Southern Atlantic,— we having more calms, more gales, more fogs, more rains, and more thunder than they do farther south. In the latitude of Massachusetts, by this chart, there will be in January 4 calm days, 27 gales, 13 rainy days, 2 foggy ones, and 1 thunder-storm; in February 6 calm days, in March only 3; but there will be 16 rainy days and 6 foggy ones, with only 16 gales. At the War Office I was introduced to Dr. Wood, an army surgeon, nephew of the late President Taylor, and resembling him enough to have been his son. We visited the Washington Monument, which has reached a height of 170 feet. It is to be 518 feet, just a *leetle* higher than any other artificial structure in the world, except the Great Pyramid. But I am inclined to think it will not be completed in my day. The "Know-nothings" got the management of it about a year ago, and were to finish it immediately; but hitherto they have not laid a stone.

"Know-nothing" was the name colloquially given to the short-lived "American" party, organized in 1854, in secret, oath-bound societies, the members of which, when questioned, "knew nothing" about it. By this party a great many Congressmen had been elected, among them Mr. Banks, the Speaker, who was at this very time a prominent candidate of that party for President in the election of November, 1856. He was nominated, but declined in favor of Fremont, the Republican, who was defeated by James Buchanan, of Pennsylvania.

* A good friend of Miss Dix; see her Life.

Sunday, February 24.—Accompanied Dr. Nichols to the small Unitarian church, and there heard a most excellent sermon from Moncure Daniel Conway, a young Virginian, lately in the Divinity School at Harvard College, of apparently great intellect and originality. The sermon aimed to maintain the rights of the *individual*, his supremacy within those rights, over all associations,— a progressive sermon, it would usually be called. He claimed that every man should lay aside all precedents, discard the ideas and conventionalities of his predecessors, rid himself of his own prejudices, and boldly think for himself, arraigning nations and their institutions before the tribunal of his own soul, and judge of them by the standard of conscience and the "light within." * Among the audience were John P. Hale, senator from New Hampshire, and Mr. Seaton, partner of the English publisher, Joseph Gales, of the well-known firm of Gales & Seaton, of the *National Intelligencer*. Mr. Webb, a young lawyer, related to James Watson Webb of the New York *Courier and Enquirer*, drove home with us, and dined at the hospital, where we passed a very sociable afternoon.

February 25.— After a call on a former pupil of mine at Providence, Dr. Daniel Breed, who was afterwards a pupil of Liebig in Germany, and is now an examiner in the Patent Office, I went to the Senate Chamber, where a speech was expected from Senator Jones of Tennessee. The galleries were crowded, so that I could only reach the outside of the doorway ; but, waiting patiently, I got in at last, among a crowd as dense as the Leicester sheep used to be in our stable at shearing-time, and I looked down on the assembled wisdom of the nation. I recognized Houston of Texas, Cass of Michigan (my Paris acquaintance of 1838), Seward of New York, Hale of New Hampshire, Charles Sumner and Henry Wilson of Massachusetts ; but no one pointed out to me the other senators. Jones was speaking on the admission of Kansas, without slavery, in

---

* As a follower of Fox and Penn, this was acceptable doctrine to Dr. Earle in its religious aspect ; but he was hardly ready to go so far in political and social radicalism as this young Virginian, the friend of Emerson and Theodore Parker, and afterwards of Carlyle and Browning, during his long residence in London as the successor of William J. Fox at the South Place Chapel. He did not remain long in Washington, then had a church at Cincinnati, which divided in 1862, and Mr. Conway came to Concord, Mass., whence early in 1863 he went to England. He now lives in New York. Mr. Hale and the other senators named below were friends of Mr. Conway (most of them), and often heard him preach. Mr. Hale had been in the Senate nearly ten years, where he was the first distinctly anti-slavery senator, but was re-enforced in 1849 and subsequent years by Chase of Ohio, Seward, Sumner, and Wilson, and many others. His son-in-law, Mr. Chandler, is now a senator from New Hampshire.

answer to a speech by Wilson a few days ago. He took the Southern view of the question with energy and eloquence for about three hours. Some remark of his called up Hale, who spoke as energetically and eloquently for twenty minutes, and at adjournment gave notice that he would answer Mr. Jones at length on Thursday Strong language was used on both sides, and there were sallies of wit by both senators. Had a foreigner, unversed in our politics, listened, he would have carried away a fear that everybody in this country is going to kill every other body in course of a few days. I walked back to the hospital, to find refuge with the insane — who don't talk so.

February 26.— In the afternoon of this Tuesday (the day when the wives of the cabinet officers receive calls each week) I called with Dr. Nichols at Mr. McClelland's, the Secretary of the Interior, under whose jurisdiction is the hospital, and from whom Dr. Nichols receives his appointment. We were received by Mrs. McClelland, her very handsome niece, and a young lady from Baltimore. I had seen the young ladies before, at the hospital, whither they came with the Secretary the day I reached Washington. Mrs. McClelland is from Williamstown, Mass., but has long lived in Michigan, where her husband has been governor. We took tea at Dr. Breed's, the only guest besides ourselves being a handsome, bright-eyed, intellectual-looking Miss Coues from Portsmouth, N.H., whose father, Samuel E. Coues, author of a queer book about the planetary system, is employed in the Patent Office.* To-day the ice in the Potomac is still unbroken, though much softened; but the snow has mostly gone, and Pennsylvania Avenue is slightly dusty.

February 28.— I went to the Senate Chamber, crowded almost to suffocation in the galleries, and listened to a speech of nearly two hours, on the Kansas question, by John P. Hale, of a higher degree of eloquence than I had believed him capable. He was followed, on the other side, by Senator Robert Toombs of Georgia, one of the most able and eloquent members of the Senate, whatever may be thought of him by those who dislike his view of slavery. I had previously met the architect of the Capitol extension, and examined his plans. If completed as now designed, we shall have one American building (the first) to compare with the palaces and public buildings of Europe.

* Father of the present Professor Coues.

Thus the diary continues, with calls in the city, speeches in the Senate and House on some phase of the Kansas question, visits of Congressmen and others to the hospital, dinner parties, receptions at the White House and elsewhere, and remarks on the weather and passing events. It was a winter of unusual severity, snow and frost continuing until late March, and the ice in the great Potomac lingering a month longer than common. He hears Douglas, of Illinois, "the little giant," speak on the Kansas issue which Douglas himself brought upon the country, and which nothing but the Civil War could finally settle. He goes to the sermons of Mr. Conway, and meets him at a hospital dinner, with this comment in the diary : —

Sunday, March 23.— We drove to hear Mr. Conway's sermon to-day ; and he came home with us, dined, and passed the afternoon. He is as interesting in conversation as in the pulpit, a man of superior intellect and of moral qualities of a very high order ; yet his religion is that of the extreme Unitarians, or nearly so. He says he believes in the divinity of Jesus Christ, but not in his Deity. Neither does he believe in the miracles. Among his reasons for this disbelief he alleges that not one of the books of the New Testament was written until fifty years or more after the birth of Christ, and long after his death,— time enough, he thinks, for a story to grow considerably, if stories grew then as rapidly as now. He questions that Matthew, Mark, Luke, and John were the authors of the four Gospels. Indeed, the book of Matthew, he says, bears internal evidence of having been written by four different men, containing four styles of composition, each as different from either of the others as the style of Webster differs from that of Henry A. Wise, of Virginia. This heterodoxy of his does not divide his church so much as his anti-slavery sermons, which please Horace Greeley and Senator Hale, both of whom I have seen there. But nine families have withdrawn because of one anti-slavery sermon.

At this time Dr. Earle's theological opinions were hardly so positive as Mr. Conway's, on one side, or those of the Gurney-ite branch of the Quakers, on the other. He had not joined in the Hicksite schism, mentioned in a former chapter, though his opinions must have inclined that way. Soon after leaving the hospital, where he had this conversation with Mr. Conway, he was present in Philadelphia at Yearly Meeting, and in his diary thus expresses himself on the points of difference in the Society of Friends : —

It appears to me that the "Wilburites" in this Yearly Meeting are just about the same in opinion that Moses Brown, of Providence, Elisha Thornton, and David Buffum, Sr., were forty years ago, and what the "Body of Friends" were in 1826. The Hicksites have gone off towards Unitarianism : the Gurneyites (followers of Joseph John Gurney, of England) have gone and are going off towards all forms of what is called Orthodoxy,— Episcopalianism, Trinitarianism, Presbyterianism. But the Wilburites wage the war rather too bitterly. They are too intolerant and denunciatory to comport with my idea of Christianity. They are at one extreme in this meeting, the Gurneyites at the other. And there are middlemen who will urge a temporizing course. If there be a split, it will be from the secession of the Gurneyites, who, being by far the weaker party in Philadelphia, will have to leave the books in the hands of the Wilburites. In 1844, before I left Philadelphia to go to Bloomingdale, I gave my opinion that the society had better separate then,— the sooner, the better,— and thus save a vast amount of scandal, ill-feeling, and backbiting. It was my belief then that no religious schism which had advanced so far as this had in 1844 was ever settled; and time has shown that I was right, for once. But I hardly think there will be a separation this year. The Gurney party perhaps think they are too weak to venture on so important a step.

This does not indicate a very enthusiastic partisan of any theological opinion. Indeed, he was ever more concerned for the spirit of Christianity than for dogma of any kind.

It was much the same in the political schism then going on between the North and the South on the slavery question. Dr. Earle, though his heart and conscience were on the anti-slavery side, could not support extreme views. In Washington he went to hear the debates of Congress on both sides of the Kansas issue. Thus on March 20 he pressed into the crowded Senate gallery to hear Stephen A. Douglas, the author of the Kansas-Nebraska bill, and afterwards the great opponent of Abraham

Lincoln in contests for the Senate and the Presidency. He
says : —

Douglas spoke to a very silent audience for two hours and more.
Some allusion to remarks made by his colleague from Illinois, Lyman
Trumbull, called up Trumbull, who proved himself fully able to meet
his antagonist at all points. Trumbull is a new senator, and has
made but one speech before this day, but already has put himself in
the front rank among senators as an able, eloquent debater. As for
Douglas, all knew long ago that he is a very able man. This, with
his short stature, gave him years since the name of the "little giant."
He is a widower ; and, while he was speaking, Senator Hale, seeing
that many ladies could get no seats in their gallery, proposed — since
much interest was felt in the speech, and peculiarly among the
ladies — that they should be admitted to seats on the floor of the
Senate. This required unanimous consent ; and Weller, of California, objected. So the ladies were obliged to stay out.

March 30, Mr. Conway's pulpit was occupied by the eloquent
Thomas Starr King, then of Boston, but afterwards of San
Francisco, where he did good service on the Union side in the
Civil War. The church was unusually full ; and among those
present were Senator Sumner, Speaker Banks, Anson Burlin-
game, and Senator Hale. Less than two months after this
Sumner was brutally attacked in the Senate Chamber by Brooks,
of South Carolina ; and civil war on a small scale broke out in
Kansas,— the prelude to the great Civil War of 1861.

Early in 1857 Dr. Earle was again in Washington, and frequent in his attendance on Congress and the Supreme Court.
Jan. 21, 1857, he writes : —

I sat for a few minutes in the Supreme Court, Judge Taney and
seven of his associate justices (all but one) being on the bench.
They are as fine-looking men as you can find anywhere. It seemed
to me that Justice B. R. Curtis, of Boston, has the most strongly
intellectual aspect, and Justice John McLean, of Cincinnati, the
most striking external appearance of high moral faculties. George T.
Curtis, of Boston, was arguing a case relating to the insurance of

Donald McKay's big ship, the "Great Republic," burned in New York four years ago.*

It was commonly said in Washington and Philadelphia in this winter of 1856–57 that, if Judge McLean had been nominated by the Republicans for the Presidency instead of Colonel Fremont, Mr. Buchanan would have been defeated. But he was chosen, and was now on his way to Washington to succeed General Pierce in the White House. In other respects the political and personal situation was changed. Charles Sumner, not yet recovered from the attack of Brooks, was preparing to sail for Europe; and Brooks himself, whom Dr. Earle saw and described in the Senate Chamber, January 23, as "lounging upon one of the seats not far from Sumner's vacant chair, his hair black and profuse, his complexion ruddy, wearing a *goatee*, but neither mustache nor whiskers, and almost always with a black glove on his left hand," was dead on the 27th and buried on the 29th. Senator Douglas was married, and Dr. Earle met him and his handsome wife at a dancing party in the house of Secretary McClelland. He portrays her as "four inches taller than her husband,—almost as tall as he is, including his hat,—with dark hair and eyebrows, and in the form of her head and features almost precisely like cousin Mary S., but taller and heavier." Of the Senate in 1857 he says : —

As contrasted with the Senate of last winter, it is as broadly different as a battlefield is from a Quaker meeting. Then it seemed soaked in gall and wormwood : this winter it is smeared with honey. If my eyes did not play me false, I actually saw Douglas leave his seat, and come almost the whole length of the chamber to shake hands and chat with Seward; while Hale was cosily talking with Evans, of South Carolina, and Butler (uncle of Brooks) laughing and joking with Foote, of Vermont. Mason, of Virginia, acting president of the Senate, left the chair, and called upon Foote to fill it in his absence.

There was much tea-drinking and dining and evening festivity this winter, in which Dr. Earle took a kindly share; his friend,

* The court had not yet pronounced its notorious Dred Scott decision of 1857, intended to be the bulwark of negro slavery.

Dr. Nichols, being in love, and often seeking the society of the young ladies.   Of one Washington house he says : —

Mrs. M.'s eldest son is a great friend of Dr. Nichols.   This sufficiently accounts for our visits there.   Were it not unphilosophical to look for more causes than this sufficient one, I might add that his sister, aged twenty, is a handsome brunette.   Other brunettes are coming up after her.   There are Alice and Isabella, and Nannie and Sallie, and Jeanie and Lucy,— interspersed with several brothers, — in a regularly descending series.   Great havoc will be made one of these years under the jacket pockets of Washington beaux.

Dr. Earle was ever a discriminating admirer of beauty.   In describing a party at General Webb's, he says : —

We arrived precisely at 10 P.M., and were very early; for people kept coming till midnight.   It was the most " sectional " and " partisan " of any that I ever attended in Washington,— decidedly Northern and emphatically Republican.   Hardly a Southern man of note was there, except Mr. Crittenden, of Kentucky, with his magnificently dressed wife and two young ladies.   Neither were there many Democratic members of Congress.   The Republicans in great numbers, from Banks downward, were there.   Among other notables were Judge McLean and Mr. Stoeckel, the Russian ambassador, who has recently married an American, Miss Howard, of Springfield. She was present, and among the finest-looking of the company.   In the ball-room the solemnities were concluded with a Virginia reel about 2 A.M.   As the ladies with us were relatives of the host, we were among the last who left; and we reached home a little before 3 A.M.   The next morning (January 29) was the first day since my coming that I have not risen before the sun.   However, I was downstairs before eight o'clock.

Dr. Earle was frequently meeting his former pupils, either of the Fall River school, where he taught so early, or of the Friends' School at Providence.   In the preceding winter, going upon the floor of the House of Representatives, whom should he encounter but a " Know-nothing " member of Congress from Fall River,— James Buffington, who long continued to represent that light-house and post-office district as a Republican, when the American party had merged in the new Republican party.

I looked at him, and he looked at me (I had not seen him since 1836). Then I looked a little harder, and he looked a little harder. I extended my hand, and said, "I believe this is the man, but am not positive." He took my hand, and said, "I should call this Pliny Earle." Whereupon I was convinced that he knew some things, though politically a "Know-nothing." "I have grown old faster than you have," said he; "you don't look any older to me than you did twenty years ago." That may well be, thought I; and yet a vast change may have come over me.

He met his friend again repeatedly in this second winter, and saw him taking part in the counting of votes for Buchanan and Fremont and in the other proceedings of Congress. He met him at the White House receptions, which were greatly crowded, and which he thus describes, speaking of the last one held by President Pierce before giving up the chair to James Buchanan, the last pro-slavery President : —

Dr. Nichols and I went to the White House about 9 P.M., February 27. If some of the former *soirées* had been "jams," this was "jamnation." We met many persons coming away, either because they could not get in or because they had been in and were only too glad to get out again. Every apartment in the great house was a complete, if not boundless, "continuity" of human nature. After getting to the upper step of the portico, it was some fifteen minutes before we could enter the door, the crowd being so great.

My arduous and perilous journey through the entrance hall, the corridor, the Red, Blue, and Green Rooms, into the great East Room, and so back to the corridor, was mostly performed alone; for, at the door between Red and Blue, Dr. Nichols and I got separated, and thenceforth, like Ulysses and Telemachus, in Fénelon's fable, we wandered up and down apart, each subject to his own series of adventures. As we escaped from the portico into the front hall, our misery, which loved company, was softened by seeing just in front of us Mr. Guthrie, the Secretary of the Treasury, pursuing his President under difficulties. His hat-brim was turned up defiantly, and his elephantine form was yielding submissive to the human current. At the middle hall, or corridor, the crowd grew more intolerable; for there the ladies, who had entered a side room, joined the gentlemen to force a way into the Blue Room, where stood President Pierce. Alas for the fashionable crinolines now! Willing or unwilling, they must shrink to their least compass, reversing Milton's account of those other distressed angels,

> Who in their own dimensions, like themselves,
> In close recess and secret conclave sat,
> Frequent and full;

for here they were reduced to their lowest terms and least common multiple. As I was entering the Red Room doorway, Mr. Whitfield, the pro-slavery M.C. from Kansas, attempted to edge himself in on the right, past the door-post. I thought his crowding interfered with my rights as a free citizen of Massachusetts, so I paid him in his own coin, upon which, evidently intending to keep all he had and get all he could, he put his hands and knees against the door-post. This gave him what Archimedes said he lacked in order to move the globe, a firm basis; and, thus braced, he gave a tremendous push backwards, but somewhat towards the Red Room. As good luck would have it, his back was almost directly against mine, so that he forced me, as by a catapult, very suddenly, but safe and sound, into the Red Room, whence I advanced slowly, with the stream, to the Blue Room. The doorway between the two will long be remembered by me for one of those marvellous escapes which occur at intervals of our life on earth. I was lucky enough to enter the doorway about its middle; and, the walls being thick, it is, in fact, a short entry. Once fairly in it, I took an observation of my surroundings. Five young ladies, all strangers to me, encompassed me round about, the whole six of us so closely grouped that a middle-sized crinoline would have encased us, as a thimble does the finger's end. And there stood I in the midst of them, like — like — well, like the handle of a castor, rising in the midst of pepper-box, mustard-pot, sweet-oil, and vinegar-cruet. I was on the point of saying, "How are you, gals?" when we emerged, all in a lump, from the doorway. The ladies laughed, shook out their crinolines, chatted, and pursued their way, as I did mine, to where we were introduced to the President. I told him I thought he was to be pitied, but he was so busy talking to the five girls that he did not hear me. Then I slowly passed into the Green Room, and around the usual promenade course of the East Room, in the centre of which is a marble table, under the chandelier. A girl, ten years old, was upon the table (placed there for safety); and General Houston, of Texas, was leaning against it. As I came away, one of the last noteworthy sights indoors was the Russian ambassador and his lady, clambering over a huge pile of hats, coats, and shawls in the entrance hall.

The next important function described by Dr. Earle was the inauguration of President Buchanan, March 4, 1857, as follows : —

This day rose bright and clear over Washington, the temperature such that you might be comfortable without an overcoat, yet not uncomfortable with one. All the world was agog when Dr. Nichols and I drove into the city at 10 A.M., the road thronged with people, like those which lead into Worcester on a cattle-show day. The grounds at the east front of the Capitol were already occupied by multitudes, and the street of the procession greatly crowded. Upper windows and even roofs along the route were occupied. A large platform was erected over the eastern steps of the Capitol for the incoming and the outgoing President, the Supreme Court judges, senators and members of Congress, and such other persons as could get upon it. This placed them where a concourse of 100,000 people might see them distinctly. Directly in front of this there was another platform, some four feet high, to protect numerous pieces of ornamental marble lying there until warmer weather shall permit putting them in place in the new Capitol. This platform, upon which I got a position, would perhaps hold 10,000 persons. My place was almost directly in front of the chair intended for Mr. Buchanan. At length, after long waiting, there was great hurrahing by the crowd, and much noise from the bands of music, intimating the coming of Mr. Buchanan, whom a covered passage protected on his way from the street to the Capitol (west front). Fifteen or twenty minutes later the door leading to the eastern portico was opened; and President Pierce, with Mr. Buchanan, made his appearance, followed by the judges of the Supreme Court in their

black silk gowns.   Advancing to the front of the platform, in the
centre, they took seats amidst applause from the surrounding "sov-
ereigns."   Then foreign ambassadors, members of Congress, and a
pell-mell crowd of men, women, and children followed, all running
to secure the best places.   Gold-laced, small-clothed, and cock-
hatted ministers plenipotentiary were elbowed by farmers' boys and
pushed aside by firemen rigged in fire dresses.   Contrasting these
ceremonies (unceremonious) with those of great State occasions I
had seen in Europe, I could imagine the foreign ministers saying in
their hearts, "All republicanism."

When Buchanan began to read his inaugural, and the crowd's
attention was consequently centred on him, I felt a fumbling near
my coat pocket.   I edged aside a little, but the fumbling soon
began again; and I looked round.   Directly behind me stood a
blear-eyed, sandy-haired young man, in snuff-colored coat, who,
seeing my motion, gazed point-blank into vacancy, with the most
innocent expression ever seen on the face of man.   I looked
point-blank into those innocent blear eyes, and said, "If you
don't look out, we'll have hold of you pretty soon."   With a
voice as innocent as his expression had been, he said, "What
for?"   "Oh," said I, "you are rather short; and I want to lift
you up so you can see."   I then turned to my neighbor, Dr. Brown,
of Bloomingdale, and said, "Look out for your pockets."   Whereupon the innocent snuff-colored coat wedged its way among the
people, and disappeared.

After the short inaugural was read, Chief Justice Taney administered the oath of office to Mr. Buchanan.   There was a great
shaking of hands on the platform.   The Vice-President, Breckenridge, who had already taken the oath of his office in the Senate,
came forward, and bowed to the people; and then the great multitude dispersed.   Miss Harriet Lane, the President's niece, rode
away in a barouche drawn by four white horses, and Buchanan,
Pierce, and Breckenridge in another, drawn by two whites.   There
were twenty times as many people about the Capitol and in Pennsylvania Avenue to-day as at the first inauguration I witnessed here,
— March 4, 1837, — when President Van Buren, who had been
Vice-President, was inaugurated.   While Buchanan was escorted
to-day by many military companies, Van Buren then rode from the
White House to the Capitol alone with General Jackson and with

no escort whatever.* So we advance towards the form and ceremony of monarchies.

In the twenty years that intervened between the retirement
of Presidents Jackson and Pierce, no less than seven Presidents
had been in power at Washington, no one of them exceeding
four years in office, and one (General W. H. Harrison) surviv-
ing his accession only a month. He had been succeeded by
John Tyler in April, 1841; and in July, 1850, General Taylor
had been succeeded by his Vice-President, Millard Fillmore.
In Pierce's administration his Vice-President, W. R. King, had
died, so that this period of twenty years was more marked
than any other by the short terms of these high officers. Buchanan was succeeded by Abraham Lincoln, who was assassinated at the beginning of his second four years, and, twenty
years after Lincoln's accession, President Garfield was assassinated, so that there were again but seven Presidents in the
twenty-eight years from 1857 to 1885, all of whom Dr. Earle saw.
Andrew Johnson he saw and heard for the first time in the
Senate in January, 1859, when Dr. Earle was again in Washington on a visit to Dr. Nichols at the Government Hospital,
which was still small (130 patients only), but gave to its director and his guests access to all that was distinguished in
Washington society of that time. Consequently, Dr. Earle
was again thrown into a tide of social festivity, by no means
disagreeable to the recluse of Leicester, when he came forth
from his cottage into the active world. Since the winter of
1857 Dr. Nichols had married Miss Maury, the brunette with
so many sisters; and in her circle of friends Dr. Earle assisted
at dinner parties, one of which, almost an official gathering, he
has described in a letter to his sister at Leicester.

Jan. 28, 1859.—I dined to-day with Mr. Parker, who lives in
Washington not far from Mrs. Maury's, the mother of Mrs. Nichols.
The dinner hour being six, I presented myself then. The door was
opened by a negro in white gloves. Thinks I : " I'm in for it. This

---

* It might be said that to be escorted by the hero of New Orleans was equal to many militia
companies. Railroad-building had wrought the change in the multitude present.

is a white-glove dinner." Guests in the entry were putting on white gloves; while I, not expecting this grade of dinner, had come without my gloves. I felt a little mortification, but put a bold face on, and determined to make the best of it. So I went into the parlor, spoke to my host and hostess, and was introduced to all the guests who had arrived,—about half the expected twenty,—all of them gauntleted in white kid. But this is a free country; and, as all these people were democrats, I consoled myself with the thought that I was setting them a good democratic example. The party being all assembled, two broad doors opened, one from the front and one from the back parlor, and behold the dining-room, running parallel with the parlors, of the same length and somewhat wider. We are each informed what lady he is to escort to the table; and the procession is formed in this order, as near as I recollect: 1. Hon. Isaac Toucey, of Hartford, Secretary of the Navy, with Mrs. Jacob Thompson, wife of the Secretary of the Interior; 2. Postmaster-general Brown, of Tennessee, with Mrs. Parker, our hostess; 3. Colonel Drinkard, chief clerk in the Navy Department, with Mrs. Brown; 4. Dr. Thomas Maury, who married a daughter of Mr. Parker, with Miss Pillow, daughter of General Pillow, of Tennessee; 5. Mr. Schell, brother of the New York collector, Augustus Schell, and Mrs. Dr. Maury; 6. Hon. J. Thompson, Secretary of the Interior, with Mrs. Schell; 7. Mr. John Maury and Miss Saunders, stepdaughter of the Postmaster-general; 8. Mr. Thompson, son of the Secretary, and Miss Mary Parker; 9. Mr. Trotter, of Philadelphia, and Miss Alice Maury; 10. Dr. Earle and Miss Fanny Parker. Then there were Mr. Parker, and a lady and gentleman whose names I do not recall. The table was set for twenty-four, and all the chairs but one occupied. Every gentleman, save one, is between two ladies, and every lady, save one, between two gentlemen. A vase, with a beautiful bouquet, each containing camellias, etc., is in front of each lady, who will take the flowers home with her. The table is twenty-four feet long and ten feet wide. Over either end is a massive chandelier, with eight gas-burners. Two candelabra, each with ten candles, stand on the table, between them vases of flowers. Pyramids, temples, etc., made of confectionery, are here and there on the tables. All the food is in an adjoining room, and is served in sixteen or twenty courses by four colored men in white gloves. At each plate is a decanter of water, with a goblet. Also there are five wine-glasses, no two of them alike, and two of them colored cut Bohemian glass. These drinking implements not being thought quite enough, a small tumbler of Roman punch was added, after the soup, and a cup of coffee as the *finale*. We were at the table nearly three hours, and it was altogether a very sociable and pleasant affair. We departed at 9.30, Miss Saunders having first given me an invitation to a ball at the Postmaster-general's, to-morrow evening, with six hundred other guests.

Dr. Earle went to this ball, to the White House receptions, where Miss Harriet Lane presided with grace, and to a reception at Dr. Bailey's (the anti-slavery editor who first published "Uncle Tom's Cabin"), where the company were all Republicans, with their wives and daughters, and where he met Senators Seward, Wilson, Hale, etc., Richard Mott, brother-in-law of Lucretia Mott, and Justice McLean. In the Senate they were discussing Cuba and a bill appropriating $30,000,-000 for acquiring it, while the House admitted Oregon as a State. No one then looked forward seriously to disunion, though it had long been threatened, and John Brown, in Kansas, had just made the first forcible emancipation of slaves,— —an example which the President followed less than four years later. Senator Sumner was still in Europe, recovering slowly from his injuries of 1856; and General Banks had become Governor of Massachusetts.

The Civil War broke out in April, 1861. A year later we find Dr. Earle in Washington, on business of the census, but much occupied with thoughts of the sick and wounded soldiers and the unsuccessful conduct of the campaigns around the capital. In July, 1862, he offered his services as surgeon to the Sanitary Commission, through Dr. S. G. Howe; but no occasion for his joining the army in the field occurred. Writing from Washington to his nephew, Pliny Earle Chase, in Philadelphia, April 12, 1862, he says : —

I am very busy looking through the army hospitals, listening to the proceedings in Congress, finishing the special business with Mr.

Kennedy, superintendent of the census, for which I came, and noticing the many changes which have taken place since I was last here, in 1859. The city is comparatively quiet since General McClellan and his army left to go to the York River; but officers and soldiers are no rarity in Pennsylvania Avenue and the suburbs on the east, as well as on the heights of Georgetown and Arlington. Across the Potomac the encampments of many regiments are to be seen.

The stress of war had doubled the extent of the work done at the Government Hospital, which now not only received the insane of the army and navy, but gave shelter and treatment to the sick and wounded of both army and navy, so that in the beginning of 1863 it contained nearly 600 patients instead of the 130 of 1859. Pressed with all these duties, Dr. Nichols (Jan. 15, 1863) gave Dr. Earle the charge of the west wing of the hospital, containing 175 insane patients, all men, and many of them recently from the camps and battlefields. This duty detained him in Washington for some months in 1863, and called him there again early in 1864. But so important are his records of the army experiences and political events of this period that a chapter must be devoted to them.

CHAPTER XII

IT was a natural but perplexing situation which the Civil War created at the national capital. Washington had been politically and socially a Southern village. Slavery existed there, and was maintained and cherished by Congress, and by every President since Jefferson, although several of them had been opposed to slavery in the abstract. The rebellion of Virginia brought the forces of the pro-slavery army within easy reach of the seat of government for the loyal States, which to them was at the extreme verge of the territory they controlled; and this both made attacks on Washington by the rebels feasible and expedient and exposed its defenders to great inconvenience and risk. Moreover, a large part of the resident population of Washington sympathized with the rebellion, either actively, in all its aims, or virtually, as agreeing with some of them,—to grant no rights to the negroes, for one. The officers of the regular army, too, were mostly hostile to the anti-slavery cause,—some of them bitterly so; while others looked on the slave-question as having little to do with the issue of the war. On the other hand, the tide of anti-slavery sentiment was constantly and rapidly rising, and finding expression more and more in the debates of Congress. In the autumn of 1862 President Lincoln threw his great influence and matchless sagacity on the side of emancipation. But the army officers, and particularly McClellan and his friends, still hoped for some political compromise which would save slavery, and restore the old governing class of politicians to power. This was the situation when Dr. Earle took up his residence at the Government Hospital, and came into intimate relations with General Hooker and other prominent persons at Washington. His diary is cautiously written, but contains some facts and suggestions which have not yet got into the authentic

books of history and biography. It will therefore be cited
more fully than in the preceding chapters.

As has been said, Dr. Earle passed most of the winter of
1862–63 in the Government Hospital for the Insane, as an
unofficial medical assistant to his friend Dr. Nichols. He
found there many new patients, sent up from the army in the
field and the navy in active service along the Atlantic coast
and in the Gulf of Mexico; but they were chiefly drawn from
the rank and file of the infantry,— the same class as those
among whom Whitman, the Long Island poet, had just then
begun his self-sacrificing labors in the field and the Washington
hospitals. Some of Dr. Earle's insane patients had before been
in other asylums; and instances were not a few where the
patient had been discharged from the asylum for the purpose
of enlisting in the Union army. He writes (Jan. 27, 1863) : —

At my first visit to this hospital, seven years ago, it was but a
small building, with about 30 patients. It has now grown into a
great establishment,— all the original design having been built upon,
— and is occupied for three nearly distinct hospitals. One of these
is for the insane, who are under my care; a second is for the sick
and wounded men from the army; and the third is for the disabled
men of the navy,— in all three, almost 600 patients. As I walked
about the grounds some days ago, I came to a settee so placed
as to command a fine view of the river (the Eastern Branch of the
Potomac), of Washington and Georgetown. Its four occupants,
soldiers, had but four legs among them. One of the men was a very
talkative Frenchman, who lost his leg at Antietam last September,
but had before been in all the battles of the peninsula, under General McClellan. He gave his views very fully concerning his general
and the whole conduct of the Army of the Potomac. They were not
favorable to either. At the next Sunday service in the chapel I
counted 13 men with only 13 legs, but 25 crutches ; and the whole
number of one-legged men in the hospital is about 40. A manufactory of jointed wooden legs, which the government supplies gratis to
such men, is established on our premises. On the 15th of January
Dr. Nichols gave me charge of the west wing of the chief hospital
building, containing 175 insane men, about 20 of whom (all from the
army) have been admitted in the twelve days since I took charge. It

was a most fortunate thing that the government could complete this hospital before the war : otherwise there would have been no place for these insane soldiers and sailors.

The army, from whose command General McClellan was finally removed last November, is now quiet along the Rappahannock, excepting the inquietude caused by the change of commanders. The McClellan men in Washington have been looking for their favorite's reinstatement; but he never will be reappointed, unless much greater changes take place. Fitz-John Porter has met with his reward. It is now generally conceded that there was a regular attempt, not to say conspiracy, to break down General Pope. It succeeded for the time, but its most serious consequences have begun to fall in the proper place. I have heard a naval officer (a McClellan man) say that Porter ought to be shot, and I have also heard one of our major-generals say that in England or France Porter would have been hanged. There is no longer a doubt in my mind that our army might have been in Richmond long ago if all the officers had really tried to get there. Some officers have been incompetent; but private piques and jealousies, and a determination not to fight in earnest, have been the real causes of our failure. It is known that in the battle of Fredericksburg (Dec. 13, 1862) General W. B. Franklin's division contained 60,000 men, 6,000 of whom went into action under General Meade, and drove the rebels nearly a mile. General Meade then looked back, expecting reinforcements, but saw nothing coming, and retreated. Here the battle on the left wing ended; yet 54,000 soldiers there did not fire a shot, and were not ordered into action. A man of excellent judgment, who immediately after the battle went over the ground where Meade fought, says there is no doubt, had the whole division gone into action, the enemy's right flank could have been turned, and the victory been ours. He also says that our army will not succeed until it has submitted to more thorough discipline, that in this battle one whole regiment scattered at the mere sound of the first shell that came screaming over them, and "ran in all directions like a flock of sheep." However, sheep don't generally run in *all* directions, was my reflection.

Fredericksburg, on the Rappahannock, was almost wholly evacuated by its inhabitants. Whereupon our soldiers took large liberties with the houses and furniture. At least 30,000 soldiers slept there one night, nearly all in the streets, and about six times as many as the usual population, men, women, and children. Their beds were odd: stacking arms in the streets, they tore off doors, window shutters, house-boards, and fence-boards, laid one end of each board on the curbstone, the other on the pavement, and slept on them. My informant, who rode through these streets at midnight, estimates that one hundred houses, at least, of the poorer sort, were thus stripped of their enclosing boards as high as the top of the first story, and stood there, as if on stilts, upon their bared timbers. When the army recrossed the river after the fight, one of the trophies borne away was a great pier-glass mirror, which an enthusiastic soldier had strapped on his back. An officer, an army surgeon, fell in love with a richly sculptured marble mantel-piece at Fredericksburg, tore it from its place, and with the aid of two soldiers brought it away.

Well, there is a man at the head of the army now [General Joseph Hooker, appointed upon General Burnside's resignation, January 26] who will fight whenever he has a fair opportunity, and not only so, but will make his subordinates of the Army of the Potomac fight, too. General Hooker breakfasted with us yesterday morning, having come up from the Rappahannock in the night. He then went into Washington, had an interview with the President, issued his address to the army on taking command, and returned to the army at night.

No doubt General Hooker was the "man of excellent judgment" who went over the battlefield after the retreat of General Meade, and was also the informant about those midnight slumberers in Fredericksburg streets. He had been impatient of the delays of McClellan and the incompetence of other generals, and was known in the army and the country as "Fighting Joe Hooker." Dr. Earle, Quaker as he was, expressed the hope that he would now "stick to his antecedents." He goes on : —

February 3.—General Hooker dined with us on Saturday last, remaining at the hospital about three hours. Of course, we made the most of him by asking all proper questions regarding the army, the prospects, etc. He says the rebels will remain in their present intrenchments until he shall attack them; and he certainly will attack them, but not till the roads are better and the army fully reorganized and in better discipline. He means to fight, and does not mean to have any officer under him who will not fight. He would not have accepted the command unless he could put men of his own choice at the head of his three divisions. He has not meddled in politics hitherto, believing that the rebellion must be put down by hard blows, and that, the sooner these blows are given, the better. Judging from what I now know, I am not surprised that the Potomac Army has not been victorious heretofore, but shall be both surprised and disappointed if it does not conquer now. I am in a strong anti-McClellan and pro-Hooker atmosphere; and this, together with a slight acquaintance with Hooker, may have unfitted me to judge impartially. Still, it is evident that McClellan spoiled his army, and that he has not even the merit of being a good disciplinarian. His opponents here say that he did not manage the retreat after the fights before Richmond, but made sure of the safety of Number One, and left the whole conduct of the retreat to under officers. If that be so, he is shorn of his last glory.

Notwithstanding these facts about General McClellan, which have turned out substantially as stated by Dr. Earle, the displaced and dissatisfied general was nominated for President the following year, against President Lincoln, by the party which favored peace, with a compromise on the slavery question, but was totally defeated in November, 1864. By that time General Hooker had yielded the command of the army first to General Meade, and then to General Grant, under whom, at Chattanooga, he performed his most brilliant feat,—the capture of Lookout Mountain. For this and other military services he has received the first honor of an equestrian statue from the State of Massachusetts, as his native State. Dr. Earle goes on : —

February 7.— I was at the Capitol to-day, and heard the Senate debate a bill appropriating $20,000,000 to assist Missouri in emancipating her slaves, who did not come under the effect of the President's emancipation proclamation of January 1. While I was in the House of Representatives, General Burnside appeared on the floor, and for awhile was the greatest Shaker in Washington, every one being eager to grasp his hand. After the representatives had done him this honor, the pages thronged about him with books and scraps

of paper for his autograph.   So great was the demand that he finally
had to refuse, and departed.   Last week Miss Dorothy Dix told me
that there was very little sickness in the soldiers' hospitals, of which
she has a general oversight, the patients being mostly convalescent,
so that there was " nothing for the nurses to do."

February 22.— But I have work enough to keep me out of mis-
chief.   This is my 39th day at the hospital; and, since I came,
45 men patients, 43 from the army and 2 from the navy, have been
admitted,— insane patients, I mean, who all come under my care,
and, being all recent cases of insanity, they make me much work.
In all we have 190 insane patients, about 150 of them from the army.
Many are Germans and Irishmen, 2 or 3 Italians, 1 Frenchman, and
1 Pole, the last a man with an enormous head, who speaks six
languages.   His brain is too powerful for his body.   He is very
insane, and will probably die.   If our army is to be judged by some
of the specimens that come to us, its physique is not in high condition, whatever its morals may be.   Day before yesterday four men
were brought in a squad, looking like Italian brigands, and very
evidently belonging to the "great unwashed."   To place the living
beings they brought with them at 4,000 would be a low estimate.
They were brought from the guard-house, which is an old slave-pen
in Alexandria.   From all I hear of that old Virginia town, it has
become what some call a most God-forsaken place, reeking with filth
and all the abominations of warfare.   Steamboats run hourly from
Washington thither.   We get similar samples of soldiers from the
regular Washington guard-house.

Our soldier-patients are from nearly every Northern State, from
Maine to Kansas (which became a State two years ago, and is
represented in the House by another Conway, Martin, not Moncure,
— the latter now living at Concord).   Coming, as they do, from
various commands and many regiments, they can give us much news
about war matters, in spite of their insanity.   Then I make it a
rule to talk with every one who recovers, as many do ; and I follow
Captain Cuttle's rule of making a note of all that is noteworthy.
Last evening I wrote the war history of an Irishman as he related
it to me, who was pressed at New Orleans into the rebel service,
fought against us at Big Bethel and Williamsburg, deserted, and got
back to New Orleans, whence General Butler, then in command
there, shipped him to Boston.   He afterwards enlisted in a New

York regiment. Two or three days ago I was talking with a man who has been nearly a year and a half in the Army of the Potomac. When I asked him if the soldiers liked General Hooker, he said, "Some do, but there are many who don't: there isn't one soldier in a dozen who likes an officer who rushes into a fight."

Miss Dix lunched with us a few days ago (we breakfast at eight, lunch at twelve, and dine at five). She says there is great mortality among the soldiers who were wounded at the battle of Murfreesboro, and thence brought to the hospitals at Alexandria and other places near Washington. They were carried (by the rebels) from Murfreesboro to Chattanooga, thence by way of Richmond to Norfolk or Fortress Monroe; and it was twenty-six days from the time they were wounded till their wounds were dressed. No wonder their mortality is great.

Religious services on the Sabbath have been held for a year past in the chapel; but, until I came, no secular lecture had been given there. On the 14th of February I consecrated it to that purpose, having an audience of 200 persons gathered from the several departments of the hospital; and I also lectured on the 17th and 20th. I expect to continue this service twice a week while I remain here. It breaks the monotony of the hospital evenings, pleases many of the insane, makes the government of them easier, and increases their attachment to the person in general charge of them,—if he is also the lecturer. All the one-legged men who are well enough are in my audiences; and, as the chapel is in the third story and they walk with crutches up the forty-seven steps of the two flights of stairs, the noise they make is appalling to sensitive persons. It reminds me of the negro song,—

> Sich a-gittin' upstairs I nebber did see.

March 1.— 15 more insane patients have come in; and, of the whole 60, 57 have come into my department. A fine young man was brought here two days ago from one of the Connecticut regiments, with three of his toes so badly frozen that they are likely to slough off, unless amputated. His wife, a young woman apparently under twenty-three, arrived from Connecticut to-day, having been informed of his illness when he was in one of the general hospitals here. He is so much bewildered that he told her it was only a week since he had seen her, yet the physicians at his hospital thought him feigning insanity. One minute's observation by a person of experience with the insane would prove that he is not feigning. A Michigan soldier, whose case is sadly interesting, died a few days ago. He was brought here in November with a bullet wound received at the second battle of Bull Run,— a wound in the left temple directly over the outer extremity of the eyebrow. He could give no account of it, except he said the bullet had been taken out. At intervals here he had spasmodic attacks resembling epilepsy, his mind being weak between the fits. In one of these paroxysms he died; and then the bullet was found lying at the base of the brain, over the back of the eye-socket, partly flattened, and divided for half its length into two horn-like projections. Its pressure on the brain had caused the growth of a sac-like tumor as large as a hen's egg; and the discharge from the external wound came from the interior of this tumor.

I have been talking this evening with a recovered patient who has been more than a year in the Potomac Army. He acknowledged that McClellan is no disciplinarian, and has permitted his soldiers to do much as they pleased, that his dilatoriness has caused the death of 30,000 men, needlessly, of course; but yet he is in favor of McClellan for our next President, because he "was so kind to his men." He allowed, further, that his want of success was owing to lack of discipline in his army, that he might, more than once, have gone into Richmond, and that his neglect to pursue Lee's army after Antietam was a great blunder. On the other hand, he says that, if General Hooker had not been wounded so early as he was at Antietam, his achievements would have been such that he would then have been promoted to the chief command, as he has been of late. He complimented Hooker's courage, saying that he "would never retreat on the battlefield, but would conquer or die"; yet this soldier does not like Hooker, and says, "the army don't like him, because he is so strict." There's a long story behind what this soldier says, and a deal of meaning in his talk. We have so far failed, and, should we finally fail, must continue to fail to the end, because our generals are seeking popularity rather than victory, while the men are unwilling to submit to a discipline which alone will give us victory.

On Monday last, February 23, General Hooker again dined with us, and spent the night, giving us a long evening's talk with him.

He wished to have General Stone — of Ball's Bluff notoriety — for his chief of staff, believing him to be loyal. But President Lincoln told him that, if he knew all the circumstances of the case, he would not ask it; and so he selected General Butterfield, of whose industry and efficiency he now speaks in the highest terms. In course of the evening Mrs. Nichols intimated to the general, apparently in joke, the possibility that the rebels might make another raid, and ride round his army, as happened to his predecessor. General Hooker answered very seriously that they would never ride round his army; and, not more than three days after, General Stuart, their cavalry leader, tried the experiment, and failed. I believe Hooker would rather be shot than have such an attempt succeed. He says he knows everything that the rebels are doing, their camp is full of his spies, and he supposes that his own camp is as full of their spies. One of them, an Englishman, who acted as a spy for both sides, running between Richmond and Washington, and delivering all letters, despatches, etc., which he carried for individuals directly to the government on the other side, has been detected in his double treachery, and shot. In the famous retreat from McClellan's intrenchments around Richmond to the James River, Hooker says that, after the first order to retreat, neither he nor General Kearney either saw McClellan or received an order from him, and that, on a day when Kearney saw some movement of a part of the army which he did not understand, Kearney rode rapidly to Hooker, and said, "There is either cowardice or treachery here somewhere." It is evident that Hooker believes that McClellan is greatly responsible for the present state of things in the country.

March 3.— Saturday last Dr. Nichols and I went to the White House to call on "Abraham and Mary Anne," as we Friends say, it being their regular day of reception. The evening "levees" have not been held this winter; but in their stead there have been "*soirées*" in the morning,— that is, from one to three o'clock in the afternoon. We arrived about two, and found a moderate number of people there, which was largely increased later. "Mary Anne" was doing the honors and receiving the honors without the assistance of her husband, who had unexpectedly been called to the Capitol by some business in the Senate. Mrs. President was dressed in a rich black silk, with a wide lace flounce, and a train which lay on the floor a foot behind her. She wore a set of jewels,— brooch, earrings, two bracelets, and a head-band,— all made, apparently, of jet and pearls set in gold. A man-servant stood behind her,— a new custom never practised by ladies of the White House before, and perhaps introduced to prevent visitors from treading on that train; and a gentleman usher was very busy introducing all comers to Mrs. Lincoln. The Blue Room, where this occurred, was so far darkened by its heavy blue curtains as to give a twilight aspect to everything. To tell the truth, Mrs. President acquitted herself exceedingly well, even better than I had expected. When I saw her last spring, with her bonnet on, in full mourning, I thought her homely, and, in fact, she can lay no claim to beauty; but she is a better-looking woman and did this reception better than either Mrs. President Polk or Mrs. Pierce, as I saw them. A great deal has been said by the secessionists and aristocrats and those out of office concerning her homeliness and vulgarity of manners; but, if her manners were "green" when she came to Washington, two years ago, she has succeeded in ripening them fast. She told Dr. Nichols and myself that she was very sorry "my husband" could not be present to welcome us, but that, to make amends, a special reception was to be given Monday evening,— that is, last night. We then took a walk through the extensive greenhouses, and came away; but, as we were on the portico,— a continuous train of carriages arriving,— the President's carriage appeared, and, while two full coaches were still in front of it, "Father Abraham" slipped quietly out of it, and made his way to the door, almost wholly unobserved. There was a crowd at the door. The President took his place in it, unnoticed by those near him, and, without saying a word, quietly waited for the moving of the waters; but he tucked his hands into his overcoat pockets, and drew the skirts around him, the air being rather chill. As they came to the doorway, the President and a small, brown-coated, fur-capped man were about even in advantage of position for entering; but the advantage was a little in favor of Mr. Lincoln. He perceived it, and gave a gentle "crowd," in order to get ahead. But Browncoat had no notion of being beaten by such a lank-looking fellow as he felt pushing him. So he went at it in earnest, and wormed himself in ahead of Father Abraham. It was very characteristic.

Well, time moved on; and, some fifty hours after this scene, the Monday evening mentioned by Mary Anne had come along. So

Dr. Nichols and I went again to the White House, leaving our overcoats at Miss Dix's, as we went, for fear of losing them in the crowd.
'Twas a calm, sweet night, with a bright moon; and, though both
houses of Congress were in session, their galleries crowded with
visitors, there was no lack of callers on the President. We got to
the rear of the entering crowd about nine o'clock; and there were
not less than one thousand to enter before our turn came, and the
house was already so full that many men were jumping out from one
of the windows. After we got inside, there were several hundred
people between us and the President; and the crowd was such that
Dr. Nichols took a short cut to the great East Room, without trying
to see Mr. and Mrs. Lincoln. I persevered, and was triumphant. I
communed with Abraham, and told him there was a lady in my
neighborhood who sent her love to him. And Abraham inquired,
"What is the lady's name?" And I lifted up my voice, and said
unto him, "Her name is Mrs. Marshall." Thereupon Abraham
exalted *his* voice (though it is and was then as soft as that of a
delicate woman, and as gentle), and said, "My respects to her."
The crowd pressed on behind me. I was taking up precious time.
My message was delivered, my promise kept: why then should I
delay? So I passed on with the multitude into the East Room,
where was the same old story I have seen and heard for many winters,
— a jam of men and women, but an entirely new set of men and
women. With the exception of three or four public men, I saw but
two persons I could remember ever to have seen before; and even
Dr. Nichols, long resident here, said he did not recognize more than
a dozen of his acquaintance. There was less dress, less style, much
fewer persons of really polished manners than in former times,— a
change due in part to the political change of administration, but still
more to the war, and its effect in bringing certain classes of people
to Washington, and keeping others at home or in the campaigns.
As Congress was just closing its session, its members were otherwise engaged; and I saw only one member of the cabinet,— Gideon
Welles, of Connecticut. I spoke with Cassius M. Clay, now a
general in the Union army, with General Sumner,— a distant cousin
of Charles Sumner,— and with General Fremont, still a popular man
from the events of the last ten years. When it was whispered that
Fremont was in the East Room, there was a general rush, or an
attempt at rushing, to find him. Seeing this, he made the circuit of

the great room as quickly as he could, through a dense body of bodies, with outstretched hands, eager for a shake, and immediately and quietly left. He is a smaller man than I had fancied him, his head hardly above my shoulder.

As by this time Dr. Earle had a very wide acquaintance all over the United States, this remark of his about the new and strange faces at the White House receptions has much meaning. The political and military revolution of 1861 had been followed by a social revolution; and the power of the United States, which had been lodged in a few slaveholders at the South, controlling the army and navy, whose officers were largely their relatives, and a few politicians at the North, represented by Buchanan, Pierce, Caleb Cushing, the Van Burens, and Douglas,— this power was again returned to the hands of the people, who were carrying on the war and freeing the slaves in their own fashion, without heeding the old men or the old traditions. These for the moment were represented at the North by the displaced General McClellan, at this very time receiving honors and applause from the Northern men with Southern principles, who had lost office and influence when Lincoln became President. It was a covert — and soon to be open — attack on the administration; to overthrow which McClellan was brought forward as a Presidential candidate the next year, 1864, but signally defeated in the popular vote.

A similar change was noted at Washington when Andrew Jackson succeeded John Quincy Adams as President in 1829; and the sweeping change in officials then made was much more than repeated under President Lincoln, whose first act on assuming power was to fill the offices, great and small, with his own supporters. As the war went on, he appointed many " War Democrats "; but the McClellan episode threw many of that class back into their old party relations, imbittered for a time by the emancipation decrees of Lincoln, which had culminated a few weeks after McClellan's removal in November, 1862. The same men in Boston who had attacked the emancipation policy in August and September, 1862, united with others of the military profession in April, 1863, in giving McClellan a sword, which he was invited to use "for the administration, when it behaves itself"; that is, when it should give up its policy of freeing and arming the blacks.

Monday, April 6, 1863.— This month came in with as delightful spring weather as could be wished,— with bird-songs, the bursting of lilac-buds in the Washington gardens, green lawns, and other pledges of summer.   But now we are in the midst of snow and frost,— yesterday morning six inches of snow, which to-morrow will be all gone, leaving its postscript of mud.   And along with these changes of weather we are having an epidemic of small-pox,— no less than ten cases of it in this hospital,— yet no one of our five hundred inmates manifests any alarm at it; while one case in the city of Worcester would set Leicester and all Worcester County in an uproar of alarm. Such is man's power of adapting himself to his miseries.

On the evening of March 31 I went to the great Union meeting at the Capitol, at which the President and his cabinet were present. I succeeded in getting a place directly beside the Speaker's desk in the great House Chamber; and directly in front of me sat the President, and Secretaries Seward, Chase, and Usher, and the Postmaster-general, Montgomery Blair.   So for three hours I looked our government in the face, at only a few feet distance.   The President looked no fatter nor handsomer than usual.   His little boy [Tad] was with him, sitting, most of the time, in his lap, and now and then bearding his face.   Seward looked old and worn; Chase, fat, good-humored, and hearty, just like his face on the dollar greenbacks; Blair, rather lean and nervous.   The long speech of the evening was by Andrew Johnson, military governor of Tennessee, which State he used to represent in Congress.   It was a loyal and patriotic speech, with many good points; but it showed that "Andy" never wore out many grammars at school, and was never mentally disciplined by chopping logic.   He often brought down the house, got many thumps from Seward's cane on the floor, and once, at least, set the President's feet "dancing the hard-heeled shuffle." *

While waiting for the meeting to assemble, and wandering about

---

* When the legal-tender paper currency was issued by Mr. Chase as Secretary of the Treasury, he was allowed to have his own handsome head engraved on the most numerous issue,— the dollar-bills,— so that his face became known to more of the soldiers and other citizens than that of any other living statesman in America.   It was afterwards said that this was one of his bids for the Presidency, which never came to him.

the House to see whom I knew and whom I knew not, I reached the west end of the chamber, and there found seated in the back row of representatives' chairs, behind those formerly occupied by Giddings of Ohio and my pupil of olden time, Buffington of Fall River, an interesting group of Ute Indians from the Rocky Mountains. This warlike tribe has always been friendly to Uncle Sam; and now they have been brought here to show them how big a man our Uncle is, and so preserve their friendship, and keep them from going over to the rebels, as some of the Southern tribes have done. A delicate, smooth-faced young white man sat with them, who said he had them in charge; and thereupon I had much conversation with him. He told me their tribe numbers about twenty-three thousand,—men, women, and children. They regard us whites as an inferior race, and one of this party told the Indian Commissioner the day before that in case of war they could whip us. He was going to take them the next day to see the Army of the Potomac, after which, he thought, they would change their minds.

Soon after this date Dr. Earle returned to Leicester for the summer of 1863, and was then chosen Professor of Psychologic Medicine in the Berkshire Medical Institute, a temporary medical school, where for several years Dr. Holmes, the poet-anatomist, had lectured. This was the first time in the United States that mental diseases were recognized as a necessary part of the study of medical science, though they had long been so considered in Germany and other European countries. Indeed, the University of Zurich has many years had for its professor of psychiatry the director of the Cantonal Asylum of Burg-hoelzli, near by; and such would have been Dr. Earle's position at Pittsfield, after his election to the superintendency of the Northampton Hospital, had the Medical Institute continued. He gave his introductory address at the Commencement in November, 1863, and then proceeded to Washington again, where for six months he was once more associated with Dr. Nichols at the Government Hospital. The admissions of army patients had much increased, as the war went on, and during this winter of 1863–64 were nearly forty a month, or more than one a day. His diary recommences thus:—

Washington, Dec. 2, 1863.— I was nearly a week on my way here by Pittsfield, New York, and Philadelphia. November 24 I gave my address at Pittsfield on " Psychologic Medicine " to a small audience. It seemed to give general satisfaction. The next day I went to New York, and on Thanksgiving Day, the 27th, went across the ferry to Brooklyn, and attended Henry Ward Beecher's church there. Every spot large enough for a standing-place was occupied, and the *Express* newspaper (no friend to Beecher) says more people were turned away than could get in. His sermon had for object to show what we have to be thankful for, as a nation. This naturally led him to speak of the war and the condition of the country since emancipation. He had been speaking but a few minutes when a few of the audience ventured to applaud him. The ice thus broken, more and more joined in the applause, until finally, when he said that the names of Washington and Lincoln would go down to posterity linked together, the whole audience "came down" with a tremendous clapping of hands.

Immediately after my arrival here I settled quietly down into the hospital routine, and have thus continued. My duties are much less arduous than last winter, Dr. W. W. Godding,* who came here in September last, filling the place I then had, while I have charge of the insane women and negroes; and Dr. Stevens has the sole care of the sick and wounded soldiers in St. Elizabeth's Hospital, and Dr. Gunnell still acts as surgeon to the naval hospital, as last year. I continue my lectures to the inmates of all the hospitals on the evenings of Monday and Friday each week, while on Wednesday evening there is a dance or some other entertainment; and we have an excellent musical choir.

The farm which joins the hospital farm on the south was taken by the government last summer as a cavalry depot; and the number of horses kept there varies from 10,000 to 15,000. The extent of this establishment, as well as the fate of horses in war-time, may be conceived from the fact that the government is advertising for twenty-five men skilled in skinning horses. In consequence of this accession to our neighborhood the travel on our road has increased tenfold; and there is an almost constant procession of cavalry, of newly bought horses, of condemned ones, of soldiers, and of army wagons with supplies. One night several thousand horses broke from the

* Now at the head of the Government Hospital.

enclosure, and the next morning were scattered in roads and fields all about the neighborhood, nearly a hundred having been drowned in the Eastern Branch by the bridge where we cross in driving to Washington.

Dr. Godding, here first mentioned, remained an assistant physician at the Washington Hospital until he was chosen to succeed Dr. G. C. S. Choate as superintendent of the Taunton (Massachusetts) Hospital. Remaining there until 1877, he was then placed at the head of the Washington Hospital, of which he is still the honored superintendent. He has given me some recollections of Dr. Earle during their early acquaintance, as follows: —

I first knew Dr. Earle here in the autumn of 1863, he having charge of the female department and I of the male patients,— both assistants to Dr. Nichols, the superintendent. It was while serving here, in the spring of 1864, that he was visited by a committee of the trustees of the Northampton Hospital, and shortly after appointed to its superintendency. I was intimately associated with the doctor during that six months of 1863–64; and later, when from 1870 to 1877 I was in charge of the State Hospital at Taunton, I frequently met him.

Dr. Earle in 1863, then in his fifty-fourth year, was still a remarkably good-looking man; and, though myself twenty-one years younger, I found him very companionable and agreeable. He had already a reputation as a statistician, and had published much in the *Journal of Insanity* and elsewhere on mental disorders. He had travelled in Europe, had been assistant physician at the Frankford Asylum, and had been in charge at Bloomingdale. Earlier he had been a teacher in the Friends' School at Providence, R.I., and had that thorough equipment in the fundamental branches, including English grammar, for which those " Friends' " Schools are famous. I profited by his knowledge; and, such leisure moments as we had, I enjoyed conversing and associating with him. I say *associating*, for he was fond of games; and Dr. Stevens and I, after the evening work was over, often utilized the office table for a game of cards with him. Dr. Earle preferred to beat. Indeed, he did not take being beaten kindly; and we, early discovering his foible, and not having the fear of his superior age and wisdom before our eyes, often combined to throw the game into one or the other of our two hands. He, honest and un-suspecting, sometimes was so outrageously beaten as to need all his will-power and philosophy to withdraw in anything like a devotional frame of mind. The same was true of billiards. He was fond of the cue, and we were able to win on that game.

But he went up to Northampton, and there found time to perfect himself in those caroms and curves, so that, returning on a visit to St. Elizabeth some years later, he challenged the knights of the cue, and "laid out" every one of us. I have somewhere among my papers an interesting souvenir of the good doctor,— an illustrated pen and ink series, sent after his return to Northampton,— illustrating "Ye Visit of Ye Earle of Leicester to his friend Kinge Nicholas at Ye St. Elizabeth, with serratim views of ye overthrow and dis-comforture of ye Philistines."

He was a most methodic and painstaking, conscientious man. He introduced many methods at St. Elizabeth that bore testimony to this. He evolved a form for registry of cases, and induced the superintendent to adopt it in place of that in use, which — when I came, years later, to take charge of the same side — I found both exhaustive and exhausting.

Another instance of his methodic ways while I was associated with him was the episode of his chewing tobacco. He decided one morning that he was using too much tobacco,— that he would gradu-ally withdraw, and cut off his ration altogether. He was nothing, unless methodic; and every morning for a week or more he daily weighed out five grains less of his "fine cut." He would call atten-tion to it, and dilate on the ease with which a resolute man could conquer an appetite that had begun to control him. This ingenious process continued for perhaps a week longer, when one morning, noticing a cloud on his face, I ventured to ask how many grains he had taken off that morning. He replied "that he wasn't well, that he was in no condition to continue it at that time." I never saw him resort to the scales after that, but I think the tobacco pouch remained by him.

These facts simply show that my friend was human, like all the rest of us. Foibles he had, but they touch not one whit the integ-rity of his life or the value of his work.

Dr. Earle's diary continues:—

Jan. 28, 1864.— I have some leisure from hospital duties, and devote the time to medical reading for my first course of lectures at Pittsfield next autumn. I have received and declined an invitation to deliver the address at the annual Commencement of the Medical School in the University of Michigan, at Ann Arbor, in the latter part of March. The number of insane soldiers much increases here, in spite of the public assertion of Rev. Dr. Bellows, of the Sanitary Commission, that no man in the Union army had become insane since the beginning of the war. But upwards of 40 have been admitted here since January 1 from the armies of the East and South alone, besides 27 who all came at once, each under charge of another soldier, from General Grant's army. Thus more than 70 have been received in twenty-seven days. Last year they only came at the rate of 6 a week.

I notice a remarkable change of sentiment in Washington since last winter. Emancipation is generally accepted as an established fact, even by those most opposed to it; and it is admitted, even by the friends of General McClellan, that Lincoln is to be re-elected President this year. And so (since it would be hard to give up all court society for five years longer) "old Abe" has risen in the estimation of Washington people of the old régime, and Mrs. Lincoln has callers who formerly "turned up the nose" at her. In general, society is accommodating itself to the new state of things, and gradually returning to its smooth current of outward harmony. There are more evening parties, more sociability. Since the middle of January the weather has been such as we have on the hills of Leicester in May,— no frost in the ground, some fields quite green, overcoats often a burden, windows open for comfort, etc.

February 21.— My course of life in the midst of war is very even. Breakfast, a walk through the wards of the women's department, the preparation of medicine for my patients, a look at the morning newspaper, lunch, sometimes with visitors, as formerly, the reading of medical books or insanity statistics, perhaps a game of billiards with one of the men patients, then dinner at five, and an evening occupation varying between lectures, reading, and a second visit to my wards,— such is the sum of my existence. I sometimes go to the weekly dance, but only as a spectator.

In January I went to the anti-slavery meeting in the hall of the
House of Representatives, which was addressed by the celebrated
young political lecturer from Philadelphia, Anna Dickinson. The
lowest price of tickets was fifty cents; yet the hall was full, with
many standing in the doorways and sitting on the steps in the
galleries.   The President, Vice-President, Speaker of the House,
many senators and representatives, and some 1,800 other persons
were there to hear an out-and-out anti-slavery address, which at
every expression of radical sentiment was greeted with an uproar
of applause.   It was evidently repeated from memory, yet in every
respect well delivered.   She was perfectly composed, though in the
presence of an audience that would discompose most men; but who
would have thought ten years ago, when the Kansas-Nebraska bill
was forced through Congress to extend and perpetuate slavery,
that in January, 1864, a woman would stand there and glory in
emancipation proclaimed by the President of the United States?
Verily, the world does move; and when will "the Union as it was"
come back again?

This month I was at a party at the house of Mr. Kennedy, the
superintendent of the census, whose parlors are not large, and who
generally gives parties for men alone.   More distinguished men were
at this one than I ever met before at a private party anywhere.
Members of the Senate and House, Judge Usher, Secretary of the
Interior, officers of the army and navy, among them Admiral Charles
Wilkes, who took Mason and Slidell from the "Trent," and almost
brought on war with England thereby, Dr. Peter Parker, many years
a missionary in China, Judge Holt of Kentucky, and many of the
foreign ambassadors were present, among them Lord Lyons and
Baron Stoeckel, the Russian envoy.

Miss Dix came to this hospital yesterday, and is still here.   She
lately visited the Virginia Insane Hospital at Williamsburg, now
supported by the Federal government, and reports it in excellent
order and well supplied.   On her return she travelled in company
with twenty-five of our army officers, who had escaped from the Libby
Prison in Richmond, and heard some sad tales from them, so that
she is not much in love with the rebels.   Dr. Stevens has had letters
from General Hooker at the South-west, who writes that there is little
to prevent our armies in that quarter from going to Mobile or
Charleston when they choose.

By this time General Hooker, who had resigned the command of the Potomac Army just before the battle of Gettysburg, and had won renown at Lookout Mountain in September, 1863, was in command of the Army of the Cumberland in Tennessee, and General Grant had been selected to take command of all the armies in the field. He came to Washington early in March, and there met the President for the first time, though both had been citizens of Illinois for years. Late in April he took personal command of the Potomac Army, and moved against Richmond, proposing "to fight it out on this line if it takes all summer." It did take all summer and the next winter; but Dr. Earle did not remain in Washington to see the close of the war in April, 1865. His last entry at the Government Hospital is dated May 24, 1864, when the annual meeting of the American Association of Medical Superintendents of the Insane, a body which he had helped to found twenty years before, had just closed its sessions in Washington. His diary for May says :—

The number of our insane has so much increased, as the war goes on, that it has been concluded to break up the hospital for sick and wounded soldiers (St. Elizabeth's), which for almost three years has occupied the eastern part of these large buildings. Other hospitals have been provided for them. So the one-legged and the sick were removed May 2 and 3, and their places are henceforth devoted to the insane. General Grant crossed the Rapidan on the 3d, and we are making preparations here and at the army hospitals for the great swath of men who are now being cut down by the scythe of war. It has been a lovely spring. On May Day I took a long walk through the fields and woods of our premises, while everything was in the full flush of early spring. The forests were tenderly green with the foliage of the tulip-tree (liriodendron) and the maples, and the ground beneath was sprinkled with many flowers. The blood-root, hepatica, and epigæa had bloomed and gone. The anemones, claytonia, violets, and flowering cornel were then in bloom. Elsewhere the cherry and apple blossoms were abundant, the lilacs opening their first blossoms, and the grass was waving in the breeze, almost tall enough for the scythe. At the Association meeting last week, only about twenty members were present, twenty hospitals being represented out of twice that number, such being an effect of the war. We went in a body, so many as we were, to call on "Uncle Abe" at the White House. He looked thin, worn, and haggard; but we were so early he had not breakfasted. Notwithstanding our small numbers, he told us there was enough of us, he reckoned, "to keep everybody straight or else make everybody crooked."

And with this interview Dr. Earle's personal acquaintance with Abraham Lincoln seems to have ended. He was assassinated eleven months after, having in the mean time been reelected and seen the end of the Civil War. In the June following this interview Dr. Earle was chosen superintendent of the State Lunatic Hospital of Massachusetts at Northampton, and took charge of the 350 patients there July 2, 1864. About that time my acquaintance with him began; for I had then been for nine months secretary of the first Board of State Charities ever established in America, and had among my official duties the visitation and inspection of the insane under public and private treatment. In what follows, therefore, I speak from intimate acquaintance with Dr. Earle and his work.

CHAPTER XIII.

MASSACHUSETTS had aided in the establishment of the McLean Asylum for the Insane as a branch of her General Hospital before 1820, but built no State hospital until 1832, when that at Worcester (now used as a chronic asylum) was erected. A second State hospital was opened at Taunton in 1854: and so rapidly had the insane increased that a third was begun soon after at Northampton, which was the largest and costliest then existing in Massachusetts, and was opened in 1858. Its early administration was unsatisfactory. It had cost more than was estimated, and its finances never had reached a proper balance of income and outlay. Its patients were largely drawn from the chronic cases in the older hospitals, and were mostly incurable. Its first superintendent, Dr. Prince, though an agreeable man, had no special fitness for the position and no proper training in the management of large expenditures. Consequently, the hospital was usually in debt. Its medical staff was unequal to the moderate requirements of that period, — so much less exacting than our day,— and the discipline of attendants and patients left much to be desired. Finally, public criticism, too long withheld, led to the resignation of Dr. Prince. Private censure had not been withheld from early in the hospital's history. A few months after its opening, Miss Dorothea Dix, in pursuance of her habit of making unannounced visits to the hospitals for the insane, and perhaps not wholly satisfied with the selection of the superintendent (which was generally ascribed to favoritism and politics), descended upon the courteous host and hostess at the Northampton institution, and, after leaving them, wrote as follows : —

BOSTON, Oct. 22, 1858.

Dear Sir,— I have time for writing but briefly; but I desire to thank both yourself and Mrs. Prince for the very kind reception extended to your *abrupt* and uninvited guest; and to express by word to yourself the sense of quiet satisfaction I had, in seeing the Institution you direct under so favorable circumstances. Indeed, so many conditions of things and persons satisfied me so well (especially by contrasts) that I do not like to put myself in an ungracious attitude by objecting to anything which came under notice. You will excuse my candor, I am sure, if *for your sake* as well as for that of your patients, I allude to one point,—*the exposure* of your patients in the *Chapel* to the *remarks* and observations of *strangers* and *writers*, which will surely lessen *confidence* in the *public* mind,—eager as most persons are to *push* into the interior of all such Institutions, they feel differently when *their friends* are objects of curious, useless notice. . . . I have a hundred things to say, but no time now. Should you write, please direct Care of Brown & Dix, Milk Street, Boston.   yr fd

                                                        D. L. DIX.

This note, with its underscoring and abbreviation (the latter only shown above in the signature), is characteristic of the writer, who followed the advice of Tasso, and mixed honey with the "sacred bitters" (*hiera pikra*) of the censure she was not slow to impart. She shrewdly pointed at a blemish that long existed at Northampton, and increased in some ways, until it was swiftly swept away by Dr. Earle's discipline.

The new Board of State Charities secured the needful appropriation of money from the State; and, after an interval of three months, Dr. Earle, whose appointment had been favored by the State Board, took charge of the medical and general affairs of the establishment. He found the bonds of discipline much relaxed, and a very small proportion of the patients apparently curable. Out of more than 200 whom the State supported there from its own treasury, only 7 were reported to me in September, 1864, as curable, of whom, in fact, only 4 did recover. The farm was not large enough, and had been ill-cultivated. In short, everything needed the eye and hand of a skilful master. It was then seen how valuable had been the varied experience and the world-wide observation of the new superintendent, and especially how useful was his early training in frugal and practical industries.

Dr. Earle, though fifty-four years old, was then in the full vigor of life. His uncertain health, occasionally yielding to periods of depression such as led to his resignation at Bloomingdale, had been confirmed by age and by careful attention to exercise and recreation. The affairs of the nation, after years of trial and doubt, were taking the favorable turn which led to peace the following year, and to the final removal of the national plague of slavery; and he rejoiced in the opportunity of testing, in a practical way, the ideas he had long held concerning the moral treatment and manual occupation of the insane. He could have desired a more hopeful class of subjects for his treatment; yet that, also, he gradually secured by the admission of a much larger number of private patients, attracted from other States by his high professional reputation. This number soon doubled; and, at the end of five years from Dr. Earle's coming, it was trebled. This of itself gave the hospital more ease in its finances; for the price paid by the private patients was more than their cost, while the pauper patients, who made nearly nine-tenths of the whole number in 1864, were then costing more than was paid for their support. At the end of Dr. Earle's fourth year not only had the valuation of the hospital property increased by nearly $30,000 since he came, but the trustees were able to say, "For the first time since the founding of the hospital we have passed a year without borrowing money"; and they closed the year with a balance of nearly $10,000 in hand. This balance went on increasing — though often drawn upon for other than current expenses — until, when Dr. Earle resigned in 1885, it stood at $34,000; while the valuation figures had gone up from $272,000 in 1864 to more than $440,000 in 1885. This gain came from the high cultivation of the enlarged farm, the better labor of the employed patients, the systematic handling of all expenditure, and for a time the increased income from private patients.

By this prudent management of the hospital, Dr. Earle disarmed criticism on the economic side, and made his establishment popular with the legislature and the State authorities, who had been accustomed to see it a frequent applicant for appropriations, not only for repairs and new buildings (as was the case with other hospitals), but for deficiencies in its current expenses. To meet the lack of a working capital, which every new hospital feels, the Board of State Charities, in accord with Dr. Earle, procured advance payments for nine-tenths of the State patients there (which was perfectly safe, since they were permanent boarders), and thus enabled him to make cash purchases, and thereby reduce the current cost. This he also reduced materially by introducing the system of distributing supplies which he had seen practised in frugal Germany; each person employed being made accountable for the articles delivered upon his request, and thus becoming more careful against waste or theft,—the latter by no means unknown formerly in such establishments. In this way he became a model for other hospitals to follow, as they gradually did, but not till some of them had suffered from extravagance and peculation so as to attract public notice.

What the condition of his patients was in respect to curability will appear from Dr. Earle's second annual report, covering his first full year at Northampton (from Oct. 1, 1864, to the same date in 1865) : —

The size of this hospital being disproportionate to the population of the four western counties and that part of Worcester County which sends its insane to Northampton, it has constantly been made the receptacle for the incurables of the other two hospitals (at Worcester and Taunton), which are filled to overflowing from the cities and denser settlements of Eastern Massachusetts. Of the 134 patients admitted in the year, 44 were transferred from those hospitals; and the recovery of any one of these is extremely doubtful. Again, town authorities in this section of the State appear but little disposed to bring their insane to this hospital, so long as they can be taken care of in the poorhouses or at their homes ; and the same is too often true of the families of private boarders or pay-patients.*

* The usage in Massachusetts was and still is to admit three classes of patients (in respect to their means of support) to its State hospitals and asylums, of which there are now nine instead of three, as in 1865: 1. State patients, having no ascertained "settlement" or legal residence in any city or town; 2. Town patients, poor persons having such settlement in some city or town; 3. Private patients, chiefly from Massachusetts, for whom board was paid by their friends or from their own property. The first class were paid for by the State; the second, by their municipality; the third, as above stated. In October, 1865, Northampton Hospital had 235 State patients, 48 town patients, and 69 of the third class.

A few weeks since a man was received here who had been insane forty years, and during the last eleven had been chained by the leg to a staple in the floor of a room in the house of a relative. He had never before been in a hospital. For these and other reasons, out of 134 admitted in the year, the disease of only 34 was of less duration than one year. In all the rest it had passed into the chronic stage of comparative incurability.

Among this unpromising mass of patients, 468 in all, 33 recoveries were reported,— 6 State patients, 6 town patients, and 21 private patients; but 6 of these recoveries were from delirium tremens, or inebriety. The deaths were 41; and here the proportions were reversed, 24 being State cases and only 14 private patients. This excess of deaths over recoveries continued for a few years; but in 1870, with a total population of 604, there were but 33 deaths against 50 recoveries, while 2 were discharged as "not insane,"— perhaps the first patients thus frankly designated in our hospital reports. But, among the 604 of 1870, only 103 had never before been in any hospital; while at the end of the year (Oct. 1, 1870) the three classes of patients stood: State, 209; town, 73; private, 122,— the first class diminishing, and the other two considerably increasing.* Meantime an asylum for the chronic and quiet insane had been opened at Tewksbury, and a part of its inmates had been drawn from Northampton. On this point Dr. Earle said: —

The patients removed to Tewksbury are chiefly the most quiet and undemonstrative in the house; while among those brought hither from other hospitals an increasing proportion are excited, violent, and destructive. For these reasons the number of the turbulent has been gradually augmented, until it is now threefold what it was when I took charge, six years ago. Thus this hospital has been and still is in a state of transition from little more than an asylum for incurables to the status of a hospital proper, receiving all its patients directly from their homes.

* In consequence of changes in the laws of pauper settlement the proportion between these classes has now greatly changed. On the 1st of October, 1897, among the 522 patients of the enlarged Northampton Hospital, only 47 were State cases, while 388 were city and town cases, and 87 private patients. Out of 182 admissions, 135 had never been treated before.

This change, always greatly desired by him, Dr. Earle lived
to see; for in October, 1888, more than three years before his
death, his successor, Dr. Nims, reported that, of 166 patients
admitted in the year, only one was from outside the four
western counties, which had, in fact, nearly doubled their
population since 1864.

At that date (1888) there remained of the original transfers
from the other hospitals (including 100 State patients who had
been sent up from the South Boston Hospital in 1858) about 80
old cases, of whom a few yet remain, ten years later. This
persistence of old cases, together with the more frequent
admission of recent cases (always more exposed to death than
the chronics, until the latter are enfeebled by age), has made
the deaths in recent years outnumber the reported recoveries.
Thus in 1868 there were 43 deaths among 565 patients; in
1878, 23 deaths among 551, with 26 recoveries; in 1888, 31
deaths among 624 patients, with 36 recoveries; in 1885, the
year of Dr. Earle's retirement, there were 27 deaths and 29
recoveries among 588 patients; in 1892, the year of his death,
among 627 patients there were 31 deaths and 45 recoveries.
But in 1896, among 745 patients, there were 46 deaths and
only 36 recoveries; and in 1897, among 735 patients, 45 deaths
and only 30 recoveries. A marked feature of Dr. Earle's administration was the low death-rate among his patients, showing the extreme care taken by him, and also the excellent diet
which the large and well-cultivated farm enabled him to supply
at a comparatively small cost. In 1885, the last year of his
direction, there were 364 acres, or nearly double the number
he found in 1864; and each cultivated acre produced nearly
twice as much as when he began his practical management of
the farm, for which his rural life at Leicester had so well
qualified him. Thus in 1864 only 40 tons of hay were cut;
in 1885, 251. In the former year, 6,256 pounds of pork were
raised; in 1885, 17,544. The difference in the crops of fruit
was still more marked, and nearly as much so in vegetables for
the kitchen.

Next to the economic benefit of Dr. Earle's administration
may be placed its statistical value, both to the hospital itself

and to the State at large and other States. His long study of
statistics had shown him how imperfect and useless was
much of the information which hospital statistics professed
to give, and he speedily reformed the practice at Northampton. My own studies had led me in the same direction; and
when I became Inspector of Charities, in 1879, I at once con-
ferred with him in regard to the forms proper to be used in all
the Massachusetts hospitals and asylums, when reporting their
insane for the official year. Profiting by his suggestions, which
had been strikingly enforced by his then recent publications on
the Curability of Insanity, I prepared tables, which, when revised by him and approved by Dr. Allen and Dr. Hitchcock, of
the State Lunacy Board, became the official form for tabula-
tions, and have, ever since 1880, been in use in Massachusetts,
with trifling modifications, which do not improve them. Based
on the facts thus reported, the principal matters of endless
dispute, as to the age, curability, form of disease, death-rate,
occupations, etc., of many thousands of the insane, have been
partially settled, so far as Massachusetts is concerned; and
other States and countries have profited by this example to
improve their own statistical reports, so that it is no longer
possible to have those absurd results so gravely and confi-
dently stated, upon which Dr. Earle commented sarcastically
in his annual Northampton reports, and afterwards in his useful volume, exposing the old fallacies respecting curability.

Two positions taken by Dr. Earle, while in charge at
Northampton, drew on him much idle censure from his professional brethren. The first was his unsparing exposure
year by year, from 1876 onwards, of the traditional and deceptive modes of reporting recoveries, so as to make it appear to
the public that insanity in general is a malady easily curable
(only true of certain forms of the disease). This provoked for
years the most offensive imputations from some of those who
had been using, consciously or ignorantly, the old forms of
statistical report to propagate a mistaken opinion which flattered
professional pride. His only object was truth, whether agreeable to preconceived opinion or not. Yet he was charged with
mean motives, and with misrepresenting the statements of

those not yet converted by his facts. The other position, no less creditable to his love of truth and his public spirit, was his attitude towards the extravagant scale of expenditure in hospital building for the insane, which prevailed in several States in the decade from 1870 to 1880, and culminated in Massachusetts in the culpable wastefulness of the builders of the Danvers Hospital. Unjustifiable use having been made of a letter which had been extracted from Dr. Earle's good nature, to procure from the legislature an appropriation of $500,000 more, to finish the Danvers structure, than he had been assured it would cost, he felt it his duty to give his full opinion concerning the matter in his yearly report for 1876. Estimating its final cost at $1,800,000, including interest before it could be occupied, and its capacity at 500, he computed the building-cost *per capita* at $3,600, both assumptions being within bounds of the existing fact when the hospital was opened in 1878. Dr. Earle then said : —

Scattered all over Massachusetts there are hundreds, perhaps thousands, of farms, averaging 100 acres of land, with a good country dwelling-house of two stories, and from three to five rooms on the ground floor, a suitable barn, and (often) other out-buildings, and wood sufficient for the perpetual maintenance of two fires; and any one of these farms may be purchased for less than $3,600. The market value of more than 500 such farms will be spent in the construction of that hospital. For at least one-half of its cost, nothing is added to its excellence as a curative institution, and no compensation is gained, at all commensurate with the amount of money disbursed. Had the State built the hospital with one half of its appropriations (actual and in prospect), and with the other half purchased that amount of its outstanding bonds and burned them, it would, in my estimation, have done a greater work of beneficence than it will have performed by the lavish expenditure of that half. The burned bonds would no longer oppress the people with demands for either principal or interest, but the establishment at Danvers entails a perpetual and unnecessary burden to meet its current expenses. It is not a legitimate or truthful expression of the will of the people of Massachusetts. Had it been known in the beginning that it would cost even $1,500,000 (the sum already asked for), no

one will pretend that the enabling act for its foundation could ever
have been obtained.

There was no misunderstanding trenchant words like these.
They greatly angered the indolent commissioners and incompetent architects and engineers who had wasted so much public
money, and they caused much anguish of mind to the plausible
medical men who had helped support the pretension that such
costly buildings would promote recoveries. These knew that
their reputation was not equal to the task of crying down the
most eminent of their profession, one of the thirteen founders,
in 1844, of the Association of Superintendents, whose deliberate
votes against monster asylums they had helped to set aside; but
they were none the less vexed on that account. The public responded at once to the plain language of the Northampton
superintendent, which was widely copied in the press, and had
much to do with the searching legislative investigation that
followed in the winter and spring ensuing. As its result, the
commissioners were turned out, the new hospital was put into
the hands of a new board, who found all Dr. Earle's anticipa-
tions of their financial difficulties fully realized, and it was five
or six years before this crowded building could meet its yearly
outlay from its own income, as the Northampton hospital had
done, under Dr. Earle's frugal management, for nearly twenty
years.

The open and secret hostility to Dr. Earle for his outspoken
protest against extravagance soon ceased, so evidently was the
judgment of the people with him; and, when in Chicago in
June, 1879, he set forth the true theory and wise practice of
hospital building for the insane, at the meeting of the National
Conference of Charities, he received general applause from all
parts of the country. But his sin against traditional opinion
and the long delusion of his profession concerning the curability of the insane was too great to be so soon forgiven. His
tentative publication on this subject began in his Northampton
report for 1875 (Twentieth Annual Report), and was continued
for several years in the same annual. In December, 1876, he
summed up his first results in an address before the New Eng-

land Psychological Society, of which he was president, and then printed them in a pamphlet of fifty-two pages at Utica, N.Y. They were received by the majority of his associates with reluctance or positive aversion, so completely did they contravene the comfortable hypothesis upon which sumptuous hospital-palaces had been erected and large appropriations of public money or private endowment obtained. This hypothesis was that insanity is easily and rapidly curable, if only taken at once and treated in a hospital, thus saving to the community the vast sums otherwise requisite to maintain the uncured patients in asylums. It was a pleasing and convenient theory. It provided many medical men with palatial homes and exalted reputations, which some of them deserved and most of them enjoyed; but, as it proved, the facts were all against it. This Dr. Earle and others had known, and Dr. Thurnam, of the York Retreat, had stated the truth years before, but no man had demonstrated it on a large scale, extending research over many lands and many thousand cases; and so the plausible and comfortable fallacy continued to hold sway during the grotesque inadequacy of the hospital statistics, on the revision of which the demonstration must depend. Dr. Earle had been for decades laboring at this revision. The farther he advanced, the more clearly he saw what the final inference must be; and he gave his colleagues credit for the same penetration and singleness of purpose which he had. For the time he found himself mistaken and disappointed. His figures were unassailable; but their meaning was so unpleasing to professional pride of opinion, and so fatal to the system of error long and carefully built up, that it is no wonder they were slowly accepted, even where they were fully understood. For, in the modest inquiry which the Northampton superintendent undertook to make, he soon came upon blunders that so touched his sense of the humorous that he could not refrain from exposing them mirthfully, thus adding a barb to the dart he threw with mild efficiency. His earliest victim was that gay and captious Briton, Captain Basil Hall, who travelled in America seventy years ago, and gave Wordsworth and others such a sad picture of the American defects. Hall had visited the Hartford Retreat, October,

1827, and there had found something to praise. He said in his second volume : —

Dr. Todd, the eminent and kind physician of the Retreat, showed us over every part of this noble establishment,— a model, I venture to say, from which any country might take instruction. During the last year there have been admitted here 23 recent cases, of which 21 recovered, equivalent to 91.3 per cent. The whole number of recent cases during the year was 28, of which 25 have recovered, equal to 89.2 per cent.

"Thus recognized and indorsed," said Dr. Earle, "the report of the Hartford visiting physicians, otherwise comparatively unknown, was sent by the newspapers through the length and breadth of the land; and the people received their first impression that insanity is largely curable. By a few strokes of his magic pen Captain Hall did what, were it not for him, would have required the labor of years." He then quoted the curious boast of Dr. Galt, of the Williamsburg Asylum in Virginia, made in 1842, that he had cured 100 per cent. of his recent cases, leading this sanguine statistician, reasoning from thirteen cases, " to believe there is no insane institution, either in Europe or America, in which such success is met with as in our own." Dr. Earle slyly added : —

Dr. Galt had produced the maximum of percentage figures, including deaths. Nay, had he not (under a recognized principle) mathematically demonstrated the curability of *all* the insane? What said Dr. Luther Bell, of the McLean Asylum, in his report for 1840? "Our records justify the declaration that *all cases, certainly recent*,— that is, whose origin does not, either directly or obscurely, run back more than a year,— recover under a fair trial. This is the general law. The occasional instances to the contrary are the exception." The spring-tide of mathematical curability had now attained its highest point; and Dr. Galt was upon the crest of its topmost wave, with Dr. Bell beside him in opinionative curability.

Warnings against this self-deception of the men whom the public trusted were not wanting. Dr. Ray, then at the head of the Maine Hospital at Augusta, said in 1842, "Nothing can be made more deceptive than statistics, and I have yet to learn that those of insanity form any exception." His successor, Dr. Bates, in his report for 1850, exposed the juggle with figures at which Dr. Ray may have hinted : —

I am sure figures are sometimes made the instruments of deception. Suppose, at the end of each year, instead of reporting all cases *as recent* which were admitted within one year of the attack, I should, for the purpose of appearing to cure 90 per cent. of recent cases discharged, report only such as recent as had not become old by remaining with us. I might impose the belief on the *uninitiated* that 90 per cent. of recent cases could be cured. Yet every man acquainted with the subject knows that no instance can be shown in which 90 out of 100 cases, admitted in succession, *no matter how recent*, were ever cured.

And Dr. Earle's English friend, Samuel Tuke, of York, had in 1841, when introducing the German Jacobi, of Siegburg, to the English reader, said this : —

The mode of reporting the results of our institutions for the insane calls loudly for attention, if we would arrive at any useful statistical comparisons as to the effect of treatment and other circumstances . . . in regard to the cure of this greatest of human maladies.*

Notwithstanding these warnings, Dr. Earle himself, naturally hopeful, and yielding to the common drift of opinion in his youth, had said in his first Bloomingdale report (for 1844) : —

Of cases in which there is no eccentricity or constitutional weakness of intellect, and when the proper remedial measures are adopted in the early stages of the disorder, no less than 80 in every 100 are cured. There are but few diseases from which so large a percentage of the persons attacked are restored.

* This passage, and many of the citations before, are from Dr. Earle's "Curability of Insanity," a complete demonstration of the falsity of statistical representations of its easy curability, and of the proper method of reporting recoveries. It should be in every hospital library and every collection of works concerning the insane, not only for its statistical information (nowhere else in English so extensive), but for its calm and scientific spirit.

Cautious as these exceptions were, the percentage was far too high; and Dr. Earle apologized for his error in his masterly volume,* saying : —

Thirty-two years ago Dr. Earle was younger than now, and had not the benefit of so extensive an experience. His practical knowledge of the treatment of insanity in 1844-45 had been derived from a number of cases considerably less than were under his care at one time in 1876 (494). He has had time and opportunity and reason to modify many of his opinions; and among those modified is that of the curability of insanity. Doubtless there are others of the writers he has quoted who would now seek protection, and who deserve it, under a similar plea.

It seems that Dr. Bell, one of the most able and outspoken of the deluded and deluding alienists of the decade from 1840 to 1850, did reach a conclusion more extreme in regard to incurability than Dr. Earle, who quotes him as saying in 1857, " I have come to the conclusion that, when once a man becomes insane, he is about used up for this world." And even Dr. Ray, who attacked Dr. Earle's conclusions in rather too partisan a spirit, as late as 1879, took occasion to say then : —

It may well be doubted whether the terms "recovered," "improved," "much improved," have been of any use not more than balanced by their inevitable tendency to mislead the reader respecting the curability of insanity. The public, as often happens, thought that the information sought for was to be found in a parade of vague, general expressions.

The peculiar merit of Dr. Earle's whole career at Northampton was to destroy the value and check the parade of "vague, general expressions " and impressions.

In the year 1870 Dr. Earle was subjected to one of those persecutions by a discharged patient, possessed of money and local influence, which so often fall to the lot of those who care for diseased minds. It was alleged that he was detaining at

---

* This was written in 1876, while the volume only came out in 1886.

Northampton patients who were not insane, that his treatment was sometimes abusive and sometimes neglectful, and that he had not complied with certain exacting and quite needless requirements of law in regard to notifying distant relatives of his patients. The last charge appeared to be true. I believe the law has since been practically abrogated. The other charges were wholly disproved; and a former patient of education and character, who had been relied on to give testimony unfavorable to the physicians, came forward, and said : —

I consider them competent men, and that the care and treatment bestowed by them could not be improved. If at any time I had a different opinion, it was owing to a diseased mental condition. I am of the opinion now that Dr. Earle conducts the affairs of the hospital with humanity, competence, and kindness.

Such was the conclusion of all the official persons called on to investigate the complaints, myself among them. And one of the chief qualifications of a superintendent for such a difficult position was as marked in Dr. Earle as in any of the hundred superintendents and directors of hospitals and asylums whom I have personally known, in an experience now covering thirty-five years, — his strictness of discipline, both for patients and attendants. This, which sometimes passed for unkindness, and was really exacting now and then, was the truest kindness when the real interest of all persons was considered. The inflexible justice of a most kindly nature thus displayed itself, often at the cost of much pain to the doctor himself. In the case above mentioned it gave him so much concern, though conscious of doing his duty, that it seriously affected his health, and led to a third visit to Europe, which he made in the year 1871.

Though rapid, this journey was more extensive than either of his former ones, so far as the inspection of insane asylums was involved. He revisited several that he had seen in 1837–38 and in 1849, and he gave attention to the many new ones that had sprung up everywhere. He received, as he deserved, the most distinguished welcome in all the countries visited; and he noted with keen eye the many changes that had occurred since he was in Great Britain, France, Germany, and Austria twenty-two years before. He could not quite accept the peculiar institution of Gheel in Belgium, as adapted to America or even Scotland; and his caution made him distrustful of the Scotch system of Family Care (a considerable improvement on Gheel, because under more exact control and classification by the government of the whole country), though it has since amply justified itself and been copied in other countries. The remarkably well-built and well-managed colony-asylum of Alt-Scherbitz was not founded until five years later, and was never seen by Dr. Earle. Had it been, it would have overcome, by its great practical success, some of his objections to a combination of hospital and asylum in detached buildings. There are nearly forty such buildings at this Saxon Anstalt. But he admired the newer Scotch asylums, with their combination of buildings for the recent and the chronic cases. He made the acquaintance of Sir James Coxe, Dr. (now Sir Arthur) Mitchell, and Dr. Clouston, not yet at the head of the Edinburgh Asylum; praised the Scotch Lunacy Commission, which his American friend, Miss Dix, had some hand in creating in 1857, disliked the monster asylums of London and Paris, found the condition of the Vienna and the Munich insane greatly advanced since 1849, and was particularly pleased with the public spirit of Zurich in providing asylum room for 1,000 insane, when the population of the whole canton was less than 300,000. He saw what was then the new hospital of Burghölzli, over which Dr. Auguste Forel so long presided, and won such a reputation throughout Europe, and thought the size of this Zurich establishment (250 patients) a model for Massachusetts. In his report for 1872 Dr. Earle briefly sketched his plan for the Massachusetts insane, then estimated at about 3,000 in number: —

Were a system for the care and custody of our insane now to be devised, I would recommend a series of small hospitals, designed for not more than 250 patients each, and so situated in the several counties or quarters of Massachusetts that some one of them should be easily accessible to every citizen. Whether they should be founded, owned, and conducted by the State, or by the counties or districts respectively, is perhaps a matter of but little importance.

This passage shows that he adhered to his early opinion in favor of small establishments (like those at Cupar in Scotland and Zurich, which he specially mentioned), and foreshows, in a modified form, the Wisconsin system of county asylums, which was instituted by Mr. Andrew Elmore and Mr. Henry Giles in 1881. It was soon after his return from Europe in 1871 that Dr. Earle arranged for building a small hospital for recent cases (not more than fifty) on land which he had bought for the State across the street from the main hospital,—a plan which, unfortunately, he found himself too old to carry out in face of the difficulties created by professional opinion and the extravagant outlay at Worcester and Danvers. But it has been practically adopted by the trustees of the Westboro Insane Hospital, and such a building is now going up there.

It was characteristic of the open mind and capacity for new impressions which Dr. Earle's insatiable love of travel indicated that he should continually advance in his opinions concerning the care of the insane, as the increase and the changed conditions of that class required changes in their care. Thus, in 1879, at his first appearance before the National Conference of Charities in Chicago, with his elaborate report for the committee of which he was chairman on " Management of the Insane," he was found to have modified in detail (while adhering in principle) the extent and nature of that State management which he had always held desirable and obligatory. The aim, as he stated it, was "a general scheme, by the kindly operation of which every insane person requiring curative treatment, parental care, or custodial restraint, shall be suitably provided for, in such places and manner as will be effective, without transcending the true pecuniary ability of the people." How then reach that aim? Not by palace hospitals: on that topic he was plain and convincing : —

The argument used to be, " The better the hospital, the greater will be the number cured"; and the word "better" was in some places interpreted "more costly." Under this rendering the ambition of architects, the pride of commissioners and superintendents, and the universal extravagance of the people during the years next following the Civil War strongly fortified the argument ; and the consequences are now apparent in hospitals which have cost from $2,500 to $4,000, perhaps $5,000, for every patient to whom they can offer a comfortable domicile. Hence during the last few years it has cost Massachusetts $1,000 a day, Sabbaths included, to supply the shelter of a hospital (to say nothing of support) for the mere *current increase* in the numbers of its insane. . . . No nation or State has ever been able to afford such expenditure from the public treasury. The wealthy may and can bear it, but its burden weighs grievously upon tens of thousands in the humbler spheres of society. The life's blood of many is drawn, under the forms of law, in providing an ostentatious charity for a few.

What, then, was to be done in the face of this increasing multitude, who must somehow be provided for, since the inadequacy of hospitals is shown by decreased recoveries and overcrowding everywhere ? First, maintain curative hospitals and small ones, never exceeding three hundred in the number of patients. Next, vary the monotonous forms of architecture, as is done in England and Germany. Then provide separate asylums for the incurable, grouped around or near the hospitals. Finally, place some of the harmless insane in families, though that is to be done cautiously.

It is in the directions thus pointed out, nearly twenty years ago, that enlightened opinion has since been moving; and, when Dr. Earle saw the continued success of the Family Care system of Scotland and Belgium, his doubts gave way, and he heartily approved, in 1885 and the following years, my introduction of the Scotch system into Massachusetts, even selecting himself a few of the old cases which were to be boarded out from the Northampton Hospital. In January, 1890, at the age of eighty, he joined with Dr. Talbot, of Boston, Mr. Allen, of Medfield, Mr. Barrus (now a trustee of the Northampton

Hospital), and others,—a committee of the National Conference of Charities,—in this recommendation to the Massachusetts legislature : —

That there should be in Massachusetts a *qualified* Lunacy Commission, which, with other official boards, should provide for the
chronic insane in asylums and families.   Particularly should permis-
sive power be given to the hospitals and asylums to board out their
patients, and to take them back when necessary, without waiting for
the action of a central board.   This is a power natural and necessary
to such establishments, if they are to give their patients the best and
most varied opportunities for improvement.   It frequently happens
that the convalesence of poor persons would be promoted by their
removal from the hospitals into private families.   For convalescing
patients, whether rich or poor, the boarding-out system furnishes
advantages of which most of the hospital superintendents have
expressed a desire to partake.*

It will be noticed that these suggestions are in line with
those made by the Massachusetts Commission of 1896, and of
Dr. Dewey, Dr. Stedman, and others, who in 1897 recommended "after-care of the insane"; but they were made six
years before the drift of professional opinion settled in that
way.   This is a good example of the advanced position usually
held by Dr. Earle in all questions affecting the insane, and of
the practical view which he took of matters too often discussed
theoretically.

In the late years of Dr. Earle's superintendency at Northampton, opinion had come round most gratifyingly to his position
on the main questions.   He had become the Nestor of American alienists, and was so recognized in places where he had
been sometimes viewed with aversion as "one that troubleth
Israel."   But his physical powers yielded to the advance of age.
A tendency to pulmonary disease also manifested itself, and
kept him housed much of the long, harsh winters of Northamp-

---

*See the Boston *Evening Transcript* of Jan. 24, 1890. The date of the committee's report,
however, was January 4. It was presented to the legislative Committee on Charitable Institutions
about the 23d. A lunacy commission, called the "State Board of Insanity," has been established
this year (1898) in place of the unsatisfactory board existing in 1890.

ton. He therefore, with his usual prudence and unselfishness, withdrew from his position of command, gave in his resignation seven years before his death (in 1885), and was relieved of the cares of office. At the invitation of the State he continued to reside in the hospital, busy with his correspondence, his Earle Genealogy, and his manuscripts, and died there May 17, 1892, in his eighty-third year. He had already provided his burial-place and monument in the rural cemetery of that lovely city,* to which he left a large public bequest and the memory and example of a good public servant.

At Dr. Earle's resignation the Northampton Hospital passed into the charge of Dr. Edward Nims, who had long been the first assistant physician, and who understood and carried out Dr. Earle's methods.†   Mention should also be made of the long and active service of Miss Fanny Earle, as clerk,— the daughter of Dr. Earle's eldest brother,— who for many years relieved her uncle of much of the labor, both of public and private cor-respondence, and materially aided him in the preparation of the Genealogy.

---

* Northampton had been celebrated, long before Dr. Earle became its most distinguished citizen, for the beauty of its scenery and the fame of its residents. Jonathan Edwards preached there, and wrote some of his works in Northampton. George Bancroft was a teacher in Dr. Cogswell's Round Hill School, where Motley was fitted for college; and it was in Northampton that Bancroft began his History of the United States. It was the lifelong home of John Clarke, who there founded the Clarke School for the Deaf (which made oral instruction popular in America) in 1867, a few years after Dr. Earle went there to reside.

† The vote of the trustees of the Northampton Hospital, upon his resignation, was as follows: —

Resolved, That, in accepting the resignation of Dr. Pliny Earle, superintendent of this hospital, the trustees have reluctantly yielded to the conviction that his advancing years and impaired health demand rest and relief from the responsibilities and labor of his position.

Dr. Earle has been at the head of this institution twenty-one years, and during nearly all that period has also been its treasurer. In its management he has combined the highest professional skill and acquirement with rare executive ability. By his thorough knowledge, his long experience, his patient attention to details, by his wisdom and firmness, his absolute fidelity to duty, and devotion to the interests of the hospital, he has rendered invaluable services to the institution and to the com-munity which it serves. The trustees are deeply sensible of the assistance which he has given them in the discharge of their duties, and follow him, in his retirement, with the assurance of their highest respect and esteem.

Resolved, That the trustees indulge the hope that Dr. Earle will continue to make his home in this institution, that they may continue to profit by his counsels; and they will provide that his rooms shall always be open and ready for his use.

Resolved, That these resolutions be entered upon the records of the board, and that a copy thereof, attested by the chairman and secretary, be transmitted to Dr. Earle.

HENRY W. TAFT, *Chairman*.
LYMAN D. JAMES, *Secretary*.

(JULY, 1885.)

CHAPTER XIV

THESE pages have exhibited Dr. Earle in the whole extent of a life protracted beyond the ordinary limit, and occupied for fourscore years with an unresting and fruitful activity. His brief infancy, soon passing into the eager pursuit and acquirement of varied knowledge, which he instantly applied to some purpose deemed needful, and the few years that followed his retirement from the actual control of a large establishment for the treatment, shelter, and observation of mental disease,— these were the only parts of Dr. Earle's life when he was not actively engaged in important pursuits, useful to himself, his kindred and friends, or to mankind at large. The story has been told as much as possible in his own words. Here it is to be summed up from his account, and from the observation of those who knew him in his various periods of life and spheres of action. Of such the witnesses of his earlier years are now few. He outlived all his nearest kindred and most of his early friends and acquaintances, and even the pupils of his half-dozen years of class instruction are now few and fast passing away. He was the last survivor, I think, of the old and now extensive organization which, in its first form, was the American Association of Medical Superintendents of Institutions for the Insane, and which now has another name. Of its original thirteen members, who founded or early contributed to the *American Journal of Insanity*, Dr. Earle, if I am not mistaken, died last. He held its presidency in his last year of control at Northampton, and resigned it when he gave up the superintendency. And in the years since his death many of his colleagues, younger than himself, in this and other countries, have passed away,— Drs. Bucknill, Hack Tuke, Lockhart Robertson, Heinrich Laehr, J. P. Gray, Bancroft, Andrews, and others ; so that comparatively few are now left who saw his

ABOUT 1818.

Yours truly,
Pliny Earle

professional work in the hospital with the trained vision of practical experience. I have supposed that he selected me as his biographer and editor partly because circumstances made me officially cognizant of that work at Northampton, without previous bias for or against him from professional brotherhood or jealousy,—as Tacitus says, *sine ira et studio, quorum causas procul habeo.* It was by that work and by his demonstration of the true theory of Curability — which his success at Northampton allowed him the opportunity to develop and publish — that he desired to be judged in the field of science and practice to which he consecrated fifty years of his life.

Consecration is the right word to describe his care for the insane. With all his worldly prudence and common sense, and notwithstanding his broad toleration of theological differences, he was from the first, and essentially, a religious man, governed in all the important actions of life by a sense of religious duty and that regard for the fatherhood of God and the brotherhood of man, which the small sect of his family and forefathers especially cherishes. Of the narrowness of the Quaker Church he had nothing : of its profound instinct of divine guidance and the worth of the human soul he had much. In the growing strength of materialism among scientific men and physicians, he still maintained the spiritual and immortal nature of our minds, and could have said with Shakespeare, "I think more nobly of the soul, and no way approve their opinion." In one of his lectures to physicians in middle life, he thus stated his view : —

Were the arguments for the hypothesis that in insanity the mind itself is diseased tenfold more numerous than they are, and more weighty, I could not accept them. My ideas of the human mind are such that I cannot hold for a moment that it can be diseased, as we understand disease. That implies death as its final consequence, but Mind is eternal. In its very essence and structure (to use the terms we apply to matter), in its elemental composition and its organization, it was created for immortality. Consequently, it is superior to the bodily structure, and beyond the scope of the wear and tear and disorganization and final destruction of the mortal part of our being.

It required some courage and firm religious conviction to adhere to this noble opinion during the latter half of the passing century; but Dr. Earle continued to maintain it, and it gave a dignity to his special occupations which nothing else could so well provide. It was in this spirit that he took them up as a medical student in Philadelphia, and thus he fulfilled his whole duty in them through life.

From his brethren and sisters of the Society of Friends exhortations were not lacking to a more active proselyting effort among his patients, not in the narrow sense of making them Quakers, but to bring them into the general Christian fold. Thus his English friend, Anne Knight, who was associated with Mrs. Fry in her labors at Paris in 1838, and whom Dr. Earle found there on his return from Italy and Greece in April, 1839, had this advice to give him, when about to sail for America (April 28) : —

Dear Pliny Earle,— Excuse my dismissing the formality of doctor and addressing thee, in the freedom of Christian sisterhood, a few words which I can hardly withhold on this prospect of thy departure (forever, perhaps) from us. To-day I ventured, in wishing thee *every blessing*, to hope thou wouldst "minister to a *mind* diseased" as well as to its afflicted earthen vessel. It has remained with me, augmenting into earnest desire, that the stability of thy mind, enlarged by this European experience, with increased ability to help thy diseased fellow-creatures, may be ever engaged in directing their hearts to that only and best fountain of healing, which can raise them up to life eternal. Oh, never lose sight of thy power, in the *endearing* function of alleviating the pains of others, to hold up to their view that Saviour by whose stripes we are healed ! . . . Opportunities for spiritual help are far more in the power of a medical than a *pastoral* man. Thou art admitted where a *preacher ordained* is rejected,— at the couch of the dying infidel, in the last scene of the daughter of wickedness. How may such *be allured* to the Saviour by gentle and gradual means, without saying a word of death ! How often does vitality spring up to utilize our honest endeavors with our fellow earth-worms ! . . . In fear of having been too free, and feeling my own unworthiness and presumption in so doing, I remain, with every good earthly and heavenly wish, thy sincere friend.

Two years later an American lady, who had been a pupil both of Dr. Earle and his sister, gave him the same religious warning, introduced with praise for his youthful prosperity in his chosen work (April, 1841) : —

My best wishes for success and eminence in all thy undertakings. I often hear thee spoken of in the most respectful terms, and I read comments upon what thou offers to the public; and all is of a flattering nature. Now forgive me, dear Pliny, if I say, " Remember from whom all good comes." Thou must know that I feel myself much indebted to thy family, and a lively interest in every member of it. Should thou come to Massachusetts [from Philadelphia] it would afford me much joy to receive thee here [At Sandwich, where the oldest American Quaker meeting is].

The early promise implied in these affectionate suggestions was fully kept, but hardly in the manner then hoped by Pliny Earle and his friends, — a pronounced literary career, combined with his philanthropic efforts.   For it is to be regretted that he was not gifted (along with his higher qualities) with a genius for expression, nor had acquired by training a better style ; since it must be confessed that he seldom charms or even convinces by his *manner* of writing.   He lacked imagination ; and his very fancy, though quick to see the common and even the grotesque features of nature and life, seldom imparted actual liveliness to his style.   He was educated at a period when the standard of rhetoric in New England was very low, and when the common style of those who passed for good writers, unless they had a touch of genius, like Channing, Emerson, and Hawthorne, was diffuse and languid, given to long periods and roundabout forms of expression.   The genius of Dr. Earle was for observation and faithful study, not for expression.   Therefore, in the tens of thousands of pages which he wrote and published, while he conveyed impressive and indispensable fact, he did not charm by his presentation of the subject.   Like his father, as he depicts him in my early pages, Pliny Earle the younger was mathematical.   His mind found its shortest road and its best vehicle in numerical statement.   Consequently, he has put the statis-

tics of his subject, whatever it might be, on the soundest and
clearest basis; and the inferences which he drew from the
figures he marshalled were not the startling fallacies of the
amateur in statistics, but the reasonable conclusions which,
sooner or later, the world must and would accept.

Upon this mathematical foundation rested his great economic
success in the management of his hospital. He knew exactly
the weight and measure and number of each thing needed, the
value of every dollar to be expended, and the times and seasons
in which that value would be greatest. Before his time there
had been no remarkable economic management of the insane
in Massachusetts, and hardly in the country anywhere. Profusion and stinginess by turns marked the outlay for them; and
the worth of their manual labor, both sanatory and pecuniary,
was ill understood. Dr. Earle saw what his patients could do,
computed in his calculating head how much that meant in
money saved, how much in nerves quieted, muscles strength-
ened, power of will developed, discipline gradually infused into
wayward natures; and so, out of a most unpromising collection
of patients, the refuse and *débris* of treatment in other hospitals
or neglect in unsuitable places, he produced a band of odd-
looking but cheerful and productive workers. His process was
viewed by other superintendents at first with amused scepticism,
then with aroused interest, then with some jealousy; but, finally,
they gave to his methods of employment the sincere compliment
of imitation.

It was this same arithmetical turn of mind which made him
so impatient of the glaring, useless extravagance in asylum
building, and gave to his censure of it the convincing pungency
which those on whom it fell found hard to endure, though useless to resent. Somebody has defined the highest happiness of
the New Englander as consisting in the power to do good and
at the same time make money by it. The contrary of this,—
to do harm to his friends, the poor insane, and to throw away
millions of money in doing it,— when seen going on all about
him, moved Dr. Earle to unwonted severity of comment. His
nature was kindly beyond that of most men, or even women.
He abhorred cruelty or harshness in any form, and would rather

praise or keep silent than inflict pain by censure. But this wave of profusion in the care of the insane which he saw over-running the country drew from him the severest rebuke he ever uttered, except when he saw the helpless insane abused or sadly neglected.   •

Dr. Earle's kindness was the natural expression of a warm sympathy with human nature in its manifestations, great and small, provided they were not cruel or vicious. That delightful expression of Terence's —"I am a man: nothing that con-cerns man lacks interest for me"— was more descriptive of this Quaker dancer, this smiling tourist, this susceptible ad-mirer of beauty, than of most men I have known. He did not expect, nor even wish, all mankind to resemble himself or be governed by his strict moral sense. He was ready to allow leeway to the thoughtless, the ignorant, the young, and espe-cially to the grotesque. His sense of humor was quick and keen, though he had not the Attic salt of witty expression in much readiness; and whatever appealed to his toleration of the grotesque was inwardly pleasing. Like Jaques, when he met Touchstone in the forest of Arden,

> His lungs began to crow like Chanticleer

whenever he encountered those oddities that every traveller must meet as he passes from country to country. The best-natured man in the world, he was an admirable travelling com-panion and the happiest kind of tourist; for nothing pleased him more than travel. In return, he made friends everywhere, saw the best company wherever he might be, and had no glum, unsocial ways, such as might have been associated by the un-thinking with his Quaker garb and some traces of early rus-ticity which long adhered to him. Whist-playing, dancing, music, and the lighter recreations of young or old were ever agreeable to him. His unquenchable curiosity and his love of pleasing made him acceptable everywhere. His own comment on his first visit to Europe, of which so much has been said in the early chapters, is worth citing. When he was again in England in 1849, he thus wrote to his sister Lucy : —

My introductions have opened to me a new circle of acquaintance; and, either because I was formerly much in London or because I am a little older and somewhat less verdant, I find I am directing my observation differently. Boys of ten in yellow breeches, with Quaker coats big-buttoned, and buckled shoes, are no longer a novelty. Processions of girls in blue frocks, long yellow gloves, and white caps decked with red ribbons, pass by me like the idle wind. Lord mayors and sheriffs in gilded coaches, their footmen in tinselled velvet, plush, and silk, are now to me like the dancing figures on a wandering hand-organ. When I was here before, I gave my attention almost wholly to acquiring popular rather than permanently useful knowledge. Now I am seeking the *utile cum dulce*.

This self-condemnation was hardly warranted by the facts of 1837–39, but he had passed through much of the serious pathway of life in the intervening ten years. Among other experiences he had cherished an unsuccessful love for an American lady whom he met in Europe on his first visit, the recollection of which may have been the decisive reason why, with all his susceptibility and all the favor with which he was received by women, he never married. In this instance calm friendship had followed the temporary interruption of correspondence, renewed years after, and containing, on the lady's part, some passages concerning spiritual subjects, which should be quoted as giving a higher view of the faith held by women in the Society of Friends than might be inferred from some of the citations already made regarding theological disputes. Miss X. writes : —

I perceive that you incline to the spiritual acceptation of some of the phenomena [of mind-reading, etc.]. All minds cultivated in the Quaker faith are more inclined to admit such an interpretation than the rationalistic and philosophic many. . . . I say *rationalistic* instead of *rational*, as opposed to spiritual, in my definition, because I think the spiritual and the rational are intimately allied. Indeed, a truly spiritual being must be rational, since the greater includes the less. But I mean that casuistry of thought, self-styled philosophy, which assumes independence of the religious element, and explains all facts, all laws, all miracles, by its own infallible insight, becoming absurd through egotism. To these there is no sacredness, no mystery, even in the manifestations of Supreme Power: miracles are not, because they do not need them. The true Quaker, on the contrary, should be a humble, gentle, self-distrusting spirit, leaning on a Power so vast, so incomprehensible, yet so ever-present, that he borrows its serenity through fidelity and inmost obedience. This influence inclines Quakers more than other men to receive any new manifestation of the spiritual with great readiness, because they believe the universe of matter and of mind to be pervaded by the living power of an ever-creating God. To me the strongest evidence of the miracles of the New Testament is in the conviction of my own soul. They commend themselves to me as true by their harmony with the super-human nature of him who wrought them, by their lofty lessons of benevolence, self-sacrifice, and triumph over common circumstances. They prove the superiority of God to all the known laws of his universe, but they reach beyond our sight to that world of spirit that we believe lies all around us here. Fidelity is the key-note to that eternal harmony of which we only dream in this mode of being, but whose faint echoes come to us now and then, to reconcile us to many privations, and bind us more firmly to the great task of life's duties.

How superior this spiritual insight and assured faith in the unseen even to that sublime passage of Latin verse * which the Pythagorean Avienus prefixed to his paraphrase of the astronomical poem of the Greek Aratus ! and which may thus be rendered, in the measure so familiar to Dr. Earle and his contemporaries,— the iambic pentameter of Pope and Goldsmith : —

> Yonder the hall, and there the primal throne
> Of God, the Father, is in lightnings shown,—
> Germ of all motion, elemental might,
> Æthereal fire, earth's heat, and core of light;

---

* Hic statio, hic sedes primi Patris; iste paterni
Principium motus, vis fulminis iste corusci,
Vita elementorum, mundi calor, aetheris ignis,
Astrorumque vigor, perpes substantia lucis,
Et numerus celsi modulaminis; hic tener aer
Materiaeque gravis concretio; succus ab alto
Corporibus coelo; cunctarum alimonia rerum ;
Flos et flamma animae, qui discurrente meatu,
Molis primigenae penetralia dura resolvens,
Implevit largo venas operatus amore, *et seq.*

Impulse of stars, from whose aye-rolling spheres
Their lofty music still my spirit hears.
Soft air concurring with material dense,
This universe its life-blood draws from thence,
Till all its parts receive their aliments.
Through primal Chaos in diffusion rolls
Thy vital stream, the flame and flower of souls,
Fills every channel with thy potent aids,
As Love immense the impenetrable pervades.

   .   .   .   .   .   .

A secret voice doth on our hearing fall : —
" Me first and last and midmost shalt thou call !
One and the Same these acts diverse bespeak,
Be the apparent impulse strong or weak.
The Lord thy shepherd is.   The widest rove
Draws not his flock beyond his sacred love :
All earthly things in his fixed groove must go,
Grand master of the uplifted and the low.
He governs well the swift-revolving pole,
Where each unsocial orb finds path and goal ;
Leads the fair dance of Seasons in the year,
Where Winter's frosts no longer chill with fear,
Since softly smiling Spring comes on amain,
And dusty Summer parches up the plain,
Till Autumn's burden falls of fruit and grain."

Here it is the visible universe on which the thought of the
poet is fixed : in the exhortation of the disciple of Fox and
Woolman, it is the Inner Light, more attractive than all the suns
and stars and abrupt fires of heaven, which carries confidence
to her mind.   Her remarks were called out by some account
which Dr. Earle had written of the "manifestations" of so-
called "Spiritualism," then common ; and this, again, had been
in response to her observations on Feuchtersleben and his
theory of Imagination, concerning which she said : —

How striking is his expression, "There is no other entity but
activity,— the purest, the only true enjoyment of living beings"!
How much philosophy in this epigram : "Annoyance is man's
leaven, the element of movement.   Without it we should grow
mouldy"!   How keen, yet how true, that hypochondriasis is

egoism carried to excess, and that egoism arises from want of cultivation! How beautiful this tribute to Nature, "Her significant silence develops man"! His remarks upon Imagination seem to me to explain many of the phenomena attributed to mesmeric or spiritual agencies, some of which I have witnessed lately [June, 1853] with curious interest. The undoubted integrity of the medium left no other rational interpretation of the result save that of "the vital effects of one individual reacting on another who is unconscious of the influence." Is it equally true that "all Nature is but an echo of the mind; and from her we learn the highest of all laws,—that the Real springs from the Ideal, and the Ideal by degrees remodels the world"?

It was not often that Dr. Earle found himself debating these high philosophical questions in his correspondence, but he was long interested in that unexplained side of nature which is here touched upon. He had seen many experiments in mesmerism and its related semi-sciences, from 1840 onwards, both in America and Europe; but he reached no definite conclusion, except that much was imposture and much also inexplicable.

Perhaps, after all, the true explanation of Dr. Earle's remaining single through life is that given concerning the banker-poet, Rogers, with whom he dined at the hospitable house of Charles Dickens in London, July 5, 1849. He told the anecdote in an account of the dinner sent to his sister a day or two later:—

I was punctual to the hour named in the invitation, 6.15 P.M., and was met in the entrance hall by two white-gloved men-servants, who showed me to the library, where I was received by Mr. Dickens, his wife, and a young lady of one-and-twenty, with an intelligent, amiable countenance and a profusion of curling hair. In a few minutes Mr. Prescott, of Boston, entered,—a son of our historian of Mexico,—soon followed by Mrs. Macready, wife of the actor, and she by George Sumner, the brother of Charles. Conversation ran briskly for half an hour, when Mr. Dickens said it was dinner time, but they were waiting for Mr. Rogers. Hardly had he spoken when the door opened, and a man entered, burdened with the weight of eighty years, short of stature, robust of body, his head large, bald, but with some hair perfectly white,— in his general appearance much resem-

bling the late John Quincy Adams. This was the poet, the author of
"Italy" and the "Pleasures of Memory." There were no more
guests, Mr. Bancroft, our ambassador, having been invited, but detained by a previous engagement,— the annual Speech Day at
Harrow-on-the-Hill, the school of Byron, Sir Robert Peel, and other
celebrities.

At our dinner there was no learned or literary talk, but Dickens's
readiness and fund of anecdote were always at hand to fill any gap
in the conversation. Mr. Rogers was mirthful, or, rather, showed a
quaint, quiet, piquant humor. He seemed much disposed to talk
with the ladies, still exhibiting that general preference for the sex
which, as the curling-haired young lady afterwards remarked, has
prevented him from forming any individual alliance with a partner
for life. He suggested going to Vauxhall in a party, and the ladies
promised to go. Soon after, talking of women, he said that, much as
he liked them, they had one fault — they take other people at their own
valuation, and so always fall in love with coxcombs. Mrs. Macready
cried out upon this as the most ungallant speech she had ever heard
from him, and she with the other ladies declared they wouldn't
go with him to Vauxhall. "However, you are right," said Mrs.
Macready.

Dr. Earle's "general preference for the sex" did not prevent
him from strongly favorable impressions in regard to particular
ladies, one of whom, Fräulein Fanny Martini, daughter of Dr.
Martini, of Leubus in Silesia, corresponded with him for a year
or two after meeting him at her father's asylum, where he spent
several days in the summer of 1849. Her letters display a
lively, cultivated mind, fond of poetry and novels, and thus appealing to his literary tastes. Her personal charms must have
been marked, from the solicitude of Dr. Earle to continue the
acquaintance; for he was ever captivated by beauty. She had
begun their conversation at Leubus by some smart saying about
"dreadful Quakers," which led him in his first letter from Paris
to give her an account of who and what Quakers are. To
this she replied in sprightly English : —

I am vain enough to believe all the kind words in which you remember Leubus, especially as I presume Quakers are not allowed to

flatter. Believe, my dear sir, that I not only found nothing "dreadful" in receiving your letter, but we all were very glad and happy
that you had not forgotten us.   May you sometimes when at home
and with your family remember your German friends, and may you
not quite forget the thoughtless girl who gave the best evidence of
her ignorance by calling the Quakers dreadful!   And still, my good
sir, can I not blame so much the said forwardness; for without it I
fear I should never have heard of all those truly Christian and moral
laws and institutions of which you were kind enough to tell me in
your letter. . . . As to the reading of novels, I am sure that the
human heart, and especially that of woman, is almost the same in
every land and nation; that it is ever eager to dream; and then that
charming and pernicious butterfly, Fancy!   I must tell you that I
read now "Dombey and Son," and am perfectly charmed by the
description of Florence.   It is indeed a pity that she is less curious
than myself, and never thinks of reading the manuscripts of her poor
beautiful mamma.   If you ever see Mr. Dickens once more, ah! tell
him that, if he has many admirers in Germany, there are none who
like more his genius and the excellent heart he must possess than
my mother and myself. . . . Balls, an amusement very seldom afforded
to me at Leubus, gave me great pleasure at Dresden and delight in
dancing.   I hope you have not forgotten the Française (or, rather,
quadrille) on my birthday; and I am sure that, if it depended on
your decision, you would not only allow your amiable and beautiful
Quaker ladies a little dancing, but help them even in doing so. . . .
I would commit to you to read the prosaic works of our dear Schiller,
and for common usage the German newspapers.   Unfortunately, we
have but few well-written novels in German, nothing but bad trans-
lations, the politics and philosophical literature being solely cultivated
by our literators.   Novels are left to the care of lady writers, who,
unfortunately, try to copy George Sand, producing books that have
neither morality, religion, or real good taste, and not having even
the excuse of an erratic genius and the charm of originality.   We
have most charming poems by Geibel, Uhland, Chamisso, and the
delicious little poems of Goethe.

It seems a pity that this *spirituelle* Silesian Fanny could not
be induced to cross the Atlantic,— she does not seem to have
been unwilling,— and become the bride of the Quaker whom

she found no longer "dreadful." She waited three years for the proposal which might have been expected but never came, and then married in Germany, communicating the engagement to Dr. Earle in a letter of January, 1853, which also expressed her deep interest in "Uncle Tom's Cabin," just read, and her unfavorable verdict on Thackeray, whom she had met in Dresden. Of him she wrote : —

The most interesting of our new Dresden acquaintances was Mr. R. Noel, the phrenologist, himself very amiable ; and in his house we saw Thackeray, the great English novelist. Perhaps you have become acquainted with him in America, for he was on his way there. I must confess that his person is very different from what I supposed him to be, and that I was not a little disappointed by his serious and inaccessible manners.

This description of Thackeray's manners could never apply to Dr. Earle, who was ever kindly and gracious, with a touch of courtliness as he grew older, and became the protector of so many helpless and unfortunate persons. He had written to Miss Fanny from Cuba or soon after his return in 1852, and awakened in her the old desire to travel and know the world by sight, in which she strongly resembled her American friend. She says : —

Your description of the isle of Cuba highly interested me, and once more made my heart thrill with the evident desire to see the world and its wonders. I am sure it is a shame and a pity I am not a man. How I would roam through lands and seas, always eager to learn, to see new and various scenes of life, new customs, and foreign people! A woman's lot is beautiful, very true ; but the tranquillity, the limitedness, of a homeward life is not for all. And my only comfort is books, enabling me at least to hear of things I shall perhaps never see. . . . I hope you believe that I am no more afraid of Quakers or think them to be dreadful, even if you had not told me of the meeting, where the young people do quite the same as everywhere, in all countries and in every tongue,— flirting and making love. And so I believe almost, my dear sir, that you, too, found, perhaps, at that same meeting the friend whose love and care shall

embellish your life and soothe every sorrow. May it be so! for a
being so kind as you are is not made for solitude and a single life.
You see I have become an advocate for marriage. You know I was
resolved never to marry, but Heaven would not have me an old
maid.

As Landor said,—

> " I will not love." This word has often
>   Come from a troubled breast,
> Seldom from one no sighs can soften,
>   Seldom from one at rest.

The advice of Fanny Martini was good, but her friend never
availed of it.

Probably the best explanation of Dr. Earle's celibacy was
the care which circumstances required him to take of some
members of his own family. A brother of great mechanical
ingenuity, but of little worldly prudence, a sister who claimed
much tenderness and consideration, and to whom he wrote
more frequently than to any other person, a younger brother
who, in the words of a Leicester neighbor,* "had less than his
equal share of the mind and capacity of the family, but a gift
at 'the plain language' in more than mere words," — all these
had a claim on a brother's thoughtfulness which his marriage
might have impaired or set aside. As years went stealthily
by, at times darkened by his depressed moods, a feeling of this
kind would gain strength in his equitable mind ; and, if it
could not keep him from falling in love, it might prevent those
indissoluble ties which bind the married man.

Dr. Earle has been mentioned as "one of the founders" of
the *American Journal of Insanity*, but the remark is not literally true. That long-established quarterly was the sole venture of Dr. Brigham, then (in 1844) the head of the New York
State Asylum at Utica, N.Y. But Dr. Earle was the first colleague whom he took into his confidence, writing to him thus
at Bloomingdale, May 28, 1844 : —

---

* Rev. Samuel May, the veteran Abolitionist, a classmate of Dr. O. W. Holmes, and one of the
small band which early rallied round Garrison, with his cousins, S. J. May, S. E. Sewall, and Bronson Alcott. See his general reminiscences of the Earle family in the Appendix, page 383.

I am about starting an *American Journal of Insanity*, quarterly, octavo, pages ninety-six, edited by the officers of this asylum. The first number will be published early in July. It is intended for the general public as well as for the profession. This is an entire secret, as I have mentioned it to no one except Dr. [T. Romeyne] Beck, of Albany. The first number I must prepare myself; but after this I ought and must have help, and I shall look to you, and hope to interest you in the work. I will send you immediately the first number, when out, and shall want your opinion, advice, and assistance. . . . *June* 10.— I feel under great obligation to you for your kind words of encouragement about the *Journal*. I shall adapt it to the general reader, though I hope to make it useful to the profession, especially after I get you and others to contribute to it.

This soon happened; and Dr. Earle had a long article, adapted to the "general reader," on " The Poetry of Insanity," in the number for January, 1845, which, as Dr. Brigham wrote, " has brought in letters many fine compliments for you from school-dames up, or down, to grave doctors of divinity." In connection with Dr. Earle's innovation of reading lectures to his Bloomingdale patients, Dr. Brigham makes these suggestive remarks in a letter of February 27 : —

I see that you lecture. It is a good idea; but suppose you lecture to them on insanity,— that is, in a way to instruct them about the nature of their disease, its prevention, etc.? I find it does no harm, and to some patients it does good to talk with them about insanity, etc. One patient now here, a physician, says his knowledge of diseases, especially insanity, enabled him to guard against attacks repeatedly. I believe, if people were well instructed on insanity, there would be less of it.

It was the same belief which kept Dr. Earle assiduously writing for so many years on a subject in itself unattractive and for readers too often inattentive. But he did not regret this labor, nor consider it lost, any more than his German contemporary, Dr. Heinrich Laehr (mentioned in his " German Asylums "), who continued to exchange publications with Dr. Earle, and wrote to him repeatedly in their old age. In one of these letters of 1887 Dr. Laehr says : —

I recall with great pleasure both occasions (in 1849 and 1871) when I met you in Halle, and here at Zehlendorf, in my Schweizerhof.* Though I have read that you have given up the public office you so long held, and intrusted to other hands the fruitful labor of so many years, yet I am certain you did not thereby renounce our calling, to which your life has been devoted. Rather have you gained leisure for the improvement of our science, without losing interest in it. You have not only witnessed the chief development of it in America, but have had a share in that development; and I fancy that a glance into the past, such as my " Gedenktäge der Psychiatrie aller Länder " permits, will receive more sympathy from you than from our younger brethren, who are inclined to look forward, and too easily forget that they stand on the shoulders of others. May God grant you strength for effort and pleasure in the work of our noble profession!

The last work done by Dr. Earle in this line was the chapter on "Curability" in Dr. Tuke's Dictionary of Psychological Medicine, published in 1892, in which Dr. Laehr also had a chapter on the "History of the Insane in Germany." But Dr. Earle did not live to see the volumes issued, though he read the proof of his article.

In 1846, when Dr. Brigham had made his quarterly successful, he desired Dr. Earle to become its owner and editor, recognizing in him the qualities which made him so long the collector and disseminator of truths which the profession and the public needed to know. He wrote to him (Nov. 11, 1847): "I am getting old and averse to labor, and cannot, I think, take charge of the *Journal* another year. Will you not take it? Under your charge it would do much good. There are now subscribers enough to pay, and it brings many exchanges. I hope you will think favorably of it." The offer could not be accepted; and, when given up by Dr. Brigham, it passed, for long years, into the control of an able man who made it too much the organ of his own opinions and interests, so that from 1854 to 1867 no article by Dr. Earle appeared in its pages. In its first ten

---

* This was a private asylum which Dr. Laehr had long directed, and which he gave over to his son in 1889. In 1849 he had been an assistant of Dr. Damerow, at Halle, where Dr. Earle first met him.

years he had published fifteen articles there, and his work on the German Asylums made four of these articles in 1852–53. In 1867–68 he published four articles there, three of them being public addresses, and in 1877 a portion of his work on "Curability." Could he have edited the *Journal* in the spirit of its founder, it would much sooner have reached that comprehensive, scientific position which it has held for some years past.

Dr. Earle's medium of communication with the public, here and in Europe, was the much earlier established Philadelphia quarterly, the *American Journal of the Medical Sciences*, to which he contributed not less than fifteen original papers and eighty-five reviews of books and reports between August, 1838 (when a part of his graduating thesis of the year before was printed), and January, 1869, when he reviewed the annual reports of fifteen American hospitals for the insane. When the New York Academy of Medicine was founded, he read the first paper before its members, a "History of Insane Hospitals in the United States," which was published by the Academy, and afterwards used in his long chapter on "Insanity" in the census volume for 1860, and in a shorter article on the same subject in the American Almanac of G. W. Childs, the celebrated Philadelphia journalist and publisher.

He also contributed occasionally to the London *Journal of Mental Science*, while under the editorship of his English friends, Drs. Bucknill and D. H. Tuke, with the latter of whom he maintained correspondence as long as he lived. The death of Dr. Tuke has prevented me from obtaining the letters of Dr. Earle; but from those of the Tuke family, of which he knew three generations, a few passages may be cited : —

York, 16, 8 *mo.*, 1841.— [Samuel Tuke.] I must in the first place thank thee for a copy of thy "Notes on a Visit to the Asylums for the Insane in Europe," with which I was much interested. In the second place I must express my satisfaction and pleasure in finding that thou art applying thy knowledge and skill to that department of thy profession which treats the diseases of the mind, and that thy talents are engaged in connection with the Asylum for Friends at Philadelphia. It is matter of deep satisfaction to me to see how many intelligent and right-minded persons are now earnestly engaged in studying the alleviation and care of the most grievous of maladies. I hope the work of Dr. Jacobi [of Siegburg,] which I have had translated, will prove acceptable to those engaged in the management of our hospitals for the insane. I have gone, in the Introduction, into the question of the prevalence of insanity in England, and particularly in the Society of Friends. I wish you would investigate that subject *thoroughly* in your State. Thou wilt, I think, be interested in our "statistical tables," which have just been printed, and of which I send six copies. I was much interested in yours, which has lately come to hand [Report of the Friends' Asylum].

It was these tables of the York Retreat which first put Dr. Earle upon his lifelong inquiry into the curability of the insane. Samuel Tuke's opinion was that insanity among Quakers was much promoted by their close intermarriages, and this was why he wished his young friend to make thorough investigation in a matter of some delicacy.

Falmouth, Feb. 1, 1873.—[D. H. Tuke.] The arrival of your annual report, which I have studied with much interest, induces me to write now. I shall find the statistics of use in revising, as I am now doing, our "Manual of Psychological Medicine" for a third edition. What is the most recent ascertained proportion of lunatics (insane and idiots) in the United States? As it stands in the Manual, it is 1 in 738, as reported in 1860. Can thou at the same time give me any statistical evidence, beyond what appears in your report, that in America over-education and excessive emotional excitement materially increase the number of the insane? I have always maintained they do; but at present it is hard to prove it in England, where statistics are all in favor of the lunacy-producing effects of ignorance. Dr. Thurnam is a convert to this view, which has been ably supported by Dr. Benjamin Richardson.

I sent a copy of my book, "The Influence of the Mind upon the Body in Health and Diseases," in October, 1872, for thy acceptance. Has the *Journal of Insanity* or any other journal noticed it? It lays claim to no original views, but I hope it will be found a useful book, and may induce some to employ psycho-therapeutics more definitely. What address would find Miss Dix now?

In the autumn of 1884 Dr. Tuke visited America, and spent a day or two with Dr. Earle at the Northampton Hospital, which then for the first time came under his observant eye. His comments, taken from his book, "The Insane in the United States and Canada,"— a very fair account of the conditions then existing,— are as follows : —

The name of Dr. Earle is almost as well known to English as to American alienists.   He and Dr. J. S. Butler are now the only survivors of the original thirteen who founded (in 1844) the American Association of Superintendents of Hospitals for the Insane, and he was in 1884 its president.   Among the noteworthy features of his hospital is its financial success.   No doubt this might be associated with a far from satisfactory condition of the patients, but the reverse is the case.   The amount of work performed by the patients has been a point of special attention with Dr. Earle.   Thus the laundry work for an average of 530 persons is done with only two assistants (women), whose aggregate wage is $35 a month.   For the last fifteen years two-thirds of all the necessary manual labor upon the premises, Dr. Earle says, has been performed by the patients.   With an average of over 30 cows, the milking is all done by patients, an employee overseeing them.   The poultry-house is under the sole charge of a patient.   I may mention the remarkable extent to which indoor recreation in some form is carried out : The patients assemble in the chapel almost every evening for instruction, entertainment, and amusement; and Dr. Earle is convinced that the labor and expense thus bestowed bring a liberal recompense in the contentment and satisfaction of the patients, and their greater self-control and orderly conduct, not only during these meetings, but at other times and places. . . . The farm is one of the important means in the hygienic and restorative treatment of patients, and affords no inconsiderable source of income,— upwards of $10,000 per annum.

From frequent visits, official and otherwise, to Dr. Earle's hospital, I can fully confirm these statements.   Probably I have "assisted," as the French say, at fifty of these evening lectures and readings in Northampton, once or twice with Miss Dix in her visits there.   Dr. Earle began the system of lectures to patients at Frankford in the winter of 1840–41, the first instance of the kind known. At Northampton he proceeded on a more liberal scale, bought costly apparatus for illustrating chemistry and physics, and indulged his taste for travel by collecting views of foreign cities and countries, and exhibiting them to his patients with illustrative lectures. In his third winter at Northampton (1866–67) there were 45 lectures, 6 of them on brain disease and mental disorder ; and these last were heard by an average audience of 256 patients, the average of employees and patients for the whole course being 282, when the whole hospital population was less than 500. Dr. Tuke's "every evening" must be taken with some limitation. Dr. Earle kept the account, and has recorded, with his usual exact-ness, that in eighteen years, 1867–84, both included, "the average annual number of days on which assemblages of the patients occurred was 332 ; and the largest percentage of patients in attendance was 76, or more than three-fourths." It is believed this experience is unique in the history of asylums.

As for the labor done by patients, I was also personally cognizant of that for more than twenty years ; and no such example has been known to me, before or since, in American hospitals. It was to this steady but not compulsory discipline of labor that the financial success of the hospital was due in great part ; and, though the record of recoveries at Northamp-ton showed small numbers, because the cases were so largely chronic, yet there were many unrecorded *virtual* recoveries,—patients who, while still insane, were capable of self-support and self-direction under kindly supervision. So, when I came to select patients of the chronic class for boarding in families, in 1885 and three subsequent years, I found the largest pro-portion of desirable cases at Northampton. Some of these, after ten years of family life and perhaps thirty years of in-sanity, are still living comfortably in rural households.

The allusion to Whittier, the Quaker poet, in the next letter recalls the curious fact (mentioned by Dr. Earle in his paper on color-blindness in 1845) that so good an observer of nature was insensible to certain colors,— could not, for instance, distinguish between strawberries and their leaves by color alone, and saw but three colors in the rainbow. This might better qualify him for a Quaker poet than for any other kind. Dr. Worthington had succeeded Dr. Earle at Frankford.

Returned to his pleasant suburban retreat, Lyndon Lodge, at Hanwell, where so many American friends have been hospitably received, Dr. Tuke thus wrote the next year after his book appeared : —

Jan. 31, 1886.— I was grieved to hear of the death of Dr. Worthington and Dr. Sawyer, to both of whom I had become attached. I first saw Dr. Worthington at York some thirty years ago. Then we met at Bournemouth, when he was last in England, and in London, where he was ill and I attended him. I visited him at Baltimore in 1884 very pleasantly. His disposition was gentle and affectionate to an unusual degree. For the conflicts of our present age (as affecting psychological politics) he evidently had no heart, and was disposed to say, "Non possumus," to the calls for reform in asylum and almshouse, contrasting strongly with Dr. Godding herein. Dr. Sawyer seemed the right man in the right place at the Butler Hospital in Providence, and it was very agreeable to see him and his wife at Lyndon Lodge. I suppose the church would label him a heretic; but, if so, there will be many heretics in heaven among those you and I have known and valued on earth.

I am glad to see that Whittier has expressed his unity with the little book I sent you. I find in his poetry a continuous charm and comfort. As I am almost always absorbed in insane studies and people, I find it necessary to break away from them at times, and then generally resort to Whittier.

Jan. 6, 1888.— I should much like to add to my collection of "Pliny's Letters." I profit by the occasion of the new year to congratulate my old friend on having lived to see 1888, and hope it finds him still able to enjoy life and occupy his retirement and well-earned leisure with congenial pursuits. [It was in this year that Dr. Earle closed his antiquarian researches of fifty years by the publication and distribution of his Earle Genealogy, a volume of more than five hundred octavo pages, which cost him thousands of dollars, as well as almost endless correspondence and labor, his affectionate tribute to his American ancestors and kindred to the number of more than 4,000.] Did I tell you of my delightful autumn holiday last year in the Black Forest, and my attendance at German medical meetings, in one of which I met Snell, whom you visited at Eich-berg? I went with him to the old asylum there, but he is now at Hildesheim. Why are German memories so particularly delightful to us? I hear that you are pedigree-hunting. Remember that, if the elision of one letter would make you an Earl, the change of one would make me a Duke.

Dec. 2, 1888.— I am sorry to know that the state of your health precludes the fulfilment of the dream of revisiting old England. Be assured we should have welcomed you under our roof. I am in-terested in all the particulars you send me of your present mode of life. When I visited Dr. Nugent, the Irish inspector of asylums, who is at least eighty-four, I found him with Cicero's De Senectute in his hand. What surprising mental and physical powers (I will not say judgment) Gladstone displays at seventy-eight! John Bright is supposed to be nearing his end. Strange whirligig of fate that he should live to have two empresses (our Queen-Empress of India and the Empress Frederick) anxiously interested in his state, and liking him much better than they do Gladstone. Gladstone has shown his nice feeling by speaking kindly of Bright, and frequently wiring to know how he is.

The Earle pedigree must have been a very agreeable pastime. I used to have a hobby that way myself, but the cares of life have forced me to think mostly of my own concerns. My only daughter, Maria, is to be married next spring to a doctor (not a Friend), to whom I can intrust her with every confidence. Our consulting rooms are in the same house in Cavendish Square.

It was in his London house that I called on Dr. Tuke in July, 1890; and his first inquiry was for Dr. Earle. On my second visit to Europe, in 1892, our good old friend had died, and I engaged Dr. Tuke to write some reminiscences for this Memoir; but he died too soon for that. At his urgency I visited the Alt-Scherbitz Asylum in Saxony, which I agreed with him in thinking even better than the Northampton Hospi-tal, because its houses were better arranged and its system of employment quite equal to that of Dr. Earle.

Dr. Earle was for forty-eight years an honorary member of the Medico-Psychological Association of Great Britain and Ireland,— longer, I think, than his friend Dr. Tuke was; and he had contributed more than once to the long-established *Journal of Mental Science*, of which, at his death, Dr. Tuke was an editor.   In the first number (CLXIII.) of the *Journal* after this event (July, 1892) appeared this notice : —

Dr. Earle, as is well known, attracted great attention at one time to the question of the degree to which the insane recover, and caused much surprise, not unaccompanied with incredulity, by demonstrating from statistics that the percentage of recoveries was smaller than supposed and the proportion of relapses greater.   He was foremost in exploding the constant and seductive fallacy of confounding persons with cases ; and, unfortunately, not a few remain unable to understand or appreciate the distinction between the two.   He revelled in figures, whether scientific or financial, and in regard to the former may be compared to Dr. Thurnam, for whose laborious researches he entertained the greatest respect.   In regard to asylum construction, he favored a departure from the orthodox views current among the old school of American alienists.   In this and other respects he was a man of independent opinion.   In religion he was broad and catholic in his views and a foe to theological intolerance.   Ministers of all shades of belief officiated in turn at the Sunday services held in the asylum.

Earlier in the same year (May 6, 1892), in his address at the centenary meeting of the York Retreat, Dr. Tuke, who was the great-grandson of William Tuke, the virtual founder of that pioneer establishment, alluded to the visit made there in 1838 by Dr. Earle, and spoke more at length of Dr. John Thurnam, its physician, who was for years a correspondent of his American friend.   I find several of his letters preserved by Dr. Earle, and may cite a passage or two from this first sober reasoner on the curability of the insane.   Dr. Thurnam wrote from the York Retreat, Oct. 14, 1845, thus : —

Respected Friend,— In reply to thine of the 15th ult., I may state that through Dr. [Luther] Bell I heard with much pleasure of the Committee on Statistics, appointed at the meeting of your Association last year, and that it would afford me much pleasure to do anything in my power which might forward its objects.   I am not, however, aware of any works on the subject which have of late issued from the British press. MM. Parchappe and Debonteville, of the Rouen Asylum, have recently produced a valuable report, under the title of "Notice Statistique sur l'Asile des Aliénés de la Seine Inférieure" (Rouen, 1845), which they express their readiness to exchange for the reports of other asylums. The notices of British asylums in Dr. Julius's "Beiträge zur Britischen Heilkunde" (Berlin, 1844) are also interesting and valuable.

My own book was announced for the present month, but I fear it may not be actually out till a month later. Though not my own publisher, I naturally feel interested in the success of the publication, and should be glad of any suggestion from thee as to the best method of introducing the book amongst you. We have had the pleasure of seeing here both Dr. Bell and Dr. Ray from your country. The continuance of such intercourse between the superintendents of the two countries, I think, augurs well for the prospects of asylums on both sides of the Atlantic. I wish more of us had visited you than have yet done so. A member of our committee, James H. Tuke, has, I expect, before this called on thee; and I hope he will see many of your best asylums before he returns.

This gentleman (J. H. Tuke) was the son of Samuel Tuke, who had welcomed Dr. Earle to his father's house in 1837, when he was making his first visit in York; and the account of this given by the young American at the time, in a letter home, is worth citing here. He said :—

Soon after dinner, on the day of my arrival in this city, a son of Samuel Tuke called at the hotel, with an invitation from his father for me to make a home at his house during my stay in York. This politely proffered hospitality was accepted, and I shall ever remember with pleasure the hours which I have spent beneath this roof in the society of an intellectual and intelligent family. Samuel Tuke is well known in the United States, by those interested in the treatment of lunatics, for the attention which he has devoted to the subject, and the essays connected with it which have emanated from his pen. It is probable that no other man living without the pale of the medical profession is so well acquainted with the proper management of the insane and the most suitable construction, arrangement, and dis-

cipline of lunatic asylums.   His grandfather was the projector of the
Retreat, an institution of the kind near York, which, under the
auspices of the son and others, has attained a high reputation.   This
asylum was one of the pioneers in that great and important revolution
which has taken place in the moral treatment of the insane.   " The
Retreat near York " has long been quoted in the United States as
approaching nearer to perfection in its management and as giving
a higher percentage of cures than any other public establishment in
England.   It was established by members of the Society of Friends,
the funds being obtained by annuities, donations, and annual sub-
scriptions.   The original cost was £5,971 sterling, including the expense of eleven acres of ground which constitutes the farm.   The
receipts from patients were inadequate to defray the current expenses
for several years.   Our countryman, Lindley Murray, was an early
and active promoter of the interests of this establishment.

I breakfasted yesterday with Dr. Caleb H. Williams, the visiting
physician of the Retreat, and he went with me to the asylum, and
accompanied us through the several departments.   There are four
classes of patients according to price.   In the lowest class the sum
of 4 shillings sterling per week is paid, while in the highest it varies
from 20 to 80 shillings.

Probably the York Retreat was the first of the European
asylums inspected by Dr. Earle, who afterwards saw so many ;
and there was none among his colleagues whom he valued more
than Dr. Thurnam, who lived to welcome him to England again
in 1871.   Dr. Thurnam was not superintendent of the York
Retreat at the date of Dr. Earle's first visit there in 1837, not
having been appointed until 1838 ; and he left there in 1849,
the same year that Dr. Earle left the Bloomingdale Asylum.
He then took charge of the Wiltshire County Asylum, and
died there Sept. 24, 1873.   It was more than a year before
Dr. Earle, at Northampton learned of his friend's death ; and
I find a letter of Mrs. Thurnam, of January, 1875, informing
him of the sad event.   She wrote : —

Dr. Thurnam died quite suddenly ; and I have no hesitation in
asserting that his ceaseless industry, his devotion to his suffering
fellow-creatures, and his conscientious, even overpowering, sense of

the responsibilities of his office wore him out prematurely. From 1838, when he was appointed to the Friends' Retreat, to the time of his death, thirty-five years, he had been unremittingly at work, dying at last, as he himself expressed it, "in harness." No man should give more than twenty years to such work. Be warned in time! and, if possible, let me urge upon you to retire from the battlefield while you can yet enjoy some well-earned repose and leisure. . . . I venture to request that, if Miss Dix be still living, and yon can learn her address, you will do me the favor to inform her of my irreparable loss. I think she will be sorry for me.

Miss Dix did in fact survive until July, 1887; and the mention of her illustrious name gives occasion to speak of her long acquaintance and friendship with Dr. Earle. She was his senior by seven years, although careful not to disclose her exact age, and must have met him while at Frankford or, perhaps, even earlier. Like the sisters of Dr. Earle, she had been a teacher of girls, contemporaneously with them, and would naturally have known the family. But the earliest letter of hers which I find is one written from Ohio, in severe illness, while Dr. Earle was at Bloomingdale, and after one of her self-sacrificing campaigns in the cause of the suffering insane. From that time forward they met and corresponded often ; and it was at the Northampton hospital, as Dr. Earle's guest, that I first met Miss Dix. I had often heard of her from Dr. Howe and others who had aided her in her work or had been her pupils ; but when I met her, in 1865, age had lessened her activity and given even more rigidity to her opinions than they had by force of her positive and exacting nature. With much dignity of character and great acquired experience of the world, there remained something of the schoolmistress in her mode of presenting her subjects and meeting those differences of opinion that occur even among the most philanthropic. A Quaker education, with its repression of self and its deference to others, would have modified that imperiousness which she seems to have inherited, and which she had learned to restrain through tact, where her great objects were fully in view. Advancing years had lessened this tact, without rendering her less positive. They had also seen her peculiar work mainly accomplished, while for the needs of the situation which her own heroic activity had so largely created she had neither the vital force nor the special knowledge and discrimination required. Through her it was, campaigning for the neglected insane from State to State and from country to country, that so many new asylums had been built, so many old ones enlarged; but they had in too many instances become centres of intellectual indolence or of semi-political intrigue; to whose busy and well-paid medical men new ideas were irksome, and any forward step in the care of their patients or the guidance of public opinion was a kind of reproach to their imbibed complacency of attained perfection. It was the familiar story of goodness going to seed and planting the surrounding fields with a growth which was not goodness, or at least was a degenerate and reverting form thereof,—a fact familiar to poets. Wordsworth saw at his university —

> Honor misplaced, and Dignity astray;
> Feuds, factions, flatteries, enmity, and guile,
> The idol weak as the idolater;
> And Decency and Custom starving Truth,
> And blind Authority beating with his staff
> The child that might have led him; Emptiness
> Followed as of good omen, and meek Worth
> Left to herself, unheard of and unknown.

Miss Dix had done her work. The fame of it remained and will not be forgotten. It was, however, a work for a time of ignorance and developing civilization, and by no means a permanent model for all coming time. This fact she hardly recognized, nor was it natural she should. Like all strong natures of her type, she saw what she was appointed to see, wrought her task therein with zeal and swift accomplishment, but she saw little beyond. Nor could she well understand that saying of Wordsworth's successor,—

> The old order changeth, yielding place to new,
> And God fulfils himself in many ways,
> Lest one good custom should corrupt the world.

In her own chosen sphere, however, at the time of her
activity, she had the range and the success of Peter the Hermit
in preaching his crusade; and she might go by the name of
Dorothy the Hermitess, so retired was her private life (often
that of a suffering invalid) and so brilliant her public successes.
Her achievement in drawing $50,000 from the bank account of
Cyrus Butler, of Providence (equivalent to half a million in
these days of trooping and syndicated millionaires), more than
half a century ago, has been narrated by her lively biographer,
Mr. Tiffany. But there are some circumstances of the interview which he does not relate, and which, perhaps, are doubtful
in their accuracy, though certainly *ben trovate* when the two
personages are recalled. There was a small asylum for the insane in Rhode Island; but, as usual then and not unknown
now, the poor, who need the most care, got the least there.
Miss Dix entered the field, provided herself with the startling
facts of number and neglect, and then inquired who, in the city
of Roger Williams and Francis Wayland, might give the needful money. Several names were shown her, among them Mr.
Butler's, a bachelor, a rich man, but not till then suspected of
much munificence. Accompanied to his door by her friend, the
Unitarian minister, but without an introduction, she entered, and
found an elderly man and a silent clerk within the office. Inquiring for Mr. Butler, the clerk pointed to the old gentleman, who wheeled round, looked at her, and asked what she
wanted. "If not intruding, I wish to make a statement to you
that will hurt no one, but give you the opportunity of a monument to your name as a benefactor of the poor which will never
be forgotten." "Be brief, and tell me what this means," was
the ungracious reply. "Briefly, then, I have learned that the
poor insane of your town are without a suitable hospital; and
I am looking for a citizen who has both the means and the
liberality to start a movement which cannot fail to succeed."
"Are you Miss Dix? If so, sit down." She took a chair; and,
before she left her auditor, she had given him the facts of the
situation, not without an appeal to that rigid New England
conscience which was her own impelling force. "What do
you wish me to do?" "To subscribe $50,000 for the enlarge-

ment of your insane asylum, and let it be called henceforth the
'Butler Hospital.'"   He turned to his check-book, wrote a draft
for the sum asked, and Miss Dix went forth the marvel of
Rhode Island, which had always been hearing how Moses
smote the rock, and the Israelites drank the gushing stream, but
had never seen the miracle wrought.

Miss Dix was among the constant correspondents of Dr.
Earle; and he was one of the few persons from whom she took
pleasure in receiving instruction rather than imparting it, when
the care of the insane was involved.   And with reason: for he
had studied the subject in many lands, and had practised the
art before a kind of accident brought the sufferings of the insane to her notice, and engaged her sympathetic heart in their
behalf.   They did not agree in opinion always, for Dr. Earle
was conscious of defects in his professional brethren which
Miss Dix was not quick to perceive in her friends; but she
recognized his devotion to the cause she had taken up, and it
was ever a pleasure for her to see the ease and quiet command
with which he moved among her friends, the patients.   It was
apparently a real disappointment to her, though a pleasant one,
when she reached Constantinople in 1856, and found that Dr.
Earle's Timar-hané, that place of torment in 1838, had been
replaced by a well-kept Turkish asylum.   She was fresh from
her victory over neglect and ill-timed levity in the high officials
of Scotland, where, by her own activity and pathetic eloquence, she had secured the appointment of a royal commission, out of which grew in time the admirable lunacy system
of Scotland, in some points the best in the world; and she
would have rejoiced in a trial of strength with the Sultan.   But
all had changed since Dr. Earle's visit.   A young Turk of influence had been a student in Paris, like Dr. Earle.   Like him,
he had visited a good French asylum.   Then he returned to
Constantinople, and introduced the French methods of care,
themselves much improved since the *douche* period.   Miss Dix
went to Suleiman's Mosque and Hospital, and was delighted.
"The insane of Constantinople are in far better condition than
those of Rome or Trieste, and in some respects better cared
for than in Turin, Milan, or Ancona.   The superintendent

proposes further improvements. I had little to suggest and nothing to urge."

The sphere of the two friends was very different: hers was a public career, influencing the powerful in behalf of the helpless; his, though public in its result, was among the helpless themselves. And it was by his perception of their specific needs, not their general condition of neglect, that he was able to improve that condition. He dealt in details and particulars, in figures of arithmetic rather than figures of speech; and he saw with clear foresight the evils that may come from beneficence itself. Miss Dix in later life became aware of these, in some measure, and intimated what the remedy might be. She objected, like Dr. Earle, to extravagant outlay; and, after her experience in army nursing during the Civil War, she began to perceive the need of training attendants for the insane, to which some medical superintendents are yet blind. In October, 1875, she wrote to Dr. Earle after a brief visit to Northampton:—

Regretting only that no opportunity occurred for full conversation upon some questions of wide concern to hospitals for the insane, now very numerous and popular institutions, I suppose the knowledge and direct influence of successful and long-experienced practitioners was never of more real consequence as "helping means" to those whose connection with institutions is but recent, and whose acquaintance with the Protean phases of insanity is deficient both by study and observation. I have been sorry to hear much complaint of hall attendants, by outside parties, much more than in ordinary seasons. ... When less money is extravagantly consumed in new and spacious buildings, there will be fuller ability for employing a more numerous, and perhaps more informed and trained, force of nurses and attendants than are in service at present.

This was written in the heyday of that outrageous expenditure in hospital building of which two new structures in Massachusetts were then instant examples, and against which, as was seen, Dr. Earle was roused to protest. He did so with much effect at the Chicago Conference of Charities in 1879; and, in the widely circulated address made by him there, he paid his brief, emphatic tribute to his more prominent friend, then seventy-seven years old, saying: —

In 1841 Miss Dix began that long and laborious career of phil-anthropic devotion to the interests of the insane with which her name is indissolubly connected, and to which the annals of all history furnish no parallel.   To Dr. Woodward and Miss Dix, more than to any other two persons, are the insane of our country indebted for the awakened interest of the people in their behalf, and, consequently, for that rapidity of practical action manifested in the erection of asylums and hospitals for their benefit, which has in no other country been exceeded, even if it has been equalled.

Retiring from his hospital in 1885 (October 1), the trustees recorded their estimate of Dr. Earle's worth in the vote already printed in the previous chapter.   It fell to me, as an editor of the Springfield *Republican* (the local newspaper of that section of New England), to speak of him then; and some passages of the article may here be cited : —

Perhaps no hospital superintendent ever attended more system-atically to all the details of his work or carried them more completely in his mind, while at the same time he knew how to throw upon others the work that properly belonged to them.   His discipline has been strict and exacting, particularly in regard to industry and frugality; while the condition of most of his patients and the location of his hospital have denied to him those brilliant results which are oftener claimed than attained in this specialty.   He has cared little for show or for fame, but has done his daily duty with accurate fidelity,

As ever in his great Taskmaster's eye.

His reward has come in the gradual recognition of his services by many who were once slow to admit them, and still slower to allow that the quiet veteran, in his old-fashioned hospital and among his dry statistics, was the real head of his profession in America.   Such has been the fact, however, for years; and it is this which makes Dr. Earle's withdrawal from active duty an event of more than local con-sequence.   He will remain a citizen of Northampton, and will there prepare for final publication the writings on which he has long been engaged.

These writings were the Earle Genealogy, concerning which some curious particulars will be found in the Appendix, and the final edition of his "Curability of Insanity." Both involved and had long compelled a large correspondence and frequent reference to the special library he had collected at Northampton, where, by invitation of the authorities, he continued to live at the hospital. This library enabled him to bring before the Association of American Medical Superintendents of Institutions for the Insane (of which he was president in his last year at Northampton), in his address of June 16, 1885, a mass of facts concerning recoveries and curability which that learned and at last persuaded body had never before considered. And, as many of its members had chafed at Dr. Earle's frank censure of the waste of public money in building the Danvers Hospital, he felt warranted in recurring to that subject in this address, which he soon after revised for publication. He said :

The Danvers Hospital was opened for the reception of patients on the 18th of May, 1878. It is, emphatically, one of the establishments upon which a flood of money has been poured for the purpose of creating a curative institution as nearly perfect as possible, under the light of existing knowledge. If abundance of pecuniary means in construction, together with what was believed to be the highest embodied ideal of architectural arrangements, could cure insanity more rapidly than a less costly and more simple structure, that hospital, most assuredly, was prepared for a demonstration of the proposition. It was evident that great efforts were made to arrive at such a demonstration, and thus to prove that the curative advantages of the institution were an adequate compensation for the excess of expenditure.

I may observe in passing, so true is this statement, that, when I questioned several of the then superintendents of the Massachusetts State Hospitals (who appeared in excuse for the outlay at an investigation by the legislature of 1877, which I conducted), they gave as a sufficient reason for spending

$1,500,000 where $750,000 had solemnly been declared ample by the architect that the excess of money would promote recoveries. When I asked them to point out exactly how it would do that, they took refuge in generalities, well knowing, I fear, that the money had been lavished on the comfort of the officers and attendants rather than for the cure of patients, and more in ignorance of what was really needed than with any very definite aim at even luxury of living. Dr. Earle went on:

The usual custom of a large transfer of incurable cases from older hospitals and asylums was omitted at Danvers, and the supply of patients was derived chiefly from current commitments. By this means the proportion of recent cases was much higher than usual from the first; and, as Boston and five other large centres of population (which usually furnish a larger ratio of recent cases than the rural districts) are within a short distance from Danvers, that proportion was raised still higher. And now for the results. In course of the first five fiscal years, out of more than 2,500 cases admitted, 554 cases were discharged recovered; but 115 persons, who had recovered a total of 121 times, had returned to the hospital. So that the net recoveries were but 433, or less than 17 per cent. of the admissions. Within the three years ending Sept. 30, 1884, the recoveries were but 265; while 80 persons, representing 86 recoveries, were readmitted. So that the actual recoveries were but 179, only 11.70 per cent. of the admissions during the three years.

Here was the dilemma of the extravagant hospital builders coolly stated in a way from which there was no escape. They had said the outlay at Danvers and similar places must promote recovery. This was either true or false. If true, why had not the cures occurred? If false, why had the statement been made? Dr. Earle believed it was made in careless ignorance, because the statistics of American asylums had not been so reported as to convey the truth. In 1879 he had revised, and I had introduced in Massachusetts, such forms of statistical report as brought the true facts to light. In this way the failure at Danvers to come up to the promise of the builders was clearly revealed. And, in closing his final address to his colleagues, Dr. Earle said: —

I would express the hope that the time is not far distant when our
Association will so far perfect its statistical system as to make a distinction between *persons* and *cases*, and thus enable the reader to
learn how many of the reported recoveries are first recoveries, and
how many are subsequent.   This improvement was made in the
Massachusetts tables in 1879, and in those of the British Medico-
Psychological Association in 1883.   Surely, the American Association ought not to lag far behind.*

Valuable as statistical exactness is, recoveries are not
secured thereby, but by close observation, personal care, and
the wise use of moral and medical means.   Nor is it always
possible to indicate the means or cause of recovery.   When
Dr. Earle and I were arranging the form of the Massachusetts
tables just mentioned, we provided for one showing the cause
of death in asylum patients.   This was retained and is still in
use; but another form, providing for a report by the physicians on "Cause of Recovery" in patients recovered, was
stricken out at the request of the asylum physicians.   As I
remember the incident, Dr. Earle said concerning that table,
"If you can get the cause truthfully stated, it will be of much
value; but it will be exceptional that the true cause will be
known, or, if known, truly stated."   He allowed it to pass,
however, and was ready to make such reports himself; but his
foresight proved exact, and the form was set aside.   His
friends were perhaps inclined to claim more for him in the
matter of recoveries under his care than he would have allowed
for himself.   His cousin, Mrs. Spring, in a letter from Los
Angeles in the summer of 1897, made these statements, quite
new to me, concerning the first motive for his choice of the
alienist's specialty, and his early success in treatment: —

My kinsman, Pliny Earle, was one of many children; and I think
of them in their orderly Quaker home, with their wonderful mother
and noble father, as one of the most intellectual families I have ever
known.   They had a very dear, beautiful, brilliant cousin,— so
lovely and charming that mothers said to their daughters, "Be like

* Yet this simple change has not yet been generally made in the United States.

Mary Earle." From a terrible illness she recovered, all but the
brain, and, after many years, died a wretched death in an insane
asylum. This called Pliny's attention to such sufferers, and so he
devoted his life to their cure or alleviation. Dr. Brown-Sequard
once said to me, "He is the only one of us who *does* cure them."
Dr. Earle had a remarkable power of organization, of peaceful influence and enduring patience. He was prepared for any emergency,
knew the tendencies of each patient, and kept untiring, vigilant
watch of them all. I remember in one of the dancing evenings
at Bloomingdale, when Margaret Fuller, William Henry Channing,
Marcus Spring, and I were present, one of the patients darted out
of the dance, and, putting up her hand on Dr. Earle's shoulder, said,
"Thou model of a man!" and then took her place again. Long
afterwards I went there alone, and for weeks watched his treatment
of those unfortunates,— not as a mass, but as individuals. Before
he took charge, they had been subjects of amusement for visitors
[the thing Miss Dix had censured at Northampton before he took
charge], but Dr. Earle never allowed them to be intruded upon. I
was told in New York that his testimony was the first legal evidence
where insanity was claimed or suspected, and I knew a case where
his evidence saved a man's life. It was he who settled the difficult
Parish Will case.

Mrs. Spring adds, "A disappointment in early life turned
his interest still more upon the life he had chosen." At all
events, he gave to it his most sacred thought, and expended in
hospitals and asylums the gayety of his nature, in all forms of
entertainment, as well as his serious studies and his incessant
care. Then, at the unmistakable summons of age, he prudently
withdrew from his responsible position, attended to those persons and affairs that had claims on his consideration, designated his biographer, and gave him both needful explanations
and ample discretion for editing or omitting, and calmly prepared for the last scenes. He distributed his printed works to
friends and to libraries, made provision for the perpetuation
of his memory at Northampton, which he had come to love as
a home, by generous bequests to the local library of broadest
scope and most liberal management, erected his own funeral
monument there, and took care, in perpetuity, for the plain

tombstones of ancestors and kindred at Leicester. He forgave
his enemies (if any such remained), said farewell to kinsmen
and dear friends, and awaited the inevitable hour with quiet
trust in the good Power that had guided his way of more
than fourscore years, with outward and inward illumination.
He died, after a short illness, on the 17th of May, 1892.

Pliny Earle, as these pages have disclosed, however faintly,
was a personage as marked as his name was unusual. Along
with strong family traits, he yet had an individuality which
gave him distinction, from childhood to old age, and could not
be defined or limited by his social, religious, or national environ-
ment. "To define," said our friend Alcott, "is to confine";
but no such imprisonment fell to the lot of Dr. Earle. Of singular personal beauty (which the portraits here engraved but
partly recall), and with a grace of manner that was but the
native expression of the kindliest heart, he attracted notice
wherever he might go, and awakened expectation which his
success in life, for some years, did not seem to justify. He
won no high name in literature, was neither a brilliant orator
nor a noted man of science, secured few of those glittering
prizes which even his modesty would have valued, and held no
position of wide command or conspicuous influence. In all
this he shared the common lot, which awards even temporary distinction to but few, and that for the most varied
reasons, compelling praise or blame. But he slowly rose above
most of his contemporaries in the zeal and perseverance with
which he sought the good of mankind ; and in a profession in-
trinsically noble, where he found errors abundant, ideas few,
and a level of mediocrity veiled, but not concealed, from keen
observers like himself, by vague rhetoric and complacent routine. To this he opposed the singleness of purpose and simplicity of character which belonged by nature to his race and
name. He was favored by long life and providential opportunities ; and thus the features of his intellectual and moral
nature became better known, and had their foreordained effect.
Few men, perhaps none in America, have done more to clear
the way for the best treatment of the classes to whom he consecrated his powers, or have been of better example to the
future man of science or the philanthropist.

APPENDIX.

I. THE PUBLICATIONS OF DR. EARLE.

LEAVING out of view the young scholar and poet's contributions to the Worcester *Talisman*, *Spy*, and other local periodicals, some of which he gathered into his Philadelphia volume of 1841, "Marathon, and Other Poems," the following is believed to be the fullest list of his acknowledged writings that has appeared in print : —

Books and Papers.

(I.) (1841) *A Visit to Thirteen Asylums for the Insane in Europe.* (Philadelphia : J. Dobson. pp. 144.) This had before appeared in the *American Journal of the Medical Sciences* for October, 1839 (Vol. XXV., pp. 99–134). It was reprinted later, with many changes and additions. However, many of the original errors, arising from imperfect observation or dependence on untrustworthy authority, remained in the reprint. For example, the account of the traditional origin of the "Community Asylum at Gheel," as he called the famous colony at that Belgian town, is wholly incorrect, and the statistics much in arrears, coming down no later than 1821. Dr. Earle placed in the hands of his biographer a corrected copy of this reprint. An extract or two will be given from this, to show his earlier style. The visits describe conditions extending from July, 1837, to January, 1839.

(II.) (1848) *History, Description, and Statistics of the Bloomingdale Asylum for the Insane.* (New York : Egbert, Hovey & King. pp. 136.) To this was added, for completion,—

(III.) (1848) *Four Annual Reports of the Bloomingdale Asylum for the Insane.* (1845, 1846, 1847, 1848, all for the years preceding their date. pp. 55, 48, 32, 28 ; in all, 163.) Up to their date, these two volumes contained the fullest account of the operation and results of an American asylum which had ever been published ; and the presentation of its statistics in new forms, after much labor in tabulation, made it the first essay in the reformation of statistics of insanity in America.

(IV.) (1853) *Institutions for the Insane in Prussia, Austria, and Germany.* (Utica : New York Asylum, Printers. pp. 229.) These visits

were all made in the year 1849, with many others upon which Dr.
Earle did not report, but which served to correct former impressions,
and to make his comments on the annual reports of European asylums
of great value.   To his volume Dr. Earle added a supplement of sixteen pages, containing information furnished by Laehr in 1852, and a
list of German asylums at that date, tabulated by Dr. Earle, which, as
containing information curious in itself, and nowhere else accessible in
English, is reprinted in this Appendix.   The mere political changes
made in the past half-century, largely by the genius and energy of
Bismarck, give these minute divisions of German-speaking Europe
curious interest.   The first form of the volume was published in the
American Journal of Insanity, then printed at the Utica Asylum,
where Dr. Brigham had begun it.   I have made use of a corrected
copy of the volume of 1853, put in my hands by Dr. Earle.

(V.) (1853) *European Institutions for Idiots*. (New York: William Saun-
derson, Printer. pp. 22.)

(VI.) (1854) *The Practice of Blood-letting in Mental Disorders*. (New
York: S. S. & William Wood. pp. 126.)

(VII.) (1857) *Medical Opinion in the Parish Will Case*. (pp. 50.)

(VIII.) (1862) *Chapter on Insanity in United States Census: Quarto
Volume for* 1860. (Printed by the Government Printers.)

(IX.) (1864–85) *Reports of the State Lunatic Hospital at Northampton,
Mass*. (Printed by the State Printers at Boston. Pp. nearly 2,000 in
all.)

(X.) (1877) *The Curability of Insanity*. (First form of this work in a
pamphlet issued by the New England Psychological Society. Boston.)

(XI.) (1879) *The Management of the Insane in the American States*.
(Proceedings of the Sixth Annual Conference of Charities at Chicago,
June, 1879, pp. 42–59.) (Boston: A. Williams & Co.)

(XII.) (1887) *The Curability of Insanity: A Series of Studies*. (Philadelphia: J. B. Lippincott Company. pp. 232.)

(XIII.) (1888) *The Earle Family: Ralph Earle and his Descendants*.
(Compiled by Pliny Earle, of Northampton, Mass. Printed for the
Family.) (Worcester, Mass.: Press of Charles Hamilton. pp. xxiv,
480.) This may be considered Dr. Earle's *magnum opus*, since it
occupied him, at intervals, for half a century, and involved an expenditure on his part of some thousands of dollars. It is a masterly work,
of incredible labor almost, and yet deals with only one of the eight or
ten families in America named Earl, Earll, or Earle. It contains more
than 4,000 names of the cousins, near or remote, of Dr. Earle, and yet
omits more than 1,000 as not coming within the scope of the book.
In connection with what the volume tells of the artistic branch of the
Leicester Earles, this Appendix will contain something about the two

Ralphs, James and Augustus Earle, who were the art-contingent, and were divided between New and Old England in the political separation of the two countries; James being the husband and Augustus the son of a Tory mother, though the grandson of a patriot soldier of the Revolution. Ralph drew the first sketches of the early fights at Concord and Lexington. An uncle of the last English artist of the family married into the family of General Jackson, the hero of New Orleans, and painted his great kinsman's portrait; his nephew was sailing the Mediteranean with Admiral Smyth or acting as draughtsman to the " Beagle," in which Darwin made his grand voyage round the world.

(XIV.) (1838–92) An incomplete list of Dr. Earle's contributions to Reviews, Annuals, Dictionaries, etc., follows : —

1838. *Insanity: Its Causes, Duration, Termination, and Moral Treatment.* (Part of his Medical Thesis of 1837.)

1840. *The Climate, Population, Diseases, etc., of Malta.*

1840. *Medical Institutions, Diseases, etc., at Athens and Constantinople.*

1841. *The Royal College of Physicians and Surgeons in London.*

1842–45. *Observations on the Rapidity of the Pulse of the Insane.*

1843. *The Curability of Insanity.* (First paper.)

1845. *The Inability to distinguish Colors.*

1845. *Experiments with Conium maculatum.*

1847. *Cases of Paralysis Peculiar to the Insane.*

1849–57. *Cases of Partio-General Paralysis, or Paralysis of the Insane.*

1840–42. *Reviews* of Sir William Ellis, of Dr. F. Leuret, of the Statistics of the York Retreat, of Eleven Hospitals.

1843–44. *Reviews* of Reports of Twenty-five American Hospitals, of the Retreat near Leeds, and the Bridewell and Bethlehem Hospitals in England.

1845. *Reviews* of the Reports of Twenty American Hospitals and Eight English Hospitals.

1846. *Indian Hemp and Mental Alienation.* (Review of J. Moreau.)

1846. *Reviews* of Reports of English Lunacy Commission and of Fifteen American Hospitals.

1844–47. *The Poetry of Insanity, Contributions to the Pathology of Insanity, Cases and a Leaf from the Annals of Insanity.*

1847. *Reviews* of Reports of Nineteen American Hospitals.

1848. *Reviews* of Reports of Eighteen American Hospitals.

1851. *The Insane at Gheel.*

1852. *The Lunatic Hospital at Havana.*

1849–52. *Reviews* of the Reports of Twenty-six American Hospitals.

1853–55. *Reviews* of the Reports of Forty American Hospitals.

1856. *Reviews* and Report of Twenty-three American Hospitals.

1856. *Insanity and Idiocy in Massachusetts.*

1857. *New American Institutions for the Insane.*
1857. *Reviews* of the Reports of Twenty-five American Hospitals.
1858. *Reviews* of the Reports of Twenty-eight American Hospitals.
1859. *Reviews* of the Reports of Thirty-four American Hospitals.
1860. *Reviews* of the Reports of Thirty-three American Hospitals.
1861. *Reviews* of the Reports of Fifteen American Hospitals.
1862. *Reviews* of the Reports of Thirty-six American Hospitals.
1863. *Hospitals in British America.*
1863. *Reviews* of the Reports of Ten American Hospitals.
1864. *Reviews* of the Reports of Thirty-nine American Hospitals.
1865. *Reviews* of the Reports of Thirty-six American Hospitals.
1866. *Reviews* of the Reports of Thirty-five American Hospitals.
1867. *Reviews* of the Reports of Thirty-three American Hospitals.
1867. *History and Description of the Northampton Lunatic Hospital.*
1867. *Psycopathic Hospital of the Future.*
1868. *Psychologic Medicine in the Medical Curriculum.*
1868. *Prospective Provision for the Insane.*
1868. *Reviews* of the Reports of Twenty American Hospitals.
1869. *Reviews* of the Reports of Fifteen American Hospitals.*

In addition to these articles, Dr. Earle published in 1846 a review of "Esquirol on Mental Diseases," in a New York periodical; a "History of Insane Hospitals in the United States," the first paper read before the New York Academy of Medicine, and published in its records; in 1863 an article in the American Almanac on "Insanity"; in 1881 an article on the "Curability of the Insane" in the Proceedings of the Conference of Charities; and in 1892 a long article on the same subject in Dr. D. H. Tuke's "Dictionary of Psychological Medicine," published in London two months after Dr. Earle's death. In the *Journal of Social Science* he published in 1890 his paper on "Popular Fallacies concerning the Insane." In his early days he had written copiously for the literary and daily journals, and contributed, in 1837, 1838, 1839, many letters to the Worcester *Spy*, describing his journeys about Europe.

A paper on Color Blindness, exhibiting what may be called Dr. Earle's middle style, when writing for the people rather than for physicians, appears in this Appendix; and, to show his latest style and condensed form of statement, the Social Science paper on "Popular Fallacies concerning the Insane" and his contribution to Dr. Tuke's "Dictionary of Psychological Medicine" are reprinted.

---

* See also Dr. Earle's later "Reminiscences" in this Appendix. It is difficult to be sure that all he so copiously wrote is catalogued, and his manuscripts are not here noticed.

II. SELECTIONS FROM "THIRTEEN VISITS."

An English Asylum.

The number of patients in the Wakefield Pauper Asylum at the time of my visit, in the summer of 1837, was 334, of whom a small minority were women. Fifty or sixty of the men labor, regularly, either in the manufacture of the articles above mentioned, in gardening, or in some mechanical trade. All the utensils used by the patients at their meals, unless necessarily metallic, are made of wood. The working patients are furnished, besides their regular meals, with two "drinkings" during the day, each of them consisting of three-fourths of a pint of beer and four ounces of bread. Nearly two hundred dollars per annum is paid for tobacco, which is also divided among the laborers, each being entitled to a weekly ration of one ounce. Many of the patients, as we passed through the wards, begged for tobacco, or for money to purchase it with. One of them, after having thus played the mendicant, put into my hands a piece of cloth, upon one side of which he had written, in large letters, "*Millennium. Green, blue, and yellow united.*" And upon the other, "*Victoria 1st, July* 28, 1837. *Virgin Queen of Peace. Amen. Aquila.*" It will be perceived from the date that this was but a short time subsequent to the accession of Victoria to the throne of Great Britain. The universal popularity which the youthful queen enjoyed at that time among her sane subjects thus seems to have penetrated the walls of the institutions for lunatics. And this poor, infatuated maniac beheld the "green, blue, and yellow," the insignia of the different political parties of the realm, united through her means, and hence the "consummation devoutly to be wished," the immediate advent of the millennium ! "Eh, eh," said he, after I had read the above ; and, as he spoke, he looked up into my face with a piercing glance and a most significant smile, "do you know what Aquila signifies in English ? " Being answered in the affirmative, "Well, sir," he continued, "*I* am the Eagle " ; and he placed a most emphatic stress upon the pronoun, in order to give an adequate idea of the dignity of his person.

The women were supping when we went through their department, each eating her ration from a small wooden dish, similar to a pail.

That air of neatness and comfort which reigns throughout the establishment is particularly conspicuous in the section for the females.
One of the women, who had been refractory, had her arms confined.
I had previously observed, in the men's department, that confinement by straps, in chairs and beds, is also resorted to in cases of
violent mania.

"Who are you?" inquired one of the women who were eating,
after having scrutinized me with the wild and searching gaze of a
maniac. "Are you a Methodist minister?" "No," said I, "I am an
American." This answer was perfectly satisfactory; and no sooner
was it uttered than half a dozen patients suddenly rose, "Oh, you are
from *America:* then you know my brother," said one. "Do you
know J. F.?" inquired a second. "Have you ever seen —— ——?"
asked a third: "he is my husband's brother." "I have a sister in
America," remarked a young woman, looking up with a smile so
gentle and an expression of countenance so calm and subdued that
one beheld in it more of the attractive innocence and beauty of sane
and healthy childhood than the fierceness and wildness of confirmed
lunacy.

The Utrecht Asylum.

The building, though still small, has been enlarged; the courts
have been planted with trees and flowers; and at the time of my
visit, in July, 1838, their size was being much increased by extending their limits over the sites of some ancient buildings, purchased
by the "Regents" of the asylum, and demolished by their order.
The building is shaped like the letter L. The room of the superintendent is in the angle, in the second story, so situated that he
can see every patient who is out of doors. The wards have dormitories on but one side, the remaining space being a gallery,
which is used as a place of promenade in bad weather. There is a
common sitting-room for each class of the inmates. Their number
was 94, that of the two sexes being about equal. They are divided
into three classes: those of the first class pay 812 florins, equal to
about $125, per annum; those of the second, 412 florins, or
$65; and those of the third, 100 and 150 florins. The third
class is composed of paupers. Those who pay but 100 florins are
natives of Utrecht: those who pay 150 come from other places.
The rooms of the first class are furnished handsomely, but not with

that elegance which is seen in those of the similar classes in some asylums.

When necessary, the camisole, or the strait-jacket, fetters, the douche, and the dungeon are put in requisition as means of restraint and coercion. The stream of water forming the douche is but one-fourth of an inch in diameter, while those of Salpêtrière and Bicêtre, at Paris, are about seven-eighths of an inch. The quantity of water flowing from the latter must, consequently, be nearly twelve times as great as from the former. There is but one bathing-tub in the establishment. The patients resort to reading, writing, drawing, music, cards, billiards, chequers, or draughts, and some other games, for entertainment and amusement. There is a library intended for their use. The billiard table, a large and handsome one, was made by two of the former patients. In one of the men's rooms several patients were occupied in drawing and reading; and, had it not been for the wildness of the eye and the characteristic traits of countenance, which cannot be mistaken, in one or two others who were present, I could hardly have believed myself to be in a mad-house. Most of the men in the first class were in the court devoted to their use. Among them was a physician. He conversed freely upon his situation, gave an account of his commencement of practice, and the success which attended his efforts, until his friends thought it best for him to take lodgings in the lunatic asylum. At length he asked me if I thought him deranged. He had talked so rationally, and this question was put so directly and so earnestly, that to avoid answering it was almost impossible. An evasive reply, if any, must be given. "It is difficult to define derangement," said I; "and, if we should accept the definition given by some authors, we should include almost the majority of mankind." He appeared satisfied with the answer, and only remarked, with a melancholy tone, "Je crois bien que la plupart des gens soient des aliénés." Poor man! although reason was dethroned, it was evident, from his conversation, that the affections retained their empire.

[There has been some confusion of dates, even in France, until recently, in regard to the world-renowned deed of Pinel. Dr. D. H. Tuke, writing of his ancestor, William Tuke, who did for England more than Pinel did for France, set this matter right in 1892, soon after Dr. Earle's death. He said: "Pinel's nephew, Casimir Pinel, discovered in the registers of Bicêtre that the exact date of his noble inspiration was 1793. 'On doit croire que ce fût vers les derniers mois de 1793, et non de 1792, que Pinel se présenta à l'Hôtel de Ville pour demander l'autorisation à la Commune de faire enlever les chaînes aux aliénés de Bicêtre.' ('Lettres de Pinel,' 1859.) M. Semelaigne, the great-grand-nephew of Pinel, gives the date of his nomination to Bicêtre as Aug. 25, 1793, and the day of entering upon his duties there as Sept. 11, 1793. ('Philippe Pinel et son œuvre.')   Then followed the like humane deed at the Salpêtrière.'" Dr. Semelaigne was present at York in 1892 when the story of William Tuke was told by his descendants and successors, in celebrating the Centenary of the York Retreat, July 21, 1892.]

Pinel, the Younger, describes his Father's Deed.

The Bicêtre is hallowed as being the scene of the boldest and noblest achievement recorded in the annals of insanity.   Here morning first dispelled the midnight gloom of lunacy; and the guiltless maniac was released from the thraldom which associated him with criminals and brutes, taken by the hand as a brother, and acknowledged to be worthy of the kindest attention, commiseration, and sympathy.

The following brief account of the commencement of the labors of Pinel, extracted from a paper read by his son before the Royal Academy of Sciences, commends itself to the attention of every reader : —

"Towards the end of 1792,* Pinel, after having many times urged the government to allow him to unchain the maniacs of the Bicêtre, but in vain, went himself to the authorities, and with much earnestness and warmth advocated the removal of this monstrous abuse. Couthon, a member of the Commune, gave way to M. Pinel's arguments, and agreed to meet him at the Bicêtre.   Couthon then interrogated those who were chained; but the abuse he received, and the confused sounds of cries, vociferations, and clanking of chains, in the filthy and damp cells, made him recoil from Pinel's proposition. 'You may do what you will with them,' said he, 'but I fear you will become their victim.'   Pinel instantly commenced his undertaking. There were about fifty who he considered might, without danger to the others, be unchained; and he began by releasing twelve, with the sole precaution of having previously prepared the same number of strong waistcoats,† with long sleeves, which could be tied behind the back, if necessary.   The first man on whom the experiment was to be

---

* Really, 1793.   † A garment now known by its French name, *camisole*.

tried was an English captain, whose history no one knew, as he had
been in chains for forty years. He was thought to be one of the
most furious among them. His keepers approached him with caution, as he had, in a fit of fury, killed one of them on the spot with
a blow from his manacles. He was chained more rigorously than
any of the others. Pinel entered his cell unattended, and calmly said
to him, 'Captain, I will order your chains to be taken off, and give
you liberty to walk in the court, if you promise me to behave well, and
injure no one.' 'Yes, I promise you,' said the maniac; 'but you are
laughing at me,—you are all too much afraid of me.' 'I have six
men,' said Pinel, 'ready to enforce my commands, if necessary.
Believe me then, on my word, I will give you your liberty if you will
put on this waistcoat.'

"He submitted to this willingly, without a word. His chains were
removed; and the keepers retired, leaving the door open. He raised
himself many times from his seat, but fell again on it; for he had
been in a sitting posture so long that he had lost the use of his legs.
In a quarter of an hour he succeeded in maintaining his balance, and
with tottering steps came to the door of his dark cell. His first look
was at the sky; and he cried out enthusiastically, 'How beautiful!'
During the rest of the day he was constantly in motion, walking up
and down the staircases, and uttering short exclamations of delight.
In the evening he returned of his own accord into his cell, where a
better bed than he had been accustomed to had been prepared for
him, and he slept tranquilly. During the two succeeding years
which he spent in the Bicêtre, he had no return of his previous
paroxysms, but even rendered himself useful by exercising a kind
of authority over the insane patients, whom he ruled in his own
fashion.

"The next unfortunate being whom Pinel visited was a soldier of
the French guards, whose only fault was drunkenness. When once
he lost his self-command by drink, he became quarrelsome and
violent, and the more dangerous from his great bodily strength.
From his frequent excesses he had been discharged from his corps,
and he had speedily dissipated his scanty means. Disgrace and
misery so depressed him that he became insane. In his paroxysms
he believed himself a general, and fought those who would not acknowledge his rank. After a furious struggle of this sort he was
brought to the Bicêtre in a state of great excitement. He had now

been chained for ten years, and with greater care than the others, from his frequently having broken his chains with his hands only. Once, when he broke loose, he defied all his keepers to enter his cell until they had each passed under his legs; and he compelled eight men to obey this strange command. Pinel, on his previous visits to him, regarded him as a man of original good nature, but under excitement incessantly kept up by cruel treatment; and he had promised speedily to ameliorate his condition, which promise alone had made him more calm. Now he announced to him that he should be chained no longer; and, to prove that he had confidence in him, and believed him to be a man capable of better things, he called upon him to assist in releasing those others who had not reason like himself, and promised, if he conducted himself well, to take him into his own service. The change was sudden and complete. No sooner was he liberated than he became attentive, following with his eye every motion of Pinel, and executing his orders with as much address as promptness. He spoke kindly and reasonably to the other patients, and during the rest of his life was entirely devoted to his deliverer. 'I can never hear without emotion,' says Pinel's son, 'the name of this man, who some years after this occurrence shared with me the games of my childhood, and to whom I shall always feel attached.'

"In the next cell were three Prussian soldiers, who had been in chains for many years, but on what account no one knew. They were, in general, calm and inoffensive, becoming animated only when conversing together in their own language, which was unintelligible to others. They were allowed the only consolation of which they appeared sensible,— to live together. The preparations taken to release them alarmed them, as they imagined the keepers were come to inflict new severities; and they opposed them violently, when removing their irons. When released, they were not willing to leave their prison, and remained in their habitual posture. Either grief or loss of intellect had rendered them indifferent to liberty.*

"Near them was an old priest, who was possessed with the idea that he was Christ. His appearance indicated his belief. He was grave and solemn, his smile soft, and at the same time severe, repelling all familiarity. His hair was long, and hung on each side of his face, which was pale, intelligent, and resigned. On his being once taunted with a question that, 'if he was Christ, he could break

* Dements, of course.

his chains,' he solemnly replied, ' Frustra tentaris Dominum tuum.' His whole life was a romance of religious excitement. He undertook, on foot, pilgrimages to Cologne and Rome, and made a voyage to America for the purpose of converting the Indians. His dominant idea became changed into an actual mania, and on his return to France he announced himself as the Saviour. He was taken by the police before the Archbishop of Paris, by whose orders he was confined in the Bicêtre as either impious or insane. His hands and feet were loaded with heavy chains, and during twelve years he bore with exemplary patience martyrdom and constant sarcasms.

" Pinel did not attempt to reason with him, but ordered him to be unchained in silence, directing, at the same time, that every one should imitate the old man's reserve, and never speak to him. This order was rigorously observed, and produced on the patient a more decided effect than either chains or the dungeon. He became humiliated by this unusual isolation, and introduced himself to the society of the other patients. From this time his notions became more just and sensible; and in less than a year he acknowledged the absurdity of his previous prepossessions, and was dismissed from the Bicêtre.

" In the course of a few days Pinel released fifty-three maniacs from their chains. Among them were men of all conditions and countries,— workmen, merchants, soldiers, lawyers, etc. The result was beyond his hopes. Tranquillity and harmony succeeded to tumult and disorder; and the whole discipline was marked with a regularity and kindness which had the most favorable effect on the insane themselves, rendering even the most furious more tractable."

The Asylum at Charenton.

Dr. Louis favored me with a letter of introduction to M. Esquirol, the *médecin en chef* of the asylum at Charenton, and the distinguished veteran in the treatment of the insane. With this I went to the asylum, where I had the pleasure of meeting him to whom it was addressed, in the scene of his present labors among the unfortunate people who love and honor him as a father, and in whose welfare his interest continues, unrepressed by the weight of accumulated years. After his visit to the patients was completed, I sat an hour with him in the parlor of the institution, during which time he conversed chiefly upon the subjects of lunacy and of lunatic asylums. After speaking of the comparative merits of the various establishments of the kind in Europe, and giving the preference to that at Reggio, in Italy, over all others that he had ever visited, he made many inquiries with regard to those of the United States, and expressed much interest in the progress of improvement in the treatment of the insane upon this side of the Atlantic.

The asylum of Charenton, in a village of the same name, is about five miles eastwardly from the city of Paris. It is situated upon the southern declivity of a hill, which runs parallel to the river Marne near its shores, and but a short distance from its junction with the Seine. It was originally a hospital, under the care of the Brothers of Charity. About the beginning of the eighteenth century a department was for the first time devoted to the reception of persons afflicted with mental alienation. In 1795 the hospital was suppressed; but in 1797 it was re-established, and devoted exclusively to the treatment of the insane. It is now called, in common with some other establishments of the kind in other parts of France, "Maison Royale d'Aliénés." It includes many edifices, which have been erected at various periods, and extensive gardens and promenades, which extend to the summit of the hill upon the declivity of which it is situated. The following description is translated from the recent elaborate work of M. Esquirol, to which I am also indebted for most of the subject-matter for the remarks upon this asylum:* "The section for men is composed of four courts (of which three are planted), three infirmaries, one ward for patients of a suicidal propensity, one dormitory, one gallery and six corridors into which open the doors of the several rooms; one bathing-room, and six rooms where the patients assemble. These last-mentioned can be heated. The section for women has a garden, four planted courts, two infirmaries, one ward for women disposed to commit suicide, two bathing-rooms, seven dormitories, six galleries and corridors into which open the doors of the apartments, and five rooms in common, which may be heated."

An extensive additional department for females, combining most of the modern improvements, was erected about twelve years ago, and first occupied in 1829. This is one of the best-arranged and most neatly kept establishments of the kind that I have had the

* Des Maladies Mentales, considérées sous les Rapports Medical, Hygiénique, et Médico-légal. Par E. Esquirol. Paris, 1838.

opportunity to examine. The furniture is good and sufficiently handsome, without being extravagant. The beds of the dormitories are hung with white curtains. No corresponding department for the men has hitherto been erected.

The Milan Asylum.

Manual labor is pursued to a considerable extent by the patients. A large garden belonging to the asylum furnishes employment to nearly one hundred of them during the warm season. In one room, through which we passed, between forty and fifty men were engaged in braiding *paglia di Spagna* — Spanish straw — for carpets. They worked as steadily, and appeared as orderly, as if they had not been lunatics. In another apartment several men were employed in making shoes, and as many more in tailoring. One of the latter was cutting clothes. Soon after we entered he commenced talking to me, and conversed so rationally that I supposed him to be a sane person, acting as overseer to the others. Under this supposition I inquired of him if all those under his care were insane, to which he answered in the affirmative. Perceiving that he conversed in French, I asked him if he was a Frenchman. He replied that he was not, and added, "Je suppose que vous êtes Anglais." "No," said I, "I am an American." "Ah! vraiment," he responded, dropping his shears and lifting both hands as if agreeably surprised, "vous êtes Américain. Eh bien, vous êtes très-heureux, vous êtes *carbonaro*. Tous les Américains sont des *carbonari*. Je voudrais bien être dans ce pays-là." Knowing the subject of the *carbonari* to be rather a delicate one in Italy, these remarks, together with some others subsequently made, induced me to suspect him insane, and this suspicion, upon inquiry of the *direttore* of the asylum, who accompanied me, proved correct.

An artist, in the same apartment with the patient above mentioned, was occupied in cutting designs in paper. He showed me a representation of Bonaparte at St. Helena, and another of the garden of Eden. They were, indisputably, the most elegant workmanship of the kind that I have ever examined. I attempted to purchase the latter, but he informed me that it was already disposed of.

Many of the women were making lint, or *charpie*, for the use of the hospital in the city; and in one apartment there were about

ninety sewing and spinning tow upon throstles whirled by the hand.
For coercion and restraint the douche and confinement in bed, or of
the limbs, are effectual means. I observed one patient manacled
with irons, and strong leather mittens upon his hands. He tears off
his clothes whenever his arms are unrestrained. Several others
wore strong leathern belts, to which their arms were fastened. In
the same ward with these men there was another, very gentleman-
like in appearance, who was exceedingly anxious lest I should go
away unaware of his dignity or of the distinguished honor I had received by admission into his presence. Accordingly, he approached
me, and repeated, with the utmost volubility, a long list of titles,
which *he graced*, such as "prince" of one place, "king" of another,
"emperor" of a third, and, finally, "ruler of the world." In his
anxiety to furnish me with this important information, he followed us
far out of the ward.

The only means of amusement which I saw were a swing and a
giustra, if I rightly understood the word. The latter is so constructed that four, or, indeed, eight persons seated at the extremities
of two beams which cross each other at right angles, in the centre,
may revolve horizontally in a circle. These are in the principal
court occupied by the men. The court is shaded by two parallel
rows of sycamore-trees, beneath which are many seats for the patients, permanently fastened to the ground.

The Asylum at Constantinople.

Connected with some of the mosques there are buildings for the
reception of the sick,— a kind of hospital, in which the poor who
are suffering under disease may have their wants ministered to by
the hand of charity. That which is adjacent to Suliman-yé, or the
mosque of Suliman, is devoted exclusively to the insane. There
none but men are admitted, the women according to Turkish custom, as well as in conformity with the precepts of the religion of
Mahomet, being kept in private seclusion. The building is but one
story in height, and, like the cloisters of many Gothic cathedrals, and
the khans or caravanserais of Turkey and Natolia, completely sur-
rounds a central court. The entrances to all the rooms are beneath
the corridor at which the court, upon all sides, is limited.

I visited this asylum during the feast of Bairam, near the

close of the year 1838, in company with two American gentlemen, residents at Constantinople. We entered the court, passing several miserably clad people, " sitting at the gate," not " to ask alms," but to receive it, if voluntarily offered. Within the court were many people, mostly young men and boys, who had come either for the gratification of curiosity or to administer to the wants of the afflicted. We passed along the corridor to the first window. From between the bars of the iron grating with which this was defended a heavy chain, ominous of the sad reality within, protruded, and was fastened to the external surface of the wall. It was about six feet in length. The opposite extremity was attached to a heavy iron ring, surrounding the neck of a patient who was sitting, within the grating, upon the window-seat. We entered the room, and found two other patients, similarly fastened, at the two windows upon the opposite side of the room. It was a most cheerless apartment. A jug to contain water, and, for each of the patients, a few boards laid upon the floor, or elevated three or four inches, at most, and covered with a couple of blankets, were all the articles of comfort or convenience with which, aside from their clothing, these miserable creatures were supplied. Although in the latter part of December, they had no fire. Nor were the windows glazed ; but close shutters, attached to each, rendered it possible measurably to shield the inmates from severe weather, whenever it might occur. The length of the chain of each patient is barely sufficient to enable him to lie down upon his comfortless bed of boards and blankets. Leaving this apartment, we proceeded successively to the others, twelve or fifteen in number, in all of which we found the patients in a very similar condition to those whom we had first seen. There was but one who was not chained. He was an elderly man, though still retaining much of the vivacity of earlier years. His long and profuse hair and beard were nearly white, and his complexion very delicate. He was formerly a priest of the Islam faith. He has been deranged and confined in this place nearly fifteen years, during which time he has thrice broken the chain with which he was secured. He is now alone in his apartment, within which no one is permitted to enter. He talked and raved incessantly, threatening to kill those who were making him their gazing-stock.

Like those in the apartment first mentioned, all the patients, with one exception, were without fire. The person forming this exception was one of the most hideous of undeformed human beings. He

has been in the Timar-hané, as this asylum is called by the Turks,
more than forty years. His hair and beard, both naturally abundant, curly, and black as ebony, appeared as if they had not been
cut or combed since his entrance. They nearly concealed his face,
and the former hung in a profusion of literally "dishevelled locks"
about his neck and shoulders. His head would have been a
nonpareil for an original to the figure of Cain, in David's celebrated
picture of "Cain meditating the Death of Abel." He lay crouched
upon all fours, resting upon his knees and elbows, and holding his
head and hands over a *manghale* of living embers. Whatsoever was
said, whether addressed to him or otherwise, could only induce him
slowly to turn his huge head, and present his hideous face more
directly to view. His case was a striking example of dementia.

The patients, generally, appeared to enjoy pretty good health,
aside from the lesion producing insanity. I was informed that a
physician attends them regularly. There is a person who has the
charge of supplying them with food, and they receive considerable
attention from those who visit them. While we were there, many
visitors were conversing with them, giving them articles of food,
money, and tobacco, and doing them a kind office by filling and
lighting their "chebouks." These patients presented a diversity of
forms of insanity, and a variety of hallucinations. One of them was
seated against the bars of his window, cross-legged, and with arms
folded upon his breast, in all the counterfeited dignity of a sovereign,
and the imperturbable gravity of a saint. It was evident by his de-
meanor that he esteemed himself one of the rulers of the earth,— a
Mahmoud, a Mahomet, or a Great Mogul. Upon being informed
that I was an American, "Please," said he, turning towards me
slowly, and without the slightest change of countenance,— " please,
effendi, to give my respects to the Sultan of America." This said,
he assumed his former position, and maintained it with the most
scrupulous exactitude.

There was another, one of the finest-looking Mussulmans that
ever worshipped before the altars of Stamboul. His beard might
acknowledge no rival in beauty excepting that of Mahmoud II.
and his eye possessed all the mingled fire and softness of the
Orient. He was occupied in sewing. He was surrounded by
several young Turks, but continued his labor, regardless of any of
those who were present. The gentleman of our party who speaks
the Turkish language addressed him, and at length won him, al-

though with considerable reluctance on his part, into conversation.
I have never witnessed a greater blandness and suavity of manners
than in him.   Upon being asked the cause for which he had come to
that place, "Please, gentlemen," said he, "to be seated, and I will
relate the whole history."   Inasmuch as the uncovered stone floor
presented an aspect rather uninviting as a seat, we excused ourselves; and he was requested to proceed.   Thereupon he placed
himself in an attitude worthy of the orators of antiquity, and related
a long story in a most amusing but graceful manner.   The whole
substance of it was that people began by calling him a fool, and,
going from bad to worse, at length ended by bringing him to the
Timar-hané of Suliman-yé.

Such, then, is the gloomy picture with which these sketches of
some of the asylums for suffering humanity are brought to a conclusion.   It presents us with an additional motive for hoping that
the stream of knowledge, which, taking its rise in Chaldea, has
flowed to us, constantly augmented in its course, through Egypt,
Greece, Rome, and the nations of Western Europe, may reverse its
course or release a branch, once more to fertilize the desolate
regions of intellect throughout the East.   It is a proposition the
truth of which cannot be questioned that in proportion as a nation
advances in intellectual cultivation, its practical benevolence assumes
a loftier standard.   When, then, the light of science shall gild with
brighter rays the empire of the Ottoman, we doubt not that the
chains of the maniac will be broken, and his condition rendered
such as to leave a hope that alienated reason may reassume her
proper throne.

It is difficult to reconcile the treatment of the patients in the
Timar-hané with the testimony of physicians in regard to the
attention paid to unconfined lunatics in Turkey, and with the prevalent opinion among the followers of Mahomet that the insane are
the especial favorites of heaven, that their "discord" is

Harmony not understood,

that their language appears to us to be incoherent and unmeaning
merely because the minds of the sane are not sufficiently spiritualized
to comprehend it.   Dr. Millingen, an English physician who had
practised nearly twenty years in Constantinople, informed me that he
had known the wandering lunatic to be received by strangers, and
for weeks in succession receive all the kindness of the most cordial
hospitality.

III. THE GERMAN ASYLUMS IN 1852.

PUBLIC INSTITUTIONS FOR THE INSANE IN PRUSSIA.

Institutions.		Opened.	Physicians.	No. of Patients.	Remarks.
RHINE PROVINCE:					
Alexian Brothers	Incurables	16 cent'y	Dr. Raeckel	9　Dec., 1851	487 square miles. Population, 2,830,936.
Alexian Brothers	"	14 cent'y	Dr. Schumacher	50　Dec., 1851	At Cologne.
Annunciaten	"	—	Dr. Hartung	95　End 1851	At Aix la Chapelle.
Cologne	"	1802	Dr. Raeckel	126　Dec., 1851	At Aix la Chapelle.
Düsseldorf	"	—	Dr. Bournye	111　Dec., 1851	Takes incurables from Siegburg.
Kaiserswerth	Mixed	1852	Dr. Hintzé	For 40 females	Pastor Fliedner, director.
Neuss	Incurables	—	Dr. Hellersberg	25　End 1851	For men, opened more than 100 years ago.
Siegburg	Curables	1825	Dr. Jacobi	228　Nov., 1851	Dr. Focke, second physician.
St. Thomas	Incurables	1835	Dr. Lux	117　Dec., 1851	Andernach. Incurables from Siegburg.
Trèves	"	1835	Dr. Tobias	98　Dec., 1851	
WESTPHALIA:					
Gesecke	Incurables	1841	Dr. Schupmann	28　End 1851	638 square miles. Population, 1,468,998.
Marsberg	Rel.-united	1835	Dr. Knable	334　Dec., 1851	Dr. Schwartz, second physician.
Münster	Mixed	—	Dr. Pellengahr	4　End 1850	
SAXONY:					
Halle	Rel.-united	1844	Dr. Damerow,	313　Dec., 1851	460 square miles. Population, 1,799,240.
Magdeburg	Incurables	—	Dr. Neide	19　Dec., 1851	Dr. H. Laehr, second physician.
POMERANIA:					
Greifswald	Curables	1834	Dr. Berndt	21　Dec., 1851	576 square miles. Population, 1,197,701.
Rueggenwald	Incurables	1841	Dr. Steinhauer	69　Dec., 1850	
Stralsund	"	1842	Dr. Von Wulff-Crona	27　End 1851	
BRANDENBURG:					
Arbeitshaus	Incurables	—	Dr. Leubuscher	176　End 1851	734 square miles. Population, 2,200,000. Berlin.
Charité	Mixed	1798	Dr. Ideler	128　End 1851	Berlin.
Neu Ruppin	"	1801	Dr. Wallis	148　End 1850	Berlin. Dr. Goecke, second physician.

PUBLIC INSTITUTIONS FOR THE INSANE IN PRUSSIA, *Continued.*

Institutions.		Opened.	Physicians.	No. of Patients.	Remarks.
BRANDENBURG, *con.*—					
Soran	Mixed	1812	Dr. Schneiber	160 Nov., 1851	741 square miles. Population, 3,065,800.
Wittstock	Inc. & idiots	—	Dr. Schultze	101 Dec., 1851	
SILESIA:					
Breslau	Mixed	1820	Dr. Ebers	41 Dec., 1851	
Brieg	Incurables		Dr. Ehrlich	170 End 1851	
Leubus	Curables	1830	Dr. Martini	144 Dec., 1851	Dr. Hoffman, second physician.
Plagwitz	Incurables	1826	Dr. Pohl	110 Dec., 1851	
POSEN:					
Owinsk	Mixed	1838	Dr. Beschorner	94 1850	536,51 square miles. Population, 1,364,000.
Posen	Incurables	—		18 1852	
PRUSSIA:					
Dantzig	Mixed	16 cent'y	Dr. Goetz	69 Dec., 1851	1,178 square miles. Population, 2,499,400.
Koenigsberg	"	18 cent'y	Dr. Bernhardi	71 Nov., 1851	Patients to be removed to Schwetz.
Schwetz	"	1822	Dr. Butzke	16 End 1851	To be abolished when Wehlau is opened.
Schwetz	Rel-united	—		For 200	General hospital; patients not separated. Expected to open in 1852.
Wehlau	"	—		For 200	Expected to open in 1852.

Total number of patients, 3,130.
The Hohenzollern Lands, with 21¼ square miles and 66,000 inhabitants, have from 10 to 12 insane in the general hospital.

INSTITUTIONS IN GERMANIC AUSTRIA.

Institutions.		Opened.	Physicians.	No. of Patients.	Remarks.
UPPER AUSTRIA:					
Lintz	Mixed	—	Dr. Knörlein	114 End 1850	208 square miles. Population, 720,000.
LOWER AUSTRIA:					Dr. Schassing, house physician.
Vienna Gen. Hosp'l	Mixed	1784	Dr. Viszanik	427 July, 1851	359¼ square miles. Population, 1,538,047.
" New	Curables	1852	Dr. Riedel	For 400	
Ybbs	Mixed	1817	Dr. Spurzheim	278 End 1851	Dr. Horning, second physician.
SALZBURG:					130 square miles. Population, 152,000.
Salzburg	Mixed	—	Dr. Ozlberger	16 Dec., 1851	Dr. Zellner, acting physician.
MORAVIA:					
Bruenn	Mixed	—	Dr. Alexik	118 End 1851	404½ square miles. Population, 1,833,200.
SILESIA:					92½ square miles. Population, 476,800.
Troppau	—	—	Dr. Rokita	—	Has but 6 rooms.
STEYERMARK:					
Graetz	Mixed	1796	Dr. Koestel	172 End 1851	408 square miles. Population, 1,000,000.
BOHEMIA:					943¼ square miles. Population, 4,600,000.
Prague	Rel.-united	1846	Dr. Fischel	594 Nov., 1851	Drs. Ezermak and Spielman, assistants. Opened in 1790 as department of hospital.
CARINTHIA:					
Klagenfurt	Mixed	—	Dr. Kumpf	32 End 1851	188¼ square miles. Population, 340,000.
CARNIOLA:					
Laibach	Mixed	—	Dr. Zhuber	24 End 1851	181¼ square miles. Population, 500,000.
TYROL:					523 square miles. Population, 900,000.
Hall	Mixed	1830	Dr. Tschallener	102 Dec., 1851	Dr. Stoltz, second physician.
Trient	"	—	—	40 Feb., 1849	
COASTLANDS:					
Trieste	Mixed	—	Dr. de Dreer	66 Dec., 1851	138.3 square miles. Population, 505,831.

Total number of patients, 1,833.
The duchies Auschwitz and Zator, with 70 square miles and 365,000 inhabitants, have no institutions for the insane.

OTHER INSTITUTIONS FOR THE INSANE IN GERMANY.

Institutions.		Opened.	Physicians.	No. of Patients.	Remarks.
KINGDOM OF SAXONY:					
Colditz	Incurables	1829	Dr. Weiss	376 Oct., 1851	272 square miles. Population, 1,894,636.
Hubertusburg	"	—	Dr. Weigel	About 100	For men. Dr. Voppel, second physician.
Leipzig	"	1701	Dr. Radius	—	Females, mostly idiots.
Sonnenstein	Curables	1811	Dr. Lessing	35 Dec., 1851 / 241 Jan., 1850	Formerly for curables. At Pirma, Dr. Klotz, house physician. 1,394 square miles. Population 4,526,650.
KINGDOM BAVARIA:					
Baireuth	Mixed	—	Dr. Marc	54 Dec., 1851	
Bamberg	"	—	Dr. Schwappach	39 End 1851	
Erlangen	Rel.-united	1846	Dr. Solbrig	143 Jan., 1850	
Frankenthal	Incurables	—	Dr. Bettinger	230 Jan., 1852	
Giesing	Mixed	1803	Dr. Christmuller	45 Dec., 1850	Near and for Munich.
Irsee	"	1849	Dr. Hagen	118 Nov., 1851	Dr. Engelman, assistant physician.
Klingenmunster	Curables	—	Dr. Kiderle	—	Not opened. For 350 to 400.
Regensburg	Mixed	1852	Dr. Marcus	—	
Würtzburg	"	1743		80 End 1851	Dr. Gegenbauer, assistant physician. 354½ square miles. Population, 1,805,558.
KING. WÜRTEMBERG:					
Winnenthal	Curables	1834	Dr. Zeller	103 End 1846	
Ziviafalten	Incurables	1812	Dr. Schaeffer	160 Nov., 1851	
Marialberg	Cretins	1841	Dr. Zimmer	52 Jan., 1852	
Rieth	"	1848	Dr. Muller	12 End 1850	At Winterbach. 695 square miles. Population, 1,799,000.
KINGDOM HANOVER:					
Hildesheim {	Curables	1827	Dr. Bergmann and three assistants	190 End 1851	1st relative-united institution in Germany.
	Incu. men	1827		212 End "	
	"	1849		160 " "	
GRAND DUCHY BADEN					
Illenau	Rel.-united	1842	Dr. Roller	414 End 1851	278½ square miles. Population, 1,379,000.
Pforzheim	Incurables	14 cent'y	Dr. Muller	177 Jan., 1850	Near Achern, Drs. Hergt and Fischer, ass'ts.

OTHER INSTITUTIONS FOR THE INSANE IN GERMANY, *Continued.*

Institutions.		Opened.	Physicians.	No. of Patients.	Remarks.
G. D. MECHLENBURG SCHWERIN:					
Dömitz	Incurables	1851	Dr. Fiedler	65 in 1850	228 square miles. Population, 536,724.
Sachsenberg	Curables	1830	Dr. Flemming	201 Jan., 1851	Takes incurables from Sachsenberg. Near Schwerin, Dr. Lechler, 2d physician.
G. D. OLDENBURG:					
Blankenburg	Incurables	1786	Dr. Kindt	85 in 1848	113 square miles. Population, 278,030.
G. D. HESSE:					
Hofheim	Mixed	—	Dr. Hohenschild	367 End 1851	152 square miles. Population, 62,917. Near Darmstadt.
G. D. MECHLENBURG STRELITZ:					
Strelitz	Mixed	—	Dr. Berlin	50 Dec., 1851	52 square miles. Population, 524,000.
G. D. WEIMAR:					
Jena	Mixed	1821	Dr. Kieser	61 Jan., 1851	67 square miles. Population, 261,370.
G. D. LUXEMBURG & D. LIMBURG:					
Luxemburg	Mixed	—	Dr. Wirth	29 End 1851	65½ square miles. Population, 282,000. Dr. Pondron, associate physician.
DUCHY BRUNSWICK:					
Brunswick	Mixed	1829	Dr. Mansfeld	61 Jan., 1851	72 square miles. Population, 270,100.
DUCHY NASSAU:					
Eichberg	Rel.-united	1849	Dr. Snell	153 End 1850	84 square miles. Population, 427,915. Dr. Jlasting, 2d phys. Eberbach open'd 1812.
D. SAXE-MEININGEN:					
Hildburghausen	Mixed	1830	Dr. Harmisch	32 Jan., 1852	45½ square miles. Population, 163,323.
D. SCHLESWIG AND HOLSTEIN:					
Schleswig	Mixed	1820	Dr. Rueppell	469 Dec., 1851	163½ square miles. Population, 163,000. 157½ square miles. Population, 525,050. Dr. Gage, second physician.
DUCHY ANHALT:					
Dessau	Mixed	—	Dr. Bobbe	48 End 1851	48 square miles. Population, 158,000.

OTHER INSTITUTIONS FOR THE INSANE IN GERMANY, *Continued.*

Institutions.		Opened.	Physicians.	No. of Patients.	Remarks.
D. SAXE-COBURG:					
Gotha	Mixed	—	Dr. Ortley	18 Sept., 1851	37 square miles. Population, 149,753.
D. SAXE-ALTENBURG:					
Roda	Mixed	1848	Dr. Richter	78 Nov., 1851	24¼ square miles. Population, 131,789. 2 geographical miles from Jena.
Elec've HESSE CASSEL:					
Hainai	Incu. men	—	Dr. Amelung	154 Dec., 1851	208.9 square miles. Population, 754,590.
Merxhausen . .	Incu. women	1533	Dr. Hildebrand	111 Dec., 1851	20 cretins. School to be opened for them.
PR. LIPPE DETMOLD:					
Brake	Mixed	—	Dr. Meyer	74 Dec., 1851	21 square miles. Population, 108,000. New buildings to be erected.
PR. SCHWARZBURG:					
Arnstadt . . .	Mixed	1820	Dr. Nicolai	12 End 1851	31 square miles. Population, 129,652.
Rudolstadt . .		—	Dr. Otto	29 Dec., 1851	
PR. REUSS:					
Gera	Mixed	—	Dr. Buelau	13 End 1851	27.9 square miles. Population, 112,175.
Free City Hamburg	"	—	Dr. Maier	495 Jan., 1851	7 square miles. Population, 188,054.
Bremen . . .	"	—	Dr. Eschenburg	26 End 1851	5 square miles. Population, 76,000.
Lubeck . . .	"	—		31 End 1851	7½ square miles. Population, 47,685.
Frankfort on Main	Mixed	—	Dr. Hoffman	67 Nov., 1851	1⅓ square miles. Population, 71,678.

Total number of patients, 10,808 approximately.

The principality Waldeck, with 21¼ square miles and 62,000 inhabitants, has a few insane in the asylum for chronic disorders at Flechtdorf. The principality Schaumburg-Lippe, with 9¼ square miles and 30,000 inhabitants, has a few in its prison and almshouse. The principality Liechtenstein, with 2¼ square miles and 6,400 inhabitants, has no receptacle for the insane. The landgravine Hesse Homburg, with 6 square miles and 26,000 inhabitants, sends its insane (six in 1851) to Hofheim.

PRIVATE INSTITUTIONS.

The following table, compiled from the work of Dr. Laehr, includes all the private establishments recognized by him in the Germanic countries. He notices, however, only "those which are directed by a physician, and which, by their internal and external regulations, can be considered, by persons who understand the subject, as *Private Institutions for the Cure* and Care of the Insane." How many are thus ignored I know not; but among them is that of Mrs. Klinsmann in Berlin, as well as several others in the same city, which, though licensed by the government, certainly can present but feeble claims to the title of "Institution."

Institutions.	Countries.	Opened.	Director.	No. of Patients.	Land.	Remarks.
Bendorf	Prussia: Rhine Province	1847	Dr. Erlenmeyer	22 End 1851	—	Near Coblentz. For insane and idiots.
Bonn	"	—	Dr. M. Nasse	—	—	Established by Dr. F. Nasse, father of present proprietor, who died in 1851.
Bonn	"	1849	Dr. Herz	16 rooms	2 large gardens	
Bonn	"	—	Dr. Albers			Between Cologne and Bonn.
Endenich	"	1844	Dr. Richards	For 20	7 acres	For 25. 3 geographical miles from Bonn,
Eitorf	"	1846	Dr. Meyer	8 in 1850	50 acres	2 from Siegburg.
Moers	"	1843	Dr. Whitfield	15 End 1850		
Berlin	Brandenburg	1849	Dr. Posner	4 End 1850		
Kowanowko	Posen	—	Dr. Zelasko			
Vienna	Austria: Lower Austria	1831	Dr. Görgen	About 30	Large park	Founded at Sumpendorf, in 1819, by the father of Dr. Görgen.
Lindenhof	Germany: Kingd'm Saxony	—	Dr. Matthias	For 20	—	Near Dresden; founded by Dr. Braunlich.
Poina	"	1833	Dr. Pienits	For 20	—	Dr. Dietrich, second physician.
Thonberg	"	1838	Dr. Guentz	25 in 1844		Near Leipzig.
Kennenburg	Würtemberg	1844	Dr. Stimmel	—	6 acres	Formerly Heimbach; near Esslingen.
Schöndorf	"	—	Dr. Schnurrer / M. Rauer, prop.	—		14 English miles from Stuttgard. Founded by Dr. Schnurrer, senior.
Jena	Saxe-Weimar	1848	Dr. Kieser	—	2½ acres	In the suburbs of Jena.
Marienthal	Saxe-Meiningen	1846	Dr. Marting			
Oberneuland	Near Bremen	—	Dr. F. Engelken	For 25		
Rockwinkel	"	1770	Dr. H. Engelken			
Hornheim	Schleswig	1845	Dr. P. Jessen	For 50-60	20 acres	Near Kiel, Dr. W. Jessen, 2d physician.

Total patients about 250.

*General View of the German Institutions for the Insane
with Reference to their Destination.*

AA. PRIVATE INSTITUTIONS.

Bendorf, Berlin, Bonn 3, Eitorf, Endenich, Hornheim, Jena, Kennenburg, Kowanowko, Lindenhof, Marienthal, Moers, Oberneuland, Pirna, Rockwinkel, Schöndorf, Thonberg, Vienna.

BB. PUBLIC INSTITUTIONS.

I. CONNECTED WITH OTHER INSTITUTIONS.

A. WITH PENAL INSTITUTIONS.

1. *Curables and Incurables.*— Strelitz, Gera.

2. *For Incurables.*— Berlin.

B. WITH OTHER HOSPITALS.

(*a*) In the same building.

1. *For Curables and Incurables.*— Berlin, Breslau, Brünn, Dantzig, Grätz, Hamburg, Klagenfurt, Münster, Schwetz, Trient, Würtzburg.

2. *For Incurables.*— Cologne, Leipzig.

(*b*) In separate buildings.

1. *For Curables and Incurables.*— Bremen, Kaiserswerth, Laibach, Luxemburg, Roda, Trieste, Vienna, Hubertusburg, Trèves.

C. WITH ASYLUMS FOR CHRONIC AND INCURABLE CASES.

1. *For Curables and Incurables.*— Hofheim.

2. *For Incurables.*— Aix-la-Chapelle, Frankenthal, Gesecke, Hainai, Merxhausen, Pforzheim, Stralsund, Wittstock.

II. INDEPENDENT INSTITUTIONS.

1. *Mixed, Curables and Incurables together.*— Armstadt, Bamberg, Baireuth, Brake, Brunswick, Dessau, Frankfort on the Main, Gotha, Hall, Hildburghausen, Irsee, Jena, Königsberg, Lintz, Lubec, Mariaberg, Munich, Neu Ruppin, Owinsk, Regensburg, Rudolstadt, Salzburg, Schleswig, Soran, Winterbach, Ybbs.

2. (*a*) *For Incurables.*— Aix-la-Chapelle, Blankenburg, Brieg, Cologne, Colditz, Dömitz, Düsseldorf, Magdeburg, Neuss, Plagowitz, Posen, Rügenwald, St. Thomas (Andernach), Zwiefalten.

2. (*b*) *For Curables.*— Greifswald, Klingenmunster, Leubus, Sachsenberg, Sonnenstein, Siegburg, Vienna, Winnenthal.

3. *Relative-connected Institutions, the Curables and Incurables being in separate buildings.*— Eichberg, Erlangen, Halle, Hildesheim, Illenau, Marsberg, Prague, Schwetz, Wehlau.

IV. COLOR-BLINDNESS IN 1844-45.

[This paper was printed in part in the *American Journal of the Medical Sciences*, but is here given with some of the names substituted for initials, and with other variations which make it interesting. When written, the subject was almost unknown in America, and had been but little studied in Europe. It is now well understood; and seamen, railway officials, army officers, and others act upon the knowledge which fifty years ago was the possession of only a few men of exact observation, like Dr. Earle. He seems to have used the paper as a lecture. It is here printed from his manuscript.]

"Know thyself!" Such was the important and comprehensive injunction inscribed upon the entablature of the portico of the temple at Delphos; and from the time of the first establishment of the Delphian oracle down to the present time man has endeavored, in a greater or less degree, to act in obedience to the command. He has attempted to reveal the hidden secrets of his physical as well as of his mental existence through the agency of every available means. The elements of antiquity (fire, air, earth, and water) have been called upon to contribute towards the attainment of this end. Observation and research have exerted their influence. Matter and mind have united their energies for its acquisition. Astrologers have invoked the agency of the starry hosts. Theologians and metaphysicians have spent their lives in speculations, have promulgated theory after theory, until "of the making of many books there is no end." Anatomists have plied the scalpel with an assiduity which has left hardly a fibre of the human system undissected from its neighbor. Physiologists have theorized until their doctrines are nearly as various as the languages of Babel. Chemists have called into requisition every agent reacting upon the tissues and their products, and have brought the powerful means of analysis and synthesis to their aid. And what is the result? Mind is still unknown to itself, except by some of its attributes. Its abstract nature and its connection with the body are as truly among the arcana of nature at the present day as in the time of Adam. What is our knowledge of the body? The scalpel has revealed the form, and the microscope, to some extent, the intimate structure, of the several organic systems of which it is composed; but in what utter darkness are we still groping in regard to the functions of those organs! The thymus, the thyroid and the bronchial glands, the spleen, the *appendicula vermiformis*, the pineal gland,— that Cartesian throne of the immortal soul,— the *for-nix*, the *pons Varolii*, and, one might almost say, the whole mass of the encephalon,— what are these but *terra incognita*, even to the most "transcendental" anatomist and the most profound physiologist?

Receding one step farther, how is our knowledge confounded, in relation even to those organs of which we are acquainted with the immediate use, by the simple question, "*How* does it act?"

I nothing know but that I am,

says the poet; and in a similar manner, in relation to the functions of the organs in question (that of secretion, for example), the physiologist may assert, with a becoming humility, "I nothing know but that *it is*." For what is the benefit, what the advancement of knowledge, if we attempt to explain the phenomenon of secretion by resorting to the undefinable and uncomprehended terms or phrases "vitality," "organic forces," "*vis vitae*," "*vis animae*," and the like? Is it not a subterfuge approximating in absurdity to that of the early natural philosophers, who, having declared that "Nature abhors a vacuum," were compelled to draw the inference, and assert accordingly, that, "although Nature abhors a vacuum, yet she does not abhor a vacuum above the height of thirty-two feet."

These reflections have been suggested by the nature of the subject about to engage our attention. It is a fact long known to physiologists (but of which a very large proportion of the community appears to be ignorant) that there are persons who, although their organs of vision are apparently perfect in every respect appreciable to the senses, do not possess the power of an accurate discrimination of colors. To these persons, colors appear identical which to others are nearly as opposite as white and black. Red and green, sufficiently dissimilar to ordinary perceptions, almost invariably appear to them to be alike; while in respect to most of the other colors, primary or secondary, they are involved, to a greater or less extent, in the same difficulty.

So far as my own researches have extended, here are all the cases of this peculiar physiological trait that have been published:—

1. Mr. HARRIS, of Allonsby, England (Cumberland).— Black and white were the only colors of which he had an accurate perception, and he could distinguish between red cherries and the surrounding leaves by their form alone. He had two brothers with the same

defect, one of whom always mistook orange for grass green, and light green for yellow.   (Case described in Philosophical Transactions for 1777, p. 260.)

2. SCOTT.— He mistook pink for pale blue, and red for green. His father and a maternal uncle, one of his sisters, and two of his sons had the same defect.   (Related by himself in Philosophical Transactions, 1778, p. 613.)

3. ROBERT TUCKER, of Ashburton, England.— Orange and green were identical to him, so were blue and pink.   He could generally discriminate yellow, but mistook red for brown, and blue or violet for purple.   (Transactions of Phrenological Society, p. 209.)

4. J. B., a tailor of Plymouth, England.— The solar spectrum appeared to him as if composed of the two colors, yellow and blue. Indigo and Prussian blue looked like black, purple like a modification of blue, dark green like brown, and light green like a pale orange.   He once patched the elbow of a blue coat with crimson, and at another time repaired a garment with crimson silk, supposing it to be black.   Yellow, white, and gray were the only colors he could distinguish with certainty.   (Transactions Philosophical Society of Edinburgh, vol. x. p. 253.)

5. DUGALD STEWART, the mental philosopher, could not distinguish the scarlet fruit of the Siberian crab from its leaves.

6. DR. DALTON, the eminent English chemist, and his brother.— In the solar spectrum he can perceive yellow and blue, the red being "scarcely visible," and the other colors unperceived.   Blue and pink are alike to him by daylight.   (Memoirs of the Literary and Philosophical Society of Manchester, vol. v. p. 28.)

7. Mr. TROUGHTON, an eminent optician of London.— The whole solar spectrum appeared to him of but two colors, yellow and blue, all the least refrangible rays being of the former tint and the most refrangible of the latter.   (Brewster's Optics, American edition, p. 260.)

8. Another man seen by Sir David Brewster, who could perceive only yellow and blue in the spectrum.   (*Ibid.*)

9. A man in the British navy of whom it is said that he purchased a blue "uniform" coat, with vest, and red breeches to match.   He had one brother similarly affected.   (Dr. Nicholl in Medico-chirurgical Transactions of London, vol. vii.)

10. A grand-nephew of the gentleman last mentioned.— He con-

founded green with red, and called light red and pink blue. Paper stained with radish-root he called "blue," and spoke of green spectacles as "red glasses." Indeed, it appeared that light yellow was the only color that he could accurately distinguish.

11. Another gentleman, whose case is published by Dr. Nicholl.— In his own words he says: "My eyes are gray with a yellow tinge around the pupil. The color I am most at a loss with is green, and in attempting to distinguish it from red it is merely guess-work. Scarlet, in most cases, I can distinguish; but a dark bottle-green I could not, with any certainty, tell from brown. Light yellow I know; but a dark yellow I might confound with light brown, though in most cases I think I should know them from red. All the shades of light red, pink, purple, etc., I call light blue; but dark blue and black I think I know with certainty. Though I see different shades in looking at the rainbow, I should say it is a mixture of yellow and blue, yellow in the centre and blue towards the edges. I have red crimson curtains in the windows of my bed-room, which appear red to me by candle-light and blue by daylight. The grass in full verdure appears to me what other people call red; and the fruit on trees, when red, I cannot distinguish from the leaves unless, when I am near it, the more from the difference of shape than color. A cucumber and a boiled lobster I should call the same color, making allowance for the difference of shade to be found in both; and a leek, in luxuriance of growth, is to me more like a stick of red sealing-wax than anything I can compare it with." (Medico-chirurgical Transactions, vol. ix. p. 359.)

(This man's eyes, when fatigued by looking at red and green spots on a white ground, became much affected; but no incidental color made its appearance.)

12. JAMES MILNE.—(One of the three brothers of No. 15.) See below. (Transactions Phrenological Society, p. 222.)

13. Mr. C.— No details. (*Glasgow Medical Journal*, vol. ii. p. 15.)

14. Two cases detailed by Dr. Elliotson. In one of them the rainbow appeared as a band of a brighter color than the rest of the sky, but a little darker at one side than the other, and gradually shaded off between the two sides. (*American Journal Medical Sciences*, vol. xxiii. p. 446.)

15. Three brothers and a cousin mentioned in G. Combe's "System of Phrenology" and in the Edinburgh Transactions of the Phreno-

logical Society. They inherited color-blindness from their maternal grandfather, there being none of the intermediate generation who had the same peculiarity.

16. M. M. — A case recently published by M. Boys de Loury. He was a draper, but obliged to give up his business on account of the defect. The irides of his eyes were light blue, confounded towards the centre with yellow spots. He thought that vermilion, scarlet, and the color produced by madder were identical. Rose-color appeared to be a dirty white, and carmine a deep blue or violet. (*Annales Médico-psychologiques*, January, 1844.)

17. A boy, mentioned by Dr. Szokalski, who always confounded blue and red. (*Ibid.*)

18. MARY BISHOP.— A most interesting case, in which the defect was temporary, being induced by (or at least accompanying) partial amaurosis. (*American Journal Medical Sciences*, vol. xxvi. p. 277.)

Dr. Hays remarks that several cases of this natural defect have come under his notice. He is the editor of the *Journal*.

These eighteen are all the cases mentioned in the scientific works which I have consulted. I proceed to notice several others within my personal knowledge, some of them in my own family. The initials are not in all cases the true ones.

1. JOHN ADAMS, a preceptor of Leicester Academy.— One evening during the period when fashion required a bow of ribbon, corresponding in color with the garment, upon the lower extremity of each side of the pantaloons, this gentleman was engaged for an evening party. The tailor was remiss, the new garment did not arrive in season, and the preceptor called upon the knight of the shears. It was complete with the exception of the ornament. The owner took them, purchased some ribbon on the way home, and with deft fingers arranged the bows and fastened them with pins in their destined situation. His duty was now fulfilled, his mind at rest. The fastidious spirit of fashion was appeased, the shade of Beau Nash honored, and the dictum of the living Brummell obeyed. What, then, should prevent the most worthy preceptor from figuring (as he did) at the *soirée* in a pair of light-blue pantaloons, decorated, *à la mode de la Légion d'Honneur*, with bows most magnificent in size and glaringly red in their color?

2. C. D.— He confounds green, red, and brown. A young man, color-blind, purchased a piece of light-blue cassimere for a pair of

pantaloons, and a skein of pink silk with which to make them. Having carried these to a "tailoress" (the wife of C. D.), she opened them, and, perceiving the incongruity, asked the young man if he could not procure silk more nearly to match the cassimere. Somewhat astonished, he took up the silk, scrutinized it and the cloth, and, throwing it down upon the latter with an air of the most perfect confidence and assurance, exclaimed, "What could be a nearer match?" The tailoress, together with her husband, C. D. (who was present), thereupon enjoyed a hearty laugh at the expense of her employer. In a few days, however, an incident occurred which proved that C. D. himself could distinguish colors hardly better than the young man. He spoke of "a little red dog," but the canine race in the nineteenth century rarely rejoice in a roseate or carmine hue. It was no more red than the pink silk was blue. The purchaser now enjoyed his turn of risibility.

3. Z. G.— He confounded red and green.

4. R. M. had the same peculiarity as Z. G. He was for many years a minister in the Society of Friends, and dressed in drab throughout, except his cravat, which was invariably of a brownish red, the "bandanna" so much used in days gone by. He believed it to correspond with his other garments.

5. J. M., a young man of seventeen years. — I was passing a few weeks during the early summer in the country; and this young man, together with his sister, stopped at the same place as myself. I one day accompanied him upon a long ramble through the neighboring fields and woods. At length, upon arriving at a partial opening in an otherwise dense forest, we found a portion of the ground most abundantly covered with the wintergreen, or checkerberry, the *Gaultheria procumbens* of the botanists. Being fatigued, we sat down in the midst of it, where the berries were as numerous as the leaves, peering out from beneath them by tens of thousands, and presenting their round and rosy cheeks to the blessed light. One would have believed that no person, unless he were blind or marvellously nearsighted, could stand even at the distance of ten feet and direct his eyes towards this prolific bed without beholding them in myriads. But, as I soon discovered, my companion was obliged either to place his head very near the ground or to take hold of the leaves with one hand and feel under them with the other to procure the berries, yet his eyes were not myopic. Immediately suspecting that an inability

to distinguish colors was the cause of his difficulty, I commenced a
conversation with him upon the subject of colors in general, without
alluding to my suspicion. I then picked some of the green and some
of the red leaves of the Gaultheria, and with these, the berries, grass,
and other leaves, made a series of comparisons and contrasts, sufficiently apparent to ordinary vision, but they were all alike in color
to my companion. Upon returning to the house, and when in the
presence of his sister, I placed a bright scarlet bandanna handkerchief upon a green table-cover, and asked him the difference of the
two. He asserted most positively that there was no difference, to
the utter astonishment of his sister; for neither he nor any of his
family had ever suspected the defect.

6. U. R.— At the age of twenty-five he first found that he could
not distinguish colors, thinking a bright scarlet tape exactly to correspond with a steel-blue ruler.

7. Mrs. A. — When merino shawls with broad, flowered borders
were in fashion, a merchant in the country purchased a lot which
were soon disposed of, with the exception of one. The border of
this was so pale, dingy, and ugly that it remained on hand a long
time. The merchant had begun to suspect that he should be compelled to place the amount of its cost in the account of profit and
loss, when Mrs. A. appeared as a customer. She was fairly charmed
with the beauty of the border, thought it as handsome as any she
ever saw, and purchased the shawl at its full price.

8. J. W., a man thirty-five years of age. Green, red, and brown
are said to appear alike to him.

9. Mr. A.— A young man in the State of New York.

10. A gentleman in the city of New York.

As will appear from an inspection of the first series of cases, the
inability to distinguish colors prevails in certain families, and appears
to be hereditary. Mr. Harris had two brothers defective like himself,
but the vision of his parents and of two other brothers and sisters
was normal. Scott's father and maternal uncle, one sister, and two
of her sons had the defect; while another sister and his own two sons
were free from it. Tucker's maternal grandfather and a brother of
Dr. Dalton had the same defect. In one of Nicholl's cases the
mother and father and his four sisters were free from it, but his
mother's father had it. This last had two brothers and one sister.
One brother had the defect, the others not. In the other case

several of the family were similarly affected.   Dr. Hays says, "We know of a family in this country similarly circumstanced."* Dr. Elliotson, in his "System of Physiology," remarks that in families in which the peculiarity is hereditary it sometimes overleaps one generation.   This was the fact in one of the cases related by Dr. Nicholl, as well as in that of Robert Tucker.   Another example will be presented hereafter.

In none of the cases hitherto published do we find the peculiarity prevailing to so great an extent (in any family) as it does among my own kindred.   My maternal grandfather and two of his brothers were characterized by it, and among his descendants there are seventeen persons in whom it is found.   I have not extended my observations among the collateral branches of the family, but have heard of one individual in one of them who was similarly affected.

Nothing is known of the first of five generations in regard to color-blindness.   In the second, of a family consisting of seven brothers and eight sisters, three of the brothers, one of whom was my grandfather, had the defect in question.   In the third generation (the children of this grandfather), three brothers and six sisters, there was no trace of the defect.   This forms the instance alluded to above, in which the peculiarity overleaped one generation.   In the fourth generation the first family is composed of five brothers and four sisters, and two brothers have the defect.   In the second there was but one child, a daughter, whose vision was normal.   In the third there are seven brothers, of whom four have the defect; in the fifth, seven sisters and three brothers, in all of whom the vision is perfect in this respect; in the sixth, four brothers and five sisters, of whom two brothers and two sisters have the defect; in the seventh, two brothers and three sisters, both of the former having the defect.   In the eighth there was no issue, and in the ninth there are two sisters, both of them able to appreciate colors. Thus, of twenty-four males and twenty-eight females, a total of fifty-two persons, in the fourth generation the peculiarity is found in thirteen males and two females, fifteen in all, or about three-tenths of the whole number.   Seventeen of the persons in this generation are married, and the whole number of their children is fifty-three. Many of them are very young, some of them not living; and, as the defective perception has been detected in but two of the families,

* American Journal Medical Sciences, vol. xxvi. p. 283.

those alone are placed in the chart as the fifth generation. In one of these families, consisting of three brothers and three sisters, one of the brothers has the defect; and in the other, a male, an only child, is similarly affected.

Of the twenty individuals marked as having the peculiarity, but fifteen are now living, and these so widely scattered that it has been impossible for me to make anything like a series of similar observations in their several cases. I believe, however, I am warranted in saying that in every instance there was an inability to distinguish between red and green,— two colors almost as dissimilar, to ordinary vision, as black and white. Instances of this are mentioned in each of the first two series of cases given above, and I know many anecdotes illustrating the same in the third series.

Several young men, among whom was one who could not distinguish colors, were conversing upon the defect, when the latter was asked if he could tell the color of a neighboring corn-barn. "Oh, that," said he, "is evidently red." The man for once was right, although it is probable that he was aware of the fact that such buildings are never painted green in that section of the country; and he would have come off well, had he not attempted to demonstrate his position even beyond a necessary Q. E. D. "It is evidently red," said he; "but I'll tell you what it resembles: it looks precisely the color of yonder pine-tree." Rich and variegated as are the autumnal forests of America, yet neither native author nor sage and sagacious traveller from the Old World has ever given them credit for a rubicund fir-tree. And, doubtless, the stern and sturdy McGregors, while singing to the honor and blessing of the "evergreen pine," the emblematic "saint" of Clan Alpine, never dreamed of the day in which its verdant hue would be pronounced identical with that of a granary smeared with Spanish brown.

A child ran into the room of his grandmother, where scraps of variously colored paper were lying upon the floor. "Oh," exclaimed he, in childish joy, "here's some *red* paper," and immediately collected all the pieces of *green*. When he became old enough to wield a pencil, he manifested some skill in drawing; but the yellow bears, and the black birds of paradise, and the green men, and the ladies with green cheeks, red eyes, and blue hair, that were brought into existence by his truly original genius, would have astonished Paul Potter, confounded Correggio, and made Titian, Guido, and Raphael

believe they had mistaken their calling. Such specimens of humanity as emanated from his pencil would have ruined the glorious
dream of the youthful Michel Angelo Buonarotti.

Another boy, when picking or attempting to pick some strawberries, asked of his companion the best method of ascertaining if
the berries were ripe, adding that he "always took hold of each
berry, *pinched* it, and, if it were soft, picked it," therefrom supposing
it to be ripe.

A third experienced the same difficulty in picking strawberries,
the berries of the Gaultheria, etc.; and the consequent want of success in his berrying expeditions was the source of much youthful
affliction. In later years he purchased a sleigh which was painted
dark green on the outside and a bright vermilion red within. After
it had been in use several years, some incidental allusion was made
to its colors, when he remarked that he had never suspected that it
was not of the same color throughout.

To many of those who have this anomaly of vision it appears that
red, green, brown, and even drab, appear identical, and look to them
nearly of the same hue as a dingy brown or mud-color does to those
whose perception of coloring is accurate.

A young gentleman of social tastes and habits could never detect
beauty in a lady having one of the most important elements of that
characteristic,— rosy cheeks. The rouge of the toilet and the carna-
tion redolent of ruddy health were, to his warped optics, mere daubs
of muddy brown.

An elderly man who lived in the country was called on by some
neighbors who were "breaking out" the roads after a violent snow-
storm. Being told that an ox had hurt his foot, and was bleeding
profusely, he followed the track where were thousands of bright
scarlet spots on the white snow. Then he told his neighbors they
were mistaken, the spots were nothing but traces of mud, thrown up
from the ground beneath.

One of the persons mentioned in my list of ten (J. W. or J. M.)
was the poet Whittier, to whom I shall again allude. He was visiting an acquaintance of local reputation as an amateur horticulturist,
and upon the centre-table stood a vase of the most choicely selected
dahlias. Among them was one larger and more perfect than the
rest, its color white, but the borders of its petals, like the clouds of
an American sunset, tipped with a gorgeous red,— a magnificent

flower, at the acme of bloom and coloring. Mr. Whittier's attention being called to the bouquet, he looked rather indifferently (for a poet, whose genius seems allied to flowers), thought the dahlias very well,— indeed, some of them were "quite pretty." Then, selecting the flower described, he remarked that it would be "very pretty, but the edges of the petals looked as if it had been frost-bitten or dropped in the mud." He says that, before knowing that his power of perceiving colors was imperfect, he always wondered that people should talk of "glorious sunsets" or "beautiful sunsets"; for he could detect neither beauty nor glory in them. Moreover, that model of perfect beauty, the rainbow, whose delicate tints,

> Shade unperceived, so softening into shade,

delight the ordinary eye, appears to Whittier but different shades of one color, and that a dingy brown. The prismatic arch, in this poet's eye, degenerates into a "Charles's wain" of mud. Yet from his writings no evidence of this peculiarity of vision can be detected. The *poet* throws his gossamer veil of ideality before the vision of the *man*, converting his sombre world into a paradise like that of the Persian.

As not quite alien to our subject, it may be mentioned that Whittier is deficient in another faculty which, at first view, would seem to be necessary to the true poet. Although he has music in his soul, yet he has not "a musical ear." He cannot distinguish one tune or air from another; yet his poetry is not deficient in perfect cadence, harmony, and rhythm. This apparently inconsistent union of high poetical genius with an inability to distinguish color or tune must be considered a most wonderful psychological phenomenon.

Another gentleman of my acquaintance in whom this peculiarity exists is a well-known professor in one of the prominent medical schools of the United States. His poetical talents are such that, had he immolated to them the truths of natural science, he might undoubtedly have gained a reputation no less extensive and no less amply deserved than that of the author just mentioned. In him, also, the inability to appreciate musical sounds is coexistent with that to distinguish colors.

In an extract from a letter of my brother he states that his ear was similarly defective, and it may be asserted of the whole family that they are no less generally characterized by this peculiarity of organization than for color-blindness. In some of the branches, however, where there was a high degree of musical talent inherited *from the other side*, several of the individuals have it ; and among them are two who cannot distinguish colors, yet have a most delicate "musical ear," and are remarkably quick at "catching a tune."

In no work that I have consulted is the alliance or simultaneous existence of these two defects mentioned. Other examples in less distinguished persons occur to me. Defective vision being under discussion at a social party where I was, a young man present selected two figures in the carpet which to him appeared precisely alike. One of them was, in fact, composed of different shades of green, the other of similar shades of brown, or "butternut" color. Another gentleman purchased a piece of red flannel, supposing it to be brown; and that there is identity of resemblance, in some instances, between red, green, and drab, has been shown by the anecdote of the Quaker minister. An elderly man, also a Quaker, accustomed to dress in drab, being in want of a new coat, selected cloth that accorded with his taste, but, when the draper was about to cut it off, found that it was marked "green." Again, having a drab overcoat in the hands of his tailor, he purchased a green lining to match it. A brother of this last-mentioned Friend bought drab cloth for a coat and a red material for lining, supposing them to be the same color.

A man with this defect kept a shop in the country, where a lady one day asked for some "quality" binding. Several pieces were then lying in view on the shelves. His customer was asked which she would have. "The red." "Well, which?" She answered as before, "The red." A third time was his question put, in the hope that some specification other than that of color would be given. The customer, beginning to think herself trifled with, cut him short with, "Why, you fool, the red." The man extricated himself by taking down all the colors (as he ought at first to have done) and allowing her to select.

A boy of fourteen, having to speak of a domestic fowl upon his father's farm, described her as "the yellow hen with a blue tail." In after years, being rallied on this combination of colors, he was somewhat piqued, and declared, with much positiveness, "If the tail was not blue, it was pink." Several of my acquaintance having this peculiarity believe that they have improved by practice. Some main-

tain stoutly that they can perceive colors as accurately as anybody;
and I have known one or two to declare, like some of the insane,
that they are right, and the rest of us wrong.   There is thus a
delicacy (very unphilosophical, to be sure) at having the defect
alluded to; and some are particularly sensitive when brought to
judge of matters of color, lest they expose themselves, like the shop-
. keeper.

The Case of Dr. Earle's Brother.

I have found illustrations of this defect in one of my brothers (it
exists in two).   From notes which I took of his case several years
since, I extract the following: —

Red and green appear alike to him. So do green, brown, and olive;
pink, violet, and pale blue; blue and lilac; and light green and drab.
He perceives but three colors, yellow, orange, and blue, in the rainbow.   The yellow predominates, the blue is very faint.   The orange
and yellow are but different shades of the same color, so that, in
reality, it is but the yellow and blue that he detects in the prismatic
arch.   He can see but little difference between the summer and the
autumnal foliage of the forests.   For many years he has cultivated
with much assiduity the power of detecting colors, and evidently improved therein.   These extracts are from a letter received from him
a few days since: —

" The general appearance of the rainbow to me is that of an object
striped with three colors, gradually blended into each other, and
themselves varying in their shades.   I am unable to say whether,
with a good prism, I could, using care, distinguish and mark the
seven distinct colors produced by it.

" As a general rule, however, it seems true that the difference
between me and others is more a want, on my part, of a quick and
vivid perception of distinctions than an absolute inability to discern
them; for I rarely find two colors which appear different to others, if
placed in juxtaposition, without my being able to perceive that they
differ. Yet the impression upon my mind is so imperfect that, on
seeing them again, at least in some cases, I might be unable to give
their respective names correctly.   In some few instances, where
colors are really different, perhaps I might not discern that difference
if they were placed side by side. This would be where the ground
color of both was the same, but one of them slightly tinged with red,

such as pale blue and lilac of about equal depth of color, or deep blue and violet.

"I can always distinguish correctly a full blue, a scarlet, or a yellow, and generally orange also, if near my eyes and examined with care. *I can discern yellow and blue of moderate depth at a great distance. But at any considerable distance I might not know whether a red was really a red or a deep green, brown, or olive.* I cannot, in general, know whether some olive cloths are really olive or brown; but there are some browns that I can be sure of as being of that color.

"I cannot see red apples or red cherries or red strawberries at any considerable distance, so as to distinguish them from the foliage; or, *where I do distinguish them, it is not so clearly as I see the green ones.* Red, I think, appears brighter and plainer to me by candlelight than in the day. So does blue, but yellow more faint than by daylight. I sometimes have mistaken a light green for a drab. The red which has some mixture of yellow is more vivid to my eyes: that which is crimson, or nearly so, resembles blue to some degree. Of the three principal colors, yellow is most distinct. All colors are agreeable to me, though I suspect red is less so than to people in general. Those red flowers which have a tinge either of yellow or blue are, I think, more pleasing than those which are of a pure red.

"In the vast variety of compound colors, where there is a slight predominance of the blue over the red, but the degree of illumination equal, I am, in general, unable to tell whether the blue or red tinge predominates, and, of course, am liable to miscall the names. I find, however, that my perception of shades has improved by practice, as it has of musical notes, in which I was deficient; and I am disposed to think that, with application, I might perfect myself so as to be rarely mistaken."

That he has improved to some extent I have not the least doubt; but the perfection which he believes attainable is, probably, altogether Utopian. Some years since, at a time when he was more positive than at present (for years have, as usual, tempered assurance in doubtful matters of philosophy) that he had learned to distinguish colors, he was conversing upon the subject in company, and asserted his belief that he could discriminate between red and green. At that moment a child with *green* morocco shoes entered the room. "If that be true," said one of the guests, "pray tell us the color of that child's shoes." "Pooh!" said he: "those are evidently *red.*"

A case similar to the last is this: Two young men, both unable to distinguish colors, were requested, by the sister of one of them, to purchase a skein of green sewing-silk; and, fearing that they might forget or mistake the color, she directed their attention to the morocco facing of the cushions to their gig as being precisely the shade she wanted. On their way to the city the question of the color of the silk became the subject of serious and deliberate debate; and it was decided that the sister had been greatly mistaken in saying that the morocco of the cushion was green. Once in the city, they went — mutual mentors — "a-shopping." One of them asked for some "green sewing-silk," hoping that a package of that color alone would be handed down. Alas for the pleasures of hope! A large package, flaunting as many colors as the coat of Joseph, was displayed upon the counter. The customers, unwilling to expose their defect, were in a quandary. At this critical juncture some blessed incident directed the attention of the clerk another way. One of them "took time by the forelock," seized a skein which he supposed to be green, and stuffed it, unwrapped and "all in a muss," into his pocket. When the clerk returned, "I have taken a skein," said the young man: "what is the price?" "Was it a *large* skein or a *small* one?" inquired the clerk. The young man began to think that the silk was no Ariadne's thread, since it involved him more deeply in difficulties instead of showing him the way out. Determined not to withdraw it from his pocket, since, for all he knew, it might be red, brown, drab, or almost any color, he quietly answered "A large one," and paid the increased price accordingly. Fortunately, when they returned, the silk proved to be green.

These cases are mostly given without the true names. I may add, however, that my grandfather, William Buffum, of Smithfield, R.I., had this defect, and that the father of my uncle Thomas Buffum's wife could not distinguish colors, so that both grandfathers of my cousins Horace, Peleg, John, etc., Buffum, were in this predicament. In June, 1846, while Dr. D. T. Brown, of the Utica Asylum for the Insane, and Dr. Rufus Woodward, of the Worcester Hospital, were with me in the garden of the Bloomingdale Asylum, picking strawberries, I detected this defect in Dr. Brown. Melatiah Green, a brother of Dr. John Green, of Worcester, cannot well distinguish colors. The cases of my own brothers and of Dr. Elisha Bartlett, a professor in Dartmouth College, have been cited above.

Causes of Color-blindness.

The question may now be asked, What is the cause of this defect in the discrimination of color? I might answer, in the words of the moral poet : —

> Presumptuous man! the reason wouldst thou find
> Why formed so weak, so little, and so blind?
> First, if thou canst, the harder reason guess,
> Why formed no weaker, blinder, and no less.

There are those who maintain that there is no standard for the perception of colors, no criterion by which, in comparing the powers of one individual with those of another, we may say one is right and another wrong. "There is among mankind," say they, "as great a diversity of perception in regard to colors as there is of mental capacity. Furthermore, we have no evidence that, in any two individuals whose vision is called perfect, the impression of any color is identical : that which is green to the 'mind's eye' of one may be red to that of another, and so of any two colors."

Strictly speaking, the position here advanced is true. No person can describe the impressions received by the mind through the organs of vision : no one can "give color to an idea." The questions involved can never be positively determined in the present state of human knowledge and with our present means of observation and investigation. They are beyond the reach of an *experimentum crucis*. No true philosopher, however, would resort to an argument of this kind. It is specious, but unsound ; and he who would admit it must inevitably become involved in a difficulty with reference to every department of philosophy, from which he could hardly extricate himself without adopting the alleged doctrine of Bishop Berkeley, that "all matter is but ideal."

Certain rays of light, impinging upon the retina, produce an effect which, transmitted to the sensorium (whether modified or not we cannot tell in its passage through the optic nerve), give an impression or perception of color which the mass of mankind are consentaneous in calling *red*. As the anatomical structure and the functions concerned in this process are, if normal, identical in different individuals, it is rational to infer that the results will be similar, to say nothing of the many other arguments in favor of their being so.

The several theories which have been promulgated as explanatory of the phenomenon in question may be divided into two classes: —

1. Those which place the cause of the defect in the apparatus of vision.

2. Those which suppose it to be in the organ of perception.

1. (*a*) Dr. Dalton, in attempting to account for the defect as existing in himself, suggests that the vitreous humor of the eye is tinged with blue and absorbs all the rays of red light. But, as was accurately remarked by Dr. Hays, "this is a mere conjecture, which is not confirmed by the most minute examination of the eye, and does not even explain all the phenomena."

(*b*) Dr. Young attributes the defect to a want or a paralysis of those fibres of the retina whose office is the perception of red light. The basis of this theory is the mere hypothesis of an anatomical defect or a pathological condition of which there is no proof; and, as is also observed by Dr. Hays, it "does not embrace all the degrees of the defect."

(*c*) Sir David Brewster first endeavored to explain the phenomenon by supposing that the eye is insensible to the rays of light at one (the most refracted) extreme of the spectrum, analogous to the ear, which in some persons, as demonstrated by Dr. Wollaston, is not affected by the notes at one extremity of the musical scale. This theory would account for but a small part of the phenomena observed in these cases. He subsequently promulgated another, less satisfactory in our apprehension, than the foregoing, inasmuch as (so far as I can comprehend it) it leaves off where it begins, making the *reason* of the inability to distinguish colors the "blindness to red light."

(*d*) Mr. Wardrop supposes the defect to arise from a greater susceptibility of the retina to the influence of the blue and yellow rays, not so much, it would seem, from an abnormal condition of the retina itself as from the refractive power of the humors by which these rays are brought to a focus more perfectly than the others upon this nervous tissue.

(*e*) M. Boys de Loury believes the defect a consequence of an abnormal structure of the retina or the optic nerve, placing those organs in a condition similar to atrophy.

Of all the foregoing theories, there is no one to which it may not be objected either that it is merely hypothetical and entirely unsupported by proofs or that it does not include all varieties of the defect. Hence none is at all satisfactory. We now proceed to those of the second class.

2 (a). "I am inclined to suspect," says Dugald Stewart, in the third chapter of his "Elements of the Philosophy of the Human Mind," "that the greater number of the instances of the supposed defects of sight ought to be rather ascribed to a defect in the power of conception, probably in consequence of some early habit of inattention."

(In the foregoing letter from my brother a similar idea is advanced.)

(b). "We have examined with some attention," says Sir John W. F. Herschel, "a very eminent optician, whose eyes (or rather eye, he having lost the sight of one by accident) have this peculiarity, and have satisfied ourselves, contrary to received opinion, that all the prismatic rays have the power of exciting and affecting them with the sensation of light, and producing distinct vision, so that the defect arises from no insensibility of the retina to rays of any particular refrangibility nor to any coloring matter in the humors of the eye, preventing certain rays from reaching the retina (as has been ingeniously supposed), but from a defect in the sensorium, by which it is rendered incapable of appreciating exactly those differences between rays on which their color depends." Dr. Dunglison, espousing the same doctrine, says, in his "Human Physiology," "The nerve of sight is probably accurately impressed; and the deficiency is in the part of the brain whither the impression is conveyed, and where perception is effected."

(c). Dr. Elliotson, a zealous disciple in phrenology of Drs. Gall and Spurzheim, says: "In all the cases in which the point has been examined, the part of the cranium under which, according to Gall, the organ for judging of the harmony of colors is placed, is flat or depressed. I have seen several of these cases, and in all this was the fact." Dr. Hays remarks that the case of Mary Bishop favors the phrenological theory, "her affection having been the sequel to an attack of cerebral disease."

(d). In the *Annales Médico-psychologiques* for January, 1844, there is an article which says: "M. Chevreuil has shown that there is a harmony and a system of laws in colors as well as in sounds; that there are false colors, as there are false notes, which shock delicate natures, and colors which, like certain notes, cannot accompany each other without profoundly wounding. It is not necessary, then, to regard the incapacity for distinguishing colors as the constant result of an alteration of the retina or the optic nerve, but as being often the effect of a predisposition, natural or acquired."

The four theories placed in the second class are but modifications of that of the phrenologists. However, there is sufficient difference between them to justify placing them separately. Thus Dr. Elliotson believes the defect to arise from an insufficient development of the "organ of color," while the theory last mentioned attributes it to the peculiar combination of colors.

In the interesting report of the case of Mary Bishop, already mentioned, Dr. Isaac Hays, after an examination of all the detailed cases upon record, arrives at the following conclusions: —

" 1. As a natural defect, inability to distinguish colors may exist in different degrees.

" 2. In the worst degree the individual is able merely to distinguish shades: the perception of color is entirely absent.

" 3. In the next degree the individual can distinguish only a single color, and that color is always yellow.

" 4. We may consider as the next degree of this defect where the individual can recognize two colors only, and these seem to be always *yellow* and *blue*. This is the most common grade of the defect.

" 5. It seems probable that individuals who are able to recognize *accurately* the three primitive colors can also distinguish the secondary ones. But persons whose perception of red is imperfect do not accurately discriminate the secondary colors."

When Mary Bishop was recovering her power of appreciating colors, she could first distinguish yellow alone, like those under the second degree above mentioned. She soon afterwards became able to perceive blue also, which advanced her to the third degree. While in the latter condition, like those who are naturally affected to the same degree, although she could accurately discriminate yellow and blue, she could not detect green, which is a mixture of the two.

My observation thus far has revealed nothing that would lead me to doubt the accuracy of these deductions by Dr. Hays. All the cases which I have now for the first time published might be arranged under the foregoing heads, most of them under the fourth. It may be proper to mention in this connection that, in one young man whose case I have given, the power of discriminating colors appears to be very variable. At times it would seem as if the functions of the "organ of color "— to use a phrase which presupposes the truth of an undemonstrated theory — were performed with nearly as great a degree of accuracy as in those who can make the most delicate chromatic distinctions, while at others he makes the most absurd mistakes. It was he who first discovered that *sui generis* specimen in American ornithology (mentioned by neither Wilson, Bonaparte, nor Audubon), the "yellow hen with a blue tail." It is evident that the colors which he usually confounds appear to him by candle-light much more nearly as they do to other people than by daylight, which is equally true in some of my other cases. The explanation of this may probably be found in the fact that our artificial light is much more yellow than that of the sun, and gives to the colors usually unrecognized a certain degree of its own hue, which is perceived by all who have the defect excepting those who come under the "worst degree" of Dr. Hays. Dr. Elliotson remarks that the defect in regard to color is found more frequently among men than women. This is supported by the cases coming within my personal knowledge. They are 31 in number, of which 28, or seven-eighths of all, are of men. In the family of Buffum, represented genealogically, there are 20 persons in whom the defect has existed ; and, of these, 18, or nine-tenths, are men. And this disparity becomes greater if the proportion of each sex having the defect or free from it is considered.

The defect is said to have been observed in both myopic and far-seeing eyes, as well as in those with the focal point at the ordinary distance, but I recall no near-sighted person among those of my acquaintance who have it.

V. Popular Fallacies in regard to Insanity.
(Written in 1885.)

Although it is impossible to demonstrate it as a fact, yet all the known data bearing upon the subject very clearly lead to the inference that insanity in the United States is increasing, not merely absolutely, in correspondence with the increase of population, but relatively, as compared with the number of inhabitants. Fifty years ago the writers upon the subject placed the ratio of the insane to

the whole population in Massachusetts at 1 in 1,000. In the last
national census it is shown that in 1880 there was 1 insane person
in each 343 of the population of the State. Had the ratio of fifty
years ago been derived from a census as carefully taken as that of
1880, it might be assumed as a demonstrated proposition that insanity had increased nearly threefold within the last half-century. But
that first-mentioned ratio was a mere estimate, based upon very imperfect, insufficient, and, doubtless, often indefinite or inaccurate
data, and hence unworthy of reliance as a truthful standard for comparison.

But under existing circumstances even the present number of
the insane in the Commonwealth do not constitute a class sufficiently large to enable the people to become acquainted with their
characters, peculiarities, habits, and propensities, both mental and
physical, as compared or contrasted with those of that portion of the
inhabitants who, by common consent, are regarded as sane. Nearly
three-fourths of them are in hospitals, and a large part of the remaining fourth in almshouses and other places of detention or surveillance, where they are withdrawn from general observation.
Hence the present generation is probably less acquainted with their
characteristics than were the people of seventy-five years ago, before
the special institutions for their care had been called into existence,
and when they were allowed, to a much larger extent than at present,
to associate or to mingle with the general population. As a necessary
consequence of this state of things, the public mind is incapable of
so far comprehending the nature of mental disorder as to be able to
discriminate between the probable and the improbable in relation to
the conduct and the language of the insane or even the physical
peculiarities which have sometimes been attributed to them. The
disorder,— not to say "disease," inasmuch as disease implies the
possibility of death,— in its essential nature, and even in its relation
to the conduct and the practical ability of those who are afflicted
with it, is an ever-abundant and an inexplicable mystery to persons who are constantly surrounded by it, and who are consequently
better informed than any others in regard to it. How much more
so must it be to those who have had little or no opportunity to
become acquainted, by personal observation, with its manifestations! Still clinging to the traditional idea of a madhouse, which,
as far back as the time of Hogarth and probably very much farther,

was derived from that class of patients who were the most insane and the most demonstrative in both language and eccentricity or violence of conduct, they couple with it the mistaken though perhaps logical notion that all the insane are so distorted in mind and perverted in body that they constitute a class of beings almost as widely separated from the average of mankind as if they did not belong to the same genus or race. With what facility, then, may errors in regard to them find a place in the public mind! Having little or no positive knowledge of them, fancy, imagination, and the love of the marvellous are left free to supply the place of such knowledge.

I have been led into this train of reflection by the perusal of some memoranda of popular errors entered in a commonplace book upon my office table, to which I shall give here a passing notice. It is not proposed to enter at large upon the subject, to point out all the contrasts between the popular impressions in regard to the insane and those opinions which are the results of long intercourse with them. Such a course would involve too much time and space. A glance at a few of the most prominent alone can here be permitted.

Perhaps no one point in the general belief in regard to the inmates of the institutions for the insane is more widely prevalent than that they are unhappy, wretched, miserable. In reference to a very few and wholly exceptional cases, this is, to a certain extent, true. But farther than that it is untrue. And the same may be said of any class or collection of human beings, wherever situated and in what mental condition soever they may be. It has been my lot to be connected with each of five such institutions sufficiently long to become acquainted with its patients; and, judging from the experience thus obtained, and writing not thoughtlessly nor hastily, but with all due deliberation, it is my opinion that, if a lasso were thrown around the first four hundred and seventy-six adults who might be met at any time upon the sidewalks of Northampton or any other city, the amount of unhappiness drawn together in its coil would be as great as exists among the four hundred and seventy-six patients to-day, or the same number any other day, within the walls of this Northampton Hospital. I do not forget, but am most free to acknowledge, that the worst wards of a hospital of this kind present a sad spectacle, even to persons familiarized with it, — a very sad spectacle to any one to whom it is an unaccustomed sight. But this aspect is the consequence of mental impairment and bodily deterioration, and is no evidence of unhappiness on the part of the patients. The observer derives his judgment from his own feelings and emotions, not from the mental and moral condition of the persons around him, which, particularly if he be a casual visitor, he cannot accurately know. It is, indeed, true that among the inmates of a hospital one may hear more expressions indicative of unhappiness than among the same number of sane persons. The latter are like boilers in which the steam is repressed, subjected to control, and generally used only as dictated by prudence and good judgment; while the former, like the open, boiling pot, permit the generated steam to rise directly to the surface, in bubbles, and immediately pass away. There is a basis of truth for the old saying that the only difference between a sane and an insane man is that the latter speaks what he thinks, while the former does not. It is the same, let it be remembered, in regard to feeling and emotion. The insane permit them, untrammelled, at once to appear in expression: the sane reduce them to restraint and condemn them to concealment, either temporary or perpetual.

Among the classes of the insane of which the subjects most painfully and depressingly impress the inexperienced observer are the melancholiacs, some of whom are continually uttering expressions of self-condemnation for acts or "sins" of either commission or of omission, and not infrequently of both. In language, in tone of speech, in facial expression, and in general appearance, they sometimes seem to embody all that goes to make up the sum of the extreme of human mental wretchedness and suffering. And yet, with a no inconsiderable part of these, all this outside show of misery is simply habit, to which anything like real feeling is an utter stranger. No person could long survive the reality of their apparently intense suffering. But their health is not impaired by it. There are some who even thrive upon it. At meals they will stop their moanings and complaints, and pay as ample a compliment as any one to palatable food. At night they will retire, and sleep as sound as the healthy but wearied laborer until morning. But, when the meal is finished and the morning comes, they rise only to return to their habitual utterances of apparent woe. I repeat that all this external show of sorrow is, in many instances, nothing more nor less than a morbid habit, which has become essentially automatic, and is no more the indication of actual and profound affliction than the word "eschec," uttered through a mechanical contrivance by Maelzel's celebrated chess-player, was the indication and evidence of an adequate intellectual comprehension, by that automaton, of the signification of what it uttered. It is from cases like these that the general character of the insane is too often judged.

It is a frequent remark that to an insane person his delusions are realities. This is undeniably true, so far as his mental impression of the subject, or object, of that delusion, and his belief in it, are concerned. But the effect of that delusion upon the conduct and the physical condition of him who has it is often far from being identical with that which must necessarily be produced, could that subjective delusion become an objective reality. The delusion, as a delusion, is a reality; but it has not the force of a substantive or absolute reality. No proposition in Euclid is more positively demonstrated than is this, by the cases just mentioned. The same holds good with another class, one of which is the subject of the following sketch.

A female now in the hospital* often tells visitors that she has millions and billions of children "up in the canopy," — an imaginary apartment of the house,— and that persons are constantly engaged in murdering them. This is with her a "fixed idea," a permanent delusion. It had possession of her at the time of her admission in 1858, and probably some years before, as she was brought from another hospital. Yet this woman is always quiet and gentle, makes no outward show of grief or unhappiness, and never attempts to force or find her way into the presence of her imaginary children. She is a perfect pattern of industry, and has good judgment in her work. For twenty-seven years she has been the best ironer of starched linen in the laundry, and until recently has worked more hours in the year than any other person in the house. It is needless for me to attempt to depict the immediate effect, or the more remote consequences, upon any *sane* mother who had positive knowledge that her children were being murdered.

Even raving and destructive maniacs, how much soever their condition is to be deplored, are not in themselves generally unhappy, but, on the contrary, in many cases happier than in their normal condition. Their very violence is the reflex of a mental exaltation

---

* From 1885 to 1896 resident in a private family, being one of the first of those boarded out in Massachusetts.

very similar to, if not identical with, that which is produced by in-
toxicating drinks, opium, and other narcotic drugs, and the nitrous
oxide, or "laughing gas." *   I was once very forcibly impressed by
a remark of a patient who for many years was subject to paroxysms
of the most violent mania, with intervals, sometimes long, of apparently perfect mental health.   He had just come out of one of these
paroxysms when I congratulated him upon his restoration.   So far
from sympathizing with me in gladness, he looked up, with a very sad
expression of countenance, as he replied, "Ah, doctor, *that* is the
happiest part of my life."

The insane themselves have no special relish for the idea that they
are regarded as unhappy or "miserable."   As a rule, they repel it.
When in charge of the Bloomingdale Asylum in New York, I one
day accompanied two ladies through some of the wards in the
department for females.   One of them met each patient with a cheerful smile, had a pleasant or agreeable remark for each, and, in short,
carried herself throughout as if she were unconscious that she was
not among the guests at a hotel.   The other folded her arms, drew
down the corners of her mouth, assumed the measured step of a
procession, and walked straight forward, looking alternately to the
right and to the left as she passed the patients, speaking to no one,
but uttering, at intervals as formal and measured as her step, the expressive comment "P-o-o-r t-h-i-n-g-s! p-o-o-r t-h-i-n-g-s!" with the
solemn tone and continuity of the tolling of a funeral bell.   She was
little aware that most of the patients were as able as ever to recognize and appreciate her peculiar manner; and doubtless she would
have been not only greatly surprised, but annoyed and mortified,
could she have heard their comments and criticisms after she left.

In conversation with a gentleman who called at the Northampton
Hospital, and who not infrequently had occasion to travel in some
of the Western States, he informed me that upon one of his journeys
he heard that no bald person becomes insane; and, as an illustrative
proof of the fact, his informant asserted that in neither of the
hospitals for the insane in Michigan was there a bald man or
woman to be found among the patients.   In reply the gentleman
was told that, howsoever it might be in the Peninsula State, it was

---

* Some forty years ago a Parisian physician (J. Moreau) published a book, the object of which
was to demonstrate the absolute identity of the mental condition in insanity and in dreams with the
delirium produced by narcotics and that which precedes death caused by heat, by cold, and by deprivation of food.

very doubtful that the rule was one of universal or of general application. We would see if it was sustained by the testimony of the Northampton Hospital. We went through the wards, and took a census of twenty-seven patients who were largely bald, to say nothing of a considerable number who had made a beginning in that direction, one who wore a wig, and one who had only a slight fringe of hair, something like a lady's narrow, standing, quilled ruff, so situated that it might require a zoölogist or a barber to decide whether it belonged to the head or to the back of the neck. If Michigan wants some specimens of baldness, say forty or fifty, merely for the sake of novelty, Massachusetts will be happy to accommodate her.

It was reported about forty years ago that blind persons are never subject to attacks of insanity. Although then in possession of sufficient evidence of untruthfulness in the assertion, yet, as it was a point of some interest, I made it a subject of inquiry at a considerable number of German institutions which I soon afterwards had occasion to visit. Several of them either then had or previously had patients who had lost their sight. In some instances it was lost before the invasion of the mental disorder, in others afterwards. Five blind persons, three of whom were men and two women, have been inmates of this hospital within the last twenty years. As at the German institutions, in some of the cases, the blindness preceded the insanity, and in others followed it. It is not impossible that we may hereafter hear that deaf-mutes are exempt from the affliction of mental alienation. In order to forestall any public declaration to that effect, it may not be amiss to state that two members of that defective class are inmates of this institution at the present time, 1885.

Within the last two or three years a paragraph has gone the rounds of the newspapers, assuring the public that the insane never shed tears until after the commencement of convalescence, and that weeping is a sure prognostic of recovery. I had never before either seen or heard of a suggestion of the kind, and it is certainly contrary to the results of my observation. There are certain classes of the insane, and among them those whose mental disorder or impairment is a consequence of paralysis, in whom the emotional nature is unnaturally sensitive. Some of these shed tears upon the most trivial occasions. Hence it is to be apprehended that the paragraph was written by some one who was not well informed upon the subject or who was willing to add one more fold to the veil of mystery through· which the subject of insanity is generally regarded.

In an interview not long ago with an intelligent gentleman from one of the most populous cities of the Union the conversation turned upon an institution for the insane within or near the limit of that city. After commending it for its excellence, the gentleman spoke of the well-merited popularity of its superintendent, and proceeded to relate the following anecdote as a proof of his remarkable shrewdness, presence of mind, and readiness of expedient in the management of the insane: "'The superintendent," said he, "had occasion to go to the summit of a tower in company with one of his patients. While admiring the extensive and beautiful prospect spread before them, the patient, with much excitement, suddenly seized the superintendent by the arm, and pressed him towards the edge of the tower, exclaiming, 'Let's jump down, and thus immortalize ourselves!' The superintendent very coolly arrested the patient's attention, and replied: 'Jump down! Why, any fool can do that. Let's go down and jump up!' The proposition struck the fancy of the patient, and thus the two were saved from their impending peril."

My informant did not say whether they did jump or not, but left me upon that point wholly in the dark; and, lest his satisfaction should be marred, I refrained from telling him that the story, in its essentials, is much older than the superintendent whom he had made the hero of it; that it was current, to my certain knowledge, not less than sixty years ago, and then had the flavor of antiquity; that it undoubtedly is an old emigrant from England, and that, had it life and the power of speech, it might not unreasonably claim to have come over in the "Mayflower."

It is barely possible, but quite improbable, that the story had its origin in some actual occurrence of the kind. While superintendents are not habitually accustomed to take their excited or excitable patients to the dangerous height of towers, yet some one might have taken an unexcitable one to such a place; and, as many a sane person on the brink of a precipice has felt an impulse to leap from it, and as there is reason for the belief that even the calmest and least excitable insane man would be somewhat more liable to that impulse than one who is not insane, it is not beyond the limits of possibility that the tale is not wholly fictitious. It has a little, though not much, greater claim upon the credulity of mankind than that other antique specimen of the history of gymnastics,—the tale of "the cow that jumped over the moon."

Whether the writer of the following account expected or intended it to be believed or not, there is no possible means of deciding; but it is nevertheless very certain that it has been published as truth:—

"A gentleman accompanying a party to inspect an asylum chanced to be left behind in the kitchen, with a number of the inmates who acted as cooks and scullions to the establishment. There was a huge caldron of boiling water on the fire, into which the madmen declared they must put him in order to boil him for broth. They would fain have assisted him into the large pot; and, as they were laying hold of him, he reflected that in a personal struggle he would have no chance with them. All he could do was to gain time. So he said: 'Very well, gentlemen. I am sure I should make good broth if you do not spoil it by boiling my clothes with it.' 'Take off your clothes!' they cried out. And he began to take off his clothes very slowly, crying out loudly the while: 'Now, gentlemen, my coat is off. I shall soon be stripped. There goes my waistcoat. I shall soon be ready,' and so on, till nothing remained but his shirt. Fortunately, the keeper, attracted by his loud speaking, hurried in just in time to save him."

To a person familiar with the inner life of an institution for the insane, this morsel of pretended history is so permeated and invested by improbabilities that the idea of its truthfulness appears to be not only perfectly absurd, but supremely ridiculous. The insane are not cannibals, even to the extent of the quality of their broth; and the medical officers of a hospital are to be credited with at least a sufficient knowledge of their patients to know, so far as can be known, whom among them can be safely trusted in performance of the work of the kitchen. They would be very unlikely to send to that work even one patient whose disease might instigate him to criminal acts, and much less a whole group of them; and if by possibility one should be sent, and should attempt any outrage or violent act, all the others would lend their assistance in opposing and securing him.

The insane form no cabals, no extensive conspiracies. They have no confidence one in another. One patient of vigorous native intellect and a strong will may indeed make a dupe, a tool, or a cat's-paw of another who is less liberally endowed by nature. This is sometimes done within the walls of an asylum for the insane, as it not infrequently is in the outside world; but the concerted action for evil, of several patients, is a thing comparatively, if not absolutely, unknown. Practical jokes are likewise sometimes perpetrated by inmates of the institution mentioned; and it is far less difficult to believe the story on the supposition that this was one of them than upon any other hypothesis whatsoever. At one of the largest of American hospitals it was formerly customary on certain days in the week to show visitors through the two or three halls for either sex. Among the patients in one of the halls for females there was a lady of brilliant intellect and large attainments, the wife of a man of wealth and eminence. She was a shrewd and acute observer, had learned much of human nature, and liked a little fun withal. She knew, or thought she knew, that, of every fifty visitors who passed through the hall, not less than forty-nine were stimulated thereto by motives no higher than those which actuate the man who goes to the menagerie to "see the lion dance" or who attends the circus to witness the antics of the clown. She thought it a pity that their curiosity should not be measurably gratified, and so she established a series of entertainments for their special benefit and her own particular enjoyment. Upon the entrance of a group of visitors she would go through a medley of eccentric and grotesque dancing, gesticulation, and speech, and wind up by sidling up to one of the company, begging a cent, and folding, with both hands, the front part of the skirt of her dress into a temporary pocket or contribution-box for its reception. The visitors were highly gratified. Their visit had not been made in vain. They doubtless went away with a memory for a lifetime, little dreaming how completely — to use a common but expressive term — they had been "sold."

From what has here been written, it may correctly be inferred that writers who, with only that extent of information upon the subject which generally prevails, attempt to delineate the peculiarities of the insane, either by description or by the language and conduct of fictitious characters, as surely betray their ignorance as they would if writing upon any other subject without sufficient knowledge. They run more or less into the extremes of extravagance, exaggeration, and caricature. Engaged upon a somewhat mysterious subject, which may easily be treated sensationally, they appear to think that, to be truthful, they must be sensational. Doubtless, they are sometimes purposely so, with the intent of producing an effect by appealing to the love of the marvellous in their readers.

The reporter of a newspaper once visited the Northampton Hospital, went through the departments for patients, and was furnished with all requested information in relation to the institution. Not many days afterwards he published a long account of his visit in the journal with which he was connected. In his description of the place he was very accurate ; but, when he came to the indications, characteristics, and manifestations of insanity, even as he was supposed to have seen them, he was evidently in water of unaccustomed depth, and floundered to such an extent that some of the patients themselves detected his awkwardness. A bright, well-educated, intelligent, and intellectually acute patient in the female department read the article, and was greatly incensed at its incongruities and inaccuracies. It gave her the text for a discourse the like of which the reporter had never heard, in college or in public hall of any kind. It partook, perhaps, of the qualities of a sermon, a lecture, and a justice's charge; but, by a usurpation of the province of a jury, it was brought to a close with the energetic announcement of the verdict : "The little puppy ! He ought to be horsewhipped."

Nor are even the responsible writers for the public journals always unwilling to cater to the popular idea of insanity and the insane. Within the last twenty years the editor of one of the newspapers of Western Massachusetts published an elaborate and detailed article in relation to this hospital, drawn largely from his personal observation. In this case, as in that of the reporter, the descriptive part was scrupulously truthful ; and the same may be said of its narrative. But, as if this wholesome dish might not prove sufficiently palatable to the partakers of his intellectual feast, he must needs throw in the spice of a paragraph of highly wrought untruth. Of five other Massachusetts newspapers which at that time regularly came to the office of the superintendent, no less than three quoted from our editor's article. Every one of them extracted the whole of the untruthful paragraph. Not one of them took even a line or a fact from that which was true.

VI. The Curability of Insanity (Dr. Earle's Last Paper.)

From Dr. D. H. Tuke's Dictionary of Psychological Medicine.

The endeavor to ascertain even the approximate curability of insanity is accompanied by difficulties; and the investigator is soon thrown upon the results of its treatment at the special institutions, as his chief resource in the search for truth. Nor are the difficulties wholly overcome by the adoption of these results. In very many cases, through the affection or the prejudices of friends or from other causes, the patient is not removed to a hospital until the prospect of recovery is either wholly or partially lost; and for reasons of a similar nature he is but too frequently removed therefrom without a sufficient test of his curability.

Another obstacle to the discovery and definite expression of the actual susceptibility of cure of the disease is found in the temperaments of the physicians by whom they are treated. There being no test for insanity, there can be no general standard equally perceptible by, and equally forcible to, the minds of all men. As a necessary consequence, each physician adopts a standard of his own, and counts his recoveries accordingly.

American hospitals furnish two remarkable instances of the effect of this "personal equation." At the Worcester (Mass.) Hospital, during the last three official years of the administration of Dr. Bemis, the reported recoveries were 43.32 per cent. of the admissions; and during the first three entire years of his successor, Dr. Eastman, they were only 22.16 per cent. of the admissions. At the McLean Asylum, during the last seven years of the superintendence of Dr. Tyler, the reported recoveries were 44.19 per cent. of the admissions: whereas, during the first seven years of his successor, Dr. Jelly, they were only 19.94 per cent. The proportion of Dr. Tyler's recoveries was to those of Dr. Jelly as 221 to 100. In neither of these instances was there any known agency which tended to render insanity less curable in the second period than in the first.

The failure, formerly, in the reports of the lunatic hospitals, clearly to discriminate between person and patients (or cases) was the source of no inconsiderable error in the minds of the readers of those reports. In cases of paroxysmal or recurrent insanity, a person is frequently both admitted to, and discharged recovered from, a hospital more than once in the course of an official year. In the numerical report of these recoveries there is no intimation that the number of persons is not equal to that of recoveries. At the Bloomingdale Asylum, New York, a woman was discharged recovered six times, and one at the Worcester Hospital seven times in one year; and in neither instance was the reader informed that the number of persons was not identical with that of cases recovered. Recoveries were also multiplied by the reported cures of the same person in more than one year. Thus the woman who, at Worcester, made seven recoveries in one year, had been discharged recovered nine times within the next two preceding years, making sixteen recoveries in the three years; and the woman who, at Bloomingdale, recovered six times in one year, was reported recovered forty-six times in the course of her life, and finally died, a raving maniac, in the asylum.

At five American asylums forty persons were reported recovered four hundred and eighty-four times, or a fraction more than ten recoveries for each person. The records of American hospitals contain the medical history of three women who were admitted as patients an aggregate of one hundred and eighteen times, and were discharged recovered one hundred and two times; and yet two of them died insane, and the third, when last heard from, had found a home, apparently for life, in an almshouse.

By new statistical tables, adopted in Massachusetts in 1879, and by the British Medico-Psychological Society in 1881, the true number of persons, as well as of cases, recovered is shown in each annual report. Hitherto no American State, other than Massachusetts, has adopted those tables.

.- The admission, at a large proportion of the institutions, of cases of not only delirium tremens and the opium habit, but alcoholism, and even *mere habitual inebriety*, and, upon their discharge, reporting them as recovered, vitiates the statistics of those institutions to an important extent, giving an apparent but fictitious curability to insanity. The published statistics of the disease include thousands of "recoveries" of this kind.

A few facts from medical history will show the method by which the popular mind, particularly in America, heretofore, received the impression that insanity is largely curable.

In the year 1820 Dr. George Man Burrows, of London, published his "Inquiry into Certain Errors relative to Insanity," in which he stated that, of all the cases (296) treated by him, the proportion of recoveries was 81 in 100; of recent cases, 91 in 100; of old cases, 35 in 100. The appendix to the "Inquiry" contained the statistics of the "Retreat" at York from 1796 to 1819. The ratio of recoveries of all those cases which were of less than three months' duration was 85.1 per cent.

The report for 1827 of the Retreat at Hartford, Conn., says: "During the last year there have been admitted twenty-three recent cases, of which twenty-one recovered, a number equivalent to 91.3 per cent."

In January, 1833, Massachusetts opened her first State Hospital, at Worcester, under the charge of Dr. Samuel B. Woodward, who was one of the original directors of the Hartford Retreat. In his second annual report, which was for the official year 1833–34, he states that the recoveries during that year were 82.25 per cent. of all the recent cases discharged. He classed as recent cases all whose origin was within one year prior to admission, and this method was followed generally at the American hospitals. So, also, was the practice of calculating the recoveries upon the number of patients discharged.

When the Worcester Hospital was opened, there were but eight other institutions in the United States specially devoted to the care of the insane; but within the ten succeeding years no less than twelve new institutions were added to their number. With the reported success of Dr. Woodward, and the other high ratios of recovery (already mentioned) before them, a generous rivalry to show the largest percentage of cures was soon manifested among the medical superintendents. For the official year 1840–41 Dr. Woodward reported 90 per cent. of recoveries of recent cases discharged, and in the next following year 91.42 per cent. In 1842, Dr. Galt, of the Williamsburg (Virginia) Asylum, claimed the recovery of twelve out of thirteen recent cases. This was a percentage of 92.3. One of the thirteen died, and of this the doctor very naïvely says, "If we deduct this case from those under treatment, the recoveries amount to 100 per cent." At length, in his report for 1843, Dr. Awl, of the Columbus (Ohio) Asylum, stated that the percentage of recoveries of recent cases discharged in that year was 100. This was the *ne plus ultra*. The same year Dr. Luther V. Bell, of the

McLean Asylum, in reviewing all his cases — "somewhat exceeding a thousand" — to that time, says that, of those cases whose duration was less than six months, "certainly nine-tenths have recovered." (The effect of fourteen years' additional experience upon Dr. Bell's opinion is apparent from the fact that in 1857 he said to one of his friends, "I have come to the conclusion that, when a man once becomes insane, he is about used up for this world.")

The inevitable and obvious result of all these publications of high ratios of recovery was to give the impression to the public mind that mental disease is far more susceptible of cure than, from facts now known, it is shown to be. Their influence was not without its effect upon the British superintendents, as is indicated by the language of Dr. W. A. F. Browne, who states that the American success "excited the envy and despair of my confrères and myself." Believing that, with regard to the subject before us, the best method of showing what can be done is to show what has been done, we proceed to mention some of the most important and reliable statistics which now illustrate the curability of insanity.

Dr. John Thurnam traced the history until death of 244 persons treated at the York Retreat, and, generalizing from these data, formulated the following rule: "In round numbers, of ten persons attacked by insanity, five recover and five die, sooner or later, during the attack. Of the five who recover, not more than two remain well during the rest of their lives: the other three sustain subsequent attacks, during which at least two of them die." In 1858 the number of persons admitted into the asylums of Scotland was 1,297. Twelve years afterwards Sir Arthur Mitchell traced their history as far as practicable, and in January, 1877, published the results in the *Journal of Mental Science*. Of 1,096 persons whose history was traced, 454 had died insane, and 367 still lived insane,— total, 821 insane; while 78 had died not insane, and 197 still lived, not insane,— total, 275 not insane (percentage of insane, 74.91; percentage not insane, 25.9). In general terms, three-fourths were insane, and one-fourth not insane. The final results in regard to these patients will probably very nearly agree with those of the 244 at the York Retreat.*

* Following the example of Sir Arthur Mitchell, I selected the first admissions to all the Massachusetts hospitals in 1880 (about 3,000), and placed them on a special list, for similar investigation, which I kept up until leaving office as Inspector of Charities in Massachusetts in November, 1888. My successors have failed to make the required investigation; but the result is much as in Scotland for those I investigated. (F. B. S.)

In 1843 Dr. Woodward published a list of 25 recent cases recovered, contrasting the cost of their treatment with that of 25 chronic cases then in the hospital.   Thirty-six years afterwards, in 1879, the present writer traced the history of those patients to that time, and found the results somewhat more unfavorable than those of the 244 at York.   Agreeably to Thurnam's rule, 10 of the 25 should never have a second attack : the remaining 15 should have a second attack, and perhaps more ; and, of those 15, 10 should die insane. The actual results were as follows : Only 7 of the patients did not have a second attack; while 18 did have a second attack or more. 7 had died insane, while 2 others were in almshouses, having long been incurably insane,— and will of course die so,— and 1 has died at home who "was never well (sane) but a few months at a time."   8 of the 25 were living in 1879, and there was more than a mere probability that some of them would die insane.

In 1883 the present writer collated the cases of duration on admission of less than twelve months — the recent cases of Americans — from the reports of several years of twenty-three British asylums. The aggregate of admissions was 15,697 ; of recoveries, 7,465.   Proportion of recoveries, 47.49 per cent.

In the *Journal of Mental Science* for July, 1884, Dr. T. A. Chapman, of the Hereford Asylum, published the collected statistics of "forty-six English County and Borough Asylums, and the Edinburgh and Glasgow Royal Asylum, for (in most instances) eleven years,— 1872 to 1882, inclusive."   Here is a collocation of the remarkable number of 93,443 cases of insanity, all of them classified as in Thurnam's table.   The whole number of recoveries was 35,468, or 37.95 per cent. of the admissions.   Of the cases of less than twelve months' duration, there were 69,983, of which the recoveries were 32,569, or 46.52 per cent.   The cases of first attack and of less than three months' duration were 38,283, of which 18,654, or 48.72 per cent., recovered.

The 5 instances of remarkably high ratios of recovery, which were so effective in producing a public impression of a large degree of curability of insanity, those of Dr. Burrows, the York Retreat, the Hartford Retreat, the Worcester Hospital, and the Williamsburg (Virginia) Asylum, were all of them derived from the treatment of an aggregate of only 395 cases.   In the light thrown upon the subject by Chapman's 93,443 cases, those five high ratios most signally fail as an authority from which to deduce a general rule of curability.

The following summary includes the results of some of the present writer's statistical researches which have not been mentioned in this article : —

1. *Cases of first attack; duration less than three months.*— (*a*) Earle's 8,316 cases, at twenty-three British asylums; recoveries, 46.71 per cent.; (*b*) Chapman's 38,283 cases, at forty-six British asylums; recoveries, 48.72 per cent.

2. *Cases of first attack; duration less than twelve months.*— (*a*) Earle's 10,929 cases, at twenty-three British asylums; recoveries, 44.06 per cent. (*b*) Chapman's 50,409 cases at forty-six British asylums; recoveries, 43.79 per cent.

3. *Not first attack; duration less than twelve months.*— (*a*) Earle's 4,768 cases at twenty-three British asylums; recoveries, 55.37 per cent. (*b*) Chapman's 19,574 cases, at forty-six British asylums; recoveries, 53.61 per cent.

4. *All cases of duration less than twelve months.*— (*a*) Earle's 15,697 cases, at twenty-three British asylums; recoveries, 47.49 per cent. (*b*) Chapman's 69,983 cases, at forty-six British asylums; recoveries, 46.52 per cent. (*c*) Earle's 8,063 cases, at fifteen American institutions; recoveries, 38.59 per cent.

5. *All recoveries; calculated on all admissions.*— (*a*) Chapman's 93,443 cases, at forty-six British asylums; recoveries, 37.95 per cent. (*b*) Earle's 33,318 cases, at thirty-nine American institutions; recoveries, 29.15 per cent. (*c*) Earle's 23,052 cases, third period of five years, 1880–1884, at twenty American institutions; recoveries, 29.91 per cent. (*d*) Earle's 14,372 cases, in one year, at fifty-eight American institutions; recoveries, 27.88 per cent.

It appears from these statistics that the reported recoveries at the British institutions exceed those at the American by from 8 to 9 per cent. of the admissions.

VII. The Artist Earles.

In the preparation of his Earle Genealogy Dr. Earle had come upon odd histories of some branches of his family; perhaps the oddest was that which connects the Leicester Earles with Concord Fight, the art studios of London, and the British navy. Ralph Earle of Leicester, son of a captain in Washington's army, and a third cousin of Dr. Earle (born 1751, died 1801), had a turn for art, and in 1775 made sketches of the fights at Lexington and Concord in the preceding April,— four pictures of some merit that were badly engraved by Amos Doolittle of New Haven, and widely circulated in that form. Like a better artist, Trumbull, he afterwards studied in London with West and got the title of R.A.; then returned to New England and painted portraits and landscapes with success,— among them several in Leicester which are preserved. Two of his family were also artists of merit,— his brother James and his own son Ralph. James had a brief career, dying in Charleston, S.C., of yellow fever in 1796, at the age of thirty-five. But he had married in 1789 the widow of an American Tory, whose only son by this first marriage was the late Admiral Sir W. H. Smyth of the English navy. In the year 1863 Sir William, gave Dr. Earle this account of his family : —

"My mother's maiden name was Caroline Georgiana Pilkington, who married Joseph Brewer Palmer Smyth, of New Jersey, a descendant of the celebrated Captain John Smith, of which marriage I am now the sole remainder. The arms of the captain and additions are worn by my family, and I enclose you an impression of my book-plate. After my father's premature death his friend, Mr. James Earle of Paxton, in Massachusetts, married the widow, by whom he had three children, Clara, Phœbe, and Augustus, of whom Phœbe alone remains. Mr. James Earle, whom I well remember, was unfortunately cut off by a fever at Charleston, just as he was preparing to return to England. There was a most friendly eulogy of him in a Charleston paper of the time (about 1796), in which they stated that he was equal to Copley, Savage, Trumbull, West, and other American geniuses of the age, instancing his power of giving 'life to the eye, and expression to every feature.' Upon this point I can safely recommend you to consult my excellent former friend, Professor Morse, himself so good an artist; for I recollect his opinion of the great merit of Mr. Earle's coloring."

It was not of James Earle, however, but of his son Augustus, that Professor Morse had knowledge, not being born until 1791, and only visiting England in 1811. He wrote to Dr. Earle that in 1812-14 he was a student in the Royal Academy with Augustus Earle, C. R. Leslie, and others, but referring him to Dunlap's "History of the Arts of Design" for notices of both James and Augustus Earle. Professor Morse adds: "When in London, in 1856, I passed the evening at a party given to me by Mr. Leslie, where I met Sir Edwin Landseer and other old friends, and among them a sister of Augustus Earle, who was married a second time to a respectable Scotch gentleman (Patrick Macintire). Her first husband was Mr. D. Dighton, an artist. The mother of Mrs. Dighton was Mrs. Maxwell, who was the widow of James Earle, if I rightly recollect. I have the impression that Mrs. Maxwell was three times married, and that the names of her several husbands were Smyth, Earle, and Maxwell.* A son by the first is one of the most distinguished admirals in the British service,— a noble-hearted and highly cultivated man,— Sir William Henry Smyth, who has written many valuable works."

By referring to Dunlap's gossiping volumes, I find that Ralph Earle (whose father Ralph refused a captain's commission from the Tory Governor Hutchinson) was himself a member of the " Governor's Guard " of Connecticut (where he lived at intervals, and where he died), and in that capacity, says Dunlap, "was marched to Cambridge, and soon afterwards to Lexington, where he made drawings of the scenery, and subsequently composed the first historical pictures, perhaps, ever attempted in America, which were engraved by his companion-in-arms, Mr. Amos Doolittle." This was after the fights at Lexington and Concord; and the pictures were four in number,— the encounter at Lexington Green, the British officers reconnoitring Concord from the Burial Hill in that village, the fight at Concord Bridge, and a fourth showing the redcoats in retreat. The original paintings may have perished: a copy or two from them exists ; and the four engravings, very badly executed by Doolittle, are often found in old houses. Earle must have been on

* In a letter of Leslie to his sister in Philadelphia, May 12, 1812, he mentions a portrait he is painting of Miss Smyth, a daughter of Mrs. Maxwell, who was governess in a family. She was sister of the admiral. Professor Morse is right in saying the widow of James Earle married again.

the spot in Concord as well as Lexington, the scenery being fairly well rendered by him. He does not seem to have remained in the army so long as Trumbull did, but went back to New Haven, where, says Dunlap, "I remember seeing two full-lengths of Rev. Timothy Dwight and his wife, painted in 1777 in the manner of Copley, as Earle thought. They showed some talent, but the shadows were black as charcoal or ink. He studied in London, under the direction of Mr. West, immediately after 1783, and returned home in 1786. He painted many portraits in New York, and more in Connecticut. He had considerable merit,—a breadth of light and shadow, facility of handling, and truth in likeness; but he prevented improvement and destroyed himself by habitual intemperance." Tuckerman relates that in 1787 Alexander Hamilton, finding him in prison for debt at New York, induced Mrs. Hamilton and other ladies to sit to him in jail, whereby he earned enough to pay his debt, and was discharged. He strolled as far as Niagara, and painted a large canvas of the Falls, which was exhibited in America and England, and was in existence in London about 1850. He also painted a large landscape of the Denny farm-house, farm, and hill, in the east part of Leicester, which still exists there, in the Denny family; and in 1800 he painted his cousin Thomas Earle, of Cherry Valley, Leicester, his fine house and sycamore-trees in the background, of which portrait Dr. Earle gives a faint copy in the Genealogy. He painted portraits of Springfield magnates and of Governor Strong and his family of Northampton shortly before his own death in 1801. His son Ralph E. Whittemore Earle, born about 1780, studied in London in 1809-10, and afterwards practised portrait painting at New Orleans and Nashville. There he came to the notice of Mrs. Rachel Jackson, wife of General Jackson, afterwards President, and married one of her nieces.

James Earle was the brother of the first Ralph, uncle of the second, and father of Augustus Earle, above-mentioned. He seems to have lived in Paxton before going abroad, as did his brother Clark Earle, who was the foster-father of Anthony Chase, brother-in-law of Dr. Earle. How early James went abroad does not appear, but probably soon after his brother Ralph. He married in London about 1789, but came over to Charleston, S.C., between 1792 and 1795, where he was seen by Thomas Sully, the Philadelphia painter, while living as a boy in Charleston. He seems to have been a

better artist than the two Ralphs; but after some success in Carolina, the birthplace of Allston and the liberal patron of Jarvis and
Professor Morse, he died of yellow fever, just as he was going back
to his family in England. His will is on record at Charleston, dated
Aug. 16, 1796; and his death was but a few days later.

His son Augustus had more art education than any of the Earles;
but his light, roving nature did not allow him to profit much by it.
He was associated in his studies with C. R. Leslie, Landseer, Professor Morse, and others of note, knew Allston, Turner, Beechey,
etc., and went sketching with Leslie and Morse, who tell adventures
of his, and knew his family.

Augustus Earle, as Professor Morse intimates, had many eccen-
tricities; but extreme reserve and modesty was not among them.
Like his uncle, Ralph, he was a rover, but over a much wider
range of the earth's surface. Attaching himself to his half-brother,
then Captain Smyth, he sailed up the Mediterranean to Sicily, Malta,
and Algiers, rambled over Carthage and Cyrene, visiting Ptolemais,
the bishopric of Synesius, then took a turn (in 1818) in the United
States, and next traversed South America, where he remained on one
coast or the other till 1824. Then he sailed for Calcutta, but was
left on shore at Tristan d'Acunha, whence, after six months' imprisonment, he went to Van Dieman's Land and Australia. Sailing for
Madras, he touched at the Carolines, the Ladrones, and Manilla,
in 1828 proceeded to Pondicherry, Mauritius, and several other out-
of-the-way places, and got back to England shortly before Admiral
Fitzroy's " Beagle," with Charles Darwin on board, was to sail on
her famous voyage round the world. As he said himself, in a
trumpery volume which he printed in 1832, " With a spirit not
at all depressed by the vicissitudes and perils he had gone through,
but with an increased and insatiable desire to visit climes which he
had read of, but never seen, he unhesitatingly accepted the situation
of draughtsman to his Majesty's ship ' Beagle ' on a voyage of discovery." He got no farther than Montevideo, and died on shore
somewhere. His uncle, Ralph Earle, who also studied abroad, became a portrait painter in America, had married a niece of General
Jackson, and painted his portrait as General and President.

Ralph E. W. Earle, married into General Jackson's family, is thus
described by Nicholas P. Trist, a well-known Virginian, who had
been Jackson's secretary for a time : —

"Colonel Earl" (it seems he went by this title in Tennessee and Washington) "had been an artist in Nashville, and there experienced the kindness of Mrs. Jackson. This was enough. By Mrs. Jackson's death this relation became sanctified for the General's heart. Earle became forthwith his protégé. From that time the painter's home was under his roof, at Washington, in Tennessee, at the President's house, as at the Hermitage, where he died in 1837. And this treatment was amply repaid. Earle's devotion was more untiring even than his brush; and its steadiness would have proved itself at any moment, by his cheerfully laying down his life in Jackson's service. If he had had a thousand lives, they would have been laid down one after the other, with the same perseverance that one canvas after another was lifted to his easel, there to keep its place till it had received the General. In 1836 President Jackson was generally accompanied in his afternoon walk by Colonel Earle." The painter died at the Hermitage, near Nashville, the next year (not at New Orleans, as Dr. Earle says); and this inscription was placed on his gravestone, beside the Jackson tomb:—

"IN MEMORY OF R. E. W. EARL,

ARTIST, FRIEND, AND COMPANION

OF

GENERAL JACKSON,

Who died, September 16, 1837."

His age at death was less than sixty. He had painted portraits of his friend for a dozen years. The likeness was easily recognized: the art was rather hard and stiff. But his attachment to the old chieftain was more pleasing than the art.

VIII. REMINISCENCES BY DR. EARLE (1889).

My last course of medical lectures at the University of Pennsylvania was in the winter of 1836–37. In the expectation of going to Europe, I succeeded in obtaining from the professors an early final examination, which set me free from the school sooner than otherwise would have occurred. As I had never previously visited Washington, I went to that city, and was present at the inauguration of Martin Van Buren as President of the United States. I also obtained an introduction to President Jackson at the White House, when no one else was present excepting the famous editor, Amos Kendall, who was widely known as a member of the so-called " Kitchen Cabinet " of the President. I then returned to my home in Leicester, and made preparations for a journey to Europe. I again returned to Philadelphia, and while there attended the sittings of the Yearly Meeting of Friends at the Arch Street Meeting-house.

On the 25th of the 4th month (April, 1837) I sailed from New York for Liverpool. Among the passengers were Captain Richard Stockton, of the United States Navy, and Joseph Sturge, one of the most prominent philanthropic Friends in England. He was then on his way homeward from the West Indies Islands, which he had visited for the purpose of investigating the operation of the seven years' apprenticeship law, which had been enacted for the British colonies as a preliminary precaution to the final and complete emancipation of the slaves. He had with him a bright young negro, about twenty years of age, whom he was taking to England as a witness to the cruelties which were practised by the planters under the law of apprenticeship. Joseph Sturge had been at home but a short time before he began to agitate the subject of the abolition of the law of apprenticeship by an exposition of the condition of things as he had found them in the colonial islands. He prosecuted this with great perseverance and zeal until he succeeded in his object through the law of emancipation enacted by the British Parliament.

Pope says, " All partial evil is universal good." If the converse of this proposition be true, then universal good must be accompanied or followed by some partial evil. The slaves of Jamaica and the other British West Indies colonies obtained their freedom, but one of the other results was the degeneracy of the young negro whom Joseph Sturge had used as a witness. He was so much elated by the prominence and attention that were given him in England by his being brought to testify before Parliamentary committees, and by being made a conspicuous personage in the mass meetings at Exeter Hall and other places, and by the limitless opportunities thrown before him for the indulgence of his appetites, that he fell into bad habits, assumed an undue self-importance, and so conducted himself that it was found necessary to send him back to his West Indies home.

I arrived in London on the evening next preceding the eighteenth anniversary of the birth of the then Princess Victoria. I remained there about six weeks, during which there were important changes in the government of Great Britain. King William IV. died, and was buried at Windsor. Victoria ascended the throne, and dissolved Parliament. London was black with the emblems of mourning, and committees of "condolence and congratulation" came from all quarters of the island in manifestation of their loyalty to the new sovereign.

* * * * * *

Three of the prominent medical societies of the United States came into existence during the time of my connection with the Bloomingdale Asylum. These are the American Medical Association, the Association of Medical Superintendents of American Institutions for the Insane, and the New York Academy of Medicine. I was a member of the preliminary convention by which each of them was founded, became a member of each, and was the author of the first original paper read before the Academy of Medicine. It was a brief history of institutions for the insane in the United States, and was published in the first volume of the Transactions of that association. In 1884 I was elected president of the Association of Medical Superintendents of Institutions for the Insane. I was also an early member and a vice-president of the American Social Science Association. Am now a member of the New England Historic-Genealogical Society, a Fellow of the New York College of Physicians and Surgeons, a member of the Massachusetts Medical Society and of the American Philosophical Society at Philadelphia, a corresponding member of the State Medical Society of Connecticut, of the New York Medico-legal Society, and of the Medical Society of Athens, Greece, and an honorary member of the British Medico-Psychological Association.

Anecdotes of Leicester and Worcester.

Miss Lucy Chase wrote to her uncle Dr. Earle soon after George Bancroft's death, who was the son of the Rev. Dr. Aaron Bancroft, of Worcester, giving these particulars of the Earles, of Leicester, by an Irishman who had worked for them: —

"We had a very interesting interview with Martin Callaghan a few days ago, April, 1891. He said: 'I remember many words of counsel which Pliny and William Earle both gave me,— we called Dr. Earle Pliny. They gave me a good deal of good advice, which has been of great service to me. I think Aunt Patience was the best woman and the most wonderful woman I ever knew. She was always a queen. She would be sitting in the kitchen mixing something for the men, and talking great thoughts. I don't think any one in the world can be her superior, even if one could be her equal. In those days I felt convinced that the country would have to suffer for its iniquity of slavery.' He seems to us to be the wholesome fruit of Mulberry Grove training. . . . We made many calls in Leicester, and saw Uncle William Earle at T. Southwick's. Uncle repeated to us the following lines: —

> 'Old age comes with sorrow,
> With wrinkle and furrow,
> No hope in to-morrow,
> None sympathy spares.
> But, unfit to rise up,
> He looks to the skies up,
> None close his old eyes up,
> He dies; and who cares?'"

"Martin drove us to Leicester, and took with him a photograph of grandmother and one of Uncle William."

William Buffum Earle, an older brother of Dr. Earle, had long been blind from an accident. He was most ingenious and inventive, but in his later life unable to support himself, and was maintained by Dr. Earle. He died in 1891. "Aunt Patience" and "grandmother" were the same noted person, the mother of Dr. Earle. Miss Chase added concerning a contemporary of her Uncle William:

"George Bancroft visited his birthplace when he was eighty-nine, and told John B. Pratt, whose mother owned the first spinet imported

from England into Worcester, that he should come to Worcester to
spend his ninetieth birthday, last October, in Mr. Pratt's house,
where he was born. But he was not well enough to do so. When
last here, he visited the Rural Cemetery; and meeting there Waldo
Lincoln and his wife, a daughter of Dr. Chandler and Josephine
Rose, he kissed the children, and said, 'I should be glad to think
they would remember this.' Speaking of Mrs. Pratt, passers-by
used to leave their wagons and carriages, and stand by her window to hear her play the spinet. One day a farmer, who had enjoyed her music, emptied his leathern purse upon the window-sill,
saying, 'This is all I have.'"

IX. REMINISCENCES OF THE EARLE FAMILY.

BY REV. SAMUEL MAY, OF LEICESTER.

Dr. Earle's father was not living when I came to Leicester in
1833. He had quite recently died. There had been five brothers,
sons of Robert Earle, namely: Pliny, father of Dr. Pliny; Jonah,
one of whose grandsons is Stephen C. Earle, the well-known architect of Worcester; Silas; Henry; and Timothy,— all men of decided
mechanical ability, all engaged in the then new and curious manufacture of card-clothing and of the machines for that purpose, and
all members of the Society of Friends. Of these relatives Dr. Earle
has given this anecdote: —

"When I was five years of age, my uncle Timothy, then one of our
nearest neighbors, erected a saw and grist mill directly south of the
Friends' Cemetery, which was about one-third of a mile from our
house. When the nether millstone had been put in place, a group
of the young men and boys of the neighborhood were one morning
at the mill for the purpose of bathing. Among them was my cousin
Amos S. Earle, the subsequent father of the architect, Stephen C.
Earle, of Worcester. He took me by the two hands, lifted me with
my arms extended upward, one on each side of my head, and let
me down through the millstone into the low apartment below it. I
have never had much occasion to laud my own sagacity; but, when
people have magnified that perspicacity which is implied by the ability to see through a millstone, I have ventured to remark that, if
such ability is a proof of intellectual acuteness, much more so is the
fact of having passed bodily through a millstone."

They lived in the north-east part of the town, where there was a Friends' meeting-house standing until within a few years, in the midst of their burial-ground. In 1833 regular religious meetings were held there every First and Fifth Day. But I believe not a single Friend or Quaker now remains in the town. There were in 1833 many such families.

Dr. Earle's mother was then living. She was of a prominent Friends' family, Patience Buffum, of Smithfield, R.I., and was known generally as "Aunt Patience" to the time of her death in 1849. When I first knew her, she was about sixty-three years of age, a woman of tall and commanding figure. As I remember her, she was of unusually large frame and rather masculine in appearance, quiet in manner, slow in speech, and of winning voice. She was a greatly respected and influential member of the local Society of Friends, and also prominent in their monthly and quarterly meetings, which were held with great regularity in Bolton, Northbridge, Uxbridge, and Leicester, as well as in Rhode Island. She was probably the leading figure in their society here at the time of which I speak.

Before as well as after the death of Pliny Earle, Sr., the house became a boarding-school for girls, being by its size and situation well adapted for such use. Two of the daughters, Sarah and Eliza, with their mother in charge of the house, established the school. It became widely known, and received a steady support, not from Friends alone. Pupils came from the neighborhood, from Worcester, and from places more remote. It was called the Mulberry Grove School, and was continued by the sisters until their marriage,— Sarah to Mr. Charles Hadwen, of Worcester, and Eliza to Mr. William E. Hacker, of Philadelphia.

As I became acquainted with the family, I found them much interested in the anti-slavery movement, and far in advance of the community generally. "Aunt Patience's" brother, Arnold Buffum, had been the first president of the New England Anti-slavery Society; and that fact, doubtless, brought them to understand and become interested in that movement. Three of the sons of Pliny and Patience Earle took a very active part in it. John Milton Earle, who was editor of the Worcester *Spy*, was a strong anti-slavery man as editor and legislator. Thomas Earle, who had become a resident of Philadelphia, was the Liberty party's candidate for the Vice-Presidency. William Buffum Earle was an effective anti-slavery writer, and one of the leaders of the movement in Worcester County. I believe that Dr. Earle received aid from his brother John Milton Earle, particularly in obtaining his education.

When I first knew Dr. Earle, he was principal of the Friends' School at Providence, the school of which Mr. Whittier has written, and which has a high reputation to the present day. In 1835 he left that position, and went to Philadelphia, to continue there the study of medicine which he had begun while connected with the Friends' School. He completed his preparatory studies at the medical school of the University of Pennsylvania, was graduated from there in March, 1837; and in April went to Europe for two years, 1837 to 1839. During those two years he was a correspondent of the Worcester *Spy*. I well remember his full and careful letters, not simply on the subjects to which he afterwards became so much devoted, but the letters of a traveller and close observer of all he saw. They were valuable, and might well have been collected in book form.

While in Europe at this time he gave special attention to the subject of insanity, and visited many asylums for the insane, so that, when he came back to this country, he was appointed resident physician at the Friends' Asylum for the Insane at Frankford, near Philadelphia. There he remained four years, and was then appointed superintendent of the Bloomingdale Insane Asylum in the city of New York,—a responsible and difficult position. He filled it, I believe, with entire satisfaction and credit, remaining in it about five years. I once visited him at Bloomingdale, and he showed me the hospital and its methods. I saw then more intimately than I had ever done before the arrangements of an insane asylum, and how valuable were his precise methods and his exactness in all practical matters. There was mechanical genius in that family, as I have said; and this talent appeared in all his work. He was afterwards a visiting physician of the New York City Lunatic Asylum on Blackwell's Island, and held the place for two years. Then his health became impaired, and he came home to Leicester to rusticate and recuperate. He had worked hard and persistently from the time when he began his active life, and well he might need rest. Leicester continued his home till 1864, though during that time he went away twice to assist in the care of cases of insanity occurring among United States soldiers and seamen at the Government Hospital for the Insane near Washington. With the exception of these intervals he was here during the nine years from 1855 to 1864. He lived during that time in a small house that his grandfather, Robert Earle, had built and occupied, still in the family and now belonging to Stephen C. Earle. It was called "the grandfather-house," and was of but one story. There he rested, reading and perfecting himself in his favorite studies during nine years. He also much enlarged his fine collection of shells and minerals, which he afterwards gave to Leicester Academy, enclosed in the handsome cases also furnished by him. The collection is conspicuous at the Academy and much prized.

It was inevitable that the town should desire his service as one of its school committee; and he so served for many years, doing a very valuable work in raising the tone of the schools. He aroused the spirit of both teachers and pupils wherever he went among the schools. There had been, to his time, no member of the school committee whose influence had been so important and marked as his since I have known the schools of Leicester.

In the establishment of our public library his influence and help were decisive. It was in March, 1861. The owners of an incorporated library of about 800 volumes (called the Leicester Social Library) had proposed to give it to the town, to be held as a public library for all the inhabitants, if the town would accept it. There was doubt in the minds of some whether the town would take it, with the responsibility of keeping it open and making annual appropriations for its support. But they did. And the credit of doing it belongs in no small degree to Dr. Earle. When the question came up in the town meeting of March, 1861, he quietly rose, and in an impressive way made the motion that the town accept and hold the library, as proposed by the proprietors, for the benefit of all the inhabitants; and the motion prevailed without a dissenting voice or vote. I was much interested myself in the success of the library, and well remember the incident. He was the constant friend of the library all his life.

On the 2d of July, 1864, the trustees of the State Lunatic Asylum of Northampton appointed him to the office of superintendent of that institution; and there he passed the rest of his life, a period of nearly twenty-eight years. In all that time, whatever reports of his professional work were published, he invariably sent a copy to the Leicester library. He was a little given to writing poetry, and always sent us his publications. At his death, by his will, he gave $6,000 to the town to help the erection of a library building, which, as he phrased it, should be "worthy of the town." He gave also a portrait of himself to be placed in the library,—an oil painting by Burleigh, a handsome and very good likeness. Many miscellaneous volumes of his private library were given to this library by his executors.

He came to Leicester each summer after he got through with his work in Northampton, and spent several weeks in the vicinity of his early home. While here, he effected a considerable improvement of the Friends' burying-ground. He also, during these more leisurely years, compiled and published his genealogy of the Earle family.

X. Portions of Dr. Earle's Will.

I, Pliny Earle of Northampton, in the county of Hampshire and Commonwealth of Massachusetts, Physician, being of sound and disposing mind and memory, do make and publish this my last will and testament, hereby revoking all former wills by me at any time heretofore made.

1. After the payment of my funeral expenses and my debts which I possibly may owe, although I am not in the habit of owing anything, I direct my executors hereinafter named to set apart out of my estate the sum of three thousand dollars. My said executors and my friend Frank B. Sanborn of Concord, Massachusetts, shall consult and advise with each other, and shall determine and decide whether said three thousand dollars or part thereof shall be devoted to preparing my biography, or to collecting, editing, and publishing my writings on insanity or any of said writings. It is my opinion that, if anything of this nature is done, it would be best to prepare a brief account of my life, which may include a reference to the places where my writings can be found; but I leave the determination of this question to Mr. Sanborn and my said executors. If they shall decide that a brief biography of the testator is desirable, I wish Mr. Sanborn to prepare it, and to have the entire charge and direction of all duties of a literary nature pertaining thereto. For his labor and services my executors are to pay the said Sanborn a liberal compen-

sation out of said sum so set apart. So much of said three thousand dollars as shall not be expended in the manner above suggested shall revert to my estate.

2. I give and bequeath to the City of Northampton one hundred dollars in trust to pay for keeping my cemetery lot in order in the future.

[Sections 3, 4, and 5 provide for legacies to his nephews and nieces, generally of $3,000 each, though there were three of $4,000, one of $5,000, and to a wealthy nephew and niece $100 each. These legacies amounted to $41,250.]

My relations with all my nephews and nieces have been very pleasant, and the sums hereinbefore given to them must not by any means be considered as indicating the relative measure of my regard.

6. To my cousin Ann V. Buffum I give and bequeath one thousand dollars.

7. I give and bequeath unto the inhabitants of the city of Northampton fifty thousand dollars, to be securely invested until the same, with the rest and residue of my estate hereinafter mentioned, shall amount to at least sixty thousand dollars. Then this whole fund of sixty thousand dollars or more shall be kept securely invested forever. Said fund shall be designated as the " Pliny Earle Aid Fund " ; and the income thereof shall be used in aid of the city of Northampton in defraying the necessary current expenses of the Forbes Library, when the same shall be ready for use. The words " necessary current expenses " shall be construed to mean in this bequest the payment of employees in and about said library, and the furnishing of fuel and lights therefor, but shall not include the payment of the salary of the librarian for said library, or any part of such salary or compensation. Although this fund is intended to be supplementary to the "Aid Fund" established in his will by the late Hon. Charles E. Forbes, the expenditure of the income of the fund herein bequeathed shall be strictly confined and limited to the objects and purposes already specified and set forth in this section.

This bequest is made and is hereby subject to the following conditions : first, that the city of Northampton shall forever keep the *corpus* of the fund herein given intact to an amount as large as sixty thousand dollars, and if, by reason of dishonesty, bad investments, incompetency, or casualty of any kind the principal shall fall below that sum, the City of Northampton shall within two years thereafter make good the deficit, and make up the amount of income lost by reason of such deficit; and, second, that the City of Northampton shall not expend or use any of income of said fund for any other object and purpose than for the objects and purposes hereinbefore specified and set forth. If the City of Northampton shall fail to fairly observe and comply with these conditions or with either of them, the bequest herein made to said city shall be thereby revoked, annulled, void, and forfeited, and the entire fund aforesaid shall vest in three trustees, residents of said Northampton, whom the Judge of Probate for the county of Hampshire or his successor shall appoint and designate under this will, to secure, collect, recover, and receive said entire fund, with all accumulations rightfully belonging to it, and said trustees shall apply and manage the same in the establishment of a Home for Aged and Invalid Men. Said Home shall be located in said Northampton, and shall be for the benefit and comfort of aged and infirm men who are legal residents of the city of Northampton or of any town in the county of Hampshire, with full power and authority to said trustees to carry out the purposes and spirit of this conditional bequest, and to have entire charge and direction of all the details of the expenditures necessary for properly establishing and managing said Home according to their views, judgment, and discretion. I recommend that, when said Home shall have been established in a manner satisfactory to said trustees, it be incorporated in a manner similar to the corporation of the Home for Aged and Invalid Women in Northampton.

8. I give and bequeath six thousand dollars to the town of Leicester, Massachusetts, to be used towards the erection of a substantial library building in said Leicester, worthy of the town.

9. To the Uxbridge Monthly Meeting of the society of Friends I give and bequeath two thousand dollars on condition that within two years after the time of my decease the society shall expend fifteen hundred dollars in grading the Friends' burial-ground in Leicester, Massachusetts, in building the wall surrounding it, in putting up an iron gate with granite posts, and in placing new gravestones therein. I hereby direct my executors to deduct from the amount of this bequest whatever money I have furnished or shall furnish towards any or all of the specific objects set forth in this section.

10. To the Home for Aged and Invalid Women in Northampton I give and bequeath two thousand dollars for the charitable objects and purposes for which said Home was created and established, and is designed to be continued and perpetuated.

11. To the Massachusetts Society for the Prevention of Cruelty to Children I give and bequeath one thousand dollars.

12. To the Massachusetts Society for the Prevention of Cruelty to Animals I give and bequeath one thousand dollars.

13. To the New England Historic Genealogical Society I give and bequeath one thousand dollars.

14. I give and bequeath to my executors one thousand dollars each in lieu of compensation for their services in that capacity.

15. I give and bequeath to my niece Frances C. Earle * my Genevese watch with monograms, as a memento of our tour in Europe, in the course of which it was purchased. [The tour was in 1871.]

16. I give and bequeath to the trustees of the Forbes Library in said Northampton, and for the uses of said library, the following books, to wit: one hundred and twelve bound volumes of the *American Journal of the Medical Sciences*, a series of the *Medical News* bound in seven volumes, the volumes in my library of Reports of the Board of Education, of Reports of the Board of State Charities, a set of twenty-two Reports of the Northampton Lunatic Hospital, bound in two volumes, and covering the period from 1864 to 1885 inclusive, and all the genealogical books in my library.

17. In no event shall any of the books belonging to my library, or any of my wearing apparel, trinkets, articles of personal ornament or for personal use, or pictures, or portraits, be sold for the procurement of funds for the payment of legacies. They may be given to my kindred, friends, or other persons, at the discretion of my executors.

18. All the rest, residue, and remainder of my estate, of whatsoever kind and wherever situated, I give, devise, and bequeath unto the inhabitants of the city of Northampton, to be added to and to become and constitute part and parcel of the "Pliny Earle Fund" bequeathed by Section 7 of this will, and to be used in all respects for the objects and purposes and subject to the conditions, revocation, annulment, voidance and forfeiture, and subsequent disposition more fully specified and set forth in said Section 7.

* On page 279 this name, " Frances" should be substituted for " Fanny."

19. I hereby constitute and appoint my nephew Charles A. Chase of Worcester, Massachusetts, my niece Anne H. Southwick of said Worcester, and my niece Sarah E. Hacker of Philadelphia, Pennsylvania, executors of this my last will and testament; and I hereby empower and authorize them to sell and convey my real or personal estate, and to do all acts, and make and execute all papers and documents, which may be convenient or necessary for the prompt and efficient performance of their duties in administering my estate. I also request that the Judge of Probate will not require any surety or sureties on the bond of them, or either of them, as such executors or as trustees, should any of the provisions of this will require their appointment *eo nomine* as trustees.

In testimony whereof, I hereunto set my hand and seal, and in the presence of the three witnesses named below declare this to be my last will and testament, this eighth day of April in the year of our Lord one thousand eight hundred and ninety-two.

                                        PLINY EARLE.   [Seal.]

Signed, sealed, published, and declared by the said Pliny Earle as and for his last will and testament in presence of us, who in his presence, in the presence of each other, and at his request hereto subscribe our names as witnesses.

        (Signed)   EDWARD B. NIMS.
                        LEWIS F. BABBITT.
                        TIMOTHY G. SPAULDING.

HAMPSHIRE COUNTY, SS.
REGISTRY OF PROBATE.
                        NORTHAMPTON, MASS., June 13, A.D. 1892.

    A true copy.

            Attest: HUBBARD M. ABBOT, *Register.*

INDEX.

ERRATA.

On page 59, for " 25th of March " read *April;* for " March 27 " read *April* 27.

Page 61, for " March " read *April.*

Page 278, line 12 from the top, read *convalescence.*

Page 279, for " Fanny " Earle read *Frances.*

Page 380, Clarke Earle of Paxton was the *step*-father of Anthony Chase.

BIOGRAPHIES BY F. B. SANBORN,

OF CONCORD, MASS.

In order of their date of Publication.

Henry David Thoreau. In the Series of "American Men of Letters." pp. viii, 317. Boston: Houghton, Mifflin & Co. 1882.

Life and Letters of John Brown, of **Kansas** and Virginia. pp. viii, 645. Boston: Little, Brown & Co. 1885.

New Connecticut. An Autobiographical Poem by A. Bronson Alcott. Edited by F. B. Sanborn. pp. xxvi, 247. Boston: Little, Brown & Co. 1887.

Life of Dr. S. G. Howe. In the Series of "American Reformers." pp. viii, 370. New York: Funk & Wagnalls. 1891.

A. Bronson Alcott, his Life and Philosophy. By F. B. Sanborn and W. T. Harris. pp. vii, 679 (up to p. 543 by F. B. Sanborn). Boston: Little, Brown & Co. 1893.

Familiar Letters of Henry David Thoreau. Edited, with an Introduction and Notes, by F. B. Sanborn. (A New Biography.) pp. xii, 483. Boston: Houghton, Mifflin & Co. 1894.

Memoirs of Pliny Earle, M.D. With Selections from his Diaries, Letters, and Professional Writings. pp. xvi, 409. Boston: Damrell & Upham. 1898.

Damrell & Upham also publish: —

The Curability of Insanity. By Pliny Earle, M.D.

In addition to the above works, Mr. Sanborn has edited: —

The Genius and Character of Emerson. Lectures at the Concord School of Philosophy. pp. xxii, 447. Boston: Houghton, Mifflin & Co. 1885.

The Life and Genius of Goethe. Lectures at the Concord School of Philosophy. pp. xxv, 454. Boston: Houghton, Mifflin & Co. 1886. (Out of print.)

Prayers by Theodore Parker. A New Edition, with a **Preface** by **Louisa** M. Alcott and a Memoir by F. B. Sanborn. pp. **xxi,** 200. **Boston:** Little, Brown & Co. 1882.

Sonnets and Canzonets. By A. Bronson Alcott. With an Introduction by F. B. Sanborn. pp. iv, 151. Boston: Little, Brown & Co. 1882.

Poems of Nature. Selected and Edited by Henry S. Salt and F. B. Sanborn. pp. xix, 122. London: John Lane. Boston: Houghton, Mifflin & Co. 1895.